WHITE SHELL WOMAN

Books by James D. Doss

WHITE SHELL WOMAN

A CHARLIE MOON MYSTERY

James D. Doss

William Morrow
An Imprint of HarperCollinsPublishers

From *The Diné: Origin Myths of the Navaho Indians*, by Aileen O'Bryan, originally published by the United States Government Printing Office, Washington, D.C., 1956, as Bulletin 163 of the Bureau of American Ethnology, Smithsonian Institution (later published by Dover Publications, Inc., as *Navaho Indian Myths*, by Aileen O'Bryan, 1993).

HarperCollins books may be purchased for educational, business, or sales promotional use. For information please write: Special Markets Department, HarperCollins Publishers Inc., 10 East 53rd Street, New York, NY 10022.

Designed by Oksana Kushnir

ISBN 0-06-019932-6

For

Linda Sue Pippins
Abilene, Texas

In the four directions from her house she undergoes a change. She comes out of her house an old woman with a white bead walking stick. She walks towards the East and returns middle aged; and she carries no walking stick. To the South she walks and returns a young woman. She walks to the West and comes back a maiden. She goes North and returns a young girl. She is called the White Bead Woman, Yol'gai esdzan. She has three names, and the second is Changeable Woman, Atsan a'layee. The third is Yol'gai atate, the White Bead girl. She has these three names, that is her power. Only one person knows the origin of her power, he is the Most High Power Whose Ways Are Beautiful.

—Above as told to Aileen O'Bryan by the first of four chiefs of the Navajo people, Sandoval, Hastin Tlo'tsi hee (Old Man Buffalo Grass) in November 1928: "You look at me," he said, "and you see only an ugly old man, but within I am filled with great beauty."

WHITE SHELL WOMAN

CHAPTER 1

The baby was the White Bead Baby . . . and her cradle is called
natsi'lid eta cote, the rainbow cut short.
    —Sandoval, Hastin Tlo'tsi hee

The Twins

The Ute horseman had seen their stern faces in all seasons.
Whether bathed in blazing sunshine or veiled in a lace of softly falling
snow, they were always the same. Massive. Silent. Awaiting the End
of Days.

On this day, Julius Santos had taken no notice of the towering sandstone monoliths. The rider was blissfully beguiled by those sweet things
a spring morning brings. On the mossy stream bank, startled willows
trembling with excitement at the arrival of an unexpected breeze. A
flood of melted snow crystals rippling over an avenue strewn with slippery cobblestones. The crisp whisper of a magpie's wing, a startled darting of rainbow-dappled fishes. He was distracted by these pleasures.
Any thought of trouble was far from him.

But the giants were infinitely patient. Relentlessly, they pulled at the corner of his eye.

Finally—unable to resist—Julius Santos turned his face toward Companion and Chimney Rocks. Separated by a three-hundred-yard gap, the towering brothers seemed isolated in stony loneliness. But it was all a matter of how one looked at them. The Ute knew of a special place—a unique, elevated point of view. From the Crag, it was possible to see the Twin War Gods as the ancients had seen them—standing near enough to exchange whispers.

On horseback, the sacred overlook was barely an hour away. It would be necessary to cross Ghost Wolf Mesa, a knobby formation dotted with kiva and pit-house ruins. A dozen winters had passed since he had ventured near that silent, sinister place where old bones moldered under lichen-encrusted rubble. But there was no other way to approach the Crag. A narrow, precipitous causeway of crumbling sandstone connected the mesa rim to that upraised, wedge-shaped platform where the Old Ones had built a splendid temple to honor the Goddess of the Moon.

During his last visit, Santos had stood on the very tip of the stone triangle, contemplating the gigantic sons of White Shell Woman. While he'd stared at the Twins, something outlandish had happened. He had found himself leaning heavily on one leg . . . then the other—as if a trillion tons of sandstone pitched and swayed under his feet. The startled pilgrim had been overwhelmed by the illusion that he was on the deck of an enormous, storm-tossed ship. It seemed the illusory vessel was under full sail, toward some dark, alien harbor.

But that had been years ago. He sat in the saddle, squinting at the distant mesa—that dark, haunted space that must be crossed to approach the sacred platform. In the Ute's lurid imagination, the lumpy sandstone formation was a massive hand reaching up from Lower World—with all fingers folded except one. That long, crooked digit pointed suggestively toward the Twins. And on this morning, it beckoned to the lone horseman.

To ward off this enticement, Santos closed his eyes. In doing so, he encountered the inner darkness. And looked too deeply. The old vision enveloped him.

He is on the Crag, standing on the very tip of the soaring bow. Santos gazes over interlocked waves of space and time. A splendid illusion grips his mind. Just ahead—separated by the merest slice of sky—the towering giants stand shoulder to shoulder, knee-deep in petrified talus dunes. They are anchored to the depths of a ghostly sea, waiting for their mother's pale face to appear between them. These are the slayers of monsters. Ready to take on sinew and muscle over bones of stone. And—as in the Beginning of Days—slay those unspeakable monsters that feed on human flesh.

Santos's peculiar fantasy was interrupted by a sudden stamping of the horse's hoof; a heavy shudder rippled through the animal's frame. The rider took a deep breath, and turned his face away from the Twins. He assured himself that the vision was nothing to be concerned about. It was a mental deception—a mystical mirage. The Ute turned his mount south. Toward home. This was a sensible decision. But . . .

The giants whispered their urgent summons.

You are needed.

Today you are needed.

The long finger beckoned.

Come.

Come quickly.

Santos pretended not to hear the call. But he turned his horse toward the mesa.

The Encounter

Though he was not a traditional Ute, Julius Santos did accept those particular elements of his culture that he considered helpful. This included sage advice on maintaining mental balance. And so—to the extent that he was able—he did not think bad thoughts. Not that a healthy man could possibly submerge his soul in gloom on such a fine day as this. The breeze was crisp as a new dollar bill and refreshingly cool against his face, the morning sun a warm smile on his back. He had a good horse between his knees. Moreover, he was feeling uncommonly young for his years. The moderately vain fellow considered himself a fine figure of a man. And believing so, he was. Santos was long and lean; his spine straight as a young aspen. He sat easily in the saddle— a fluid, graceful rider who seemed grafted to his mount.

Having ascended to the crest of the mesa, his spirit was likewise lifted. This was not really a bad place. There were purple and yellow blossoms blooming in splashes of sunlight; patches of melting snow hiding in the shadows of fragrant juniper. The rider directed his mount to the rim of the sandstone cliff. Snuffy was a steady beast who would step over a prairie rattler without so much as a shudder. She approached the edge of the precipice.

Santos inhaled a deep breath of sage-tinted sweetness.

It seemed that a man could see to the very edges of the earth. The Ute slitted his eyes, so the grand vision would not be absorbed too quickly. The endless space and deep silence engulfed and nourished his soul.

Precious moments passed away, but eternity was not diminished.

Santos was well short of the sacred overview, but even from the rim of Ghost Wolf Mesa the towers of Companion and Chimney Rocks seemed to stand near enough to touch elbows. According to the Zuni and Hopi, these were the Twin War Gods, sons of White Shell Woman. She was the moon, her muscular children the monster-slayers. The Twins had destroyed those mythical beasts who gorged themselves on human flesh. By this heroic act, the sons of the moon had made the world safe for human beings. It was a fine story, but Santos had watched the flickering television screen while men walked on the moon's dusty-gray surface. He knew for certain that the pockmarked sphere was nothing whatever like a woman. And to this modern Ute, the War Gods were the stuff of fanciful Zuni myth. Moreover, he did not believe in monsters.

Any child knows better.

Julius Santos was summoned back to earth by the shrill call of a falcon. The dreamer wondered how much time had passed. And wisely decided that it did not matter.

He made a clicking sound with his tongue. "Let's head up toward the sacred place, Snuffy." The Ute was content to let the mare proceed at a slow pace. When they got to the narrow neck of land that connected the mesa to the lofty Crag, he would get off and lead his mount. It was a narrow, twisting path, with steep talus slopes on each side.

Had the Ute kept to his plan, the future would have been quite different. But history is forever altered by the most casual decision, the seemingly irrelevant event.

The rider experienced a sudden desire to avoid the slightest evidence of modern humans. He would shun the carefully laid-out trails prepared for the summer visitors to Chimney Rock Archaeological Site. For him, no signs with printed words about an excavated pit-house ruin or the great kiva or the mysterious stone basin or what the Anasazi probably used this or that plant for. At a nudge of his knee, the mare abandoned the graveled road that led to the U.S. Forest Service parking lot—the jumping-off place for sightseers from Tokyo and Chicago and Berlin, who plodded along carefully kept pathways behind uniformed guides. Not that there were any tourists or guides around today. The archaeological site would be closed until mid-May, when the last of the snows had melted. Santos urged his mount across a shallow arroyo, into a thick grove of piñon. He was approaching a lonely region where the pit-house ruins had not been excavated. In this twilight place, the bones of ancients remained undisturbed. And at peace, he hoped. But upon the earth or beneath it, peace is a scarce commodity.

As he ducked to miss an encounter with a juniper branch, the Ute smiled at the memory of what his mother had told him countless times. He could almost see her wagging a finger at him, hear her voice: "Julius—you stay away from the places where them *Múukui-ci* used to live. Them crumbly old ruins are bad places. Some of them *Múukui-ci* ghosts are still there. Just waiting for a foolish person to come too close."

Santos assured himself that he cared nothing for the old superstitions. The Anasazi were long gone, and best forgotten. Not that he laughed at the notion of ghosts. He had seen his father sitting on the porch steps one Tuesday afternoon last autumn, hands resting on his knees. The old man had leaned forward, as if ready to arise and greet his son. And then he simply wasn't there. This had happened three days after his father was buried in the Indian cemetery at Ignacio. Julius Santos had seen the proof with his own eyes; something did remain of those who had passed over to the other side.

But what harm could a spirit do? Even if there were Anasazi ghosts lingering about these old ruins, they must be tired of nothing but each other's company. Santos forced himself to smile. They would be happy· to see a man ride by on a fine horse.

Snuffy raised her black nose in the air. Sniffed.

He spoke softly. "What is it, old swayback?"

Her eyes bulged with fear. The animal tossed her head, snorted.

The skin on his neck was prickling. *Maybe she smells a mountain lion.* There were rumors of a big she-cougar slinking around Chimney Rock. Santos had a long-barreled .357-Magnum revolver stashed in the saddlebag. *That should be more'n enough to scare off a big cat. Good thing Snuffy don't mind gunfire.* He had shot elk from her saddle without as much as a flinch from his mount. He patted the horse's muscular shoulder. "Move along, old girl. I intend to go amongst the old ruins—to where the ghosts are." A joke was the best way to dispel fear.

A few yards away, a pair of eyes watched.

The horse—who had begun moving forward cautiously—balked so suddenly that the rider was pitched up against her neck.

He shouted, "What the hell is the matter with—"

And then it was upon them with a wild, furious shriek.

Santos did not give a thought to the revolver in his saddlebag. Terror sets its own agenda.

Consciousness returned very gradually, as if he were awakening from a long, deep sleep. For a confusing moment, Julius Santos could not remember where he was. With a concentrated effort of will, he began to put the day together. One small piece at a time.

I got outta bed right after the seven o'clock news was on the radio. Took a shower. Had breakfast . . . ham and eggs. Then I saddled up Snuffy. Was going to take an easy ride along the creek, but I changed my mind. Headed over toward the big mesa. Where the ruins are. Oh yeah. Now I remember. Stupid horse was spooked by something. I must've got thrown. He had no doubt his mount was long gone. And it was a six-mile walk home. *Dammit anyway! Hope I don't have no broken bones.*

Santos squinted as the bright world above his face gradually came into focus. A gnarled piñon, bent like an old man's spine against the prevailing westerlies. A perfectly painted cloud slipping across a pale blue canvas. The Ute was surprised that he felt no pain. But except for the earthy pillow under his head, the fallen man felt . . . nothing at all. He tried to move, but could not. *What does it mean? Am I dead?* Strangely, this possibility did not frighten him. All things of this earth must come to an end. As Julius Santos pondered his situation, a shadowy form moved over him, blocking out the sky.

This frightened him.

What in hell are you?

And then he knew.

Santos heard his voice. "No—no—don't—"

A searing, white-hot pain splashed across his face. Then cool, soothing darkness.

It was finished.

Santos went away. To where the ghosts are.

CHAPTER 2

All of a sudden she heard something behind her. Looking around she saw a great white horse with black eyes. He had a long white mane, and he pranced above the ground—not on the earth itself. . . . And there was a young man sitting on the horse. The young man's moccasins and leggings and clothing were all white. All was as for a bride.

—Sandoval, Hastin Tlo'tsi hee

The Shaman

An excellent breakfast of refried beans, pork sausage, and eggs (fried in the popping sausage grease) was finished. When the sun got a smidgen higher, Daisy Perika's nephew would drive her to Ignacio for Sunday-morning mass at St. Ignatius Catholic Church. The Ute elder stood at the window, her thin forearms folded over a purple woolen shawl. Squinting at the gaping mouth of *Cañon del Espíritu*, she licked her lips in preparation for what must be said. And said it. "I won't be in Middle World much longer." The grim pronouncement was directed at the visitor in her trailer home.

Charlie Moon, his seven-foot frame folded over the small kitchen table, was engrossed in a copy of the *Southern Ute Drum*.

She waited.

Nothing.

"Did you hear what I said?" *Big jughead*.

The former tribal policeman—now a cattle rancher—did not look up from the article about falling beef prices. "Yeah." Aunt Daisy had been predicting her imminent death for two decades. *She'll likely live to bury me*.

She knew what he was thinking. "Won't be long till you'll be at my funeral."

He looked up to smile affectionately at the aged woman's bowed form. "You not feeling well?"

Daisy put a hand to the small of her back and groaned. "Haven't had a good day since that peanut farmer was president."

Charlie Moon folded the tribal newspaper, downed the last dregs of an extraordinarily strong cup of coffee. "So what's the matter?" He knew the answer. Too many years.

"Too many years," she said.

"It'll take more than old age to do you in."

He always says that. The tribal elder shook her head and sighed. Charlie was too young to understand. "When you get really old, things start to stop workin'. That's when you know the end isn't far off. And," she added with a knowing wag of her head, "the signs are plain enough."

He was obligated to ask. "What signs?" *It'll be pains in her chest*.

"Toenails," she muttered.

He wondered whether he'd heard her correctly.

The aged woman looked down, wiggled her toes. "I generally have to clip 'em at least once a month. So they won't poke holes in my stockings."

Charlie Moon wondered where this was going.

So that gaunt Rider on the Pale Horse would not hear the grim news and come a-galloping her way, Daisy whispered. "My toenails . . . they've stopped growing."

He stared at her feet. "That's bad?"

She gave him the pitying look reserved for the terminally ignorant.

Moon, who had never really understood his aunt, thought she wanted reassurance. "It's probably just some kind of dietary problem. A little more calcium, you'll be right as rain."

This uncalled-for optimism earned him a venomous stare.

He understood his error, and added in a conciliatory tone: "Or maybe you *are* about to fall off the saddle."

Pleased to have browbeaten her nephew into submission, Daisy treated herself to a deeply melancholy sigh. "It won't be long now. Some dark night, that snow-white owl will swoop down. He'll perch on that old piñon snag by my bedroom window . . . and call my name."

He looked at the pot on the stove. "You got any more coffee?"

St. Ignatius Catholic Church

Daisy Perika was mildly annoyed that Charlie Moon was not sitting beside her. Her nephew had been lured away by April Tavishuts, who was sitting across the aisle. Moon was smiling at something the young woman had whispered in his ear. Daisy scowled. *Hah. I bet you'd wipe that silly grin off your face if your yella-haired matukach sweetheart was to walk into church right now.* But the old woman was pleased that her nephew was paying some attention to a nice Ute girl. As far as Daisy knew, April didn't have herself a man. Or anything you could call a real family. Her father had died during the flu epidemic. And not long after marrying a Navajo last year, April's mother had left Middle World. Daisy said a brief prayer for the unfortunate soul. But Misfortune visits those who are foolish. *She should've known better than to get into bed with one of them Navajos. But I guess she must've been awfully lonely.* Daisy Perika closed her eyes. And wished that someone would come and sit beside her.

As he delivered his carefully crafted sermon on those twin sins of Pride and Envy, Father Raes Delfino tried not to notice the elderly woman in a pew near the rear of the church. But her form—hunched forward in an odd, froggish manner—tugged at his gaze as the gravity of a black hole bends a beam of rainbow light. The Ute elder was an enigma to the scholarly little Jesuit. He had no doubt that Daisy Perika's faith was firmly anchored in Christ. But like other traditional Utes, she was the creature of a complex culture shaped in darkest prehistory. He knew from several unsettling experiences that Daisy was haunted by it. As he was.

Daisy was, in fact, dozing. This was primarily because she was old and tired to the marrow. Only partly because in the back of the church she could not quite make out the priest's words. The syllables fluttered softly about her ears like little yucca moths. Lulling her sweetly to sleep.

But presently, something disturbed her nap. An urgent tugging at her sleeve.

Believing another member of the flock was awakening her for Holy Communion, she cleared her throat and whispered hoarsely: " 'S all right—I was just resting my eyes."

Daisy glanced across her shoulder. There was no one there.

Almost.

Another tugging at her sleeve. *Must be a child.* She looked down. And almost swallowed her tongue. *I must be dreaming.* She closed her eyes ever so tightly. Counted toward ten. At seven, she cracked the lid on one eye. The little man was still beside her. Right here in church, like a regular Sunday-go-to-meeting Christian. This was outrageous. "What are you doing *here?*" she rasped.

He scratched his belly and yawned.

She tried to speak without moving her lips. "Go 'way—before somebody sees you!"

No response from the dwarf.

Daisy stared in horror at the priest. Though he had not missed a beat in his sermon, Father Raes seemed to be looking in her direction—as if she were the chief of all sinners. But the Ute shaman remembered—to her enormous relief—that only a Ute could see the *pitukupf.* Well, that wasn't necessarily always the case. There were occasional exceptions. That *matukach* chief of police up in Granite Creek had seen the dwarf. But Scott Parris—Charlie Moon's best friend—was a very special white man. With gifts not unlike her own. Father Raes was of another sort entirely. She was certain the priest could not see the tiny fellow who sat by her side. And so she stared boldly at the man of the cloth.

Without turning her head, Daisy Perika spoke from the corner of her mouth. "Take off your hat." Still unnerved by his unexpected appearance, she had spoken in English.

The *pitukupf* did not respond.

She repeated the command in the Ute tongue.

The dwarf ignored her.

Daisy snatched the floppy green hat from his head, slammed it down on the pew between them.

The little man aimed an outraged look at the shaman. And muttered something best not heard by an old woman's ears. Especially not in church.

In the choppy Ute dialect, Daisy tersely inquired what the *pitukupf* was doing here. He knew very well that his sort had no business in God's house. He belonged in *Cañon del Espíritu*. Under the ground. In his badger hole.

Apparently unmoved, the *pitukupf* said not a word. But he did reach out to touch the Ute elder's wrist. And point upward with a crooked little finger.

Following his gesture, the shaman tilted her head. She was astonished to see flames, the church roof melting away like wax. And far above— in a sky that was unnaturally dark for late on a Sunday morning— Daisy Perika saw something like stars. Falling from the heavens.

At the door, Farther Raes had already exchanged pleasantries with April Tavishuts and Charlie Moon, who were waiting a few paces ahead of the old woman. The priest took Daisy Perika's wrinkled hand in his. The tribal elder had a peculiar look in her eye. "And how are you this morning?"

She responded with a shrug, punctuated with a grunt.

"During the sermon," he said with a wry grin, "you seemed somewhat distracted."

Confident that the *matukach* priest could not have seen her diminutive visitor, the shaman returned the crooked smile in kind. "Well, if I told you what I saw, you wouldn't believe me." *Or maybe you would.* But Father Raes strongly disapproved of her association with the *pitukupf*. He had told her so on several occasions.

"Try me."

To Daisy, a half-truth was quite as good as the whole thing. "While you was talking, I had this vision. It was very strange." She squinted up at a pale turquoise heaven. "There was something like little specks of fire, and they was falling down from the sky like"—she wriggled her fingers to illustrate the poetry of motion—"like . . . like . . ." The aged woman seemed unable to find the word.

The kindly priest tried to help. "You saw something falling—like rain?"

She shook her head. "It was like . . . mañana."

He did not respond to this nonsensical statement. *Poor old soul must still be half asleep.*

Daisy Perika waved her hand impatiently. "You know—that food that fell from heaven."

The Jesuit scholar smiled. "I believe you mean manna."

She nodded. "That's what I said—that stuff God fed to Moses. And them Philippines."

"Philistines," he said automatically.

She stared at the priest as if he'd lost his mind. "So you're sayin' it was the *Philistines* that Moses led outta slavery in Egypt?"

"Well, of course not. I was merely—"

The Ute elder cackled a raspy laugh. Right in his face.

It was hardly the first time Father Raes had been taken in by the sly old creature. This troublesome woman delighted in teasing him. But he could play the game as well. "How fascinating that you've had this revelation. And such a remarkable coincidence." The cleric clasped his hands and raised his gaze to the heavens. "On this very morning, I also had a strange vision."

Daisy's dark eyes were still sparkling with the flame of her small victory.

Father Raes wondered what the vision should be. "During my sermon, I noticed that you were talking. Though at first, I could not see with whom you were conversing." This much was true enough. "And then—for just a moment—I thought I saw someone sitting beside you." He was about to suggest that it must have been her guardian angel when he noticed an expression of alarm pass over Daisy's face. The priest—who suspected that the elder still occasionally talked to the dwarf—seized the opportunity. "Someone small it was—a most peculiar-looking little creature." His brow furrowed in feigned puzzlement. "I only saw it for a moment, and then—whatever it was—it was gone." He flicked his fingers. "Poof!" Father Raes smiled. "Now what do you think of that?"

Daisy Perika met the priest's penetrating gaze with the most brazen expression she could muster. "I think it must be something you ate." But her old legs were trembling as she hurried away.

For once, the long-suffering priest had the last laugh.

CHAPTER 3

First Man said: "I do not believe this thing. We are very poor. Why should we be visited by a Holy Being? I cannot believe what you tell me."
—Sandoval, Hastin Tlo'tsi hee

Chimney Rock Archaeological Site

As Charlie Moon gripped her arm, Daisy Perika grunted her way out of the pickup. Once her feet were firmly planted on the earth, the tribal elder leaned on an oak walking stick and glared up at the dark face shaded by the brim of a black Stetson. "I don't know why we had to come to this place."

A glint of amusement sparkled in Charlie Moon's eye. "Because the forest service opened up the archaeological site early." He patted his aunt's stooped shoulder. "Especially for us Indians."

"Hmmpf. I can see the top of Chimney Rock from where I live."

"But you can't see this." Moon waved his arm in an expansive gesture. "Pit houses all over the mesa." He pointed to the northeast. "And up there on the Crag, there's a great view of the stone towers."

She kicked at a bluetail lizard that skittered safely out of range. "It's a bunch of foolishness. Nothing up here but rocks and sand. And old ghosts."

"These haunts must be starved for news," he said. "Been waiting a thousand years for some talkative old lady to come and tell 'em the latest gossip." Aunt Daisy claimed she often chatted with ghosts who wandered out of *Cañon del Espíritu*.

Her dark eyes snapped at his teasing. "If the spirits want to come to my place to exchange a few words, that's one thing. But those who stay away from the living want to be left alone. Just like I do."

Her nephew, who could think of no useful reply, was saved when Daisy Perika saw someone she knew. "Look. Over there." She pointed her chin at two people emerging from an ancient pickup.

Charlie Moon turned to look. The 1957 Chevrolet had been brush-painted a pale shade of blue that matched the sky. The bed was covered with a homemade plywood camper shell. April Tavishuts was brushing something off her black skirt. April's stepfather—a rail-thin old man—slammed the door on the driver's side. He muttered something unintelligible, spat on the ground. Moon was surprised to see Alvah Yazzi at the ruins. The Navajo elder's attitude about avoiding such places was—if possible—more strongly held than Aunt Daisy's.

As if her nephew could not see past the end of his nose, Daisy said: "It's that Tavishuts girl you sat with in church last Sunday." *And her stepfather.* Alvah Yazzi had married April's Ute mother just over a year ago. A shrewish woman with a tongue sharp as a sliver of broken glass, she had not been that good a catch. But if Alvah's burden had been heavy, he had not been destined to carry it long. A few weeks after the marriage, his bride had died in an automobile accident west of Bayfield. The woman had not been wearing her seat belt. Her husband had. The Navajo had walked away from the overturned sedan with nothing more than scratches. Alvah was a prudent man. And though the Navajo was two decades older than April's mother, he carried his years well. Daisy Perika found herself smiling. *He's closer to my age than his dead wife's. And now he needs looking after.* She waved at the pair.

April had already seen the towering form of Charlie Moon and his aged aunt. The young woman was approaching, her Navajo stepfather following several paces behind with short, hesitant steps. Appropriate greetings and pleasantries were exchanged. Obligatory observations were made about the weather. All were in agreement that rain was needed. April looked up at Moon. Last Sunday, they hadn't exchanged more than a dozen words. "Since you took up ranching, I don't see you very much. Except at church."

"I keep fairly busy." Moon looked longingly to the north. Toward the Columbine.

April took a calculated risk. "I hear you got yourself a pretty girl-friend."

Charlie Moon didn't know what to say to this. He squinted at the sky.

Daisy seized the opportunity. "He's been nuzzling up to a yella-haired *matukach* woman." The old woman rolled her eyes. "She lives in California. Prob'ly rubs elbows with them movie stars."

April looked shyly at his polished boots. "California's a long way off."

Moon's reply was touched by melancholy. "That it is."

"You must get lonesome."

That I do.

There was a brief silence while April Tavishuts and Charlie Moon both wished she'd kept her mouth shut.

"April's got herself a job," Alvah Yazzi snapped.

Moon was relieved at this change of subject. "What kind of job?"

The young woman shrugged modestly. "Nothing much."

Her Navajo stepfather snorted. "You said that right."

April shot the old man a warning glance, then turned to face Moon. "I'm a graduate student in the department of anthropology and archae-ology at Rocky Mountain Polytechnic. Professor Axton is department chairman." She glanced toward the Crag. "We're conducting a survey here at the site."

Alvah spat the words through thin lips. "I've told her—don't disturb the places where the Old Ones lived."

Daisy nodded her approval of this sage advice, but held her tongue. *Maybe that Navajo is smarter than he looks.*

April Tavishuts looked her stepfather straight in the eye. "I'm not going to disturb anything. We'll be taking measurements—and making photographs. That's all."

"Bullshit," Alvah said. This was always an effective conversation stopper.

An uneasy silence was relieved by the approach of a tall, tanned white woman in her middle fifties. She moved with easy familiarity along a winding pathway that meandered among the pit-house ruins. Outfitted in khaki slacks and a spotless, white two-pocket shirt, she exhibited perfect posture and an almost military bearing. The newcomer directed her gaze at the young Ute woman. "Excuse me, April, but the tour is scheduled to begin in"—she paused to glance at a wristwatch—"about seven minutes."

Moon smiled at April. "You going to have a look at the ruins?"

"Me and Dr. Silk are the tour guides." April said this with a hint of pride.

"Token redskin," Alvah Yazzi observed with an ugly curl of his lip.

"Nonsense," the khakied woman said. "April is far more familiar with the site than Professor Axton's other students. She's a natural to act as my associate."

"*Leezh bee hahalkaadí asdzáá,*" Yazzi muttered.

Moon knew enough Navajo to understand. *Shovel-woman.*

Pointedly ignoring her stepfather, the young woman introduced the archaeologist to Daisy Perika and Charlie Moon. "Dr. Silk knows more about the Chimney Rock ruins than anyone."

Daisy responded with a polite nod.

The scientist reached out to shake Moon's extended hand. "Forget the doctor stuff. I'm just plain Amanda Silk."

There was nothing plain about the woman. Moon found her hand hard and callused. "You do a lot of work at Chimney Rock?"

She smiled to display a prominent but attractive set of teeth. "Just the dirty work. Salvage archaeology. Cleaning up after the occasional pothunter."

"Someone has been digging in the pit houses," April said with a grave expression. "Dr. Silk works for the NAGPRA committee."

Alvah frowned suspiciously at his stepdaughter. "What'n hell's that?"

"Native American Graves Protection and Repatriation Act," April responded in a patronizing tone. As if he should have known.

Amanda Silk glanced at a nearby pit-house ruin. "The vandals came during the winter months, while the site was closed. I've been awarded a contract to survey the area for illegal excavations. Evaluate the damage. Repair whatever harm they've done."

Moon thought there must be lots of places where a pothunter would have a better chance to dig up a salable artifact. And less chance of getting caught in the act. "The diggers do any serious damage?"

Amanda Silk shook her head. "Doesn't look like the work of professionals. Some teenagers, most likely—hoping to unearth something for their artifact collections." The archaeologist beamed upon April. "Well, young lady—we must not keep our special guests waiting."

April looked up hopefully at Charlie Moon. "You want to come along?"

He did. Moon invited his aunt to come with him and have a look at the site.

Her feet hurt, Daisy said. She would wait for his return. Which she hoped would not be too long.

Alvah Yazzi did not receive an invitation from his Ute stepdaughter.

The tour started on the Great Kiva Trail Loop, a path winding along the developed section of Ghost Wolf Mesa. The first group of Indian tourists represented several generations. An aged Paiute leaned heavily on two canes; he was so thin that it seemed a breeze might topple him. On the small end of the age scale, there were a dozen children. These ranged from babes in arms to a sullen teenager who had a Walkman earphone plugged into his ear. While more than half the participants were Utes who lived within a few miles of the stone towers, other tribes were also represented. Among those Moon recognized were an Apache family from Dulce, a Navajo hand-trembler from Teec Nos Pos, his brother who ran sheep at Naschitti. There was a famous potter from San Juan Pueblo, a Hopi elder from Shungopavi. And a Zuni woman pretty enough to turn a man's head.

Charlie Moon—unconsciously governed by his ingrained policeman's instinct—stayed near the rear of the group where he could see everyone. As the gathering was led to a sandstone shelf near the north edge of the mesa, the more senior of the tour guides paused and waited for silence. Amanda Silk pointed to a bowl-shaped depression in the stone at her feet. "This is the Stone Basin—the only one at Chimney

Rock. There are several at the Chaco Canyon ruins. Like this one, the Chaco basins are all near a Great Kiva. But we don't know what purpose they served." She looked expectantly at the group of dark faces. "Any of you care to comment?"

This invitation was met by a stony silence. The guide sighed. A typical group of tourists would have had all sorts of suggestions. It was a place for sacrificial blood to be spilled. One imaginative visitor had suggested that the depression had been filled with water and used as a mystical mirror for peering into dark places. A slack-jawed youth from St. Louis had snickered to his peers that maybe it was a toilet for coyotes. Not that his language had been so polite. But these Indians were a quiet lot. No speculation from their lips. Amanda wondered whether one of the elderly Native Americans present might actually know something useful about the basin—but did not intend to discuss such mysteries with a white woman.

At an encouraging look from her mentor, April Tavishuts found her voice and addressed the gathering of Indian tourists. "When we get up to the Crag, there's a wonderful view of Companion and Chimney Rocks. And you'll see the ruins of the Great Pueblo. It was constructed between A.D. 1076 and 1093." Uneasy with this first experience in public speaking, her voice quavered. She cleared her throat and began again. "The structure appears to be perfectly rectangular. But actually, the stone walls are not quite parallel. If you project lines along the walls, they converge right here—at the Stone Basin." April waited for some expression of appreciation for this curious little gem of information. She got none from the Indian spectators.

Dr. Silk made a slight nod to her subordinate.

"Okay," April said quickly, "let's go up to the Crag."

Charlie Moon, who was enjoying the slow pace of the day, moved along behind the small crowd. As he walked, he thought a rancher's thoughts. Maybe some rain would fall on the Columbine's vast acreage within the next few days. What would beef cattle be selling for this time next year. Would the two hundred acres along the river produce enough hay to see him through the winter. Was there any way to raise enough cash to buy that magnificent Hereford bull from the senator's ranch next door. Sure. Rob a bank.

The Tale

Daisy Perika and Alvah Yazzi sat on the rusted tailgate of Charlie Moon's F150. It was blissfully peaceful. Butter-colored butterflies fluttered by. A mountain bluebird fussed among the branches of a juniper, cocking an inquisitive head at the biped intruders.

The elders of their respective tribes were content to merely sit and look. There was much that was pleasing to the eye, and restful to the weary soul. Below the pleated skirt of the mesa was a broad valley, where a copper-hued stream slithered along like a glittering serpent, shifting ripples imitating the facets of reptilian scales. On the near side of the creek stretched a thousand acres of tender new grasses, born emerald green. In this vast pasture were sleek, white-faced cows— frisky calves cutting frolicky bovine capers.

The Ute woman and Navajo man enjoyed those things below. But up there, the faceless twins relentlessly drew their gaze. Crowned with swirling wisps of downy cloud-feathers, the sandstone monoliths looked down upon the mortals. And waited.

Daisy's eyes fairly ached from what they had seen. She closed them for a brief rest. Then made a sideways appraisal of her male companion— starting at the forked end. Alvah's feet were shod in canvas sandals. The thin man wore faded denim jeans, a checkered cotton shirt under his Albuquerque Dukes jacket. A massive silver-veined turquoise nugget was suspended from his neck on a leather cord. A sweat-stained red bandanna was fixed tightly around his head; long steel-gray braids hung between his shoulder blades.

Daisy supposed that April had done a good thing bringing her stepfather to this place amongst the Anasazi ghosts. Alvah Yazzi hated being here. He would complain about it all winter. And having something to grouch about would make him happy. Daisy thanked God that she had not become a grumpy old woman who made her nephew miserable. She was startled when the Navajo spoke.

"So how've you been?"

The Ute woman shrugged.

"Me too," he said in a voice that crackled with age. Alvah Yazzi stuffed a brier pipe with tobacco from a yellowed cotton pouch. He struck a phosphorus match across his belt buckle. After the curly-leaf was ignited, he took a long draw and fell into his customary silence.

Daisy Perika assumed that the Navajo had said his piece for the afternoon. She didn't mind. Being with a man who knew how to keep his mouth shut was fine with her.

But once again, his voice pierced the silence. "Must get lonesome for you. Living out there by the Canyon of the Spirits."

So you know where my home is. "It's not so bad. I see my nephew more often now than when he lived over by Ignacio."

He nodded to express his appreciation of this blessing.

She continued. "Charlie Moon drives down from his ranch every Sunday morning, takes me to church. After mass, we go to a restaurant."

"That's good."

"He's a nice young man." She would never have admitted this in front of her nephew. "But today," she grumped, "I haven't had my lunch yet. We passed right by that Mexican restaurant at Arboles." The thought of cheese and onion enchiladas made her mouth water. "Charlie said we'd get some eats later. He was in a big hurry to bring me up here." *Like a half-starved old woman with a brain in her head would want to hobble around and look at ugly piles of rock. Where dead people used to live.*

Alvah squinted into the sun. "Down at Window Rock, we hear some big talk about Cháala Tl'éhonaa'éi."

"About *what*?"

"Charlie Moon." He took a pull on the pipe.

She snorted. *Just like an uppity Navajo. Can't talk plain American. Got to throw his jibber-jabber around.* "Oh, you mean Charlie Muá-tagó-ci." But it pleased the Ute elder to realize that even these Navajo people had heard about her nephew.

Alvah exhaled a cloud of gray smoke, and coughed. "There was lots of talk about him being a very clever policeman."

"He did pretty good for himself." Daisy said this with a proud tilt of her chin. "And now Charlie's got himself a big ranch to run."

"April tells me you make medicines."

Pleased at his interest in her work, the Ute shaman explained about how from time to time she did gather special plants. Lechuguilla.

Thorn apple. Toad flax. Deer's ears. Some were available within walking distance of her home, others required an automobile trip. A few she purchased mail order. But, she explained, you had to know just how to prepare the roots or leaves or blossoms. Mess up and somebody could get very sick. Maybe even die. The preparation and dispensing of medicines was not to be taken lightly.

"You ever use Hisiiyaanii oil?"

"Sure. For treating cold sores. And skin cancer."

The Navajo puffed on his pipe, but seemed to be getting little pleasure from it. "April—she says you can cure most anything."

The Ute pharmacist modestly admitted that this was true. If someone needed a special medication for bleeding, or eye-popping headaches, or stomach cramps that bent you double—she could mix up just the thing. For a price.

The pipe was spent. Alvah Yazzi tapped the bowl on the edge of the tailgate, emptying the warm ashes onto the sand. He looked to the sky, where a hawk circled with sinister grace. "They say you talk to that Ute dwarf."

Daisy put on a puzzled expression. "Dwarf?"

"The one who lives in *Cañon del Espíritu*. In a badger hole."

"Hmmpf," she said. *April's been telling this Navajo snoop too much.*

"And they say you talk to spirits." He turned to stare at her. "Is this true?"

She looked straight ahead, saying nothing.

"I know an old man down by Lukachukai—they say he talks to the *chíindii*. I don't know if it is true. But my people consider this a very dangerous thing to do."

You got no business telling me what's dangerous. "Us Utes do what we please. If one of the spirits was to drop by and visit my place—and was inclined to talk to me . . . I might talk back. If I wanted to."

The Navajo seemed almost to shudder. "But what if you don't want them coming around. What if you want these *chíindii* to go away?"

Now that he was seeking her advice, the old shaman felt like boasting. "If I didn't want 'em around, I'd send 'em packing."

The old man looked doubtful. "You could do that?"

After the barest hesitation, she replied, "Sure."

Alvah Yazzi frowned at the stem of the cold pipe. As if it were a snake that might bite him on the lip. "Maybe sometime . . ." His voice trailed off.

She leaned closer. "What'd you say?"

"Maybe sometime I'll come and see you."

"I guess that'd be okay."

While the sun moved three diameters along its arc, they sat quietly.

Gradually, Alvah's head slumped. His chin rested on his chest. The pipe slipped from his grasp and fell to the earth.

Daisy sighed. *When I was young and pretty, they didn't go to sleep on me.*

With a suddenness that startled her, the Navajo's head jerked erect. He turned to look at the old woman. As if he'd never seen her before.

She thought Alvah's face looked peculiar. Almost wild. Like he was still half asleep.

His voice was raspy. "You know what those are?"

"What *what* are?" she snapped, annoyed at this old man's strange behavior.

Alvah pointed two knobby fingers at the stone monoliths. "Those are the Twin War Gods." He paused to allow the significance of this statement to sink in. "My people know all about them."

"You Navajo are a clever bunch." The Ute elder adjusted her cotton scarf to conceal a smirk.

"The Twin's father is the sun," Alvah whispered. "Their mother is Yolkaí Estsán—White Shell Woman."

Daisy was familiar with the myths. The tales varied, depending on whether a Zuni, Hopi, Apache, or Navajo was doing the telling. The situation was further complicated by the fact that various clans within these tribes had their particular version of the story. But in most accounts, White Shell Woman—also known as White Bead Girl—was the moon. From where they were sitting on the pickup tailgate, she would rise almost behind her twin sons and look over their shoulders. It was a fairly good story as stories go, Daisy thought. But the Utes had their own tales to tell. So she pitched her two cents into the bucket. "That tall one the *matukach* named Chimney Rock—my grandmother called it Yucca Flower Spike." She pronounced the Ute phrase for the Navajo's benefit. "Now there's an interesting story about how it got that name. A long time ago, there was this young Ute woman called Stone Calf. She didn't have a husband, but she had herself an ugly baby that had long black hair all over its body. That was because it was fathered by a black bear and—"

The words from Alvah's mouth cut her off. "When the world was young, there were terrible monsters. They killed human beings—and fed on their flesh. These beasts were slain by the Twin War Gods so people could live on the earth without being molested." The Navajo's dark eyes stared into empty space, as if he could see that which had long since passed away. "There was once a glorious time—and not so long ago—when the Twins received the honor due them. Father Sun and Mother Moon were worshiped. In return, they did many good things for the People."

Daisy groaned inwardly. Like most old men, this one liked to tell stories she had no particular interest in hearing.

The Navajo's voice droned on, like a dry wind in the pines. "Long before the horses came, some farmers had moved up there—onto this mesa. There were tall trees here in those times, not just the puny little piñon and juniper you see now. The farmers grew food down in the valley, by the river. Squash. Corn. Beans."

She felt a hunger pang. *Maybe Charlie Moon will take me into Pagosa for some eats.*

"These farmers lived in houses that were halfway under the ground. They kept warm in winter. No matter how cold it got—or how hard the winds blew." Unconsciously, Alvah Yazzi began to button his jacket against the light breeze slipping over the edge of the mesa. "Later on, those desert people who had come up from Mexico—they came to this place to worship . . . her." He jutted his chin to indicate where the unseen moon would rise. "They came up here because the sky had stopped giving water. The corn and beans shriveled up in the fields down by the creek. The squash were small—with black spots on them. It was very bad. We thought: If we can make White Shell Woman cry from hearing about our troubles, her tears will water the earth. So we prayed to her."

We? The truck bed was a hard place to sit. Daisy shifted uneasily, but found no comfort.

Alvah Yazzi's voice took on a bitter tone that disturbed the Ute elder. "We prayed and prayed. But White Shell Woman shed no tears upon our land."

"Droughts can be very bad," the Ute woman said. "I remember one back when my second husband was growing pinto beans down by the Piedra. It got so dry that parts of the riverbed turned to dust. My man said it was so dry even the fish had ticks. He was a big joker. Kept me laughing all the time." She smiled at her Navajo companion.

Alvah continued with a stony face, "We knew that sacrifices were necessary. We had the farmers bring fine cooking pots—and throw them over the cliff, onto the rocks."

The practical Ute woman considered this an exceedingly wasteful practice.

"They broke many pots. Still, our crops withered." He pointed to the distant Crag. "The chief priest lived up there in the big white temple. To make the Moon Goddess weep, he pierced his tongue. His blood dripped onto the sandstone altar."

Daisy's tongue responded with a sympathetic ache.

"Still, there was no rain. So slaves were sacrificed. They were bound with rawhide and thrown into the fire." The old man directed a peculiar look at his companion. "The Old Ones—they prefer to kill with flames."

This had gone far enough. "Look," she said, "I don't like this story. It's no good dredging up all these bad thoughts. Why don't we talk about something cheerful." *Like lunch.*

It was as if the Navajo had not heard her protest. "The bonfire was fueled by the bodies of slaves for many days." He turned his gaze to the arid sky. "Even this did not make White Shell Woman weep."

Daisy craned her neck in an attempt to see the tour group. *What's keeping Charlie Moon?*

"When they ran out of slaves, they started sacrificing the farmers who lived in the round houses."

"I figured they'd get around to that." She said this with cutting sarcasm.

"Men, women—even children—they put them all into the fire."

"You shouldn't tell such awful tales." *It could bring on sickness.*

"But the skies were hard," he said with a toothy grimace. "Like copper."

This Alvah Yazzi was a strange one. Even for a Navajo.

"So the chief priest, he knew things was finished here. He decided to leave the great white temple up there on the sandstone shelf. He had the temple kivas burned—and the other rooms. Then he ordered all the farmers' round houses burned. It didn't matter much, most of the people were already gone. Many had been thrown into the fire. Others had slipped away at night."

Daisy wished she could slip away.

"Before his job was finished, the chief priest had one thing left to do. He had something that belonged to White Shell Woman—something that must be left behind, where her sons could watch over it."

Daisy had heard at least a dozen tales of the treasure hidden by the Anasazi wizard. She yawned.

The Navajo paused, his lips curving into an unpleasant smile. "When the precious object was hidden, he threw himself over the cliff."

Daisy nodded her approval. "Well, I'm glad to hear it." Relieved that the dreadful tale was finally at an end, she bent forward to stretch her stiff back.

The old man sat on the tailgate, shaking his head. "Someday White Shell Woman will come back." He pointed at the stone towers. "She'll stand up there—between her sons. When she does, the Twins will become flesh again. And when they walk, the earth will tremble."

"Well, when they do," she muttered, "I hope I'm a long ways off."

"When they live again," he said, "they will slay monsters."

Best to humor him. "I've got nothing against killing monsters."

"But before this happens, there will be dark signs and terrible omens."

Being curious about such matters, Daisy perked up. "What kind of omens?"

Alvah raised his hands, as if in supplication before a dark altar. "Bones burned to ashes—that will be the sign."

She nodded as if this made perfect sense.

The man at her side was rubbing his eyes.

Daisy squinted at the sun. "It's getting late." And it was. The cosmic clock was ticking away their allotted time.

Her companion seemed drained of words.

Daisy was suddenly feeling very alone. Lonely enough to wish the old Navajo would talk some more. Even about crazy things. So she primed the pump. "Alvah, how do you come to know these stories—about the Old Ones who lived here?"

As if he had been unaware of her presence, the old man turned slowly. He stared blankly at the Ute woman. "What did you say?"

"How do you know all these things?"

His face was without expression. "What things?"

She glared at him. Either the Navajo was weak in the head or he was playing a prank on her. Either way, Alvah Yazzi was a very annoying man.

His lower lip trembled. "Have I been . . . talking?"

"No," she snapped. "You never said a word."

He slid off the tailgate.

"Nice visiting with you, Alvah." She watched the elderly Navajo walk stiffly back to his antique Chevrolet pickup. He moved around the vehicle, rapping his knuckles on the hood, kicking at a tire. He paused at the plywood shell to rub his palm across a dusty window. His lips were moving, but Daisy was too far away to make out his words. "Pitiful old man is talking to himself," she muttered. "I hope I never get like that."

The Dream

Daisy Perika seated herself inside Charlie Moon's pickup. April's Navajo stepfather had not been particularly good company. *But at least he's a man.*

Her stomach growled. She searched the glove compartment and found a cellophane-wrapped package of yellow crackers that had some kind of peanut butter paste smashed between them. Daisy ate them all. This made her thirsty. She found a plastic bottle of Pepsi behind the seat, and drank it. Following this snack, she rested her head on a rolled-up shawl and entertained fantasies about a fine meal. Big, steaming bowl of red chili with lots of hamburger and fat pinto beans. A grilled cheese sandwich. Tall glass of iced tea. For dessert, banana cream pie.

Soon, the aged woman was asleep. Dreaming her strange dream.

The Ute shaman floats. Like a golden aspen leaf on still water. She looks beneath the surface, and sees them—those violent men with blood dripping from their pierced tongues.

The solemn priests of the Cloud Wolf Clan spend their seasons watching White Shell Woman float serenely across the heavens. When the signs are right, they lift up their arms and cry out to her, pleading for favors. They ask for the power to banish sickness. And foreknowledge of those perilous times when the husband of the moon will fall into darkness—or when White Shell Woman herself is swallowed by the shadow-snake. These mystics also seek visions of those secret things beyond the misty boundaries of Middle World.

From time to time, the pale mother of the Twin War Gods will consider these requests. Most favorable of all are those occasions when White Shell Woman ascends far to the north—so that she may stand between her towering sons. When this happens, she is likely to grant any request made by the guardians of the Temple of the Moon. As one such rendezvous approaches, the rulers in the great city to the south send their strongest runner with a message to the priests. They are instructed thus: Ask for this one favor—an end to the terrible drought that is sucking away the lifeblood of our empire.

The priests launch a determined effort, intended to please their goddess. A great jubilee is organized. They don fine robes of pale yellow cotton fringed with iridescent rainbows of macaw feathers. Tiny bells of burnished copper hang from their earlobes, tinkling as they dance and chant in the principle kiva of the great white temple. Special songs are composed for a choir of children brought in from the southern metropolis for the occasion. There are feasts of roasted venison and boiled corn seasoned with dried serviceberry.

Sadly, these magnificent and joyful displays provoke no response from their goddess. The chief priest discards his ceremonial robe to read the entrails of a badger. The signs are unmistakable—it was a blunder to hold great celebrations. The Goddess of the Moon does not wish to be merry. She is melancholy, because she is far from her family. Perhaps this sadness can be used to advantage . . . perhaps she can be induced to shed tears that will fall to water the earth. The priests' faces and arms are blackened with soot from charred spruce. They fast until wasted flesh hangs limp on their bones. They offer up mournful chants, telling awful tales of pestilence, disease . . . and horrible death from starvation. It is all very dismal.

But the pale woman in the sky is unmoved. She sheds no tears to water the parched earth. The leaders of the Cloud Wolf Clan hold lengthy councils in the temple kivas. They hear a multitude of heated arguments and bold proposals—and finally come to a fearful decision. Intense pain will be inflicted upon their persons. Under the cold gaze of White Shell Woman, eyelids and tongues are pierced with slivers of bone. Priestly blood falls onto the temple plaza, gathering in sticky pools. Moreover, eyes are gouged out.

Still, the west winds bring no rain—only dust. Which the frustrated supplicants grind between their teeth.

The string of failures continues year after year. For a dozen scorching summers, branches of the vast kingdom shrivel and decay. Finally the very roots begin to die.

The hard truth finally becomes plain to even the dullest of the priestly caste—for some unfathomable reason, White Shell Woman has turned her face from those who live only to serve her.

Not by nature a patient people, the rulers and administrators gradually grow weary of the priests, who become the butt of crude jokes. In the Plaza of the Sun, the hunchbacked flute-player bellows derisive, vulgar songs about the follies of these so-called holy men. Worse still, whole communities of farmers rebel against the established authorities. They refuse to send food to the great city until the Cloud Wolf Clan has summoned the rains. Cruel punishments are meted out on the agricultural villages. In response, many lowland farmers scatter to the four winds in search of a green land where their children will not starve.

The desperate priests build great bonfires on the lofty Crag that stands before the Twin War Gods. For every night of a full phase of the moon, they bind seven slaves hand and foot. When darkness comes, these shrieking victims are cast into the roaring flames of a bonfire. At dawn,

the priests breakfast on roasted human flesh. Charred bones are piled in
great heaps where White Shell Woman can see them as she passes over
Middle World. Surely this will be enough. Surely she will weep, so that
her tears will water the beans and corn and squash that wilt in the fields.

After such terrible sacrifices, the Moon Goddess does finally
respond to their supplications. She weeps. For an entire night, her tears
fall from the sky. But this is not nourishing rain that falls from the wet
eyes of White Shell Woman. These are drops of searing fire.

The chief priest understands this omen. The Moon Goddess is dis-
pleased with their sacrifices. There is nothing more to be done.

Weary of soul, the keepers of the Temple of the Moon prepare to
abandon the sacred mesa. But not before concealing the clan's most
singular possession—an object so sacred that it cannot be moved from
the protective presence of the Twin War Gods. Those few who have
knowledge of the resting place must perish with their secret—even the
chief priest. But the old man can see far into the future. He knows that
after many winters have come and gone, his ghost will come to look
upon the treasure of his beloved. And he is plagued with this nagging
worry: Might the spirit of an aged man forget where he has hidden the
precious object? Being a cautious soul, the chief priest leaves himself an
enigmatic clue. It is easy to understand. Except for those who are too
clever to see what is so plain.

Daisy Perika awakened, gasping for breath, relieved to be back in
Middle World. *What an awful dream.* She decided that this bad experience was, in one sense, no different from many others in her life. Men
were to blame. Charlie Moon for leaving her alone and hungry while he
wandered around the ruins with April Tavishuts. And Alvah Yazzi for
exciting her imagination with his mutterings about Anasazi sacrifices.

The Child

It was a perfect time for Native American Day at Chimney Rock. As a
trout-shaped cloud passed over the sun, a refreshing breeze came from

the north to cool the sweaty brow. From the edge of Ghost Wolf Mesa, it seemed that one could see to the very rim of the world. As they approached the narrow land bridge connecting the mesa to the Crag, the Indian tourists followed their appointed leaders. And unlike those hurried, harried guides at Mesa Verde—who have little time to answer questions—Amanda Silk and April Tavishuts encouraged the visitors to make inquiries. Though the older Indians remained silent, there were now occasional questions and comments from the younger set. All queries were answered with a patient politeness, making each of their guests understand that they were important. Moreover, the guides knew everything worth knowing about the Anasazi ruins. Or so it seemed.

Charlie Moon was already familiar with the site, which was located within the boundaries of the Southern Ute Reservation. The gathering of Indians and their families was more interesting to him than the dusty jumble of long-abandoned ruins. The children were especially fascinating. Offspring of the town Indian families were easy to identify. Noisy and boisterous, ignoring their parents' urgent pleas to behave, they were much the same as other American children. Those raised by traditional Indian parents were shy and well behaved. A very cute little girl caught the Ute's eye. For this special occasion, she was outfitted in a new yellow dress and red cowboy boots. And looked to be about five years old. The tiny girl, seemingly oblivious of the other children, walked among the adults. She did slow down, occasionally to glance at a purple flower or pick up a pretty stone. *It would be nice to have a daughter just like that one.* But it took a couple to produce children. And so Moon began to think about Camilla Willow. She was a remarkably pretty woman—and very smart. Had money too. Maybe Camilla would like to have children someday. *Our children.* Moon walked along, lost in his happy daydream. What would they be like, these small human beings? Lively and smart, he hoped. Not overly shy. But not like some of these noisy town Indians' kids, who were yelling and throwing rocks at each other.

Something distracted him from this tangle of thoughts.

Far off to his right, among the juniper and piñon that covered Ghost Wolf Mesa, Charlie Moon thought he saw a flash of color. Bright yellow. Like the little girl's dress. He made a quick check of the crowd of tourists and did not see the child. But children get tired on walks like this and have to be taken back to the family car where they can have a refreshing nap. *Could be one of her parents left with her while I wasn't looking. Or maybe not.*

Not one to ponder such possibilities, Charlie Moon immediately left the trail. A few long strides brought him to the place where he'd seen the flash of color. It was not ten yards from the edge of the cliff. He hurried to the precipice and looked over. The Ute was immensely grateful that there was no sign of a yellow dress—or a yellow anything—on the talus slope below the ledge. *Maybe I didn't see anything.* But to be certain, he made his way south along the cliff.

After only a few steps, he thought he heard an echo of something. A child's voice. But from which direction?

The Ute looked up to see a red-tailed hawk circling lazily over the mesa. Aunt Daisy claimed that angels sometimes came in such feathery disguises. *What do you see, Si-gwaná-ci?*

The hawk fell as if upon prey, then slowed. And circled lower.

He walked toward the hawk's flickering shadow.

The air had fallen deathly still.

Then he heard it again. A small voice. Singing? Moon smiled.

He moved quickly, but quietly. It would not occur to one of such tender years that anyone might be worried. Or looking for her. *Don't want to scare the kid.*

And there she was, under the circling silhouette of the hawk. And only a few paces from the edge of the precipice, sitting in the shade of a fragrant juniper. She was singing to herself in a thin voice. "Mary, Mary . . . she had a little bitty lamb . . . its feets was white as snow. And ev'ry-where Mary went, her lamb was sure to . . ." She looked up.

Charlie Moon smiled. And spoke softly. "Hello, young lady."

Openmouthed, the child gazed boldly up at this man, whose black hat seemed to touch the clouds. "I know who you are."

So much for scaring her. "Okay. Who am I?"

"You're the giant—the one that chased Jack down the beanstalk."

He shook his head. "Afraid not."

The child—who knew a giant when she saw one—did not alter her opinion.

"Know why I seem so big?"

Her blank expression made it clear that she did not.

"It's because you're so little."

"Why am I little?" she asked.

"Maybe," he said thoughtfully, "you're a midget."

"I'm Peggy." She picked up a sandstone pebble, stuffed it into her mouth. "If you're not the giant, then who are you?"

"My name is Charlie. Ahh . . . I hope you're not going to swallow that."

"D'you want it?"

"Yeah." He kneeled, held out his hand.

She spat it onto his palm. "Charlie what?"

"Charlie Moon." He examined the little girl with a lawman's eye. "Are you okay?"

She nodded.

He stared at the moist pebble in his hand. "Getting hungry?"

"A little bit."

"Well, don't eat any rocks."

"Why?"

"They're bad for your teeth." He fumbled in his jacket pocket, offered her a piece of hard candy.

She unwrapped the peppermint, popped it into her mouth.

Moon sat down beside her, leaned against the tree. "I bet your mom and dad are real worried about you."

"Daddy is in heaven. With the angels."

They shared a brief silence.

"Then I guess I'd better take you back to your mom."

"No."

He closed his eyes and considered his predicament. *If I just scoop her up, she'll probably start squalling like a stuck pig.* This had to be handled with some care. "You like to go for walks by yourself?"

She nodded. "Sometimes."

They sat under the juniper, staring up at an immense sky.

A large black beetle was passing by. It paused to fold its front legs, press its segmented head to the ground.

"What's it doing?" the child asked.

"Talking to God," Moon said. That's what his grandfather had told him.

She reached for the insect.

"No," Moon said.

"Why?"

"It wouldn't taste good. Not with peppermint."

She made a face. "I wouldn't eat a *bug*."

"Why?"

This question evidently stumped her. Sensing he'd gained the upper hand, Moon was pleased with himself. "I'd have thought you'd be afraid to wander away all alone."

The little girl frowned. "I wasn't alone. He was with me."

"Who?"

"The man." She looked up at the Ute. "He wanted me to come with him."

He didn't like the sound of this. "What sort of man?"

The child's small, round face mirrored her uncertainty.

"Was he tall or short—fat or thin?"

"I guess so."

"How was he dressed?"

"Feathers."

Moon raised an eyebrow at this. "Feathers?"

She nodded. "Pretty feathers. Like a big bird."

Okay. "Was this bird young or old?"

Peggy thought about it. "Old."

Moon grinned. "Old as me?"

"How old are you?"

"I've lost count. What'd he look like?"

"Like a man."

This was a difficult interrogation. "What kind of man?"

Peggy's smooth brow furrowed with concentration. "Welllll . . . two legs. And two arms. And a head."

"Good. Now let's say you wanted to draw a picture of him. What would you put in it?"

She used a juniper twig to draw a stick figure in the sand. A rectangular body supporting a triangular head. Standing on four legs.

Moon was somewhat critical and said so. "That doesn't look much like a man."

"It's a dog," she said. "Dogs has *four* legs. And a head. And a tail." She added a curled-up tail to the sketch.

He sighed. "So the man had a dog?"

"It was on his back. Its mouth was biting his head."

He could think of no sensible response to this.

She used the stick to make an eye for the four-legged animal. "Then the man pulled the dog over him."

Moon didn't get it, and said as much. "I don't get it."

"He was really big," she said helpfully. "And hairy."

"The man or the dog?"

She squinted at him. Big people could be so silly. "His ears was pointy. And his nose was *really* long and pointy. Like Pinocchio's."

"That's because the little wooden kid told big lies," he said. Hoping she'd get the point.

Peggy giggled. "And Pinocchio's nose grew longer and longer and—"

Her little mind was drifting. "Did this dog have fleas?"

Peggy nodded her head, bobbing a short ponytail. "I guess so."

"Remember what color he was?"

"His hair was white—like Mary's little lamb."

He made a quick U-turn. "What about the man's hair?"

"I guess it was black." She squinted into the sun. "Or brownish."

Moon made a big show of looking around and seeing nothing. "This old man and the white dog, now where'd they go?"

She shrugged under the pale yellow dress. "I don't know. When you came, he went away. I guess he's 'fraid of giants." She gave the tall man an accusing look. "If you'd caught Jack before he chopped down the beanstalk—would you've eaten him up and ground up his bones for bread?"

"No," he said earnestly. "I'm on a strict diet. No bread. No bones." He licked his lips. "Don't eat nothing except boneless bananas."

She smiled, showing a set of tiny teeth.

Moon smiled back. The child looked to be fine. And it was a hundred-to-one shot she had invented the story as an excuse for wandering away from her mother. But just to be on the safe side, the question had to be asked. "Did this man . . . uh . . . touch you or anything?"

The little girl squinted at the giant. "The dog licked my ear."

"Sounds like a nice dog."

She nodded.

"Peggy—why do you think the man brought you here?"

She thought about this for a moment. "I think—to show me the picture."

"What picture?"

She pointed the toe of her red cowboy boot at the sandstone shelf beneath his feet. "That one."

He leaned to have a closer look. At the edge of some loose dirt, there were two deep scratches in the rock. One L-shaped, the other straight. Moon heard a wail off to the north. "Peggy . . . where are you . . . Pegggeee . . ." He got to his feet, grabbing the tot by her grubby little hand. "Sounds like your mother's looking for you."

"You think Mom'll be mad?"

"Maybe. She'll want to know why you wandered off."

"What should I tell her?"

Moon grinned. "I expect you'll think of something."

The child was delivered to an extremely grateful mother, who turned out to be the pretty Zuni woman. After hugging her little girl, Nancy Begay scolded her. This done, she thanked Charlie Moon. While the unrepentant child clung to her mother's leg, the adults exchanged a few words. He learned that the Zuni woman was a prosperous silversmith. The squash-blossom necklace suspended from her neck was her own work. Moon admired the silver flowers, and said so. This earned him a shy smile. It turned out that the lady was also a friend of Daisy Perika. Moon admitted his surprise that his grouchy aunt had any friends at all.

Nancy Begay laughed at this. And did not fail to notice that her daughter's rescuer was a fine-looking man. And gentle of speech and manner. Though somewhat overly tall.

He noticed that she had a dazzling smile. And was easy on the eyes. The Ute wondered whether he should ask the widow and her child to have lunch with him and his aunt. But Moon reminded himself that such an invitation would have unstated implications. And that he was spoken for. By a pale-skinned woman with hair of spun gold. *Who is very far away.* But he prudently decided that getting to know this attractive Zuni woman better wouldn't be quite the right thing to do.

An hour later, Nancy Begay departed from Chimney Rock Archaeological Site with the flock of Indian tourists. She looked back over her
shoulder. The tall Ute seemed an uncommonly kind man. He wore no
wedding band on his finger. And he had a lonely look about him. But
he had shown no interest in her. Nancy reminded herself that she was
a widow who didn't have time for fantasies. What she did have was a
daughter to raise. An imaginative, unpredictable child who made up
silly stories to excuse her misbehavior.

After watching the Zuni woman depart with her child, Moon returned
to the spot where he had found the little girl sitting under the juniper.
Walking slowly, in an ever-increasing spiral, he made a thorough
search. Except for several of his own footprints—and a few marks made
by the child's tiny boot heel—there were no traces of another presence. Which, he admitted, didn't prove what the little girl had said
she'd seen wasn't real. A man who was determined to do so could walk
from one end of the mesa to the other without getting his feet off the
sandstone. The former Ute policeman was well aware that there were
more than a few eccentrics wandering around the canyon country. He
was thankful that this one—if he existed outside the little girl's imagination—had done no harm.

Before departing, he knelt to run his finger along the lines incised in
stone. Under the loose soil, there might be a lot more. *I'll tell April
Tavishuts about it. She can pass it on to that contract archaeologist. Then I'll
find Aunt Daisy. Maybe she'll be ready for some lunch.*

CHAPTER 4

She took them to a room, and she wrapped them in the four
coverings of the Sky, the dawn, the daylight, the twilight, and
the darkness.
—Sandoval, Hastin Tlo'tsi hee

The Twin Boys were cared for . . . each had a cradle, and when
they first laughed gifts were given to all who came to the home.
Not much is told about them until the fifteenth day. By that
time they were young men.
—Sandoval, Hastin Tlo'tsi hee

The Scholars

A group of university scholars, graduate students, forest service specialists, and skilled technicians had assembled on Ghost Wolf Mesa.
They brought a wide range of knowledge, ranging from archaeology,
astronomy, and ethnography to geology, mathematics, and photogra-
phy. After a preliminary meeting at the parking lot, the team converged upon the site where Charlie Moon had found the child—and
the edge of the enigmatic petroglyph, which had now been completely
exposed. The experts assembled themselves in a loose circle around the
recently discovered illustration.

The excitement among the academics was barely submerged under
knowing nods and erudite comments about such arcane matters as
were of mutual interest. A comparison of this discovery with Chacoan

rock art. The relationship of the odd figures to Zuni and Hopi myths. The devastating effect of industrial pollution on Southwestern petroglyphs. Who was in line to get the department chairmanship once Professor Axton retired. Italian versus American hiking boots. The price of gasoline.

A bushy-haired photographer, having no time for idle gossip, busied himself by mounting a wooden view camera on a battered tripod that had been to the Gobi Desert and Antarctica. Today's best shot might, he hoped, make the cover of *National Geographic*. Or *Archaeology Today*.

A science reporter from the *Rocky Mountain News* cued his Sony tape recorder for interviews with the more notable members of the group. And hoped for some controversy.

There was a general sense that this was a rare privilege—to be present so soon after an important archaeological discovery was made. And the way this one had been found was more than a little peculiar. The experts stared hard at the petroglyph. As if by some mysterious magnetism of corporate will they could withdraw its secret.

Charlie Moon, having repeated his story a dozen times to as many inquisitive scientists, stood well outside the circle of privilege and watched. *This should be interesting.* He felt someone brush his elbow. Amanda Silk was at his side, leaning on a birch walking stick. The contract archaeologist was frowning. The Ute tipped his black Stetson. "Morning."

Her eyes measured the height of the sun. "Yes it is."

Moon looked toward the petroglyph. "So what do you think?"

"About what?"

"What the little Zuni girl found."

"It's a boojum," she muttered.

He wondered what that meant.

There was—as is common in human affairs—an unstated but clearly understood ranking. First in the pecking order was Professor Silas Axton, chairman of the Rocky Mountain Polytechnic Department of Anthropology and Archaeology. The tall, angular man stood on the southern side of the pictograph. Dr. Terry Perkins, professor of paleoastronomy, had positioned himself on the opposite side. Each made a pretense of being unaware of the other's presence. The accepted practice was that either professor's comments were directed to the respectful audience of colleagues and graduate students, certainly not to his distinguished rival.

Professor Axton had studied the highly stylized sketches of human beings with intense interest. Each had a trunk comprised of opposed triangles, arranged so the points were touching at the figure's waist, giving the impression of a highly angular hourglass. The heads were squares, with wavy lines protruding from flat scalps—presumably an indication of feathers. Legs and arms were merely lines. What made the drawing intriguing was that each of the figures had something grasped in its hands. There could be no doubt that these objects—straight lines with pointed tips—represented spears. The southerly figure—taller and thinner than his companion—held his weapon so that it was almost parallel to his body. The spear belonging to the shorter of the humanoids was leaning at a noticeable angle.

The implication of the petroglyph was obvious to each of the several scholars, but protocol required that the most eminent of them would state what was quite apparent to all. And so he did. Professor Axton cleared his throat and spoke as if he was unaware of the microphone the science reporter held within an inch of his chin. "While much detailed examination of this pictograph remains to be done, it is immediately apparent—from comparison with existing rock art in other locations—that these figures represent the Twin War Gods."

There was a murmur of agreement from his audience.

Axton moved cautiously to the "bottom" of the pictograph, where the toes of his laced boots almost touched the feet etched into the sandstone. The anthropologist frowned thoughtfully at the primitive armaments grasped by the stick figures. Then looked off into the distance at the rising towers to the northeast. "The artisan who crafted this drawing has arranged the spears in such a manner that each points toward one of the sandstone monoliths." He said this with an air of understated triumph. "Therefore," the professor continued pedantically, "the sandstone formations known as Chimney and Companion do indeed represent the mythic Twin War Gods. This petroglyph verifies the claims of several Native American groups, which I have long supported." He paused to beam upon his students, then cast a wary sideways glance at the paleoastronomer. "Surely this conclusion can be stated without fear of contradiction." And then muttered: "From any scholar worthy of the name."

There was another murmur from the gathering, mostly of appreciation. But this was salted with some amusement. It was clear to all whom Axton thought unworthy. The man who stood on the north side of the sketch in stone was the intended target of the anthropologist's poison-tipped arrows.

There were reasons for Axton's intense dislike of his junior colleague. For one thing, Terry Perkins held mere undergraduate degrees in anthropology and archaeology. For another, he had been awarded a Ph.D. in physics and astronomy. To compound his shortcomings, Perkins was a noted paleoastronomer. And in Axton's opinion, the sort of arrogant physical scientist who never doubted that he was considerably more intelligent and far better informed than the most prominent anthropologist. Perkins—like others of his ilk—had a highly annoying habit of poking around in anthropological business that should rightly be left to his betters. Which is to say, those who held the proper certification. If this were not enough, there was still another reason for Axton to detest the younger scholar. In every argument in which Professor Axton had engaged Dr. Perkins, the brilliant young paleoastronomer had—sooner or later—turned out to be demonstrably in the right. And Perkins never gloated over his victories. It was as if he had never doubted the outcome of such unequal contests. Perkins's behavior was galling to Axton. And damnably unforgivable.

There was a silence in the audience. Dr. Perkins would certainly have something to say. Though not directly to Professor Axton, of course.

And, as the reporter's microphone was aimed at his face, he did. "The assertion that these figures are meant to represent the Twin War Gods is, I should think, almost certainly correct."

Professor Axton was momentarily disarmed by this unexpected support.

Perkins flashed a dazzling smile at no one in particular. "Or at least as likely to be correct as any of the many informed speculations one

encounters in fields such as archaeology, anthropology—or meta-
physics."

The pink flesh of Professor Axton's face turned to gray stone.

The science reporter, who was recording this encounter for poster-
ity, could not suppress a smile.

Perkins continued in an affable tone. "While one need not doubt
that the artisan who created this nifty little sketch believed Companion and Chimney Rocks to be the earthly personification of the Twin
War Gods, we may rightly ask ourselves a question: Just who was this
artisan?"

Axton turned his craggy face to stare at the younger man. And
broke the unwritten rule by speaking directly to Perkins. "I daresay, you
physicists may be expected to come up with some technique for identi-
fying this individual who died a thousand years ago. Perhaps you will
lift a bit of his DNA from a crevice in the stone where his sweat has
fallen?"

There was a titter of nervous laughter from the audience.

Perkins—who had taken Axton's place at the base of the figure—
seemed not in the least offended. He squatted, closed one eye, and held
out his thumb to make a sighting, first along one spear, then the other.
"I am pleased to know that you are appreciative of the significant con-
tributions to anthropology made by those of us in the hard sciences.
And impressed that you are aware of the technology of identification
of specific individuals when samples of their DNA can be recovered . . .
from the scene of a crime. Or," his eyes glittered with amusement,
"from the site of a gross misinterpretation of evidence."

Axton's mouth fell open. He gasped for just enough breath to expel
one word. "What?"

"We physicists and astronomers," Perkins said slowly, still sighting
with the aid of an upraised thumb, "attempt to make measurements
whenever there is something to measure. And though I'll have to
repeat this with proper instruments, it seems that the spear on my left
does not point at the center of Companion. Its target is much closer to
the northern profile of that big slab of sandstone. And the other spear,"
he shifted the thumb, "points at the southern edge of Chimney Rock.
Not that this actually means anything." He looked up to see Axton
wince. "I would not worry," he added innocently, "you are probably

right. After all, many of the most firmly held conclusions drawn by anthropologists are based upon guesswork."

This was a cruel blow.

Axton, though stunned, manfully stood his ground. And laid his heavy axe on the other man's head. "Well, of course—some must always reject the simple and obvious explanations." He frowned thoughtfully. "No doubt these spears point toward the stellar location of some long-dimmed supernova . . . or a mysterious lunar standstill." He displayed a smirk for the benefit of his graduate students. "You astronomers are so fortunate—with such a great multitude of heavenly bodies, moving upon infinitely many paths, you are always able to find something in the sky that aligns with anything whatever upon the face of the earth. Yes, I imagine you'll come up with something."

Perkins was unbloodied by this assault. "Your faith in my profession is gratifying—but I'll leave the imagining to those who are more adept at it." The paleoastronomer ran his finger along one of the lines etched into the stone. "Perhaps the fellow who made this sketch simply did not know how to draw a straight line. He may have been," Perkins smiled wickedly, "an early anthropologist."

Silas Axton opened his mouth to rebuke the arrogant young bastard, then snapped it shut. Being unable to think of a response, the outraged anthropologist turned on his heel and walked stiffly away.

After Professor Axton was well out of sight, a pair of comely young women emerged from the small crowd and approached their hero. Perkins acknowledged them with a nod and a smile. These ladies had much in common. Both were anthropology students at Rocky Mountain Polytechnic. Melina Castro—tall, fair, and as coldly wholesome as a member of the Hitler Youth—was the first to speak. "Dr. Perkins—do you really think Professor Axton's views about the pictograph may be"—it was hard to say *wrong*—"I mean—could there be some other interpretation?"

The handsome young scholar laughed out loud, then signaled the science reporter to turn off his recorder. "Not for a minute. I just felt like twisting the old lion's tail."

Melina adored him with her large blue eyes. "How very naughty of you, picking on Professor Axton."

"He needs me," Perkins said with a sober look at Axton's retreating

form. "The taste of combat whets the old warrior's appetite for battle."
And for life itself.

April Tavishuts—also smitten with Perkins—felt that she must say
something. "Then you agree with Professor Axton—the pictograph
proves that the rock pillars represent the Twin War Gods?"

Perkins regarded the darkly attractive Ute woman with a gaze that
caressed from head to toe. "Whoever was responsible for this very
unusual pictograph—and I suspect it was one of the priestly Chacoan
caste—certainly intended to identify Companion and Chimney Rocks
with the fabled sons of White Shell Woman."

Melina attempted to regain Perkins's attention. "Why do you see
the pictograph as—well—unusual? The Southwest must have thousands of rock drawings and—"

He offered her a tolerant smile. "Tens of thousands, I suspect, Miss
Castro. But surely you understand why this one is so special?"

The blond blushed like a bouquet of pink roses.

The handsome scholar turned to the darker woman. "Why is this
pictograph so special, April?"

Embarrassed to suddenly be the center of attention, the Ute woman
hesitated before responding. And when she did, April was fumbling for
some relevant fact. "Well, even though the local sandstone is a perfect
canvas, this is the first real piece of rock art ever found at Chimney
Rock Archaeological Site."

Perkins nodded at the graduate student. "Very good. Anything else?"

By now she was beginning to understand. "With all the beautiful
sandstone cliff faces, why didn't he make his pictograph on a smooth
vertical surface? That's where most southwestern rock art is found. Not
on bumpy horizontal surfaces at ground level—where people are likely
to walk on them."

Well now. This one is thinking. "So despite the obvious disadvantages,
why did the artisan make this drawing on the horizontal?"

April Tavishuts stared at the stick figures. "If he wanted the spears to
point at the stone towers, that's easy on a horizontal surface. But it'd be
really hard to do if he'd used a vertical cliff wall. Even if he got over on
the south side of the mesa, he'd have to find just the right panel to
work with. And the face of a particular panel would be parallel to only
one of the stone towers." Her face brightened. "So Professor Axton

must be right. The fact that the spears are pointing at the towers isn't likely to be some sort of coincidence. It had to be deliberate."

Terry Perkins stared at the young Ute woman. *Miss April Tavishuts has a serious brain in her head. Something I must keep in mind.*

Charlie Moon watched the archaeologist leave, then followed her. Amanda Silk was unaware of the Ute's approach. "Hi," he said.

She whirled on him, wild-eyed with alarm.

He grinned. "Sorry. Didn't mean to—"

"Don't *ever* do that." She pressed a palm against her chest. "You could have scared me to death."

High-strung creature. "Guess I should wear a bell around my neck."

She took a deep breath and resumed her stride along the path. "I suppose I'm a bit nervous today."

He fell in beside her.

She gave him a sideways glance. "You're with the Ute police."

With? He'd never heard it put quite like that. "Used to be."

"Three or four years ago, a very tall tribal policeman changed a flat for me. After midnight. In the rain." She paused. "I don't suppose you remember."

The ex-policeman, who had changed a considerable number of tires for those he'd been sworn to protect and serve, admitted that he did not recall the incident.

"Well, I do. And I'm very grateful." They walked along in silence until she spoke again. "You have something of a reputation."

"Trying to live it down."

"As a lawman, I mean."

"Gave up that line of work. I'm raising cattle now."

"I like beef," she said.

The rancher was beginning to like this woman.

"Lucky thing you showed up at Chimney Rock for Native American Day," Amanda said. "Otherwise, that child might not have been missed until after she'd toppled off a cliff and broken her neck. But as fortune would have it, you *were* here. And able to find her."

He slowed his stride, to match her pace.

"Tell me about the . . ." The word tasted bitter in the archaeologist's mouth, so she spat it out. ". . . *petroglyph.*"

"Not much to tell."

"I understand some mysterious person showed the child where it was."

"Yeah. Kid claims she followed a man."

Amanda Silk brushed a wisp of hair off her face. "Did she provide any sort of description?"

Moon grinned. "Pair of legs. Couple of arms. One head. And he wore feathers."

She managed a thin smile. "Feathers?"

"Like a big bird. And he had a dog with him. Carried on his back."

The archaeologist frowned at the twisting path in front of her. "Doesn't that remind you of something?"

"You think the little girl was telling me a skin-walker tale?"

"It's a rather pervasive myth," she said. "Witch-men who wear wolf skins. Over the years, I've heard testimony from several eyewitnesses who swear they've seen skin-walkers shape-shift into wolves."

Moon tried not to smile. "You think a skin-walker might be hanging around Chimney Rock?"

"Depends on how you define the term. I certainly wouldn't rule out a lunatic with a coyote pelt draped over his back—who believes he's the reincarnation of an Anasazi priest." The scientist hesitated. "There have been reports of a peculiar old man moving about the ruins."

"There are lots of old men about," Moon said. "Some of 'em are fairly peculiar."

The archaeologist pushed away a juniper branch that was blocking the path. "Last summer, one of the grad students was out for a walk at night. She reported seeing a man on the Crag, near the temple ruins. She thought it was one of the university staff. When she called his name—" Amanda blushed. "It sounds so incredibly silly. But the student swears he dropped onto all fours, started trotting toward her. Poor thing—she ran all the way back to the camp."

"Who was this graduate student?"

Her expression was suddenly wary. "Why do you ask?"

The former policeman hoped the scientist would accept a reasoned argument. "Let's make three assumptions. First, the little Zuni girl followed a flesh-and-blood man away from the tour. Second, the graduate student saw a man up on the Crag." He waited for the count.

"And what's the third assumption?"

Moon looked toward the Crag. "Somewhere out there, there's a half-wit who believes he's half wolf."

She followed his gaze to the sandstone platform. "Such a man would be unbalanced. Perhaps dangerous."

"Which is why one of my friends at SUPD might want to talk to your graduate student."

She hesitated. "Very well. Her name is Melina Castro."

Moon decided to push a little harder. "And she first thought this strange fella was one of the university staff?"

Almost imperceptibly, Amanda nodded.

"Did she say which one?"

She glanced up at the dark man's face. "Perhaps you should ask Melina." They had arrived at the archaeologist's camping trailer. Amanda Silk paused at the flimsy door. "Come inside, if you like."

He followed her in. The small trailer rocked under his weight. After removing his hat, it was still necessary for Charlie Moon to bend over.

"Have a seat." She nodded to indicate a round table. "That's where I eat my meals. And do my paperwork."

He sat. And stared at a green plastic mule standing spraddle-legged beside a salt shaker.

Amanda seemed mildly embarrassed. "It's a pepper grinder. My nephew's in the novelty business—makes a good living selling this kind of junk. I am regularly blessed with samples of his new products."

"How d'you grind the pepper—turn his tail?"

"Right."

"Where does the pepper come out?"

"You don't want to know." She opened a cabinet drawer, removed what appeared to be a peppermint candy cane. "Another gift from my nephew." Amanda pressed a button on the device—a sizzling piezo-electric arc ignited a butane flame at the tip. She touched this to a ring on her small stove, turned a knob to open the propane gas valve. A ring of blue flame materialized under the sooty bottom of the coffeepot. "The wonders of our technological civilization," the archaeologist muttered.

After the pot had boiled, Amanda Silk poured her guest a cup.

He inquired about sugar.

She placed a fat plastic hippopotamus on the table.

He grinned at the ugly thing. "Another gift from your relative?"

"Twist his head a full turn." She laughed. "My nephew or the river-horse, take your pick."

Moon performed the operation on the hippo, which obligingly popped a lid. He spooned a generous portion of sugar into the cup, stirred the brew, took a drink. *Strong enough to melt the spoon.* It was nice to meet a woman who knew how to make coffee.

The archaeologist seated herself across the table from her guest. "Excuse me for just a moment. I must do this while things are fresh in my mind." She opened a tattered green ledger, used an old-fashioned fountain pen to make an entry on the lined page.

As an idle exercise, the Ute tried to read upside down. He was only able to make out a few words. And the page number. Ninety-eight. Looked like she had about three hundred pages to go.

Amanda noticed his interest. "This is my professional log. I record things while they're fresh in my mind." Having completed her notes, she entered the date and time with a flourish, marked her place with a strip of purple cloth, then closed the thick ledger.

"Those professors from Rocky Mountain Polytechnic seem to be pretty excited about the petroglyph." He hoped this would provoke a response.

It did. She threw up her hands in a dramatic expression of frustration. "Axton and Perkins are classroom scholars. They spend their days thinking deep thoughts and writing profound theoretical papers for the professional journals."

Moon thought he detected a hint of envy in her tone.

"Once in a blue moon, they actually get out in the field in their spiffy new hiking boots. Me, I'm just an ordinary pick-and-shovel archaeologist. But listen—"

He leaned forward. Listened.

She enunciated each word: "I-know-my-dirt."

Moon nodded with feigned earnestness. "First time I laid eyes on you, that's what I said to myself: 'This lady has a Ph.D. in dirt.' "

Dr. Amanda Silk smiled crookedly. "Tell me exactly what you saw when the little girl showed you the rock drawing."

He thought about it. "Not much. All that was showing was one corner of the picture. One of the War Gods' feet, I think. And the bottom end of his spear."

"Right. But the soil over the remainder of that pathetic cartoon was loose enough to brush away with a broom. Which is exactly what the grad students did so Professor Axton could get a look at the whole thing. But beyond the sketch, the dirt was packed quite hard—as it should be." She leaned her elbows on the table, clenched her hands together into a single knobby fist. "Now what does that suggest?"

Moon stared across the table at the woman. "Sounds like somebody had cleaned the soil away fairly recently."

She nodded. "And made a plausible sketch of the Twin War Gods—with their spears pointing at the stone towers."

He swirled the coffee in his cup. "If somebody wanted the picture to be found, why cover it up again?"

"He didn't cover it up," she said. "Not long after he finished his work—perhaps just a few days—the wind blew the loose sand back over it. Or most of it. But you can be sure he meant for it to be discovered. Anyone who goes to all that trouble wants his masterpiece seen. And appreciated. So the hoaxer waited for somebody to find it. But when nobody did, he got impatient."

"So the hoaxer showed the drawing to the little girl, hoping she'd tell somebody about it."

"It was a clever way to reveal his work to the world—while remaining anonymous."

Moon turned the cup in his hands. "You got any ideas about who might've faked the petroglyph?"

She stared at the ugly plastic hippo. "To arrive at *who*, one must first determine *why*."

He shrugged. "Maybe somebody did it for a joke."

"I, for one, am not amused."

This was going nowhere. He got up, taking care not to bang his head against the arched ceiling. "Thanks for the coffee."

Amanda followed the Ute outside. The archaeologist looked toward the Twin War Gods, where blue mists were gathering around the giants. Suddenly, she shivered.

He wondered whether she was feeling a chill in the air. Or something else entirely. "You think this petroglyph hoaxer's motive was serious?"

"Sinister is the better word."

Charlie Moon squinted at the sky. He saw the dark profile of a raven. A shadow slipping along the floor of heaven. It drifted away softly . . . into the pale blue lonesome. And was lost in eternity.

Most of Eve's daughters seek after riches—or at least a modicum of comfort and security. A very few search for fame and glory. April Tavishuts was looking for a man.

Not just any man. One whose *matukach* lady friend lived a long ways off in California. But Charlie Moon had vanished. *Well. He just walked away without saying a word to me.* Thus abandoned, she caught up with Melina Castro. The sturdy graduate student was stomping her way toward the camping area at the far end of Ghost Wolf Mesa.

Melina withdrew a dark look from her quiver of feminine weapons. She launched this missile at her innocent companion.

The projectile passed unnoticed. Blessed are the pure of heart.

Presently, the tall blond trusted herself to speak. "Well. Aren't you the clever one."

The Ute woman responded with a blank look.

Damned little hypocrite. Don't pretend you don't know what I mean. "You certainly managed to impress Dr. Perkins."

I hope so. He's so nice. April Tavishuts shrugged, but her lips curved in a soft smile. And her girlish thoughts were transformed into words that came out of their own accord. "He is so cute it's almost enough to"—she pressed her palms to her face—"to make you just want to *die*."

With the suddenness of a rattlesnake about to strike a mouse, Melina turned to tower over the shorter woman. "Don't *say* that," she hissed.

April, alarmed by the intensity of this passionate response, backed away. The Ute maiden stared at the young *matukach* woman as one mesmerized. Her eyes were wide, puzzled. "You don't think he's cute?"

Melina's face relaxed into a bitter half smile. *Cute doesn't half say it.* The pale-skinned girl looked hopefully to the heavens, from whence all blessings come. "Terry Perkins is extraordinarily good-looking."

The young women continued their way along the path in silence. As they came near the parking area, April looked at her companion. "Melina?"

"Yes?"

"Why are you upset with me?"

Melina Castro closed her eyes tightly. "Never, ever say you want to die."

"But I didn't actually mean—"

"I know it was just a figure of speech." Melina gave her companion an odd look. "But saying things . . . can make them happen."

April tried to smile at this odd statement. "I didn't know you were so, well—superstitious."

Melina bit her lip. "There are lots of things you don't know." *Or understand.*

CHAPTER 5

After passing over many difficulties, the Twins found themselves way, way, way east—standing at the door of a great turquoise house.

—Sandoval, Hastin Tlo'tsi hee

The Columbine

Pete Bushman, long-time manager of the vast ranch property, stood bowlegged on the front porch of the foreman's house, looking down his nose at the three men. They waited patiently for the straw boss to say something worth hearing.

"The new owner of the Columbine intends to make this a workin' ranch again. Turn a profit." *There are fools, and then there are damn fools.* Bushman chewed on a jawful of Mail Pouch tobacco. "There's rusty old bob-war fences that need mendin', alfalfa hay to be planted and cut, barns that need cleanin' out. I'll expect you fellas to work your asses off. If you got any ideas that this here is a soft spot to rest awhile and get fat, then hit the road now."

Silence.

He spat on the powder-dry dust at their feet. "Any questions?"

The youngest of the new hires, as if in a classroom, raised a hand. "This Mr. Moon—what can you tell us about him?"

The other two were experienced. But the Kid didn't know enough to keep his yap shut. Bushman considered his response with care. "Well, he's one of them Ute Injuns. Decent enough fella if you treat him right." The ranch foreman glared at the trio of misfits with steely-blue eyes. "The boss useta be a cop for his tribe. He never says nothin' about it, but I know for a fact he's killed at least eight men. Some of 'em with his bare hands. So don't do nothin' to get him pissed off." The foreman produced a gold-plated Hamilton pocket watch and glanced at the ivory face. "I got to go up to the big house now—you boys come along with me. Boss'll want to get a look at you." But as far as Pete Bushman was concerned, there was wide, deep river separating these common hands from the owner of the Columbine. And the foreman was the bridge over those troubled waters. "Them Ute Injuns is kinda standoffish—so you fellas keep your distance. And don't say nothin'— I'll do the talkin'."

Human Resources

Despite Bushman's insistence that the cowboys should wait on the porch while he powwowed with the Indian, the Ute invited them into his enormous parlor. They wiped their boots on the welcome mat and came inside, hats in hand. The odd-looking trio positioned themselves near the massive door, ready to exit in a hurry if this gigantic Indian lost his temper. They exchanged uneasy glances, but uttered not a word.

Charlie Moon thought the new hires seemed painfully shy. He was about to start up a conversation with the cowboys when deterred by a dark look from the foreman. Moon followed Pete Bushman to the far end of the long parlor.

The foreman kept his voice low. "Well, there they are."

And indeed, there they were. Three sets of eyes, furtively darting around the room. Taking in the antique furnishings and expensive artwork. And thinking more or less the same thoughts: *This is some sure-enough rich Indian.*

"I'd like to have a little talk with these cowboys," Moon said, "let them know who I am. What I expect of them."

Pete Bushman shook his head stubbornly. "I've already told these hands who you are. And I'll damn sure give 'em plenty of work to do."

"Thing is, I'd like to get to know—"

The foreman's eyes narrowed to angry slits. "If you want to do my job, you sure'n hell don't need me around."

Moon smiled. Which irritated Pete Bushman all the more. "I'd like to know something about these men."

"What? They're just ordinary, run-of-the-mill—"

Firmness was called for. "Pete. If they're going to be my employees, I mean to know who they are. Where they're from. What kind of work experience they have."

Knowing he was licked, the foreman shrugged. "Well, why didn't you say so?" He nodded to indicate the man on the far left. "That old one's Alfredo Marquez. He's got about nine middle names I don't recollect. Alf's up here from Mexico. I expect them federales are after him."

"Why do you think that?"

"Well, there's talk that Alf knifed some other Mexican fella. Fight over a woman, I expect."

The Ute ignored this tidbit of gossip. Maybe Mr. Marquez did have some trouble in Mexico. But Bushman tended to exaggerate. He watched as Alfredo Marquez, who was thin as a grass snake, leaned first one way. Then another. Moon shook his head. "You sure Mr. Marquez is strong enough to work?"

"Oh, he can work all right. Alf's just teeterin' some 'cause he's had a bit too much to drink." Sensing that his boss was about to express his disapproval, the foreman added quickly: "But he works cheap."

Moon let it pass. "What about the cowboy in the middle?" The man's teeth were yellowish, with exaggerated canines. The eyes, shaded by the brim of a tattered black hat, were small, dark—and mean. The man had the look of a starved rodent.

Bushman snickered. "They call him Pogo—'cause he has a kinda possum look about 'im."

"He running from the law?"

"Not now."

"What do you mean by that?"

Bushman shook his head. "He's done his time."

"Knifed somebody, did he?"

"Oh no. Nothin' like that."

"What, then?"

"Pogo, he stole some steers up in Montana."

Moon looked up at the beamed ceiling, and imagined a blue sky. Where untroubled clouds drifted by. "Pete—I don't mean to be overly critical. But do you think it's sound business practice for a rancher to hire a cattle thief?"

"Oh, don't worry so much. Pogo never steals from his employers."

"I am relieved to hear this. But I have something to say."

"I'm listnin'."

"So far, this is a sorry lot of cowboys."

Bushman bristled. "With what you're payin', you're damn lucky to get 'em."

Moon gave the third man the once-over. This one was tall and lean. His honest young face was decorated with a serious-looking handlebar mustache. Moreover, his blue cotton shirt was spotless, his gray trousers pressed, his boots shined. "That one," the Ute said, "is a bit of a dude. But he looks like a first-rate cowboy." He glanced uneasily at Bushman. "What particular felonies has he committed?"

"Far as I know, the Kid's got a clean slate."

Moon stared at the foreman in disbelief. "Kid?"

Bushman seemed proud of this one. "That there's the Wyomin' Kid."

"Surely you're joking, Mr. Bushman."

"That's just his nickname. The Wyomin' Kid's Christian name is Jerome. Jerome Kydmann."

Moon tried to be hopeful. "Well, being from Wyoming, maybe Jerome knows something about the cattle business."

"Far as I know, the Kid has never set foot in the Wyomin' you're talkin' about." Bushman waited for the boss to inquire.

Moon did not ask. He did not want to know.

Bushman told him anyway. "Jerome's from Wyomin', Rhode Island."

Still the Ute held his tongue.

"It's a little town on Route 95." Bushman chuckled under greasy whiskers. "Few miles east of Moscow. That's in Rhode Island too." His eyes sparkled with merriment. "I looked it up on a road map."

The Ute exhaled the breath he had been holding. "So what does the Wyoming Kydmann know about cattle?"

Bushman's face was rosy with Santa-like good humor. " 'Bout as much as most kids from Rhode Island. But he claims he's eager to learn."

Moon set his jaw and spoke through clenched teeth. "Listen to me, Bushman. I may be willing to take a chance on a tequila-soaked Mexican knife artist. I might even be willing to give Pogo-the-Cattle-Rustler a try after I warn him how I stake cow thieves over anthills and then pour honey on 'em. But I will not pay out hard cash to some tinhorn who don't know the difference between a Holstein milk cow and a Texas longhorn. And worst of all, calls himself the Wyoming Kid. And that's that."

"You're the boss."

"So you tell the Kid we can't use him."

"Okay. But like I said, he's eager to learn. Real eager."

Moon glared at his foreman. "How eager? You intend to exploit this young man—work him to death for bed and beans?"

The foreman looked sinfully prideful. "Better'n that."

Moon's tone softened. "What's better than him working for free?"

"The Wyoming Kid will pay *us* to work here."

"You serious?"

"Serious as a bad case of the claps."

"How much?"

"I told him we could provide a minimum of sixty hours of actual cowboyin' experience per week—for a tuition of only three hundred dollars a month."

Moon stood in awe of his crafty foreman.

"Of course, the Kid's gotta supply his own horse and saddle and such."

The bony fingers of guilt probed Moon's conscience. "This Jerome, he . . . uhh . . . not too bright?"

"The Wyomin' Kid's got hisself one of them Embee-A degrees from Harvard U. But he don't like the corporate world. Says it's a soul-killing rat race. So he's set his mind to learn the cowboyin' trade."

"Where would he get the money to pay . . . ahh . . . tuition?"

"The Kid's folks is rich as Shaker eggnog." The foreman watched his boss hesitate. "Charlie, if we don't take 'im on, he'll find a position somewheres else." Bushman threw up his hands. "But if you think we shouldn't be takin' advantage of the poor young fella like this, I'll go give him the sack right now."

"Let's not be hasty." Moon beamed a beatific smile toward the callow youth, who smiled back under the waxed handlebar mustache. "Maybe we should give this fine young fellow a chance to learn an honest trade."

Bushman, his victory won and savored, was in a generous mood. "Now if you want to, go on over and shake hands with 'em. But don't you never get too chummy with the help. First thing you know, they'll be actin' like they own the place and you're workin' for them."

"That's good advice, Pete. From now on I'll make sure my employees know who's in charge here. All of them." He gave Bushman a flinty look that made the foreman's bloodshot eyes pop.

Economics 101

By long tradition, all serious business at the Columbine Ranch headquarters was conducted in the kitchen. Charlie Moon sat across the massive oak dining table from his foreman. Pete Bushman's steel-rimmed spectacles hung low on the bridge of his nose; he was leafing slowly through a green ledger, making sums and subtractions on a yellow pad. And muttering darkly under his whiskers.

The clock on the wall pilfered the minutes one by one.

From time to time, each man helped himself to a sip of black coffee.

While the foreman fussed over the ranch records, Charlie Moon thought his happy thoughts. *By the grace of God, here I am—owner of maybe the finest ranch in Colorado. No more police work for me. No more hauling in drunks who puke on my new shirt. No more arresting wife-beaters whose wives kick me in the shins because I'm mistreating their loving husbands. Nosir. All I have to do is tell my foreman what I want done, and Pete'll see to it. Before long, I'll be able to sit right by the window in my great big parlor and watch hundreds of purebred Herefords grazing in the valley. In due season, there'll be calves. And once stock starts going to market, the greenback dollars will start falling all around me like cottonwood leaves in*

October. And I'll have all the time I need for fishing. Then he remembered the sweetest blessing of all. *Won't be long till Camilla shows up for a visit.* What a grand life.

The policeman-turned-rancher was startled by the sound of gravel caught in a coffee grinder. It was Pete Bushman, clearing his throat. The Ute blinked at his employee.

Bushman nibbled at the pink eraser on the number-two lead pencil. "I may be off a dollar or two here or there. But I got it pretty much figgered out."

"What's the bottom line?"

"Well, you want to buy two hundred head of good Hereford stock. But first we need some maintenance on the farm equipment—gotta get some alfalfa planted. Lots of fixin' up to do. Some of them south fences needs new bob-war. Barn roof is wantin' some shingles. Corner post in the west corral's all rotted. Livestock chute needs some weldin' work. And there's the pay for the cowboys." He grinned. "Just the two of 'em. And then there's taxes."

"Taxes?"

"Property taxes."

He showed the Ute last year's bill.

Moon squinted at the paper. "That much?"

"For ranchers, rates per acre aren't all that high. But then you got an awful lotta acres."

The owner groaned. "What about the black-ink side of the ledger?"

"Well, that lawyer fella down in Durango allows us a fixed allotment for certain kinds of expenses. We leased out sixteen hundred acres of grassland on the other side of the mountain to that U.S. senator who you got for a neighbor." Bushman grinned. "And then there's the three hundred dollars a month from the Wyomin' Kid."

"Don't remind me." Moon was feeling a twinge of guilt. "After a month or so we'll cancel his . . . uh . . . tuition. Once he's able to do some useful work, we'll put him on the payroll."

"Don't really matter. Three hundred greenbacks is a drop in the bucket for an outfit this size. 'Specially if you intend to invest in a bunch of purebred beef."

The Ute leaned forward to stare at Bushman's scribblings. "So what's the projected bottom line?"

The foreman scratched his head, pursed his lips, muttered a few choice curses under his breath. "I'd say—give or take a few bucks—we're lookin' at forty-five, maybe fifty thousand dollars."

Moon's relief showed on his face. "Well, we can't expect much for the start-up year. Even so, that's not much of a profit margin for a ranch this size."

The foreman's eyes popped. "Profit?"

He didn't want to ask. But he did. "You're projecting we'll *lose* fifty thousand dollars this year?"

Bushman's belly shook with laughter. "Only if we work twenty-six hours a day—including Sundays. And if we're extra lucky. Why, once we get this ranch up an' runnin', we'll be able to lose two or three hundred thousand dollars a year."

"That's not funny."

Bushman shook his grizzled head at the innocent. "You actually figured you'd make serious money raisin' beeves? Shoot—there ain't been no decent profit in the beef market for thirty years. Big supermarket chains and hamburger franchises buy beef from places like Argentina. South Africa. Australia. American ranches like this is mostly owned by rich people. And rich people are too smart to fool around with big herds a beef cows."

Moon's expression was that of the small boy who has just watched a double scoop of ice cream fall from his cone to the sidewalk. On a very hot day. And a big dog came along and licked it up.

The foreman sensed that his boss needed some encouragement. "You want to make a few dollars, we could raise some rodeo stock. There's some money in that, if you know what you're doin'. And we could raise some o' them sad-looking llamas. And buffalo. We can sell buffs to the Indians. We might even start us a flock o' them big ostrich birds. There's even some money in camels. But if we're eventually goin' to have a payin' operation, we need just a little bit of capital to get over the hump."

"I'm not going to borrow money."

"I was thinking of something else."

"I could put you to mending fences. Put the Wyoming Kid in charge of the business end of things." Moon wore his poker face. "A Harvard MBA would put this operation on a paying basis in no time flat."

"Don't get snappy. What I meant was—well—I don't hardly know how to say it."

"Just spit it out, Pete."

"You Injuns are a sensitive lot. You might not like to hear it."

"I'm always interested in hearing what's on my foreman's mind."

"Well, then I'll say it right out." Bushman looked at the ceiling. Scratched at his bushy beard. Licked his lips. Cleared his throat. "Well . . . you could get yourself a job somewheres."

Moon had not believed he could be surprised by anything this bewhiskered old grouch had to say.

The foreman continued in a more sympathetic tone. "I realize, bein' unskilled labor you prob'ly couldn't earn all that much. But anything you could scrape up would help."

Moon attempted to stare a hole through the man's forehead.

"And it's not like you're needed around here—all you'd be doin' is hangin' around, tellin' me how to do my job." Bushman scowled at this imagined outrage. "Me who was cowboyin' when you was still in diapers."

"I take it back—I'm not interested in what's on your mind."

"Well, that's all I've got to say." Having made this vow of silence, the foreman proceeded to enumerate a long list of calamities likely to cripple the Columbine. He noticed a vacant look on the boss's face, and paused. "Hmmpf."

Charlie Moon was staring at something on the table. A stray grain of barley. The little white seed looked untroubled. Even cheerful.

The foreman cleared his throat. "You haven't heard a word I've said."

The Ute didn't look up. "I'm so poor, I can't even afford to pay attention."

Bushman slammed the ledger shut, jammed a floppy hat down to his ears. And prepared to depart without so much as a good-bye.

Moon realized that this sad financial picture was not his foreman's fault. Bushman had merely framed it for him. "How about I fix us a snack?" He slapped the old man between the shoulder blades.

Bushman wheezed, then managed to regain his wind. "My missus won't like it if I don't have no appetite for lunch."

"Well, I wouldn't want to get Dolly peeved at you."

The foreman glanced at the huge refrigerator. Licked his lips. "What kinda snack did you have in mind?"

"You name it."

"How about a ham san'wich."

"Okay. I'll make you a small one."

"Well . . . not *too* small."

The Snack

The men took their sandwiches onto the front porch and seated themselves in heavy redwood rockers. The ranch house was situated on a prominent knoll. Off to the north and down a long grassy slope was the river. Roaring and crashing over glistening black boulders. To the south, at the near edge of pastureland that stretched for a day's walk was the lake—a thirty-acre melt of dark green glass. Ten miles away, to the west, blue granite mountains bulged jaggedly through the drifting vapors of late morning. From somewhere below these mists came the shrill call of a hawk.

Moon leaned back. Raised a heavy mug to his lips, took a sip of sweet black coffee. "Now this is the way for a man to live," he muttered.

Bushman nodded. "It'll do till a better one comes along." *And Glory is just over the mountains.* The foreman took a healthy bite from his sandwich. Between the thick slices of dark rye was a single slice of ham. Three quarters of an inch thick. Smeared with honey mustard.

A large, yellowish hound walked slowly toward the ranch house. Up the steps. Without taking the least notice of the men, the lean animal aimed its long nose toward a sunny spot on the south end of the porch. The dog fell to his belly with a soft whuffing sound. He yawned, exposing an impressive set of teeth. The yawn complete, the hound licked his black lips, lowered his muzzle to the planked floor. Closed his eyes. The very picture of contentment.

Moon took a bite of rye and ham. "That your dog?"

Pete Bushman swallowed a gulp of steaming coffee. "Nope."

Moon continued to relish his food. *This is maybe the best ham sandwich I ever ate.* Between bites, the Ute continued the conversation. "Whose dog is he?"

The foreman thought about the question. "Yours."

Moon shook his head. "I don't think so."

Bushman took ample time to chew his food. Swallowed it. "Oh, he's your dog all right."

The Ute took a long look at the somnolent animal. "Pete, if I had me a really ugly yella hound dog, I'm pretty sure I would know it."

The foreman thought about going inside to warm up his coffee. Decided it would be better to sit awhile longer. "Sidewinder belongs to the ranch—always has. Now the ranch belongs to you. So he's your dog."

Knowing it would be useless to protest this carefully thought out logic, Moon took another tack. Slyly, he asked: "How'd that pitiful old hound get a name like Sidewinder?" *Whoever named a dog owned it.*

Bushman, sensing the trap, smiled into his coffee cup. *You'll find out soon enough.*

Moon turned to look at Bushman. "This sickly looking dog get bit by a rattlesnake?"

Pete Bushman did not reply.

Sidewinder did.

Too late, Moon heard the thumpety-thump of large paws on the redwood planking. He had just managed to turn his head to see the hound take flight when a yellow blur passed over his chair. An instant later, the animal was at the shady end of the porch. Looking back at him.

"Damn!"

"You shouldn't cuss in front of Sidewinder," Bushman advised with an old-maidish air. "He is sensitive to bad language."

The Ute was on his feet, pointing at the yellow dog. "He grabbed my sandwich!"

The dog did not deny this charge. Neither did he attempt to conceal the evidence. Indeed, the brazen culprit had Moon's snack firmly under one paw, and was busy pulling at the ham.

"Now he's eating it," Moon growled.

Sidewinder growled back.

"Funny thing," Bushman observed. "That dog'll eat almost anything. I've seen him chow down on shriveled-up watermelon rinds. Rotten cucumbers. Lumps of coal. A plastic banana. I've even seen him slurp up old engine oil. But that skinny hound won't eat that there rye bread. He only likes the white kind."

"Besides snatching a man's food from his hand, what's this chowhound good for?"

"Not much. That's what he does best."

"You could've warned me."

"I could've." The grizzled foreman chuckled. "But a hard-workin' man don't find much entertainment out here."

Sidewinder choked down the last morsel of pig flesh. And looked hopefully at Moon.

The Ute scowled at the dog. Then at the foreman. "Why didn't he go for your sandwich?"

"For one thing, he's not interested in stealing a man's food unless he is really enjoying it. You was acting real hungry. And for another, 'cause he knows better. I'm on to all his tricks."

Tricks? "What else does he do?"

"Oh, he likes to steal things besides food. Old Sidewinder'll sneak away with your car keys if he gets half a chance. Or your boots."

Moon's scowl grew darker. "I don't much like this dog."

Sidewinder's tongue hung over his lips. He grinned at the owner of the Columbine.

Bushman considered the dog's demeanor, then glanced at his boss. "You know, Charlie—I think he's fond of you."

As if to corroborate this conjecture, Sidewinder wagged his tail. And slobbered.

The Chairman

It was well into the afternoon when Charlie Moon cocked his ear at the distant sound of an engine. Wasn't Bushman's pickup. The old Dodge eight-cylinder needed a valve job; a man could hear the clickety-clacking a quarter-mile away.

He went to a window that faced the long driveway. A maroon Buick was barely managing to stay ahead of a boiling billow of dust. Whoever it was had gotten past Bushman's place, which served as a sentry post to determine who could go on to the big house and who must return several miles to the paved highway. If Pete wasn't at home, Dolly would hear intruders coming, flag them down, and ask them to state their business with the Columbine spread. Nobody got past Dolly without a good story.

The dusty automobile rocked to a stop behind Moon's Ford pickup. The Ute knew who was driving before he saw the gray-haired, stoop-shouldered figure of Oscar Sweetwater emerge from the low-slung sedan. Oscar—having ousted Betty Flintcorn in a recent election—was now the distinguished chairman of the Southern Ute Tribal Council.

Moon went outside to greet the tribal elder, heard complaints about what the bumpy ranch road had done to the Buick's shock absorbers. After promising to grade the road, he ushered Oscar into the parlor, got him into a comfortable chair.

"You want something to drink?"

The tribal chairman nodded at the fireplace. "Something hot."

Five minutes later, Moon returned with a pot of freshly brewed coffee. "I'm glad to see you."

Oscar Sweetwater nodded. "Thought you would be." He took a sip of the coffee. "But you're wondering why I'm here. You know I don't generally drive myself this far from home."

Moon didn't admit that the chairman had read his mind.

Oscar grinned, exposing a well-crafted set of artificial dentures. "Well, I'll tell you. I'm on a secret mission."

"Sounds exciting."

"It is. Nobody knows I'm here." The grin morphed into a slight frown. "Well, except my wife. You know Nora—she's got to know everything." The old man stretched his legs. "You got a nice place here."

"Thanks."

"Being head of a big operation like this must keep you pretty busy."

"I got a foreman to look after things. And some cowboys."

The chairman eyed the magnificent furnishings. "Looks like you're a rich man now."

Uh-oh. Oscar's sniffing out a donation for his favorite tribal project. "If land was money, I'd be sitting pretty."

"Don't ever give up your land. That's a big mistake some of us Utes made a long time ago. A lot of our people sold the parcels they got from the government. That's why a map of the reservation looks like a patched blanket." He placed the empty coffee cup on a polished mahogany table. "Charlie—I heard how you found that little Zuni girl who got lost over at the ruins by Chimney Rock. Nice piece of work."

"I just happened to be in the right place."

Sweetwater thought about this. "It's a God-given talent—being in the right place. At the right time."

Moon waited.

"And you found that picture on the sandstone."

"The little girl showed it to me."

The tribal chairman stared at the fireplace. Reflected flames danced in his dark eyes. "How does a five-year-old girl find what all those educated people didn't know about?"

Moon was not about to mention Dr. Amanda Silk's theory that the petroglyph was a hoax. "Hard to say."

Oscar Sweetwater offered his host an enigmatic half smile. "There's talk going around."

"There usually is."

"Some people are saying that an old Anasazi haunt showed the little Zuni girl that picture of the Twin War Gods."

Moon sipped at his coffee. Knowing that, sooner or later, the chairman would get to the point.

Oscar rocked in the chair. "Yesterday, I stopped by to see your aunt."

"How's she doing?"

"She told me something bad is going to happen."

"Something bad is always happening."

The chairman folded wrinkled hands over his belly and closed his eyes. "Daisy say's there'll be some big trouble on Ghost Wolf Mesa. On account of that Twin War Gods rock picture."

Moon preferred to steer the conversation away from his aunt's premonitions. "So how's the tribal government getting along?"

"Not bad. But we're kind of shorthanded in some departments." Oscar Sweetwater opened an eye to peek at Moon. "Too bad you've got so many things to occupy your time."

"Why's that?"

The tribal chairman made a tent of his fingers. "Well . . . I sorta have a proposition for you."

Moon thought he knew what was coming. Wallace Whitehorse—the Northern Cheyenne the council had hired last winter—had finally had his fill of tribal politics. Sure. Whitehorse had taken a hike. "You already looking for a new chief of police?"

Oscar Sweetwater seemed surprised. "Oh no. That Cheyenne fella is doing a fine job."

"Happy to hear it."

The tribal chairman gave Moon an appraising look. Like a horse trader sizing up a promising animal. "Way I see it, a man should work at what he does best. You were always a good police officer."

Aha. They were looking for a *deputy* chief of police. Someone who knew the tribe and the reservation inside out.

"That foreman of yours—Pete Bushman—me and him are old friends. On the way down the lane, I stopped at his place. Dolly gave me a big piece of apple pie and a cold glass of sweet milk. Me and Pete, we sat around. Talked some."

"No kidding. And I bet my foreman told you to help me find a regular job."

Oscar furrowed his brow as if trying to remember. "I don't recall him saying anything like that. We mostly talked about football." The tribal chairman grinned. "But now that you mention it, I bet you and Pete would both be happier if you got off the ranch now and again. It'd be good for you, doing some police work for the tribe."

"What does Wallace Whitehorse think about this?"

The tribal chairman hesitated. "You wouldn't be reporting to Chief Whitehorse."

"How could I be a police officer for the tribe and not report to the chief of police?"

The chairman leaned toward Moon—as if someone might have an ear pressed to a keyhole—and lowered his voice to a conspiratorial whisper. "What I had in mind was a *special investigator* job. Not a direct employee of the tribe, more like a consultant with your own business—contracting your services to us."

Charlie Moon thought this sounded a little bit interesting.

Oscar Sweetwater could see that the former policeman was teetering this way and that, so the tribal chairman played his hole card. "We'd reimburse you for all reasonable expenses, including travel. A flat fee of one thousand per month to keep you on retainer. And the hourly pay is pretty good."

"How good?"

Oscar told him.

Moon almost managed to conceal his pleasure.

"Tribe can afford it," Oscar said matter-of-factly. "We have our hands in all kinds of businesses. Mining. Tourism. Gas leases . . ."

"Don't forget the casino."

Oscar Sweetwater nodded. "Gaming is a lucrative business for the tribe. I see it as a tax on those unfortunate people who don't understand the laws of probability. Am I right?"

"Probably."

"So are you interested in working for the tribe?"

"Running the ranch keeps me busy. Another full-time job is out of the question."

"You could put in as few hours as you wanted to."

"Exactly what sort of work do you have in mind?"

"Oh, this and that. Every so often, the council needs the services of a qualified investigator for"—he searched for the right words— "well . . . special projects. Issues where we can't use our own police force. I don't have to tell you that our tribal officers are pretty much limited in what they can investigate."

"Yeah." Anything beyond drunk and disorderly was handed off to the BIA cops. The really serious crime on the reservation was dealt with by the FBI.

"The tribe could hire a private agency out of Denver. But we don't want no *matukach* Dick Tracy working for us—getting his long nose deep into private tribal business. You understand?"

"I'd need a private investigator's license."

"Our attorney has already done the paperwork." Oscar patted his jacket. "I've got the application in my pocket. All you've got to do is sign it, we'll mail it in. And pay the fees."

Moon smiled. "You were pretty sure I'd be interested."

"Sure enough to have a jeweler in Durango make you a new shield.

Fourteen-karat gold plate. I'll look pretty foolish if you turn me down."

"I wouldn't want to embarrass the chairman."

"That's the first lesson of tribal politics. So do we have a deal?"

"We do."

They shook hands, and it was a binding contract.

CHAPTER 6

The Sun showed the Twins over his turquoise house and asked
them to choose whatever they wished.
——Sandoval, Hastin Tlo'tsi hee

The Grave

Those most important of modern conveniences are not to be found
on the mesa. Here is neither throbbing water pipe, nor snaking sewer
line, no electric transformer jigs in sixty-cycle time.

Ghost Wolf Mesa is gloriously sweet in the warm light of day—and
the temple Crag is lifted up to the very top of the world. But every day
must end. Dawn Raven must fly away to where the sun sleeps. Before
departing, she shakes the shadows from her wings, cloaking the land
with darkness. On those nights when the moon's thousand-thousand
cratered eyes stare off into eternity, the ruins are soaked in a cool, ivory
radiance. When White Shell Woman does not make her appearance,
white-hot stars pierce the velvet curtain of night. These thermonu-
clear furnaces are so stupifyingly distant that the wise shun any

thought of the cosmic arithmetic. Contemplating the vast journey those massless photons have made through time can unhinge the mortal mind. And there is madness enough among the prideful bipeds.

The thunder rumbled a booming commotion, a west wind arose and seconded the motion. The storm was gathering strength—and would soon envelope Ghost Wolf Mesa.

The contract archaeologist was snug in her camping trailer, which occupied a position in the center of the small parking lot. As far as Amanda Silk knew, she was the only living soul within the boundaries of Chimney Rock Archaeological Site. There were, of course, a great many nocturnal creatures out searching for food. Here and there, brittle bones of bygone ages rested beneath the sandy soil. And there were delectably eerie tales of faceless ghosts wandering hither and thither in the deepening twilight. But she entertained no thought of such things. It had been a tiring day, and there were necessary rituals to be attended to. First, a nice cup of tea. After removing the fragrant bag from a flowered tin, she poured precisely six ounces of water into a blue-enameled pot. When water must be carried in, one is not wasteful of the precious fluid. Because the propane stove in her camp trailer was not equipped with a pilot light, Amanda touched a long-stemmed butane lighter to the gas ring and was pleased at the pop, the rapid closing of a circle of blue fire. While the water heated toward a cheerful bubble, she removed a pair of vanilla wafers from a plastic bag. These were placed on a small china saucer decorated with impossibly pink primroses. Life, despite occasional setbacks, could be sweet. But it was up to a person to make it that way.

She seated herself at the kitchen table, the ledger open before her. It was a habit of long standing, closing each day by recording its events in the green ledger. Between sips of tea, she faithfully inked in the minutiae of the day. First, the professional tasks she had completed on the site. Problems encountered, problems solved. Being engrossed in this task, Amanda Silk did not hear the soft purr of a four-cylinder engine, or the crunch of rubber tires on gravel. Neither did she notice the momentary glow of headlights sweeping past a curtained window. The archaeologist did hear the car door slam, and looked up from her work.

There was a loud rapping at the door.

"Now who can that be?" There was more urgent knocking, as if the visitor was determined to dismount the flimsy aluminum door from its hinges. "I'll be right there." *Everyone is in such a hurry these days.*

Amanda took two steps to the door. "Who is it?"

"It's me."

She recognized the voice, pushed the door open. What she saw was a young woman, dressed in loose-fitting jeans and baggy sweater. The pretty face was framed with unkempt blonde hair. So stringy. *Why don't these young people ever fix their hair up nice.* Amanda stepped aside and made a delicate gesture, as if she were inviting a close friend into a cozy parlor. "Please come inside."

Melina Castro—outfitted with heavy hiking boots—clomped in with all the grace of an Idaho logger stomping an enraged rattlesnake. She looked around. "You by yourself?"

The archaeologist stared at the graduate student. "You might begin by saying 'Hello!' "

Melina blushed. "Oh. Yeah. Uh—hi." She gave the small camp trailer another once-over. "Is April here?"

The older woman smiled. "She is hiding under the bed."

The blush went crimson. "I—um—thought she might be—um—you know—I mean—in the bathroom or something."

Pity these university students do not learn to speak conventional English. "She is not here."

Melina pointed through the camp-trailer wall. "Her car's parked down the road."

The archaeologist stared blankly at the young woman. "Her car? April usually walks in from her stepfather's home."

"She was hauling her camping gear," Melina said. "The schedule for Professor Axton's Chimney Rock survey has been pushed forward."

The kettle began to whistle. "Would you like a cup of tea? I could add some water."

Melina ignored the offer. "April's not in her car," she muttered. "And I saw something in the trees."

The older woman frowned absentmindedly at a bag of Red Zinger as if she had no idea what it was. "What did you see?"

"Looked like—I guess—a large dog."

Amanda Silk dropped the tea bag into her cup. *She probably saw a coyote.*

"And I heard . . ." Melina lowered her gaze. "Something like—"

The older woman turned toward her guest. "Like what?"

"Sort of—grunting noises. Like somebody was working pretty hard."

Amanda poured steaming water into the delicate cup.

The graduate student's lips went thin. "I'm sure somebody's out there. With a dog."

Amanda nodded politely. "Do you take sugar?"

Melina pushed her face close to Amanda's. "I think they're digging."

The archaeologist paled. "You surely don't mean—"

"Damn right I do." The young woman nodded grimly. "It's one of those thieving pothunters that've been digging up half the mesa."

Their eyes met in silent agreement. To members of that profession legally certified to excavate the past, there is no creature on God's earth more to be despised than the skulking pothunter. "Reprehensible vandal," the archaeologist muttered.

The student clenched her small hands into white-knuckled fists. "Stinking, sleazy, slime-sucking maggot. It makes me so mad I could just puke."

Dr. Amanda Silk took a deep breath. "Well. I would never have thought they'd be so brazen—not when I'm right here in my camp trailer. It is just appalling."

The student tossed her head like a young mare, and snorted. "The knuckle-dragging moron probably doesn't even know you're here. I bet he didn't hear April coming. Or me. There's some wind. And it's thundering. Maybe April is already watching him—getting evidence." She stared through the wall. "I'm going to go have a look."

"Oh, I don't think so." Amanda shook her head. "That could be dangerous."

This middle-aged woman was worse than silly. She was useless. "What do you suggest we do?"

"Why, it's obvious—we should call the police."

Melina grinned cruelly. "Is your cell phone working?" She knew the answer to that.

"I'm afraid not."

"Still haven't replaced that crapped-out battery?"

"I meant to pick up a new one. But I forgot." *I must put it on my shopping list.*

The young woman set her jaw. "Well, I'm going to get a look at who's digging. Before the mud-sucking bastard gets away. Or loots the whole site." She turned toward the door.

"Wait," the archaeologist said, "I'll go with you." Amanda Silk was already pulling her coat on. "I have a small baseball bat in the closet. If he gives us any trouble, we'll club him!"

Melina smiled. *Maybe the old girl does have some spunk.*

Perhaps it was the rolling storm clouds, the rumbling mumble of thunder, or the murky twilight that had given way to true darkness. It may have been the small, still voice of common sense whispering inside the young woman's skull. Whatever the cause, Melina Castro was now feeling considerably less courageous than when she had launched her intrepid expedition.

It may have been the crisp night air, the exquisite thrill of a small adventure. Or the baseball bat clenched in her hand. Whatever the reason, the archaeologist discovered that she was made of stern stuff. Furthermore, Dr. Silk was becoming quite curious about what the graduate student had heard in the gathering darkness over Ghost Wolf Mesa. *If there is something unusual going on out here, I must know what it is.*

There was a flash of lightning, a heart-stopping boom of thunder.

But they were beyond turning back. And gradually, the young woman was emboldened by Amanda Silk's display of courage.

They moved forward resolutely, if slowly. From time to time—as if by some telepathically shared signal—the women would pause to listen intently. This was a time for Amanda Silk to strengthen her grip on the wooden club. Presently, one or the other would resume the trek. Together they moved on to an inevitable encounter with whoever—*whatever*—was out there in the night. Waiting.

The climax to this misadventure occurred as they approached the rim of rubble marking the edge of a pit-house ruin. Melina was barely a step ahead of her older comrade. She paused.

Dr. Silk stiffened. "Why are you stopping?"

"I heard something," the graduate student whispered.

"I don't hear anything."

Melina squinted, as if this would help her see into the darkness. "Must've been a squirrel or something. Maybe we should just head back—"

A brilliant electric fault sizzled across the blackness, cracking open the vault of heaven. The merest drop of light spilled out, blanching the mesa as a thousand noonday suns.

Melina screeched, stumbled backward, and was immediately reinforced by a shrill shriek from her companion. This duet was accompanied by an ear-splitting percussion of thunder.

For a moment that lasted an eternity, the women stood like small trees, firmly rooted to the earth in case the law of gravity had been repealed. There was another brief flash of lightning. "I think he's gone," Melina croaked. "The dirty, stinking, low-life, thieving sonofabitch—" She gasped for breath. "Why didn't you brain him?"

It seemed that the tables had turned again. There was only a single quanta of boldness being exchanged between them. When one woman felt a surge of courage, the other fairly whimpered. Now the older woman was trembling.

Melina Castro switched on her flashlight. "Ha! The scum-sucking grave robber is gone, all right. I'm going to have a look at the hole he dug."

Amanda Silk felt a swell of nausea, thought she was about to vomit. Her knees began to buckle. "I think I'm going to faint . . ." And she did.

All was dark. Amanda felt something hard under her shoulders and buttocks. Worse still, her left arm ached and her feet were terribly cold. *What am I doing . . . sleeping on a pile of rocks?* The distraught woman tried to clear her thoughts. *Where am I?* She felt someone slapping her face. "Hey," she protested, "stop that!"

Melina, who had retrieved the archaeologist's baseball bat, was standing over her. "Get up," the young woman whispered hoarsely. "We've got to get out of here."

Amanda Silk had considerable difficulty getting to her feet.

"Hurry," Melina muttered, practically dragging the archaeologist along.

"I'm going as fast as I can," Amanda said breathlessly. "What's the rush?"

"We've got to get out of here."

This young woman has an annoying habit of repeating herself. "Why?"

"Because," Melina said, "in the hole where that man was digging . . ." Her words trailed off.

"What's wrong?"

"Where he was digging—there's a body."

The archaeologist stopped in her tracks. "What sort of body?"

"A *dead* one."

"Are you certain?"

Melina was on the verge of hysteria. "Don't you understand—he's *killed* someone. And he was burying her in the pit-house ruin!"

Amanda's head was clearing. "Was it—anyone we know?"

"I didn't really get a good look at him."

"No," Amanda said wearily, "I mean—the dead person."

Melina identified the victim.

"Oh God—surely not."

"We've got to get off the mesa and into town. We'll get into my car and—"

"This is all very confusing." Amanda tripped over a piñon root.

Melina squeezed her companion's arm till it hurt. "The murderer—he's still out here somewhere. We've got to get away before he finds us."

They almost bumped into him.

"Eh!" he said.

This resulted in more screams.

"Excuse me. I did not mean to startle—"

Melina raised the small bat in a menacing gesture. "Get out of our way, you murderous bastard—or I'll crack your skull wide open!" Her voice quavered. "And stomp my feet in your brains."

The apparition raised his palm. "It was not my intention to alarm you. Please calm yourselves, ladies." This voice, which carried a distinct tone of authority, was a familiar one.

Melina—on the verge of carrying out her violent threat—hesitated. "Dr. Axton—is that you?"

"It is. And I would be immensely gratified if you lowered that ridiculous weapon."

The graduate student surrendered the bat to its rightful owner. "Well, it's a good thing you identified yourself. I could've killed you!"

"I think not," Silas Axton sniffed. "Now what on earth is going on out here? I arrived just minutes ago, and heard the most godawful screams. Loud enough to wake the dead."

Melina was almost stuttering with relief. "Professor Axton. It was just awful—I'm so glad to see you."

"I wish I could say the same. Now tell me—what sort of nocturnal mischief have you two been up to?"

Confronted by one of her peers, Dr. Amanda Silk had managed to regain a slight measure of her dignity. And her voice. "Silas, we were out looking for a pothunter."

His tone softened, as if this explanation sounded almost plausible. "And did you find the scoundrel?"

The archaeologist drew herself up to her full height. "Yes—and no."

"Pardon me, Amanda—but this response sounds distinctly contradictory."

Pedantic old bastard. "Yes, Melina found him. No, he was something worse than a pothunter."

"Confound it woman—then what was he?"

"According to this young lady"—Amanda took a deep breath—"he was a murderer."

Professor Silas Axton, who had once served as a high school principal on the south side of Chicago, took this grim news quite in stride. "Ah. A murderer. Well, then—do we know whom he has murdered?"

"Thankfully, I did not see the corpse." Amanda pointed the baseball bat at her youthful companion. "But if Miss Castro is not mistaken, the body is that of April Tavishuts."

Arboles, the Aztec Cafe

The men were seated at a table covered with a blue-and-white-checked oilcloth. Wallace Whitehorse, chief of Southern Ute police, raised his gaze from the steaming plate of tamales and refried beans. Just long enough to glance across the table at the formidable Ute who had come within a whisker of having the job that was now his. "So how've you been, Charlie?"

"If things was any better, I wouldn't hardly be able to stand it." Having different priorities than the Cheyenne, Charlie Moon did not look up from his plate. "How's the law-enforcement business?"

"Ahh, things are going kinda so-so. I don't think most of the officers mind that I'm not a Ute."

"I hear you've got the department operating smoothly."

"I like to think so."

"Anything new on Julius Santos?"

Whitehorse frowned at this unwelcome reference. "He's still a missing person. BIA cops are looking into it. Some of my officers have helped 'em search the boonies within a few miles of the Santos place. Didn't find a trace of him."

"It's a rugged country," the Ute said. "They might've come within ten feet of his body and not seen it."

"Yeah. Someday a deer hunter'll stumble over his bones. I expect Santos's horse throwed him."

Moon knew the horse. Snuffy was a stable mount—not one to spook. But a crusty old nag that'd step over a diamondback rattler without blinking an eye might go pie-eyed and rear up on her hind legs if a cottontail jumped up. So maybe Whitehorse was right.

The Northern Cheyenne was looking at his reflection in the restaurant window. Musing about what a big, lonesome country this Ute reservation was. "Break a leg out there, you're same as a dead man."

A slender waitress showed up to refill water glasses and coffee mugs.

Whitehorse watched her depart, then stirred artificial sweetener into the fresh coffee. "Surprised you were able to get away from your ranch. Big operation like that must keep you hopping."

Moon understood the implied questions. What had brought him to Ignacio—and why had he invited the chief of police to supper? Whitehorse had retired from the U.S. Army and the Military Police just a few months ago, and been hired as the tribe's new chief of police. *A job that I thought was mine for the asking.* Moon had been passed over in circumstances that were, at best, murky. At worst, the result of one politician's white-hot malice. There were persistent rumors that the tribal council had voted overwhelmingly for Moon as chief of police. And that the previous tribal chairman had—by some dark and clever subterfuge—cheated him out of the appointment. But whatever had happened was in the past. A man must live in the here and now. And here and now was going pretty good. Moon took a bite of beef enchilada, followed this with a sip of sweet black coffee. "Few days ago, I had a visit from Oscar Sweetwater."

The expression on the Northern Cheyenne's broad face remained neutral. But Moon, who was a skilled poker player, saw the muscles tense in Whitehorse's jaw.

The chief of police used a spoon handle to punch a hole in his sopaipilla. He picked up a sticky plastic bottle, squirted honey into the makeshift orifice. "So what did Mr. Sweetwater think of your ranch?"

Which meant: *Why did the chairman drive over a hundred miles to see you. Why not call you on the telephone. Must've been some important business.*

"I think he liked the Columbine," Moon said. "But that wasn't why he came to see me."

Whitehorse waited for the former Ute police officer to tell him.

"He offered me a job."

The Northern Cheyenne set the honey container down. Hard enough to jar the table. "Well, I've seen it coming." He shook his head. "I figured I couldn't last longer than a year in this damn job. Wondered how long it'd take the council to decide that Utes didn't want a Cheyenne running their cop shop."

"That's not what it was about," Moon said.

The sudden relief exploded on Whitehorse's face. "It wasn't?"

"Matter-of-fact, the council is happy with you." This was only a slight exaggeration. "And they should be. You've been doing a first-rate job."

"Thanks. But it's no secret that every Ute on the reservation expected you to get the position after Roy Severo retired. There's even talk that the past chairman pulled a fast one to make sure you were bypassed."

Moon waved this gossip aside. "Doesn't matter. Besides, I'm a full-time rancher now. Don't have the time to be anybody's chief of police." He smiled. "Or the inclination."

The Northern Cheyenne's smile outshined the neon sign on the window. "Well, I'm glad to hear that. I'd like to keep this job for a while."

"I expect you will." Moon helped himself to a sopaipilla. "Oscar wants me to act as a kind of consultant for the tribal council."

"Doing what?"

"Investigations. On issues that fall outside the normal jurisdiction of the Southern Ute Police Department."

Whitehorse's brow furrowed. "Sounds like PI work."

Moon nodded. "I'll be looking into matters that are officially off-limits to SUPD officers. Poking around whatever issues the tribal government is interested in. I'll be reporting directly to the chairman." He stirred his coffee. "I'll need your cooperation."

"Hey—you've got it." Whitehorse had a dozen questions, but he held his tongue. Charlie Moon was a fair man. But the big Ute would tell him only what he wanted him to know. And that would have to be enough.

They finished their meal without referring again to Moon's appointment. The Ute had just finished his strawberry ice cream when the radio transceiver on Whitehorse's belt made a garbling sound. It sounded, Moon thought, like someone strangling a goat. The chief of police stepped outside the restaurant while the tribal investigator paid the bill.

As the Ute emerged from the cafe, Whitehorse was warming up the engine on his patrol car. "There's a request for assistance up at the Chimney Rock ruins. Looks like I'm the closest officer available."

"Don't let me keep you."

"You might want to come along."

"Why would I want to do that?"

"They claim there's a dead body up there."

Back in the Saddle

Even with the accelerator pedal on the floorboard, Moon was barely able to keep in sight of the flashing emergency lights on Whitehorse's well-tuned Chevrolet patrol car. Charlie Moon's aging Ford pickup protested with the clacking of worn valves and a dozen miscellaneous rattles; the whisker-thin speedometer needle jittered just above seventy. On the top of Dutchman's Hill, a hubcap was ejected—to sail serenely over Stollsteimer Creek like a Lilliputian saucer from a tiny planet. Moon almost caught up when Whitehorse slowed to turn in at the Chimney Rock Archaeological Site entrance, where the gate was open. He got even closer to the low-slung Chevy as it rumbled along the bumpy gravel road ascending the piñon-studded rim of Ghost Wolf Mesa. When the chief of police braked to a rocking halt in the small parking lot, Charlie Moon was a mere fifty yards behind.

The living occupants of the mesa were assembled, awaiting the arrival of the authorities. Wallace Whitehorse introduced himself as chief of Southern Ute police, flashed his ID at the civilians. After a moment's hesitation, he introduced Charlie Moon as "a special investigator for the tribe."

"I," the head of the scholarly delegation said, "am Professor Silas Axton. Chairman of the Department of Anthropology and Archaeology at Rocky Mountain Polytechnic University." He turned to his colleague. "This is Dr. Amanda Silk. She is a contract archaeologist for the United States Forest Service. At present, she is performing salvage archaeology here at the Chimney Rock site."

Charlie Moon smiled at the shaken woman. "We've met before."

Whitehorse looked over Axton's shoulder at a half dozen younger people. "What about them?"

"They are graduate students," the professor said in a dismissive manner. "Part of a survey crew working under my direction. Most of them arrived within the past hour or so." He turned to nod to a young woman. "Except for this one. She is—in a sense—the reason that I summoned the police." The tone of his voice revealed his disapproval. "This young lady has actually seen the body. Or so she says."

The young woman in question, now much composed, stepped forward. "I'm Melina Castro."

Moon recognized the name. This was the grad student who'd claimed she'd seen a peculiar man up on the Crag last summer. A man who'd changed into a four-legged beast and chased her back to the encampment.

Wallace Whitehorse removed a microcassette recorder from his pocket. "Miss Castro, I'm going to ask you some questions. Mind if I tape our conversation?"

Melina shook her head. And looked at the man behind the chief of police. He was the one who had found the lost Zuni child. And he had also found the Twin War Gods petroglyph. Although he claimed the little girl had shown it to him.

Whitehorse pushed the Record button, muttered the date, time of day, and location into the tiny microphone. He shoved the instrument under the young woman's nose. "Okay. Please state your name. Then tell me what happened."

She repeated her name. "I'm a graduate student in Professor Axton's department. Last night, I got a telephone call from Professor Axton's secretary. Telling me that the schedule for our survey at Chimney Rock had been moved forward several days. The work is going to start tomorrow, so I came to the site tonight. When I got here, I saw another grad student's car parked on the gravel road. Which is unusual, if you know what I mean."

Whitehorse, who didn't know what she meant, interrupted. "Excuse me, Miss Castro. Just for the record, who is this other student?"

"April Tavishuts."

"She's a tribal member," Moon said. "Stepdaughter of Alvah Yazzi. Alvah has a place just down the road from here. April lives in an apartment in Granite Creek."

Melina continued. "I got to the site this evening." She glanced at her wristwatch. "I guess it was a little past eight. I saw April's car."

"A Toyota sedan?" Whitehorse asked. He'd passed it on the way in.

"Yeah. That's it. I stopped to have a look, but she wasn't there. And then I saw something off in the trees." She looked off into the darkness.

"What did you see?"

"A dog, I think." She hugged herself. "And when the wind was just right, I heard some odd sounds. Like someone digging. So I thought it must be a pothunter."

Whitehorse looked bewildered.

"An artifact thief," Amanda Silk explained. "Someone who unearths the Anasazi graves to remove burial goods. Like ceramics."

Melina continued her account. "So I went and found Dr. Silk in her camping trailer. We went to investigate."

Whitehorse—who had a daughter about Melina's age—shook his head at this. "Didn't that seem like a dangerous thing to do?"

"Not at the time. We would've called the police, except I don't have a cell phone. And Dr. Silk's wasn't working. Besides, she had this base-ball bat."

The chief of police grinned at the spunky young woman.

"Once we were out there," Melina said, "it was really spooky-quiet. So I started to think maybe I was hearing things. Or maybe the pothunter had already left. But when the lightning flashed, I saw him. He was on his knees—by the excavation. I guess we must have yelled. And then he was gone." She paused.

Whitehorse shook the recorder under her chin. "Go on."

"Well, I wondered how much damage he'd done, so I went to have a look in the excavation. To see if he'd disturbed anything important. Like Anasazi bones or artifacts. That's when I saw . . ." Her lips trembled.

"Take your time, miss."

Melina steeled herself. "That's when I saw the body. We'd scared him away before he could get it completely buried."

"Were you able to identify the victim?"

She nodded.

"Who was it?"

Melina said the words slowly, precisely, into the miniature microphone. "It was April Tavishuts."

Moon swallowed hard. Someone was going to have to tell Alvah Yazzi that his stepdaughter was dead. Murdered, most likely. He was relieved it wasn't going to be him.

Whitehorse poked the recorder in the young woman's face. "You recognize the man?"

Melina shook her head.

"Can you describe him?"

"Well—I didn't actually get a very good look at him."

Whitehorse turned to the archaeologist. "Dr. Silk, could you provide a description of the suspect?"

"Hardly, Officer. I did not see him."

Melina Castro opened her mouth as if to offer an explanation, then shut it.

Whitehorse directed his next remarks to Professor Silas Axton. "See that everyone stays put—nobody leaves the site until we've got their statement."

Axton nodded, well knowing that the fascinated graduate students could not be dragged away from the scene of a murder.

Wallace Whitehorse spoke softly to the graduate student. "Miss Castro, please take us to where you found the body."

Flanked by the formidable lawmen, Melina Castro fearlessly led the way. What had previously seemed a long journey into the darkness was barely a five-minute walk. The graduate student paused at the rim of the pit-house ruin, and pointed. Her voice croaked: "In there." She stood like a post while the Cheyenne swept the ruin with a clublike five-cell flashlight. Nothing unusual being evident aside from the disturbed earth, both men gingerly approached the edge of the excavation.

Moon kneeled by the edge of the freshly dug grave, illuminated by the beam from Whitehorse's light. He looked in. Wished he hadn't.

April's earth-specked face was in profile. Her dark eyes staring blankly into nothingness. There was a curved wound on her temple. A worm of black, coagulated blood wriggled past her ear. One hand was visible—fingers twisted, a painted nail broken. Without his conscious mind willing it, Moon's hand moved toward her face. He touched a finger under her chin. No pulse. He paused to close his eyes. Whispered a prayer.

He was interrupted by the Northern Cheyenne's bass voice. "Charlie, is this the Tavishuts girl?"

The newly appointed tribal investigator nodded. And took another look. This time with the cold eye of a professional. The shallow, rectangular excavation was barely a yard long. It had been necessary to bend the victim's knees. It certainly looked like April had interrupted a pothunter, who had hurriedly used the small hole he'd dug to conceal his unexpected victim. But the Ute was struck by the similarity to ancient Native American burials, where the corpse was placed in a fetal position, knees pulled to the chest.

There was a throaty cough of thunder, a sudden spitting of rain. A few drops plopped onto the disturbed soil. Wallace Whitehorse peered blindly into the dark heavens. "We'll need to get some kinda shelter rigged to protect the crime scene."

"I've got a tent in my pickup," Moon said.

Off to the east, they heard a faint whine of sirens.

Whitehorse glanced at his Ute comrade. "Sounds like we have some help coming."

Moon looked toward the valley. A scattered procession of vehicles with flashing red and blue lights was converging on Ghost Wolf Mesa. "That'll be the state police—and the Archuleta County Sheriff's Office from Pagosa. Won't be long till the FBI shows up. The U.S. Forest Service has a special agent stationed in Durango. I imagine there'll be some jurisdictional issues."

The chief of police understood that this last comment was something of an understatement. Before long, the mesa top would be the scene of a law-enforcement circus.

Moon posed an innocuous question to Melina Castro. "Do you know whether April owned a dog?"

The blonde student shook her head.

"You knew her pretty well, then?"

Melina Castro shrugged. "Sure. We live in the same—" She paused to rephrase the statement. "April's apartment is in the same building as mine."

SUPD Chief of Police Wallace Whitehorse had moved to the opposite side of the pit-house ruin, leaving Charlie Moon alone with the graduate student. The Ute investigator lowered his voice. "There's something I need to ask you about."

She turned her pale face toward his.

"Last summer, I understand you had an encounter here at the site with—" How to put it. "A kind of . . . peculiar man."

"So you heard about that."

"Tell me about it. It could turn out to be important."

Melina rocked back and forth, shifting her weight from one leg to the other. "It happened on the Crag."

As Moon waited for her to continue, a heavy silence filled the gulf between them. "This man—he look like anybody you know?"

"I'm not sure." She shrugged. "It was dark."

"What was he doing?"

"Just standing there—very still. So I called to him."

"Did you think it was somebody from the university?"

She frowned at the lawman. "Why would you think that?"

He let the question hang in the air. "What happened next?"

Melina Castro shook her head, as if attempting to dislodge the memory. "When this guy hears my voice, he drops onto his hands. Crouches there like an animal." The young woman shuddered. "He started . . ." She licked dry lips, began again: "He started loping toward me. Slow, at first. Then faster." She looked up defiantly. "You may think it's funny, but I ran like hell. And never looked back."

The tribal investigator found not the slightest humor in the young woman's story.

Melina allowed herself a long look at April's grave. She whispered something the Ute could not hear, then walked away, fading into the storm-shrouded darkness.

Charlie Moon fixed his gaze on a purple-black horizon where—God willing—the sun would eventually rise to illuminate this rugged plug of sandstone.

By the time Moon had secured his Army-surplus tent over the corpse, a full contingent of law-enforcement officials was milling about.

Wallace Whitehorse had retracted his earlier observation. This event could not properly be described as a circus. Circuses are fun. The chief of Southern Ute police—who now had the moral support of several of his junior officers—made it clear to his subordinates that they were to remain aloof from the squabble. Even if it meant assuming the role of spectators.

There were no loud voices raised among the disparate gathering of lawmen. But blunt words were exchanged. The Archuleta County sheriff made the point that this corpse had been discovered within the legal domain of Archuleta County, and was almost certainly murdered within the same. No one disputed this. The ranking state policeman present did mention—somewhat forcefully—that his jurisdiction extended over the entire state of Colorado. Including Archuleta County. Special agents Stanley Newman and George Whitmer, lately arrived from the FBI's Durango office, noted that Chimney Rock Archaeological Site was not only federal property—it was also within the boundaries of the Southern Ute Reservation. And it was hardly necessary to remind the competing lawmen that the Bureau was responsible for investigating serious crimes that occurred on Indian reservations, or that the victim has been tentatively identified as an enrolled member of the Southern Ute tribe.

As teeth were being gnashed, a ranger from the Pagosa office of the U.S. Forest Service considered this exchange of views. The scholarly fellow—a geologist by training and a gentleman by nature—had been notified of the calamity by a friend in the Archuleta County Sheriff's Office. "Excuse me," he said.

Several lawmen turned to glare at him with jaundiced eyes. What the hell did the Smoky want?

He offered an opinion. "If I am not mistaken, crimes committed on U.S. Forest Service property fall within the jurisdiction of the forest service special agent stationed in Durango. Should you wish to contact this law-enforcement official, I can provide you with her telephone number."

This information was news to most of those present. But not to the representatives of the FBI. "Special Agent Nye is in Mercy Hospital with a fractured hip," Newman said. "Until she recovers—or until the forest service assigns a replacement—the Bureau will take full responsibility for the investigation. I'll talk to her tomorrow. If she wishes to assume charge of the investigation, the Bureau will provide all the support at its disposal."

This seemed to settle things.

Special Agent Newman, somewhat mollified by this small victory, began the "official" interrogation of the principle witnesses. Once again, Melina described finding April Tavishuts's abandoned vehicle, enlisting the aid of Dr. Silk for a search of the area where she'd heard the sounds, and finally—the terrifying encounter with a presumed pothunter who wasn't trying to dig up something after all. He was in the process of burying a corpse. Amanda repeated her earlier testimony—she had seen neither the murderer nor his half-buried victim. Or, for that matter, his dog.

A state policeman took a call on his radio. He then informed the gathering of lawmen that the medical examiner would be delayed. Dr. Simpson was currently involved with some urgent work near Granite Creek. A small plane had crashed in the San Juans; the deceased included a state senator, his wife, and their two children. The ME hoped to arrive at Chimney Rock Archaeological Site early tomorrow morning. If Simpson should be unduly delayed, he would send a colleague.

Obviously, until the medical examiner showed up, the corpse must remain in place.

There was a general discussion among the lawmen. The rain would not be a problem, because a tent had been fixed over the site. In the meantime, the scene of the crime would be photographed and properly secured with the mandatory yellow tape.

Special Agent Newman observed that it would be necessary for someone to watch over the burial site. Were there any volunteers?

There were none. A few members of the local constabulary began to drift away.

And so Wallace Whitehorse made the kind of sacrifice administrators are prone to make. He volunteered Officer Bignight to keep watch over the crime scene.

Daniel Bignight was not overjoyed by this assignment, but the Taos Pueblo man departed immediately for the pit house. He seated himself under the thickest of the junipers. It was a suitable spot from which to mutter dark curses involving the Northern Cheyenne and his immediate relatives. Also his ancestors. And livestock.

Deprived of any jurisdictional rights, the sheriff's deputies and state police went into their respective huddles. The sheriff, being of a practical nature, decided that there was nothing useful he and his deputies could accomplish here. Clearly, they were neither needed nor wanted by the FBI. Without a good-bye to their colleagues, they got into their vehicles and drove away. The state police decided to hang around for a few hours and keep an eye on things. Though this activity would probably serve no useful purpose, their continued presence would be bound to annoy the federal agents. A man found his pleasure where he could.

Night Watch

It was a few minutes past three o'clock in the morning. The rain had almost stopped; the bulk of the slow-moving storm had drifted eastward to drench Pagosa Springs.

Thirty yards from the pit-house ruin—where he was spared a direct view of the tent covering the corpse—Daniel Bignight was at his post. To ward off slumber, he had swallowed a quart of sugared coffee. But what goes in must come out, and it was necessary that he relieve himself. He knew April Tavishuts's ghost would still be hovering about her grave, and realized that a Ute female spirit would likely be offended by the sight of a Taos Pueblo man emptying his bladder. So Bignight withdrew to a far clump of scrub oaks—and kept his back to the location where her broken body slept that deepest of all sleeps.

As Daniel Bignight was thus employed, it seemed that the sun was coming up behind him. But a sunrise at this early hour, he reasoned, would be highly unlikely. Miraculous, even. More likely, the medical examiner had shown up and Doc Simpson's crew was setting up battery-powered floodlights at the grave site. *So I'd better get back on the job before that hard-nosed Northern Cheyenne starts wondering where I am.* He completed his task, then turned to take a few steps toward his duty station.

Yellow-orange flames were billowing above the pit-house ruin.

CHAPTER 7

Now on the outer wall of the Sun's house, there hung a
weapon. The Twins pointed to this weapon and said that that
was what they had come for.

—Sandoval, Hastin Tlo'tsi hee

Morning

Night's dark cloak had faded deathly pale around the edges; first
light bathed the sandstone cliffs in a rosy glow. It would have been a
bright, lovely morning . . . except. Except for a gray twilight of gloom
that hung over the mesa. And the sickly-sweet scent of roasted flesh
and bone.

Special Agent George Whitmer had withdrawn several yards from
the pit-house ruin to speak with SUPD officer Daniel Bignight, who
was flanked protectively by his chief of police. "We'll need a statement
about what happened when the fire started," Whitmer said to Bignight.

Wallace Whitehorse—though highly annoyed with his subordinate—did not let it show. He would deal with Bignight later. "There's
not much Daniel can tell you."

That's because he left his post. Whitmer's speech was barely more gracious than his thoughts. He directed his next remark to the chief of Southern Ute police. "Guess that's because he didn't see all that much."

It was an inarguable fact. Bignight—who did not know how to tell a lie—admitted as much. "I had to pee," he said lamely.

"You should've peed on the fire," Whitmer said with a straight face.

The low humor was lost on Bignight. "It started behind my back," he protested. "Besides, you can't pee out a fire that big."

The good-natured Whitmer grinned at the SUPD cop. "Look, nobody's gonna give you a hard time about this. But I'll need a statement for the record."

Whitehorse glared at Bignight. "He'll give you a statement later." *After I'm done with him.*

Charlie Moon and Special Agent Stanley Newman were at the edge of the makeshift grave. There was virtually nothing left of Moon's canvas tent, which had sheltered the Ute woman's body from last night's rain. The fire had consumed all available fuel, including much of the flesh on April Tavishuts's bones.

Moon avoided looking at what was left of the charred face. The grinning teeth.

Newman—probing with a stick—was examining the remains of a few items mixed in with what remained of the corpse. A split steel ring looped through a half dozen heat-warped keys. A few blackened coins. A sooty brass button. "This's gonna make the medical examiner's job pretty tough."

Moon pointed at a charred object that looked like an oversized lady's compact. Except it had a rectangular slit in the cover. "Is that what I think it is?"

The FBI agent squatted for a better view. "Looks like a compass." Certainly an article a member of the site survey team might have in her pocket. He looked up at the sky. "If it wasn't for the rain, that damn blaze might've started a major forest fire." Newman pushed himself erect. "Like a homicide wasn't enough. Now we got an arson to boot."

"Whoever set it must've been waiting for Danny Bignight to doze off."

The special agent nodded. "And when he wandered off to relieve himself, that was opportunity enough to start the fire." He frowned at the human remains. "Perp must've soaked the corpse with an accelerant."

"Like what?"

"A gallon of high-octane unleaded, I'd guess."

Moon sniffed. There was no detectable gasoline scent. "Took a big chance. Burning the body must've been important."

Newman grunted. "Damn right it was important—whoever committed the murder was destroying incriminating evidence."

"Like the double-helix kind."

"DNA convicts." A shadow passed over Newman's face. "Unless the killer's a celebrity blessed with a jury of his adoring fans." The federal lawman—who had been working a Cortez bank robbery for the previous four days—scratched at a growth of stubble on his chin. "This looks like a straightforward enough murder. Victim's car is here, so she must've driven herself to the site. Miss Tavishuts stops her car, gets out"—he pointed the stick at the key ring—"brings the ignition key with her."

"Why?" Moon said.

The fed thought this question irrelevant. "Why did she bring the keys?"

"Why did she stop the car?"

"Who knows. Maybe she saw something that made her suspicious. Whatever the reason was, she goes to have a look—ends up out here at the pit house. Confronts the artifact thief. The perp panics. Bangs her on the head. Wound on her scalp looked like she might've been struck by a shovel. At least we got photos of that before the corpse was torched." The federal officer aimed a malignant look in Bignight's direction.

"It fits," the Ute said. "Maybe he didn't intend to kill her."

"Sure. But when a felon is cornered, he tends to get scared. And violent. So bad stuff happens. And now he has a fresh corpse to dispose of. But hey, he's also got a freshly dug grave. Small, but it'll do. So he folds the victim up, stuffs her in, proceeds to bury the body." Newman, feeling marginally better, adjusted the knot on his red tie. "Then the second student shows up. Sees Miss Tavishuts's car on the side of the road.

She stops to have a look, sees a dog. Which tells us the perp has a mutt with him. Then she hears the sound of somebody digging, figures it's a pothunter. Maybe the perp is already burying the body. So Miss Castro hotfoots it over to the campsite, tells Dr. Silk what she's heard, they go to investigate. Catch the bastard red-handed. And he runs like a deer."

"So all you got to do is find him," Moon said.

"Oh, we'll find him." Newman's mouth twisted into a self-satisfied grin. "By the way—what are you doing here?"

The Ute draped his arm around the fed's shoulders. "Having a nice talk with my favorite Bureau cop. Except," Moon added in deference to the other half of the FBI team, "for George Whitmer."

Whitmer chuckled. "Thanks, big fella."

Newman ignored this flippancy. "You're a rancher now, Charlie. Ranchers raise cows. They chew on straws and kick at cow pies. They do not hang around at murder scenes like homicide was their business."

"Wallace and me was having a meal over at Arboles when the call came in. He asked me to come along."

"Now why would he do that—because you used to be acting chief of tribal police?"

Moon pretended to think about this. "Could be."

Newman glared at Wallace Whitehorse. "Is Charlie jerking me around?"

The Northern Cheyenne's face had as much expression as an empty pie pan. "Could be."

Whitmer, who enjoyed such diversions, chuckled again.

Moon found himself staring at the charred bones. "I got a part-time job with the tribe."

Newman grunted. "So you're a cop again. Working for Wallace?"

"Not exactly."

"Not exactly a cop or not exactly working for the Southern Ute chief of police?"

"Not exactly neither."

"What the hell does that mean?"

"Excuse me," Whitmer interjected, "but I believe I know what Charlie's trying to tell you. I'll interpret if you like."

"I am wan and weary," Newman said to his partner. "Please spare me the crapola."

"Okay. Consider yourself spared." *Crabby little grouch.*

"I'm a consultant to the tribal council," Moon said. "Report directly to the chairman."

"Doing what?"

Moon thought about saying "none of your business." But there was no percentage in annoying this local representative of the FBI. Wallace Whitehorse had to work with these guys. And Stan Newman was a first-rate cop, doing his job. The Ute chose his words carefully. "I'll be conducting . . . inquiries."

"Inquiries, huh?"

The Ute investigator nodded. "Into issues of interest to the tribe."

Newman smiled. "You should never try to bullshit the Bureau, Charlie. I know you're working as a private investigator."

Moon tried not to look surprised. But he was.

"I know you're wondering how I am able to deduce this," Newman said. "It is elementary, my novice gumshoe. Paperwork for your PI license was submitted last week. As a service to the state of Colorado, the Bureau reviews all such applications. For the purpose of weeding out petty criminals. Con men. General misfits."

Whitmer couldn't resist. "Dang, there goes his license."

"In Charlie's case, we'll make an exception." Newman frowned. "You packing, cowboy?"

The Indian shook his head. "Momma told me to leave my guns at home."

Newman snorted at this. "Well, if you're gonna be snooping around amongst the violent low-life element, I'd advise you to arm yourself."

"My gun-toting days are over. Anyway, I don't intend to arrest any desperate criminals."

It was at this moment that an unfamiliar voice materialized behind them. "I beg your pardon."

The lawmen turned to eyeball the new arrival, who looked as if he'd stepped right out of a magazine advertisement for expensive sports jackets.

"Sorry to interrupt. I'm Terry Perkins."

Newman stared uncomprehendingly. "You some kind of reporter?" Television most likely. This guy looked like a second-string anchorman.

"Hardly, I'm *Dr.* Terry Perkins."

"Oh—you're standing in for Doc Simpson." Newman didn't wait for a confirmation. "Well, I'm glad to finally see a medical examiner. Bad news though—the murderer is also a damn firebug. As you can see, he has incinerated the corpse."

Moon could have cleared things up. He decided to let Newman find out for himself.

The newcomer pulled nervously at his earlobe. "You misunderstand; I am not a medical examiner—nor am I a physician."

"Then what the hell are you?"

The academic thought that short sentences might work best. "Professor Terry Perkins. My doctorate is in physics. I teach at Rocky Mountain Polytechnic. My specialty is paleoastronomy."

Newman was weary and irritable. "Wonderful. I was just saying to Charlie Moon—Charlie, I said, we're in deep trouble here. This homicide investigation is too complicated for us simpleminded cops. What we need here is a sure-enough . . . a . . . pileo—"

"Paleoastronomer," Whitmer said with a poker face.

"Yeah," Newman snapped at his snide partner. "One of them."

Perkins's face glistened pinkly in the morning sun. "I did not mean to intrude. When I heard about the tragedy, I merely thought I should report my presence to the proper authorities."

George Whitmer smiled at the miffed scientist. "Don't pay any attention to my partner. Stan gets sorta testy when somebody burns up all his evidence."

"Yeah. It's been a long night." Newman attempted to match his partner's amiable smile; the unaccustomed effort called upon little-used facial muscles. "So you knew Miss Tavishuts?"

"Certainly," Perkins said. "She is a graduate student in anthropology—that is Professor Axton's department. But April is—was—taking my spring seminar. Elements of Southwest American Paleoastronomy. She was an excellent student. Showed great promise. So I am naturally crushed by the terrible news."

All the lawmen shared more or less the same thought. *You don't look crushed.*

"So," Newman continued casually, "you just arrived at Chimney Rock?"

"A few minutes ago."

"The other people from the university showed up last night."

"My research at the archaeological site is independent of the survey team working under Professor Axton. I come and go as I please."

"What exactly is your professional interest here?"

"Astronomy—as practiced by the Anasazi. As they didn't have the luxury of optical telescopes, my task is mostly a matter of deducing the probable means by which they observed such heavenly objects as are visible to the naked eye. It's about points of observation." To demonstrate, Dr. Perkins raised his thumb and made a sighting of a distant mountain peak. "Lines of sight. Angles." He lowered the thumb. "All of which boils down to simple geometry." Perkins presented his most disarming smile. "Plus a few brilliant insights."

Newman smirked. "I find myself truly fascinated by this information."

Knuckle-dragging oaf. The academic's grin had a sharp bite in it. "It is always gratifying to find an interest in science among the masses. If you care to educate yourself, I would be happy to provide you with reprints of a few of my published papers. Or perhaps—something less challenging would be more appropriate. May I suggest *Dick and Jane Visit the Planetarium.*" It was an unkind cut. But all of Dr. Perkins's audience save one were highly amused.

Stan Newman returned the sharkish grin. As well as he was able. *Smart-ass egghead.*

Charlie Moon declared that he would be pleased to read about the professor's research. And having done so, instantly made a friend among the scholarly set. The Ute tribal investigator walked away with the paleoastronomer. "May I offer some friendly advice?"

Perkins kept his eyes on the path. "Feel free."

"There's nothing to be gained by annoying a federal cop." *Especially when he's looking for somebody to hang a murder on.*

Perkins sniffed. "Despite their exalted status in the popular culture, I am neither impressed nor intimidated by representatives of the FBI. I see this fellow as an irritable law-school graduate burdened with an unfortunate career choice."

"Try seeing him as an irritable lawyer burdened with an automatic weapon."

The academic considered this sobering image. "Sir, your point is well made."

Charlie Moon had withdrawn to the relative isolation of his pickup. He was trying to decide what to do. *I accepted the job as special investigator for the tribal council. So I ought to hang around and see this thing through.* On the other hand, there were already enough lawmen here to investigate a half dozen homicides. And it wasn't like Wallace Whitehorse needed his advice. *So maybe I should just crank up the engine and head for the ranch.* Now there was an appealing idea. He was reaching for the ignition switch when someone tapped on the door.

It was Whitehorse. Moon lowered the window.

"Hi, Charlie."

"H'lo, Wallace."

The police chief seemed mildly embarrassed. "Guess I should go see Mr. Yazzi about his stepdaughter."

This was Whitehorse's first encounter with a major crime since he'd taken over as chief of Southern Ute police. Maybe a reminder was in order. "Somebody will have to tell Alvah. But make sure you let the suits know what you're intending to do. Newman and Whitmer are decent enough fellows. But if you mess with the FBI's homicide, they'll cause you all sorts of grief."

"That's sound advice." Whitehorse grinned. "But from what I hear, you were always kinda independent when it came to cooperating with the feds."

"And look where it got me."

"Yeah. Retired from the force. And now you own the finest beef ranch in the whole state."

"I was lucky. You should be careful."

"Don't worry about me. I spent a long time in the military—I know all about chain of command." The chief of police glanced toward the small FBI contingent. Newman and Whitmer were reinterviewing several sleepy-eyed graduate students. "Would you come with me to Mr. Yazzi's place?"

Moon had been expecting this. And wanted to say no. "Sure. If you think it'd help."

Whitehorse reached into the pickup cab to give the Ute a hearty slap on the shoulder. "Good. Count it as a part of your consultant services. And charge your time to the tribe—starting with when we left Arboles on the call."

Moon thought about it. *Don't mind if I do.*

Ashes

It was a short trip on Route 151, less than four miles south from the entrance to Chimney Rock Archaeological Site. Daniel Bignight led the procession. The Northern Cheyenne chief of police was within three car lengths of Bignight's bumper. Moon's Ford pickup trailed well behind the matched pair of SUPD squad cars.

Bignight's big Chevy slowed, the turn signal flashed. He made a hard right onto a dirt lane made muddy from the past night's rain, then led the procession of vehicles up a slight rise, winding through a thicket of juniper. They entered a clearing, where Alvah Yazzi's 1957 Chevrolet pickup was parked in the shade of a red willow. The hood was up, the tailgate down. The door on the plywood shell was propped up with a broomstick. A large dog—which looked to have some German shepherd parentage—emerged from the pickup bed and shook off bits of straw. The animal croaked out three obligatory, deep-chested barks, then slowly wagged a drooping tail at the visitors.

Moon peered into the plywood shell, which evidently served as a doghouse. Inside was a bale of straw and a galvanized metal tub, half filled with water. There was also a sack of dog food, torn open at one end. The animal whined an appeal to the visitor. Moon rubbed the beast behind the ears. The tail wagged faster; the Ute got his hand licked.

The planked porch fronting the modest home was provided with a single straight-backed chair. As if Yazzi did not wish to encourage visitors to stay long enough to sit down. The Navajo was something of a recluse.

Off to the right was a sturdy barn with a new metal roof. Appended to this structure was a small corral made from creosote-soaked timbers. A swaybacked roan mare hung her long head over the crude fencing. A spotted goat stood beside the horse, his horned head poking between the greasy rails. The goat made a peculiar sound. Something between a belch and a hiccup. The mare tossed her head, as if to indicate that she was unimpressed by the visitors.

Bignight approached the house, then paused to glance back at his supervisor.

Wallace Whitehorse jammed an expensive gray felt hat over his burr-cut head; he stomped resolutely past his subordinate and mounted the front porch with steps that jarred the pine planking.

Charlie Moon, unsure of his official capacity, followed in White-horse's wake. April Tavishuts was not Alvah Yazzi's natural daughter, but the old Navajo would take her death hard. He would have preferred to leave this sad duty to the Northern Cheyenne, but reminded himself—*I am on the tribal payroll.* One way or another, a man always earned his money.

The mixed-breed dog stood in the yard, panting as he watched the men mount the porch steps.

Whitehorse raised his fist to knock. For an instant, it stopped, as if governed by some subconscious hesitation. The chief of police set his jaw and rapped his knuckles on the oak door. They waited. There was no response.

He turned to Moon. "It's early. Maybe the old man's still in bed."

"Maybe." But the Ute didn't think so.

Whitehorse sighed. He knocked again. Harder this time.

A hollow silence echoed within the Navajo's house.

"Well," the chief of police muttered, "looks like he's not here. Guess we might as well give it up." He smiled amiably at the round-headed Taos Pueblo man. "Daniel, you come back this afternoon. See if Mr. Yazzi has come home yet."

"He's here."

"How do you know that?" Whitehorse snapped.

"His truck is here," Bignight responded.

Whitehorse shot a dark look at his subordinate. "Maybe he's got another vehicle."

Bignight shook his head. "Alvah's only got that old Chevy pickup."

"Well, maybe he's gone for a walk."

"His dog is here," Bignight said stubbornly. "If he was out on a hike, that old fleabag would be right there with him."

The chief of police looked at a wasp nest attached to the porch ceiling. "His truck is here. His dog is here. That's enough to convince you he's absolutely got to be at home?"

"Well, not altogether."

Whitehorse's neck was swelling dangerously. "Then what makes you so damn sure?"

Bignight was squinting through a curtained window. "I can see his boots."

Whitehorse looked over Bignight's rounded shoulder. "Where?"

The Taos Pueblo man pointed. "There. Sticking out from behind that couch."

The chief of police muttered a Cheyenne curse under his breath. The boots were lying flat on the floor. Toes up. Most likely, there were feet in them.

Whitehorse tried the door. It was locked. He barked an order at Bignight, who hurried to the rear of the Navajo's home. The chubby man returned in less than a minute, breathing hard. "Back door's locked too—and the windows are either locked or stuck."

"We'd best go inside," Moon said. "Alvah might be sick or something."

Bignight knew what *something* was. He tried the porch windows. They were also locked.

The chief of police shook his head. "I sure hate to break into a man's house. If that's just a pair of empty boots, he could make big trouble for us."

Moon decided to take the matter in hand. "I'll try the door."

"I already tried it, Charlie. It's locked."

"Maybe it's just stuck." The Ute wrapped his big hand around the knob. And turned. Metal strained against metal. Didn't give. He turned harder. There was a sudden snapping when the stem broke, a metallic rattle as shattered parts clattered about in the cast-iron mechanism. "I think it's loosened up a bit."

Whitehorse groaned. "You busted it!"

The Ute, being a charitable soul, chose to overlook this unseemly remark. He pushed on the door. It opened, swinging smoothly on oiled hinges.

Daniel Bignight grinned. Charlie Moon always got the job done.

The lawmen, standing like a mismatched trio of bronze castings, stared without comprehension at something on the floor. It looked like what was left of a man. Where the Navajo elder's head should have been, there was a band of red cloth, several thick clumps of gray hair. No eyes looked through the steel-rimmed spectacles, but a set of dentures grinned pinkly at the intruders. Below this empty face was a blue cotton shirt, arms outstretched. A lump of turquoise the size of a hen's egg rested on the third button. This impressive pendant was attached to a leather cord that passed under the collar. The shirttail was tucked into a faded pair of OshKosh B'Gosh jeans, each leg terminating in a fine pair of ostrich-skin boots.

"Look at that," Whitehorse said. The chief of police was pointing at a spot just beyond the left cuff of the cotton shirt. There, where Alvah Yazzi's hand should have been, was a wristwatch. Still ticking. The imitation-leather band was neatly fastened, the timepiece resting on the oak floor in the fashion of a small hoop. As if the man's arm had turned to vapor.

The Ute squatted for a closer examination of the remains.

"We'd better not touch anything," Whitehorse said.

Charlie Moon unfolded a pocketknife. He used the blade to lift the shirt collar, moving the cloth just enough to reveal what was underneath. An undershirt. The skin was prickling on the back of the Ute's neck. "Five'll get you twenty, there're socks in the boots."

No one took the bet.

"Jeepers," Bignight muttered, "it looks like that Navajo just faded away into nothing."

Moon studied the spot where Yazzi's head should have been. There was a thick layer of coarse gray-white powder. He used the tip of the knife blade to lift a sample.

Whitehorse leaned close to see. "What'n hell's that?"

The Ute investigator frowned at the specimen. Better not to say it out loud. *Ashes*. And a scattering of bone chips.

Bignight backed two paces away from the whatever-it-was, crossed himself, and muttered a prayer for the soul of the Navajo.

A graveyard silence hung over the parlor. Finally, the Northern Cheyenne spoke to the Ute. "What do you make of this?"

Moon did not care to speculate.

"Yazzi was a Navajo," Daniel Bignight said. From the Taos Pueblo man's point of view, this was sufficient explanation.

Wallace Whitehorse's steely glance at his subordinate made his position clear—the chief of police was not interested in Officer Bignight's superstitions. Again, he directed his comment to the Ute investigator. "It's got to be some kinda damn prank. Somebody's made a—a scarecrow."

Moon held his silence.

The Northern Cheyenne's intense thinking twisted his face into a painful grimace. The skillful administrator reasoned that if this turned out to be a serious crime, it would not be his responsibility. It would be the Bureau's problem. He turned to Bignight. "Radio those FBI agents."

Bignight—who shared his boss's view on the matter—was eager to carry out this order. He turned quickly and almost tripped over Yazzi's homely dog. The animal—which had entered the parlor unnoticed— stood a few yards away staring at what little was left of its master.

"Go way," Bignight ordered. "Shoo!"

The animal raised his head. And bugled a long, mournful blue note.

The pair of FBI agents arrived in fifteen minutes flat after Bignight's call. They stood with brows furrowed, staring at the garish figure lying spread-eagled on the Navajo's floor.

George Whitmer turned to the odd trio of tribal lawmen. His gaze passed slowly over Wallace Whitehorse. Hung briefly on Charlie Moon. Then settled on Officer Daniel Bignight. Newman stared hard at the tribal policeman.

Bignight's hands went ice-cold. As if the owl were about to call his name.

The fed called his name. Softly. "Daniel."

"Yeah?"

The FBI agent jerked his head. "C'mere."

The tribal policeman approached the suit.

Whitmer's tone was soft. Casual. "Daniel, I understand you were the one to discover the . . . ahh . . . body."

"Not exactly," Bignight said quickly, "I was just the one that saw his boots through the window—"

"This could turn out to be a big break in our homicide investigation." Whitmer had a hard set to his jaw. "I need to verify proper police procedure has been followed."

Bignight swallowed hard. "Yessir."

"Upon approaching the remains, did you touch anything?"

The tribal policeman shook his head so hard it made him dizzy. "Not me—I didn't touch nothin'."

Whitmer leaned forward, positioning his face within inches of the policeman's. "You did not check the victim for a pulse?"

Bignight's mouth gaped open.

"Then how did you verify that he was dead?"

The tribal policeman pointed at the remains. "Well, anybody but a blind man could see that—"

Special Agent Whitmer guffawed, slapped his victim on the shoulder.

The amiable Bignight grinned back at his persecutor. *Silly bastard.*

Stanley Newman shook his head at the thing on the floor. It was a grave affront to his notion of an orderly universe. He turned on the SUPD chief of police. "Great balls of fire, Wallace, what'n hell is this supposed to be?"

Wallace Whitehorse cleared his throat. "I don't exactly know."

Newman, who had not had any serious sleep in forty hours, was not the soul of patience. "You-don't-exactly-know?"

The chief of police had also been awake all night—and was not about to take any smart mouth from this pasty-faced Easterner. "According to the rules, I'm just a glorified traffic cop. You federal guys are the experts on serious crimes." He stood nose to nose with the fed. "So you tell me—what is it?"

The special agent smiled coldly at the ex-Army cop. "Haven't forgot how to pass the buck, eh?"

Whitehorse reflected the nasty grin right back at him.

Newman looked at the floor. Truth was, he didn't know what to make of it. The federal policeman searched for something sensible to say. Anything. "Any sign of forced entry?"

"None." Whitehorse looked over Newman's head at the door lock Moon had mangled. "After Officer Bignight spotted Mr. Yazzi's boots through the window, we had to force the front door."

We? Charlie Moon appreciated the favor.

Being weary, Newman spoke without thinking. "You made a forced entry—without a search warrant?"

Whitehorse clenched his hands into fists. "Damn right we did—to find out whether Mr. Yazzi was dead or alive. You got a problem with that?"

Newman opened his mouth to reply, then—having nothing to say—shut it. He knelt to inspect Yazzi's almost-empty clothing. He started with the fancy boots, worked his way up gradually, finally stopping at the place where a face should have been. He stared.

The empty spectacles stared back.

Newman's lips drooped into a petulant frown.

Yazzi's dentures grinned at him.

Damn. What is going on here? "I wonder if there's anything in the pockets." Newman looked up at his partner. "We'd better get forensics out here."

George Whitmer was already punching the number into his cell phone.

The two-person FBI forensics team was already present at Chimney Rock Archaeological Site to investigate the April Tavishuts homicide, and so they arrived promptly at the Navajo's home. Photographs were made, samples taken and stored in labeled containers. The initial work done, they proceeded with a detailed examination of the clothing.

The younger man seated himself on a pine bench, a laptop computer balanced precariously on his knees. The senior member of the team began to search Yazzi's pockets.

The congregation of curious lawmen moved closer.

The senior scientist spoke in a clipped monotone, seemingly imitating a computer-generated voice. "Al, make an inventory."

The subordinate poised his fingers to tap on the keyboard.

His supervisor proceeded with the search. "One pouch of Virginia pipe tobacco from the shirt pocket. Three-blade Case folding knife in the right-front jeans pocket. A few coins in the left—let's see—two quarters, a dime, four pennies. Wallet in the rear pocket." He opened it. "Visa card issued to Alvah Yazzi. Colorado driver's license in the same name. Ditto for a Social Security card." He recited the number. "And a wad of folding money big enough to choke that goat in the barnyard."

The solemn technician with the laptop was a certified public accountant; he politely requested a more quantitative assay.

His supervisor counted out the bills. "Three hundred and eighty-four dollars."

Officer Bignight shook his head at the sight of so many greenbacks. "Old man Yazzi was a tight fella with a nickel. He'd never go off and leave that much money lying around. Not on purpose."

Whitmer's knees protested painfully as he kneeled by the forensics expert. "That dark powder and chips where his head and hands should be—"

"It's in his clothing too. All the way into his socks—which are in his boots."

"But what the hell *is* it?"

The forensic scientist stood up. "Ashes. And small fragments of bone."

The special agent pointed. "What about that stuff—uh—where his head should be."

The expert gave a poker-faced response. "That is what we highly technical types call—hair."

"Human hair?"

"Most probably."

Whitmer withdrew to join his friends.

Newman, feeling tolerably better after consuming a stale doughnut he'd found in Yazzi's pantry, returned to the scene of the presumed crime. He muttered to his partner. "George, we're like the last survivors of a wagon train. Got what's left of a Navajo at our feet. And we're surrounded by a Ute, a Cheyenne, and a Pueblo Indian."

"*Southern* Ute," Moon corrected.

"*Northern* Cheyenne," Whitehorse added.

"Well, *excuse me*." Newman eyed the third member of the Native American triad. "Bignight—you got nothing to say?"

The policeman grinned. "*Taos* Pueblo."

Special Agent George Whitmer had noticed that Charlie Moon had been unusually quiet. Even for a man who saved his words like silver dollars. He squinted at the Ute investigator. "Charlie, you got any thoughts to share with us?"

"Thinking is delicate work, like sewing beads on leather. Takes time." Moon gazed at the thing on the floor. It suggested a deflated man. As if someone had pulled Yazzi's valve, let all the spirit spew out.

Whitmer turned away to look out a porch window, which nicely framed Yazzi's old Chevy pickup. The antique truck didn't look so lonely now. Not with a half dozen official cars and Moon's F150 pickup for company. He slipped away into a melancholy silence.

Stanley Newman rubbed bloodshot eyes. "Consider the big picture, fellas. What we've got is a dead Ute woman. Murdered, buried up there on the mesa. And if that ain't enough to spoil your day, her corpse is set afire. This peculiar piece of arson happens *after* a dozen cops show up."

All eyes avoided Bignight, but the Taos Pueblo man's back stiffened at Newman's blunt reference to his apparent inability to manage a simple assignment—like keeping watch over a crime scene.

Newman waved both arms at his small audience. "And now you guys come to Mr. Yazzi's home to break the news about what's happened to his stepdaughter—and all you find is—is *this*."

Charlie Moon felt considerable sympathy for the FBI agent. Things had taken a pretty strange turn.

The Paleoastronomer

The lawmen had withdrawn to the Navajo's front porch. The FBI special agents listened with scant interest while Wallace Whitehorse gave Daniel Bignight detailed orders for sealing the premises from the public.

Yazzi's mixed-breed dog barked once. He did this to announce the arrival of a visitor.

"Excuse me."

Five pairs of eyes turned to focus on the new arrival. Special Agent Newman approached the newcomer, and was followed closely by George Whitmer and Chief of Police Whitehorse. Moon and Bignight watched from the porch.

"Sorry to interrupt. It's me again—Terry Perkins."

Stanley Newman hitched his thumbs under his belt. "Yeah. The pilio—uh—astrologer."

"Paleoastronomer." Perkins enunciated each syllable, as one attempting to communicate with a creature who had just sufficient mental ability to eat and excrete.

Newman eyed the scholar suspiciously. "I wonder how you manage it."

The scientist took the bait. "Manage what?"

"Showing up wherever there's trouble."

Perkins responded with wide-eyed innocence. "Is there trouble here?"

The FBI agent ignored the professor's question. "What brings you to the Yazzi residence?"

The academic's expression hardened. "It never occurred to me that I would be asked to explain my presence here."

"Humor me."

"I should have thought it obvious. I am merely stopping by to express my regrets to the father of the deceased."

"Stepfather," Newman corrected, and looked around the yard. "I don't see any transportation. How'd you get here?"

"Walked upright." He raised one booted foot for the FBI agent's inspection. "In biped fashion." Perkins grinned smugly at the federal policeman.

Newman glanced at the well-shod foot, then at the academic's happy face. "You hoofed it all the way from the archaeological site?" This seemed unlikely.

"It's not such a long walk—for a man in good condition." The trim scientist eyed the hint of a bulge around Newman's midsection.

The special agent sucked in his gut. "This morning when you showed up on the mesa, you were driving a yellow Mercedes." Newman had the license-plate number in his notebook.

"Indeed I was."

"Then why're you afoot—fancy car break down?"

Perkins was beginning to enjoy the exchange. "Allow me to clear up a minor bit of confusion on your part. I did return from the Chimney Rock site in my expensive automobile, which is currently parked at the cabin."

"Cabin—where?"

Perkins jerked his head to indicate the direction. "Approximately two hundred yards up the road. Just over yon ridge."

Newman's accusing tone was that of a poker player who suspects he has been cheated. "When we talked this morning, you didn't say anything about having a cabin around here."

"Nor did you inquire about where I was staying. And before you do ask, it is not mine own domicile. It is a rental." The professor smiled at his adversary. "I returned from the mesa only a short time ago. Took a moment to wash up, then walked over here to see Mr. Yazzi." He aimed a curious glance at the closed door. "How is the old man taking it?"

This question was met with an uneasy silence.

Perkins tried again. "April's death, I mean. Is Mr. Yazzi holding up all right?"

Newman didn't meet the academic's frank gaze. "I couldn't say."

"I don't quite understand—you have not spoken to him?"

"I have not. But I would like to."

"I assume by these somewhat cryptic remarks that Mr. Yazzi is not at home."

"You may safely assume that."

"Well, I wouldn't worry about him. He'll show up sooner or later." Perkins looked over his shoulder at Alvah Yazzi's antique Chevrolet pickup. "His truck isn't running. Distributor problem, I believe." His gaze shifted to the barren hills behind the Yazzi homestead. "He must be on one of his walks."

"Where does he walk to?"

The academic shrugged. "Wherever he wants."

Newman wondered what kind of smart-aleck answer this was supposed to be.

Charlie Moon directed a remark at the scientist. "Mr. Yazzi has a dog that'll need looking after."

"I am well acquainted with Bugle."

Pleased to hear his name, Bugle wagged his tail.

The Ute glanced at the barn. "And there's some livestock. They'll need to be fed and watered."

Perkins looked down his nose at the horse and goat. They gazed placidly back. "I'll be glad to look in on his animals." He frowned at the Ute. "Is there something you are not telling me? Is Mr. Yazzi not expected to return promptly?"

Newman shot Moon a warning glance, then scowled at Perkins. "When's the last time you saw your Navajo neighbor?"

"Let me see." The professor closed his eyes as if this would aid in the recollection process. "It was just yesterday morning—probably about eight-thirty."

"You two visit every day?"

"Hardly. Yesterday, I came to pay the rent."

"Wait a minute—you tellin' me you rent from Yazzi?"

"If I did not," Perkins said with a sting of sarcasm, "I would hardly be bringing him greenbacks every month."

The lawman's antenna went up. "Yazzi asked you to pay the rent in cash?"

"That was his preference."

"Did he give you receipts?"

Perkins regarded the federal agent with an annoying smile. "Am I to assume that Mr. Yazzi is being investigated for tax evasion? I should think arresting a single malefactor would not require such a gaggle of coppers."

Chief of Police Whitehorse kept a straight face. Charlie Moon didn't. Officer Bignight grinned ear to ear. Special Agent Whitmer laughed out loud.

"We already got us a comedian on staff." Newman glanced meaningfully at his partner. "I'd appreciate it if you'd just answer my question."

"No," Perkins said stiffly. "He did not provide me with receipts for the rental payment. Mr. Yazzi and I have a very informal business relationship."

"So how much is the rent?"

"I do not see how that is any of your business."

"I am making it my business." Newman's mouth twisted into a dangerous smile.

Perkins hesitated. "Three hundred dollars. Per month."

There was an exchange of looks among the lawmen. This accounted for the wad of bills in Alvah Yazzi's wallet.

"Three hundred bucks," Newman said. "Sounds like quite a bargain." As if there might be something sinister in the arrangement.

Professor Perkins allowed himself a rueful smile. "You have not seen my cabin. It is the sort of dwelling euphemistically described by rental agents as 'rustic.' A bevy of beady-eyed rodents boldly insist on sharing the premises with me. Cockroaches the size of terrapins eat my victuals. But," he added by way of balance, "it is conveniently close to the archaeological site. And therefore suitable for my modest needs."

The light breeze, which had been westerly, shifted to the south.

Newman changed tack. "You see anybody else over here yesterday?"

"I did not, but that is hardly surprising. As I have pointed out, my cabin is situated on the opposite side of the ridge. I cannot see Mr. Yazzi's residence from the rental. He could have been throwing a barbecue for the Denver Broncos and the Dallas Cowboys—I would not have noticed."

Special Agent Whitmer took up the questioning. "My partner means did you see anybody else when you came to pay the rent."

"No. I only saw Mr. Yazzi."

Whitmer's interrogation took the form of a friendly conversation. "How'd he seem?"

Perkins warmed to the soft-spoken federal agent. "Same as usual. Taciturn. Gloomy."

"Nothing different?"

"Well, he was more than usual somewhat *elsewhere,* if you know what I mean."

Whitmer did not know what Perkins meant.

Special Agent Newman did not particularly care. He was, in fact, tiring of this stuffy academic.

Perkins sensed that he was not communicating. "What I meant was—Mr. Yazzi seemed to be somewhat—shall we say—*distracted.*"

Whitmer decided this was getting nowhere. "We appreciate you taking care of Yazzi's horse and goat. And dog."

Perkins favored the fed with a gracious nod. "I really don't mind."

Newman felt compelled to remind the professor who was in charge. "But don't monkey around the house. Office Bignight is going to seal it off."

"It would never have occurred to me to trespass upon Mr. Yazzi's dwelling. But the fact that you are sealing it suggests that a crime has been committed here." Perkins waited for a response.

Newman allowed the implied question to hang in the air. "You can go now. But we'll be in touch."

Professor Perkins was about to protest this summary dismissal, but he thought better of it. And withdrew from the field.

George and Stanley

The FBI investigators were heading west on Route 160, barely ten miles from Durango. It being his turn to drive, George Whitmer was behind the wheel of the sleek Ford sedan. Not a word had been exchanged since they had left Alvah Yazzi's home. The driver glanced at the speedometer. Sixty-three miles per hour. Whitmer eased up on the pedal until it read an even sixty. "Stan?"

No answer.

He mimicked Perkins's haughty tone. "Excuse me, Your Honor."

"Hey—don't get started with me."

A grin creased Whitmer's cheerful face. "Just wanted to ask you something."

Newman was staring intensely at the rugged scenery, seeing neither lofty tree nor soaring mountain peak. "Ask away, partner."

"Whadda you think?"

The younger man grunted. "Same lowlife who murdered April Tavishuts also grabbed her stepfather. To throw the authorities off his trail, the perp lays out Mr. Yazzi's duds on the floor. Underwear is there. Socks in the boots. Even leaves the victim's wallet in the pocket, with credit cards, plenty of folding money—the works. Then he sprinkles some dust and crap around where Yazzi's body should be."

Whitmer, being somewhat of a stickler, thought motive an important consideration. "But, Stan—*why* did the perp do this?"

Newman shrugged under his immaculate gray jacket. "Beats hell outta me. But whoever did it—which suggests it's a local perp—planned on those superstitious Indian cops thinking Mr. Yazzi must've just went up in a puff of smoke." He snickered. "Which is pretty much what happened. That they fell for it, I mean."

George Whitmer was silent.

Newman did not like the ominous sound of this particular silence. "Go ahead. Say what you're thinking."

"I'm thinking we should keep an open mind."

Newman was feeling snappish, so he snapped: "Open mind about what?"

The older man swerved to miss a fat raccoon waddling across the highway. "Evidence."

"What evidence?"

"Yazzi's remains. The whole thing's sort of . . . mysterious."

"There's no big mystery. Somebody set it up."

"And you're sure that *somebody* is the perp who murdered Yazzi's stepdaughter."

"Who else?" But Newman was beginning to feel uneasy.

"Maybe that weird old Navajo man left some of his duds in the house and took a hike. It could be some kind of ritual thing." Whitmer shook his head. "I asked the forensics geek about that stuff that looks like ashes and bones and hair . . ."

Newman turned to stare at the driver. "And?"

"It's ashes and bones, partner. And hair."

The younger man set his jaw. "It'll turn out to be faked."

"Yazzi's false teeth were there in the ashes." Whitmer pushed his tongue against a loose set of dentures. "On occasion, a man may leave his wallet at home. Even his spectacles. But he don't go nowhere without his chompers."

Newman was willing to concede the point. "So maybe that old Indian guy was torched by somebody—just like his stepdaughter."

"Not exactly. The flames that burned the girl's corpse also burned the tent Charlie Moon set up. And a coupla piñon trees—which is what you expect from your normal, everyday fire. But whatever turned Yazzi's body to ashes didn't even scorch his clothes."

"So what's your explanation?"

Whitmer hesitated. "You ever hear of . . . SHC?"

"You know how I hate acronyms."

"Spontaneous human combustion."

Newman rolled his eyes. "Give me a break."

"There've been several cases over the years. Some of them well documented. Victim's body burned to a crisp, but there's very little or no fire damage to his or her immediate surroundings."

"But how can that happen?"

"There's never a totally satisfactory explanation," Whitmer said. "Some top-flight forensic scientists have been stymied."

"I don't want to hear this."

Whitmer muttered: "If what turned Yazzi to ashes wasn't a regular fire, maybe it was something else entirely."

"Like what?"

"I dunno. Some kind of corrosive chemical." Whitmer squinted through the windshield as if attempting to see something that was very, very far away. "An acid, maybe."

Newman felt his stomach churn.

"A real strong acid can burn human tissues to a cinder."

"George—please don't give me heartburn."

"And another thing."

"What?"

"Mark my words—ol' Charlie Moon knows a whole lot more'n he's saying."

"He knows diddledy-squat."

"Bet you ten bucks Moon'll be running his own investigation on the Tavishuts homicide."

Newman clutched his stomach. "He can't do that—this is a federal case."

"Charlie's a private cop now, Stan. And it's a free country."

"Just drive the damn car." He fumbled in his coat pocket for a package of Tums.

Durango, Colorado
The Gift

Charlie Moon had once believed he knew what was best for the aged woman. Aunt Daisy should be living in one of the comfortable tribal homes near Ignacio. But he had finally accepted the fact that he would never convince the stubborn old soul to leave her little trailer by the mouth of *Cañon del Espíritu*. Daisy had lived in the wilderness of this canyon country since her birth, never sleeping more than six miles from this spot. She would die here. That was the way it was. Perhaps even the way it should be.

After winding along the rutted surface of the lane for almost twenty minutes, his Ford pickup topped the summit of a low, rocky ridge. He braked to a stop and stared through the sand-blasted windshield. The Ute had seen this place a thousand times, but it was always new. Always alive. Like long brown fingers, four sandstone mesas reached forth to grasp the land beneath. Farthest to the south was Paiute Mesa. Then the largest and most prominent—Three Sisters. A trio of sandstone projections sat like weary old women on its summit. Lurid legends repeated around tribal campfires long ago held that these were ancient Anasazi sisters who had fled to the heights to escape raiding Apaches. *Cañon del Serpiente* wound sinuously between Paiute and Three Sisters Mesas. *Cañon del Espíritu* lay peacefully between Three Sisters and Dog Leg Mesas. Beyond the barren profile of Dog Leg and the wooded depths of Silver Dollar Canyon was Black Mule Mesa.

He let the image settle into his soul, where it could be properly contemplated. A traditional Ute could hardly find a better place to live. Or die. His mother's bones rested in a stone crypt far up the Canyon of the Spirits. That's probably where Daisy would want her body placed. Or maybe she would prefer the Indian cemetery near Ignacio, on the banks of the Piños. When the aged woman felt the time drawing very near, she would tell him.

Daisy's small house trailer was set on cinder blocks in an oval-shaped valley at the wide mouth of the Canyon of the Spirits. When Father Raes Delfino had first seen this place, the Catholic priest had immediately given it a name—The Hollow of God's Hand. And so it was. Around the Ute elder's home was a sparse gathering of piñon and juniper. Among the smaller trees was a knobby, leprous-looking ponderosa. It stood lofty and lonely—isolated from its kind. At the south side of the old woman's trailer was a small garden, watered primarily by water from her well, less from the infrequent rains. Daisy had electricity, but the telephone company was—quite understandably—

unwilling to string several miles of line to serve a single, impover-ished customer.

Moon shifted to low gear and eased the F150 down the slope. The already rough road went into the mouth of *Cañon del Espíritu* where it gradually became even more primitive, finally petering out into a deer path several miles into that deep separation between Three Sisters and Dog Leg Mesas. He made a right turn into the barely perceptible lane that ended in what passed for a front yard at Daisy's home.

The old woman, her nose pressed against an aluminum-framed window-pane, watched her nephew close the pickup door, then approach the rickety porch appended to her trailer. This was an interesting surprise. For one thing, Charlie Moon wasn't expected. For another, he had a par-cel under his arm. Wrapped in shiny blue paper. *Must be something for me.*

Charlie Moon sat at Daisy's kitchen table. She eyed the gaily-wrapped box. "What's that?"

"Your birthday present."

"That's not for six weeks."

"I could bring it back later."

She snatched the package off the table and began to pull at the blue paper.

Moon watched her, wondering what she had been like as a child . . . a little girl at Christmastime, surrounded by family. There was no rea-son she should be so completely isolated from the rest of humanity. Or from help in an emergency. This is why he had made the purchase in Durango.

She pulled a squarish-looking black canvas bag from the cardboard box. Frowned at it. *What's wrong with him. I don't need no ugly purse.*

He smiled. "Open it up."

She did. And also frowned at the contents. "What's this?"

"A cellular telephone."

Her eyes widened. "Why's it so big?"

"The little ones don't work so well out here. This is a three-watt job." He showed her the foot-long external battery and explained how to charge it off the house current. "I've paid for the standard service for the next twelve months. Long-distance calls aren't covered," he added. "You call somebody in China, you'll get a whopping bill."

"I don't know nobody in China."

He grunted. *Like that'd stop you.*

Daisy Perika studied the marvelous contraption in rapt silence. Now she would never be all alone again. *I can call Louise-Marie LaForte. Or Father Raes. Or Charlie Moon.* The Ute elder brushed away a tear and looked up at her nephew. "Thank you."

Moon searched his memory. But he couldn't recall hearing the grumpy old woman use this phrase. "You're welcome."

"All by myself and with no way to call for help—I could've died out here a hundred times. Could've been a heart attack. Double pneumonia. Rattlesnake bite. A criminal with a butcher knife, sneaking into my bedroom some dark night."

Moon took a deep breath, preparing himself for a useless confrontation. "You might want to think about spending some time up at the Columbine."

"Hah," she snorted. "I know what you think. 'Get her on the ranch for a visit, and she'll stay.'" The Ute elder shook her head like an old warhorse. "I don't care to live where summer's a good ten days long—"

"That's a bit of an exaggeration," he muttered. *But not by much.*

"—and where it snows two or three feet at a time." The very thought made her shiver.

"I just thought you might want to come stay for a week or two," Moon said. And added: "I've fixed up a nice place for you."

"I don't need a room in your big house. I got a home of my own."

"Wasn't thinking of putting you up in the ranch headquarters," he said. *Or putting up with you.* "I fixed up the guest cabin."

Guest cabin? She gave him a sideways look. "What's that—some little hut way up on the mountainside?"

Moon grinned. "It's on flat land across the lake from the ranch headquarters. Three rooms and a root cellar." He looked around the tiny trailer home. "Lots more space than you've got here. And it's got a well. LP gas for cooking and the furnace. Hot and cold running water. And," he added with a glance toward her tiny bathroom, "a good-sized old-fashioned bathtub."

The aged woman considered this significant benefit. *Every night, right before bedtime—soak my old bones in a great big tub, filled with hot water.* What a sweet blessing that would be.

"But I don't suppose you'd like the guest cabin," he said cagily. "It's way on the other side of the lake. Nobody ever goes over there. You'd probably get lonesome."

She sighed. This sounded pretty good. Privacy. And help always near at hand. A big bathtub. But she wouldn't agree to visit her nephew right away. It would make Charlie Moon think he was oh-so-smart. Daisy gave the amiable young man an accusing look. "So why didn't you buy me one of these fancy phones years ago?"

"Couldn't afford it." Even now, it was a stretch on his budget. Moon was looking over her gray head, focusing his vision on a deerskin drum. It hung by a rawhide thong from a coat hook. That had belonged to one of Daisy's three husbands. The second one, he thought.

There was a long pause as they listened to the croaking call of a raven.

She wondered what was going on in the outside world. "Any news from Ignacio?" Her interests generally stopped at the reservation boundary.

He didn't particularly want to discuss what had happened to April Tavishuts. But Daisy would find out soon enough. And she'd be furious if her nephew—the tribal investigator—hadn't told her before all the other old ladies on the reservation got the gruesome news. "There's something I need to tell you."

"About what?"

He avoided her searching look. "April Tavishuts."

Daisy closed her eyes. "She's dead."

How did you know? But from his long experience with the old shaman, he did not ask. *She'd just tell me some ghost story.* "Afraid so."

For some time, her lips moved in silent prayer for the spirit of the young woman who had departed from Middle World. Then she spoke aloud. "How did it happen?"

Moon took a deep breath. "Don't know for sure." The details were police business. *And I'm a tribal lawman again. More or less.*

The old woman pressed her lips together, then muttered darkly: "I knew it." She shot her nephew a beady-eyed look. "It's got something to do with Chimney Rock and those old ruins—don't it?"

He kept his gaze focused on the drum. "That's where her body was found."

"When?"

"Day before yesterday."

"April's stepfather—how'd he take the news?"

Moon shrugged.

"What does that mean?"

"If Alvah had anything to say, I didn't hear it."

Daisy Perika was annoyed by this evasive response. But when her nephew was determined not to talk about something, you couldn't pry a word out of him with a crowbar. Not that the shaman was greatly discouraged. There were other, more reliable ways to find out what was going on. *Now that I got me a telephone.*

CHAPTER 8

The first weapon is called *hat tslin it lish ka'*, the lightning that strikes crooked. The second weapon is *hat tsol ilthe ka'*, the lightning that flashes straight.

—Sandoval, Hastin Tlo'tsi hee

The Visitation

It was a few minutes past midnight. A silvery moon hung high in a cloudless sky. Strewn across the cosmic fabric, a spray of distant suns sparkled with inner fire. On a low, rocky ridge overlooking Daisy Perika's trailer home, a pygmy owl hunched ogrelike on the pale arm of a lightning-charred juniper skeleton. The predator blinked enormous yellow eyes at the Ute elder's domicile—but did not hoot her nightly call. Something was not right in this lonely place. The prudent fowl departed with a slow *whuff-whuff* of wings.

Daisy's dreams were infested by the skittering vermin of netherworlds. Frightening apparitions flitted about the dark landscape of her unconscious. Shadowy forms they were, sharp-toothed things with a lust for the blood in her veins. One hideous phantom pleaded mockingly for the shaman's help. *Cure me, old woman—make me a potion. I suffer so from itching, burning boils.* Others—even more malignant spirits— called hauntingly to her: *Come and be one with us . . . we are a great legion.*

The troubled sleeper groaned, and turned heavily from her right side to her left. Now there was a hollow, thumping sound. And she heard someone calling her by name. Summoning her away from this world of troubled dreams.

The shaman, instantly awake, sat up in bed. Holding the quilt to her chest, Daisy Perika listened intently. Straining to hear the slightest sound, she was relieved to hear nothing. *It wasn't real. Just a nightmare trying to come to life.* She fell back against a sweat-soaked pillow and sighed. Then heard it again.

Thump.

Her feet were on the floor in a moment. She looked out windows on both sides of her bedroom. The moonlight was bright enough to cast dark shadows under the piñons. But no one was there. No one who could be seen. Her mind searched for an explanation. Maybe an owl had flown into the aluminum trailer wall.

But again—*Thump. Thump.* As if some giant hand slapped the face of her home.

She burrowed around urgently in the closet where the twelve-gauge shotgun was kept.

Again the hand slapped. *Thump. Thump. Thump.*

She broke the double-barreled instrument to make sure it was loaded. It was.

Thump. Thump.

The Ute elder cocked both hammers. *Click-clack. Click-clack.*

Thump. Thump. Thump. Now the rhythm was faster. As if the unseen presence was losing patience.

Her old hands trembled. But Daisy Perika was always game for a fight. "Who's there?"

She thought she heard a voice. *It must be the little man.* He preferred to go abroad only when the sky was dark—this one was not a creature of the Light. This is why Father Raes Delfino had warned her against communion with the dwarf. But old habits, especially bad ones, are hard to break. And so—when the need arose—the shaman trudged into the Canyon of the Spirits to visit the reclusive creature. She would take a gift of food or tobacco, perhaps a trinket of some sort. And in return, the dwarf would share his secret knowledge with the Ute elder. Only rarely did he venture far from his badger hole in *Cañon del Espíritu*. But his recent visit to St. Ignatius Catholic Church in Ignacio in Sabbath daylight had proved that the little man was unpredictable. Daisy was at that age where surprises—especially in the middle of the night—are highly unwelcome.

"*Pitukupf*," she muttered, "is that you?"

There were windows open on opposite sides of her bedroom. The spoken reply came through both of them.

Her voice crackled with fear. "Why're you here—what do you want?"

The disembodied Voice told her.

Breakfast Lost

Charlie Moon dismounted the rusty Ford pickup with a cardboard box tucked under his arm. He had no shortage of work to do at the Columbine, and Aunt Daisy's place was a long way off the beaten track. But she was getting old and feeble. So whenever he was in the neighborhood, the rancher-lawman felt an obligation to check on his elderly relative. This was especially so since the brutal murder of April Tavishuts near Chimney Rock, which was not far from Daisy's home. It was just possible that some lunatic was running loose in the canyon country.

Whether or not this was so, the lonely old soul was always so glad to see him. Even if she hated to admit it. Daisy's face appeared at the window, but jerked away at his glance.

Every year she gets a little more peculiar. Moon took long strides toward the rickety pine porch attached to his aunt's trailer home. The unpainted steps creaked under his weight. He waited. *She knows I'm out here—why hasn't she opened the door?* Moon rapped his knuckles against the aluminum frame.

No response.

This was getting tiresome. "Aunt Daisy—I know you're in there. Open up!"

The knob turned, the door opened barely enough to let some of the cool darkness slip out. One eye peeked through the crack. Blinking as if sleepy. "What are *you* doing here?" It had the tone of an accusation.

"Picked you up some stuff at the market." He held the box so she could see the contents. Dozen extra-large eggs. Gallon of milk. Loaf of rye bread. Can of coffee. Slab of bacon. Two pounds of pork sausage.

She uttered a piggish grunt. "Leave it on the porch."

The harried man forced a hopeful smile. "Thought maybe you'd offer me a cup of coffee."

"Don't have none made," she snapped.

Moon fixed her visible eye with a look that would have ruffled an ordinary woman. It was wasted on Daisy Perika.

"I'm not dressed," she said. "Just got out of bed." She punctuated this pair of brazen lies with a forced yawn.

Something odd is going on here. "I'll wait," he said.

"I'm going back to bed," she said pitifully. "My head aches and I need some sleep." With this, she closed the door. As he attempted to look through the small kitchen window, she pulled the curtains.

Her nephew stared at the door for a long moment. Wondering what to do. Having few options, he placed the box on the porch. And left.

Daisy Perika held her ear close to the open window until the rumbles and rattles of her nephew's pickup had faded into the distance. Then— being a prudent woman—she waited awhile longer. Eventually satisfied that he was far away, she pulled on a light coat and stepped onto the porch to fetch the box of groceries. The late-morning air was crisp and sweet. "Nice day for a walk," she said as she carried the groceries into her kitchen. "Just a walk, that's all. Good for my old legs." As if saying this out loud would make the deception all the more effective.

But there were important things to do before she could take her stroll. Daisy unpacked the groceries. And fired up the propane stove.

Charlie Moon had returned on foot. His tall frame was hidden by a bushy juniper; he watched from a long ridge called Cougar's Tail. He peered through the fragrant branches, watching the old woman retrieve the box of groceries. A smile creased his face. *Looks like you took a short nap.*

While he waited, a raven came to sit on the blackened crown of a ponderosa corpse slain by fire from heaven. The black bird ruffled her feathers, cocked her head suspiciously at the hidden man.

Moon watched the trailer. *So what're you up to?*

The smell of frying pork issued forth from her kitchen window. This aroma was not alone. It was accompanied by the happy scent of freshly brewed coffee. Together, these drifted upward along the ridge called Cougar's Tail.

Charlie Moon sniffed. *She's making breakfast. But not for me.*

The minutes passed like a parade of snails. Moreover, Moon's imaginary gastropods were weakened by malnutrition.

The Ute elder prepared the meal with care. But she did not eat a bite.

Moon watched his aunt leave her trailer home. Daisy had a denim pouch looped over her shoulder, the sturdy oak walking stick in her hand. It looked as though she would head into *Cañon del Espíritu.* "Going to see the *pitukupf,* are you?"

The dwarf—according to the elderly shaman—lived far up the canyon in an abandoned badger hole. And despite the impassioned protests of Father Raes Delfino about such un-Christian activities, Daisy had a habit of ignoring the Catholic priest. Moon suspected that his aunt still made regular pilgrimages to consult with the mythical creature. From what he'd heard, she left gifts at the mouth of the badger hole. In return for such favors, the "little man" told her things. Useful things. Anyhow, that was the way it was supposed to work.

But Daisy Perika did not head west into Spirit Canyon. Instead, she turned her face to the south. And began to trudge up a rocky path toward the summit of Cougar's Tail Ridge.

Moon's mouth went dry. Had the old woman seen him return from his parked pickup? Was she coming all the way up here just to raise hell with him for violating her sacred privacy—and then send him packing like the skulking varmint he was? Unable to think of anything better to do, he remained perfectly still behind the juniper.

Not ten yards away—and breathing hard from the steep ascent—the old woman paused to lean on her walking stick. She looked up toward Three Sisters Mesa, that towering wedge of sandstone between Snake and Spirit Canyons. Then she turned, putting the mesa at her back. To stare, it seemed, directly at the bushy tree that shielded her spying nephew. Moon—already a slender man—willed himself skinny as a snake. To further enhance the hoped-for invisibility, he closed his eyes. And felt safer in the dark.

The Ute elder did not see him. And she could not possibly have seen Moon's truck, which was concealed a quarter mile away in a grassy arroyo. Satisfied that there was no one around to spy on her, the old woman headed back down the side of Cougar's Tail Ridge.

Immensely relieved, Moon watched her slow descent. She turned to the west. The old shaman was heading into the gaping mouth of *Cañon del Espíritu*. He whispered: "So—you *are* going to see the dwarf." His first thought was that he should grant this queer old woman her privacy. Aunt Daisy's business with the little man was her own. And it wasn't as if the *pitukupf* was anything more than a two-foot-tall figment of tribal imagination, destined to die with the dozen or so traditional Utes who still believed in such curious things. It was not as if there might be something to see in the Canyon of the Spirits. But Curiosity crooked her finger at the tribal investigator. He accepted the invitation.

Charlie Moon kept a good sixty paces behind his aunt, and was ready to move behind a bush or boulder whenever she paused to look over her shoulder. As she often did. But the old woman's bones were brittle, her joints stiff. These impairments caused her to turn slowly, giving him ample time to slip from her view. And so he proceeded up the steep-walled Canyon of the Spirits, following the elderly pilgrim. Even at midday, the deep crevasse was filled with bone-chilling shadows. There were long stretches on the south side of the canyon that had never felt the pleasant warmth of direct sunlight.

Daisy Perika plodded stolidly along the deer trail. The grade, though gradual, was uphill. Every two dozen paces, she would pause to lean on the walking stick. And wait for her lagging breath to catch up with her. As she rested, the shaman looked and listened with the steely-eyed intensity of a hawk. She sensed a solemn oppressiveness in the stillness. Today the air was heavy with a sour, almost fetid odor. As if it was not meant to be breathed by God's creatures. Moreover, she had the distinct sense that someone was watching. Maybe even following her. But whenever she turned, the canyon behind her was empty except for clumps of stunted piñon and a scattering of massive boulders that had tumbled off the talus slopes centuries earlier. Far above, on the facing edges of the mesas called Dog Leg and Three Sisters, the emptiness was stark against a pale blue sky. This place was unnaturally still. Haunted by free-roaming shadows, scissored loose from any solid object. She was tempted to turn back. But Daisy Perika had a mission at an appointed place. And so she pressed on. Into darkness deeper still.

His aunt was within fifty yards of the badger hole when she slowed. Charlie Moon took up a position in a shaded cleft on the south wall, seating himself on a mossy sandstone outcropping. He was certain of two things. First, Aunt Daisy had some business with the dwarf. Second, there'd be serious hell to pay if she spotted him. From what he'd picked up from her mutterings about these strange encounters, Moon thought he knew what to expect. As was the shaman's common practice, she'd sit herself down under a tree. And fall into a trance. Which meant having a nap. Her "visits" with the dwarf were the stuff of dreams. This could take hours. *Which is more time than I've got to waste.*

These were his thoughts. But he had not long to wait.

After taking a long, suspicious look at the shadowy places below, and upward at the sharp outline of a mesa rim cutting into the belly of a turquoise sky, the shaman stuffed the denim pouch into the crotch of a stunted juniper. This done, Daisy immediately headed toward the mouth of *Cañon del Espíritu*, her walking stick clomping rhythmically at her side. As she retraced her steps, her exit was quite different from her weary climb into the silent canyon. Now she hurried, as if ten invisible demons trotted along behind, plucking at her skirts. Not once did the Ute elder pause. Or look back.

Charlie Moon had long since ceased to be surprised by his eccentric relative's behavior. Having evaded discovery thus far, he thought it best to give her a long head start.

The sun was well past its zenith, a curtain of shadows pulled across the crook of the canyon. Moon wondered why he was waiting. To see the dwarf come out of the badger hole to get whatever the old woman had left for him? Of course not. *I'm waiting because . . . because I feel like waiting. A man doesn't need a reason for everything he does.*

Time passed. The dwarf did not show his face.

The shadows were growing long and diffuse. A chilly breeze whipped down the deep crevasse—an obvious hint that human visitors should depart from *Cañon del Espíritu* before nightfall.

Enough is enough.

Moon made his way across the sandy floor of the canyon. And stood before the tree where Daisy had left the denim pouch. He reached out, hesitated. It didn't feel right. *But I am a tribal investigator. And this is tribal land. It's not like I'm going to take what's in the bag. I just need to know what's in there.*

Inside the pouch he found a grease-spotted brown paper bag. Moon had a look inside. And an appreciative sniff. *Well.* A pint-sized thermos. A massive sandwich wrapped in aluminum foil. And still warm to the touch. He peeled back the foil. Wedged between the thick slices of rye bread were two fried eggs and a huge sausage pattie. *That dwarf eats better than I do. A wonder he ain't got too fat to squeeze into that badger hole.* Moon's mouth watered. *I'd sure like to finish this off.* But he knew it would be the wrong thing to do. In the Biblical sense, it was like a Christian eating food offered to idols. His stomach, which knew no such dogma, cried out pitifully for sustenance.

Which led him to examine his theology.

If Aunt Daisy comes back and the food is still in the bag, the poor old woman will think the dwarf don't like her cooking. So I'd be doing her a favor. The hungry man's conscience rebelled against this brazen rationalization. *No. I can't do it. No matter how you look at it, this isn't my food. It'd be like stealing.*

But the truth smacked him between the eyes like a brick.

This IS my food. These are the same groceries I brought her this morning.

And that ungrateful old woman who wouldn't even make me a bite of hot breakfast is giving my grub away to a figment of her imagination.

This was the gravest sort of inequity. The sort of wrong that must be made right.

In the interest of justice, Charlie Moon took a man-sized bite from the sandwich. *Delicious.* He unscrewed the cap from the thermos. The brew was steaming hot, black as tar, and heavily sugared. *So me and the little man like our coffee the same way.* He took another long drink. *Some home fries would go good with this.* But a man must be satisfied with such blessings as he has.

Moon's chief blessing at this time was that he was not being seriously molested. By the owner of a pair of dark, hungry eyes that stared viciously at him from amidst the cold shadows.

Unaware of his good fortune, the Ute finished off the sandwich. He folded the aluminum foil, capped the vacuum bottle, placed these items in the denim bag—which he pressed carefully back into the crotch of the juniper.

Thus filled with a quite satisfactory breakfast, he sighed.

The winds sighed with him.

Then suddenly grew in strength.

A roaring gust funneled furiously down the canyon. Moon grabbed at his black Stetson, closed his eyes against the sting of windblown sands. After a brief but violent thrashing, all was deathly silent again. The Ute seated his hat, wiped at his eyes.

And left the way he had come, without a worry.

Charlie Moon was now satisfied that his aged aunt was merely behaving in her normal fashion. Not up to any serious mischief.

The Call

Daisy Perika squinted through her reading spectacles at the tiny print in the instruction manual. As she read, she followed the directions faithfully. The Ute elder opened the black canvas case, made certain the telephone power cable was plugged into the battery connector. She rotated the antenna up to a vertical position. Finally, she reached forward with one fingertip hovering hesitantly over the infernal instrument. Cringing with apprehension, the Ute elder pushed the "PWR" button. She jumped when the thing beeped rudely, then leaned forward to eye the small panel glowing with hellish blue-green light. A jiggling bar graph indicated signal strength. The gadget seemed happy enough. Ready to get up and go to town.

Well. That wasn't so hard.

Proud of her triumph over modern technology, Daisy pressed a series of numbers, watching them line up like little black soldiers along the liquid-crystal display. *It's just like a regular telephone.* She pressed the receiver onto her ear. Waited. Nothing happened.

"Damned piece of junk," she muttered. The machine did not respond to this insult. And so she sat and glared at the offending device. As if by doing so she might intimidate it into doing its rightful duty.

It was resistant to all her powers.

Her stomach was beginning to flutter. *Might as well try to use a brick to call someone.* Sadly, she returned to the manual. *Oh.*

Daisy Perika pressed the Send button. She heard the familiar dial tone, the sonnet of musical beeps as the Ignacio number was dialed. *Thank God.*

"Hello?" The voice was a familiar one.

Daisy grinned wickedly, displaying most of her remaining teeth. "Louise-Marie?"

"Yes."

The Ute woman took a deep breath. *I've got you on the phone. Now if I can just get you to do it.* She hoped that some opportunity would present itself.

The French-Canadian woman was unnerved by the silence on the line. "Who's this?"

"Me."

"Daisy?"

"Sure."

"Where are you calling from?"

"My home."

The *matukach* woman's voice betrayed her surprise at this good news. "You finally got a telephone out there?"

"Don't have no phone," the shaman said slyly. "It's all done"—she paused dramatically, lowering her voice to a secretive whisper—"by calling on the hidden powers that make thunder and lightning."

Louise-Marie LaForte, who had great respect for the Ute elder's conjuring powers, could think of no response. And so she said nothing.

"Of course I got a phone," the shaman snapped.

Her friend was both relieved and disappointed to hear this news. "It must've cost a small fortune to have 'em string the line way out there."

"This phone's the kind where you don't need no wires connected to your house. Charlie Moon bought it for me."

"Your nephew is such a nice boy. I hear he owns a big ranch now."

"The biggest and best in the state," Daisy said. "And he's always badgering me to come and live with him. I think he's lonesome up there. All by himself except for them dumb cowboys."

The French-Canadian woman sighed. "I wish I had a nephew like Charlie."

"How are you getting along?"

"Well, I'm miserable."

"I'm sorry." *Sorry I asked.*

"I got this terrible, throbbing headache. And my feet are all swole up."

"Seems like you got troubles at both ends." Daisy cackled with rude laughter.

"And in the middle too," Louise-Marie whined.

"Don't tell me."

But she did. "I got the bleeding hemorrhoids."

Daisy recognized the opportunity, and immediately seized it by the neck. "Sounds like you need some medical attention."

"Doctors cost big money." A thoughtful pause. "You got any homemade medicines that'd help me?"

Artfully, the shaman hesitated. "Maybe."

"I'm suffering something awful."

"I could brew you some tea for the headache. And your swollen feet."

There was a hint of anxiety in Louise-Marie's tone. "What would you put in it?"

"Oh, a strip of birch bark. And just a tiny tad of clematis leaf." *With some aspirin.*

The sick woman brightened. "Could you do something about my hemorrhoids?"

"I could make you something special."

The patient seemed doubtful. "Special how?"

The Ute elder glanced at a row of jars and tins on a pine shelf over her kitchen table. "I could roll up some dried *yerba de la negrita* leaves with a little bit of tobacco. I generally paste it together with cow spit. When I can find a cow."

"Ugh—I don't think I could get something that awful past my lips."

"You can put it in your mouth if you want to." Daisy chuckled. "But you ought to do that *first*."

"First before what?"

This was too easy. "It's a suppository. So if you're determined to taste it, you should do that *before* you—"

"*Please* don't be so graphic," the patient said to her physician, "you're making me ill."

It was always fun talking to Louise-Marie. "I could cure you in no time at all." *Now for the good part.* "Of course I generally get paid for my services."

Louise-Marie's voice took on a pitiful tone. "You know I'm a poor old widda-woman, Daisy. I don't have much left from my Social Security after I pay the rent. And buy me a few things to eat."

"Don't worry about money. We'll barter. I fix you up some medicines, you do a little favor for me."

"Well, I don't know. Last time I let you talk me into helping you I almost got arrested."

"This won't be nothing like that," Daisy snapped at the ingrate.

"What would I have to do?"

"Just bring that old car of yours out here and I'll explain it."

Louise-Marie smiled into the telephone. "I'd rather you told me now."

"It's nothing much—I need you to drive me somewhere."

"You'll pay for the gas?"

"Sure. You come out to my place early tomorrow morning. First, we'll go to your place. I'll doctor you up real good, then I'll tell you where we're going. We'll have a real good time."

Louise-Marie's hands began to tremble. *Every time I let this old Indian woman talk me into doing something, I get into trouble.*

Daisy had set the hook. Now to reel in her catch. She took a deep breath. "So. Can I count on you?"

The French-Canadian woman's head ached. Her swollen feet hurt. Worst of all, it was painful to sit, even on a feather pillow. She desperately needed the shaman's medications.

Daisy shouted into the telephone. "Louise-Marie—are you coming out here or not?"

She hesitated. It was a full half second before her brain turned to jelly and her mouth took charge. "I'll be there."

CHAPTER 9

The Sun explained to the Twins that it was not safe for the people on the earth to possess this weapon they asked for. He said that the boys could use the weapon for a little while, but that he would have to reclaim it. . . .
—Sandoval, Hastin Tlo'tsi hee

Stood Up

It was to be a glorious day. The dawning sun paused to kiss the mountains; the bald peaks blushed crimson.

Though Charlie Moon had missed breakfast, he had stopped for coffee in Bayfield. The tribal investigator was feeling good about this Sunday morning's business. He was driving the freshly washed Expedition with "Columbine Ranch" emblazoned on the driver's door. The Ute was also freshly washed. And outfitted in his gray suit. With a new dove-gray Stetson to match. He pulled to a stop in front of Daisy's trailer, mounted the unpainted pine porch, rapped his knuckles on the door.

On a nearby ponderosa snag, a scruffy-looking raven ruffled her feathers and squawked an invective at the noisy intruder.

But there was no response from inside Daisy Perika's trailer home.

He knocked again. Harder this time. "I'm here to take you to church. Let's shake a leg."

The annoyed raven departed in a huff for the peaceful solitude of Cañon del Espíritu.

All was quiet inside Daisy's home. But it wasn't a tense silence, like she was hiding inside. It was a hollow, empty quiet. He tried the door handle. Locked. Moon stepped off the porch. For a long moment, he stood among the thirsty junipers and stared at the trailer. All the shades were drawn. *She isn't here.* He examined the ground and found her footprints. *Maybe a couple of hours old.* There were also fresh tire tracks, three of them with little tread left. And all four with different tread designs. Who would be driving a jalopy with an assortment of worn-out tires? Daisy's cousin Gorman Sweetwater might have come to get the old woman in his Dodge pickup. But these tire marks looked a bit narrow for a full-sized pickup. And Gorman had heavy mud tires on the rear. *Why do I care who it was?* Any way you sliced it, Daisy had left with someone early this Sunday morning. *Has she forgotten I was driving all the way down here to take her to church?* This duty had gotten him up very early on this fine morning. *And I missed my breakfast.*

But maybe Aunt Daisy had gotten sick, and used her new cell phone to summon a kindly neighbor to haul her to the clinic in Ignacio. Staring at the assorted tire tracks didn't make things any clearer. Moon cranked up the Expedition and departed. *After church, I'll stop in Granite Creek. Have some breakfast with Scott Parris.* April Tavishuts had been a student at the university there. Maybe the chief of police would know something about the murdered Ute woman. And about her university friends. Scott might even know something about someone who wasn't April's friend.

Driving Miss Daisy

The black Oldsmobile was much like its occupants. It had seen far better days. And it had a hard time getting started on cold mornings. As the vehicle moved along a narrow ribbon of Colorado blacktop, the tailpipe spewed a trail of noxious blue fumes in its wake.

Daisy Perika—who had never learned to drive an automobile—was hunched forward nervously in the passenger seat. Louise-Marie, whose skills as an operator of lethal machinery were just sufficient to make her dangerous, sat placidly behind the steering wheel. And because she was the very opposite of a tall person, also somewhat under it. Her view of the road was a narrow arch between the rusting hood and the black plastic circle she gripped with frail, liver-spotted hands. Her brow was knitted into a worried frown. "What if Charlie Moon is there?"

Daisy smiled. "He won't be."

"How can you be so sure?"

"Trust me."

Louise-Marie rolled her eyes.

The Ute woman cast a wary glance at her dwarfish chauffeur. "I don't know how you ever got a driver's license."

The French-Canadian woman turned up her nose. "I never asked for one."

"Thanks for telling me that. Now I feel better."

The driver squinted. "What's that up there by the road—a horse?"

"It's a sign."

"What's it say?"

Daisy squinted. " 'Speed Limit—Sixty.' "

"Sixty?" Louise-Marie frowned at her speedometer needle, which had been stuck at a point slightly below fifteen miles per hour since Mr. Nixon had occupied the Oval Office. "We're all right then." She looked merrily at Daisy and attempted a joke. "Wouldn't want to break the law, would we? Ha-ha." The old automobile veered well across the center line.

"Watch where you're going," the Ute woman yelled.

Louise-Marie overcorrected, bringing the right wheels onto the shoulder to scatter a small colony of terrified prairie dogs. "This is a terrible rough road. They ought to fix it."

"You're driving on the dirt!" *Silly old fool.*

"You know," the elderly driver said, "when you asked me to help you with this business, I almost said no."

"You can still back out," the Ute woman muttered.

The driver sighed. "You're always getting me into some kinda trouble. Like that time when we almost got put in jail. But then I said to myself: 'Louise-Marie—what are you so worried about? You're almost ninety, so you're not going to live much longer anyway.' " She chuckled. "So I said: 'Don't always be thinking of playing it safe. Take a chance. Help your friend Daisy and have some fun at the same time.' "

"Next time," Daisy grumbled, "play it safe."

As they headed up a long grade, the aged auto gasped. Coughed. Strangled. In a fruitless effort to get more gas to the engine, the driver pumped up and down on the accelerator pedal. The resultant lurching made the Ute elder nauseous.

Again, the Olds gradually drifted over the yellow stripe.

Daisy gave up worrying. *If I die, I die. Better than ten years in a nursing home.*

They topped the ridge, straddling the center line. And encountered a massive Shamrock gas tanker. The chrome-plated behemoth swerved with a sickening screech of tires, missing the Oldsmobile by a mere hand's breadth. There was an angry blatt from the diesel.

In response, Louise-Marie jammed the heel of her palm onto the Oldsmobile's horn button. "Road hog," she muttered in righteous indignation. "They shouldn't let people like that out on the road." She looked anxiously to her passenger, who had accepted this latest encounter with Death as a just reward for trusting her life to a madwoman. "We could've been killed!" Louise-Marie wailed.

Daisy clenched her jaw. *Yes. But at least it would've been over.*

The Foreman's Wife

The hairy-faced straw boss of the Columbine Ranch was off somewhere attending to his employer's business. Which is to say that Pete Bushman was replacing the alternator on a John Deere tractor. In Pete's absence, it was up to his good wife, Dolly, to look after business at home.

Having lived on the Columbine spread for much of her life, Mrs. Bushman was accustomed to the quiet of this vast space between the towering ranges of granite mountains. It was therefore not surprising that she heard the vehicle coming long before it was near the foreman's house, which served as a checkpoint for those who claimed to have business at the ranch headquarters farther down the graveled road. When the aged black Oldsmobile approached, Dolly was already stepping off the front porch. She waited under the gaunt limbs of a century-old cottonwood. The ranch foreman's wife could see only one person in this dilapidated Detroit rattler. And the woman she saw in the Oldsmobile was in the passenger seat. Who was driving this black bucket of bolts—was it guided by some sort of perverse witchcraft? Dolly stood as one quick-frozen by the icy touch of a witch's finger. As she backed away two steps, the seemingly pilotless vehicle eased to a wheezing halt under the cottonwood. Dark fumes stuttered from the puckered mouth of a dangling exhaust pipe. When the aged woman rolled down the passenger-side window, Dolly was relieved to spot the still smaller woman, her gray head barely high enough to see above the rim of the steering wheel.

The ranch woman moved cautiously forward. "Can I help you?"

The dark woman in the passenger seat responded. "I'm Daisy Perika." This was offered as if it were sufficient explanation.

Dolly leaned over to take a hard look at this odd pair of tourists, who had presumably taken a wrong turn. "Do you have business at the Columbine?"

The passenger nodded. "Sure. I'm Charlie Moon's aunt."

Dolly smiled. "Oh. Of course—you're his aunt Daisy."

This white woman is a little slow on the pickup. "We've come to see Charlie."

Louise-Marie LaForte blushed at her companion's blatant lie.

The ranch woman was warily apologetic. "Mr. Moon isn't here just now. He left before daylight. I think he's gone to Ignacio." She hesitated. "In fact, I believe he was headed down there to take you to church."

Daisy Perika waved this off. "That's what he said, did he?"

"Why yes, he—"

"These young men," Daisy said with a knowing smirk. "Always claiming they're going to do some favor for a poor old relative. But I bet you can imagine what he's up to."

Dolly could not imagine. "You're welcome to wait, of course. I'll put on a pot of fresh coffee and—"

Daisy shook her head. "Don't bother yourself. We'll go up to Charlie's house and wait there till he gets back."

The ranch foreman's wife looked uncertainly up the road. "Well, I suppose that'll be all right—seeing as how you're his aunt and everything. The place isn't locked." *Maybe it should be.*

"Charlie's been trying to get me to move up here and live with him," the Ute elder said. "He's fixed up a little shack for me—across the lake from the big house."

Dolly backed a step away from the Oldsmobile. "Mr. Moon prepared the guest cabin for you. It's really very nice—I cleaned it up myself." She pointed up the road. "Once you're at the ranch headquarters, you could drive around the lake and have a look—"

Daisy snorted. "Not me. I don't intend to live in no cowboy's shack. Prob'ly full of ticks and lice and bedbugs." She turned to her driver. "Let's go, Frenchy."

And off they went.

Dolly stood under the cottonwood, staring at the trail of yellow dust kicked up by the Oldsmobile's worn tires. "Poor Charlie Moon," she whispered.

Pete Bushman was seated at the kitchen table, nursing a cup of coffee. He listened to his wife's account without interrupting. When she had run out of breath, he shook his head.

"You don't think I did wrong, do you?"

Still he said nothing. Knowing this would unsettle the missus.

Dolly's hands twisted her apron into a rope. "I mean, she *is* his aunt. It's not like I let some strange woman go up to the ranch headquarters."

"Charlie don't say a lot about his aunt." He grinned through the grizzled beard. "But from what little he does say, she *is* kind of a strange woman. Always gettin' herself into scrapes." Pete looked up at his wife. "And you say there was two of 'em?"

Dolly nodded. "The other one was driving that old car. She never said a word."

"Welllll," he drawled, "I wouldn't worry."

Mrs. Bushman was immensely relieved. "You wouldn't?"

"Nope. Wasn't *me* who let them two old biddies go up to the ranch headquarters."

She slapped at him with a dish towel.

Pete was on a roll. "Maybe this one who says she's his kin ain't his

aunt atall. Maybe the pair of 'em went up there to steal the boss blind."
He leaned back and closed his eyes. "But me, I ain't worried. It'll be up
to you to do the explainin' to Charlie Moon."

"Oh hush, Peter. You're such an awful tease." But Dolly had a hard
time keeping the wan smile from slipping off her face.

Bad News

Charlie Moon—having attended mass at St. Ignatius—was at the
Sugar Bowl Cafe in Granite Creek. Despite the wasted trip to his aunt's
home, this Sabbath day was turning out well enough. The Ute
rancher-policeman was enjoying a late breakfast with his best friend.

"I'm glad you called," the chief of police said.

"I'm surprised you were able to get away from your fiancée."

A small shadow passed over Scott Parris's face. "Anne's off to British
Columbia. Chasing some kind of story about lumber and tariffs."

"These journalists lead complicated lives."

"I hear your life is getting complicated."

Moon thought this remark was about the love of his life. Meaning
Camilla Willow. "Meaning what?"

"Word's out you're doing investigative work for the tribe. And after
all that talk about being done with police work for good."

"It's not regular police work," Moon said.

"How so?"

"For one thing, I won't be hauling in drunks or breaking up bar
fights. Or pulling broken bodies out of car wrecks."

"That's three things. What will you be doing?"

Moon shrugged. "Not sure. I'm reporting to the tribal chairman.
When Oscar Sweetwater wants something looked into, I'll look into it."

"Sounds like regular police work to me," Parris smirked. "You got a
boss and everything. Next thing I hear, you'll be punching a time
clock."

Moon was reminded that he was required to list his hours on an official time sheet. But, as Oscar Sweetwater had said, this was just for the
auditors. "I've got some choice in the work I do."

"Is that a fact."

"Sure. If I'm too busy with ranch work, I can turn down an assign-ment. But if I'm interested in something that involves the tribe, I can spend some time working on it. Without asking Oscar's permission."

"So what are you interested in right now?" *As if I didn't know.*

"A killing." *As if you didn't know.*

"Any particular killing?"

"April Tavishuts."

Parris spread low-fat margarine on a slab of whole-wheat toast. "The young Ute woman they found down at Chimney Rock?"

Moon nodded.

"I know about her."

"Then you know she was a student here at Rocky Mountain Poly-technic."

"Of course."

"What else do you know?"

Parris frowned sourly at his toast. Murder and breakfast didn't go well together. "Miss Tavishuts had an off-campus apartment."

Moon looked up from his plate. "I suppose the FBI's been all over it."

"Bureau cops were there the day after the body was discovered. Forensics detail lifted prints, vacuumed up dust, took umpteen dozen photos. The usual."

"I guess it's taped off."

"Like the mummy's face."

"But you could get me inside if I wanted to have a look." Moon speared a greasy link of pork sausage.

Parris eyed a chunk of pale-green melon, and let it lie. "You intend to mess around in the FBI's business?"

"Yeah."

The *matukach* grinned. "When do we start?"

The Ute investigator thought about this. There were things to do at the ranch. But it was just an hour from the Columbine to Granite Creek and Rocky Mountain Polytechnic's campus. "How about I drop by your office tomorrow morning?"

The chief of police assumed a weary, harried expression. "I'll try to fit you into my busy schedule." *It'll be like old times.*

Moon's cell phone chirped anxiously, like a small bird smothering in his coat pocket. He ignored the bothersome thing.

Scott Parris spread sugarless orange marmalade on the toast. He knew how Charlie Moon detested the interruption of a telephone call. Especially when he was enjoying a tasty meal. "Might be something important."

"Should've left the danged thing in the car," the Ute said. "Pete Bushman's always calling me about some problem at the ranch. Something's always breaking down. Or getting sick." The telephone continued to chirp. *Maybe the battery will run down.*

"Might be the tribal chairman," Parris said with a sly grin. "Maybe Oscar Sweetwater wants you to do some serious police work."

With a grumble, Moon pressed the plastic contraption to his ear. "Yeah?"

"Charlie—is that you?"

He recognized the voice. "What's on your mind, Dolly? I need to pick something up before I head for home?" Last time it was a bushel of potatoes and six dozen eggs.

"Oh no. I just wanted to let you know that there's someone here to see you."

His heart did a drum roll. Maybe Camilla had shown up. Sweet Thing, who lived on her horse ranch in California, had a habit of dropping in unannounced. Nice habit. "Who?"

"Your aunt Daisy."

"You're kidding."

"At least that's who she *says* she is. Pete thinks maybe she's some thief who intends to ransack your house."

"He's an optimist." Moon laughed out loud. "No self-respecting felon would impersonate my aunt."

"There was another lady with her," the ranch foreman's wife said in a conspiratorial tone. "Tiny little thing."

This was beginning to come together. "An elderly white woman?"

"Could've been Moses' widow." There was a smile in Dolly's voice. "And she was driving a beat-up old car that smoked like a haystack on fire."

Bingo.

"They went on up to the big house. Pete says I should've kept 'em here at our place till you got home."

"Don't worry, Dolly. They're harmless." Not that they hadn't been a problem once or twice. But after that big hullabaloo a couple of years ago, they had learned their lesson. *Besides, they're too old and tired to cause any real trouble.*

Charlie Moon was an optimist.

The Deposit

Having parked near the cabin, the pair of aged women stood near the dusty automobile's rear bumper. They looked this way and that.

Louise-Marie LaForte spoke first. "This makes me awful nervous."

Daisy's hands tingled with inner electricity, her mouth was dry as sandpaper. "There's nothing to worry about."

This assertion did little to reassure the French-Canadian woman, who stared at the shimmering surface of the mountain lake.

"Go ahead," Daisy said urgently.

Louise-Marie shook her head. "Not me."

The Ute woman managed a smirk. "What's the matter—you afraid?"

"Yes." And she was. *Once things like this get started, you never know how they'll turn out.*

The Withdrawal

Charlie Moon saw a plume of dust in the distance. It was billowing up behind a black sedan. "Aha," he said.

Daisy Perika was feeling quite smug, silently congratulating herself on a job well done. Considering the unexpected difficulties, things had turned out just fine. And then she saw something she didn't want to see. It looked like Charlie Moon's car turning off the highway, into the gate. *Just five more minutes and we'd have been out of here.* She muttered an obscenity.

Louise-Marie clucked her tongue. "Shame on you, Daisy, saying such things on the Sabbath day."

Moon slowed the Expedition to a growling crawl, then stopped in the one-lane gravel road to block the path of the oncoming Oldsmobile. The sedan slowed, then stopped with an air of nervous uncertainty. Like a sitting rabbit, ready to jump at the least provocation.

Ignoring his aunt, he approached the driver's side of the old car. The Ute tipped his expensive gray Stetson at the elfin woman behind the wheel. "Well, look who's here. Is this Louise-Marie LaForte, or her good-looking twin sister?"

The tiny white woman looked up at the tall Indian. "Hello, Charlie." *Such a sweet young man.*

"You come to the ranch to buy yourself a side of beef?"

"Oh no. Daisy needed to come up here, so I drove her."

"My aunt came all the way up here just to see me?"

Louise-Marie dithered. "Well, I suppose she . . . well . . . perhaps—"

Daisy, worried that her companion's aimless mumblings might decide to go somewhere, interrupted. "Next time I come to see you, Charlie Moon, make sure you're at home."

He leaned over to look through the window at his irascible relative. "Seems to me, *you* were supposed to be at home this fine Sunday morning. At least that's where I thought I'd find you. After I drove all the way to your place."

"Why'd you do that?"

"To take you to church. Just like on every Sunday morning."

"I don't need *you* to take me to mass," she huffed. "I got plenty of friends who can drive me anywhere I want to go." She elbowed her aged chauffeur. "Let's get going."

Louise-Marie peeped under the steering-wheel rim. "I can't, dear. Your nephew's big car has got the road blocked."

Daisy wrung her hands in exasperation. "Well, go around it."

Moon didn't like the sound of this. "Hold on now—"

But Louise-Marie—who could not see the irregular landscape near the Oldsmobile—had already stepped on the accelerator pedal and hung a hard right into the sage. The slick tires spun in the sandy soil for a few seconds, then caught hold. And off they lurched in a churning cloud of dust. With a fine assortment of local flora snagged on the underside of the ancient car.

Moon watched them go. *I'd sure like to know what that was all about.* In time, he would know. But not soon enough.

Going Home

The blacktop road led south. Loath to witness Louise-Marie's erratic driving, Daisy Perika closed her eyes. She hoped her French-Canadian crony would believe she was asleep.

The smaller of the elderly women squinted under the arc of steering wheel. "I don't know," Louise-Marie LaForte said.

There was no response from her companion.

The driver repeated her words, louder this time. "I don't know."

Daisy ground her teeth. *What you don't know could fill a book. Great big book.*

Louise-Marie adjusted the steering so the painted white line on the pavement was aligned with the hood ornament. *That keeps just the same amount of space on both sides of the car. Makes me less likely to run into the ditch.* She glanced at her passenger. "Daisy?"

"You woke me up," the Ute woman grumped.

"I don't know if we did the right thing."

"Sure we did."

Louise-Marie shook her gray head. "The more I think about it, the worse I feel."

"I'll do the thinking. You keep your eyes on the road."

There was a heavy *bumpity-thump* under the aged Oldsmobile.

Daisy opened her eyes. "What was that?"

"I think I run over something—maybe a jackrabbit. Or a pig." Louise-Marie lifted her foot from the accelerator pedal. "What should I do?"

"You've already done it. Keep on driving."

CHAPTER 10

The Sun asked them what they would do with this weapon . . .
They named the monsters one by one . . . The Sun sat with his
head down and thought a great thought, for Yietso, the One-
Walking Giant, was also his son.
—Sandoval, Hastin Tlo'tsi hee

The Apartment

The chief of police and the Ute tribal investigator stood side by
side in the parking lot. They gave the U-shaped building a once-over.
Then a twice-over. In spite of a fresh coat of green paint and a glistening red-tile roof, the squat structure managed to look ugly. In the grassy
center enclosed by the U, there was a scattering of plastic lawn furniture surrounding an unattended swimming pool. Along with a Styro-
foam cup, a few thousand dead insects floated on the oily surface.

"Place looks like a third-rate motel," Moon observed.

Parris nodded his battered felt hat. "Used to be the Rest Easy Motor
Hotel. Got bypassed by the new highway. Owners remodeled. Con-
verted the place into off-campus housing for Rocky Mountain Polytechnic students."

"Where's April's apartment?" The Ute said this as if she still lived here. As if she still lived.

The *matukach* pointed his nose upward. "Second floor. Number 226."

The chief of police peeled back one edge of the yellow POLICE—DO NOT CROSS tape intended as a barrier to the apartment where the young woman had—up until her last moments—lived an ordinary life.

Parris turned a key in the slot, then stood aside. He indicated with a polite gesture that his friend should have the honor of entering first.

And so Moon did. The interior was quiet and gloomy, with the smell of an old attic. There was the unsettling sense that no one had lived here for decades. The Ute went to the window; he pulled a frayed cord that squeaked over a plastic pulley. A bright slot appeared between dark blue curtains, letting in a broad stream of sunlight. A trillion-billion dust particles swam against the current, as if to pass through the glass.

The lawmen looked around without comment. There wasn't much to see. Two small rooms and a bath. They were standing in the rectangle that served as living room and kitchenette.

Parris gestured with a jerk of his elbow. "Bedroom's over there."

Moon paused in the doorway. Beside a neatly made bed there was a small, battered desk. Like a student might find in a discount used-furniture store. He took a step inside the bedroom-study and noted that the FBI forensics specialists had worked with their usual professionalism. Which was to say there was not the slightest hint they'd been in the dead woman's apartment. Everything was precisely in its place—or precisely out of its place—just as April Tavishuts had left it. A pair of faded jeans draped over the back of a chair. Her bedroom slippers, one under a lamp table, another on the threshold of the bathroom door. As if she'd kicked them off, to remain where they landed. On her desk was a perfectly rectangular spot that was free of dust. Moon assumed that April's laptop computer had been removed by the FBI. Around the vacant space was the usual array of a college student's paraphernalia. An assortment of pens and pencils. A white plastic ruler. A football-shaped eraser. A RadioShack calculator with solar-cell power. On an unpainted shelf over the desk, there was a row of books. An *American Heritage* dictionary. *The Chaco Meridian. The Book of the Navajo. Myths and Tales of the Jicarilla Apache Indians. Ancient Ruins of the Southwest.* There were a half dozen volumes on Native American petroglyphs; most of these had library markings. Charlie Moon reached for a book he hadn't seen before: *When the Rocks Begin to Speak,* by LaVan Martineau. The Ute investigator wondered whether the rocks had spoken to April. Like a prayer book whose spine was cracked from much use, the volume opened in his hand to page 179. The heading of the section was "Cryptanalysis—The Forgotten Tool." April had left something to mark the page. The bookmark was a folded, tissue-thin sheet that had the yellowish look of parchment. Moon unfolded the delicate paper. On it was a carefully crafted sketch of the recently discovered petroglyph at Ghost Wolf Mesa—the hourglass-shaped Twin War Gods, spears in hand. There were penciled entries by the pointed weapons. A closer look revealed that these were compass markings. April had apparently recorded precisely where on Companion and Chimney Rocks the spears were pointing. There was a trace of something else on the tissue. He switched on a gooseneck desk lamp and held the makeshift chart close to the sixty-watt bulb. A pair of diverging lines had been erased, but the indentations of the sharp-pointed pencil were still visible. The marks had been made with a straightedge—probably the plastic ruler on April's desk. The erased lines were precisely aligned with the spears. Which all proved exactly nothing. Except that April had been fascinated by the petroglyph that archaeologist Amanda Silk had privately pronounced a forgery. This was hardly surprising. April was—no, make that *had been*—a graduate student in anthropology. The mysterious petroglyph was meat and potatoes for such folk. Maybe April had imagined that there was a fabulous Anasazi treasure somewhere out there where the spears pointed. But now the young woman was no more. The sudden realization of her absolute absence made him feel empty. Diminished. The Ute investigator forced his thoughts back to her sketch of the Twin War Gods. He wondered why April had drawn the lines parallel with the spears. And perhaps more interesting, why had she erased them?

"Hey," Scott said from the doorway, "we've got company."

It'll be the feds. Moon quickly replaced the book on the shelf. And realized that he still had April's sketched chart in his hand. He stuffed it into his coat pocket. The next face to appear in the doorway was young. Female. Blonde. Pretty enough to unsettle a man who had a pocketful of evidence.

She watched the startled look on Moon's face fade into one of relief. "So who were you expecting, the FBI?"

She's a mind reader. Moon grinned at the familiar face. "Don't I know you?"

"You should. I'm Melina Castro. April's friend." A gray shadow passed over her fair features. She took a deep breath, then exhaled the evil spirits away. "I met you that night at Chimney Rock." It was unnecessary to be more specific. There was only one That Night.

"Sure. You and the archaeologist—"

"Dr. Silk."

"—found the body." But that wasn't completely accurate. While this younger woman had seen the male suspect standing over April's makeshift grave, Amanda Silk had seen nothing. If the murderer was ever apprehended and put in a lineup, that fact was highly unfortunate. In the peculiar arithmetic of the law, the sum of two witnesses is infinitely greater than one. "So what brings you here?"

"I live here." She glanced over her shoulder. "My apartment's just down the hall. Number 229." *You can drop by anytime, Treetop Tall.*

The chief of police considered this answer unresponsive to Moon's question. Scott Parris assumed his official expression. "You have some interest in Miss Tavishuts's apartment?"

The blonde grad student shrugged with a slow, feline grace. "Ever since . . . you know—well, it's been taped off."

"And locked," Parris added.

She avoided his inquisitive gaze. "It's just that I went to take out the trash and saw her door open. So I came to have a look. Thought I should see who was rummaging around in April's apartment."

Okay. So you're a good citizen. "Then I suppose introductions are in order." Parris introduced himself.

She laughed. "I've been in Granite Creek long enough to know you're chief of police here."

"I see you're already acquainted with Charlie Moon." Parris said this with a hint of sarcasm. "But you may not know everything about him. Charlie's a modest fellow. I bet he hasn't told you that he's a special investigator for the Southern Ute tribe."

"My. A *special* investigator."

The *matukach* was warming to the game. "That's because Charlie deals with special crimes. The kind that are altogether too challenging for us ordinary police."

Her enormous eyes grew even larger. "Sounds terribly exciting. But dangerous work like that must really be awfully stressful."

"It does make life tense," Moon said with a harried look. "Some days I can hardly keep a meal down."

"Miss Castro?"

She turned to Parris. "Yes?"

"I want you to know that the sudden appearance of an attractive young lady like yourself is a rare treat."

"Why thank you."

"But I regret to have to tell you—these premises are currently the subject of an official police homicide investigation. And off-limits to those with no business here."

Her yellow hair seemed to bristle. "But I have a reason to be here."

"Which is?"

"April and I were good friends—we borrowed things from each other. I thought maybe I could get some of my stuff back." She added quickly: "If it's okay with you."

Moon, realizing that Parris was about to give Melina a polite heave-ho, intervened before his friend could heave. "What sort of things did she borrow?"

Melina Castro shrugged again. "We exchanged clothes sometimes. I think she still has one of my blouses. And maybe a scarf." She glanced toward April's bedroom, more particularly at the desk and bookshelf. "And I loaned her a couple of books. Stuff like that."

Moon followed her gaze. "Which books are yours?"

"Oh, I'd have to look at them to be sure. But there were some on Native American rock art. Petroglyphs. Pictographs." She gave Moon the big eye. "Could I check out what she has on the shelf?"

Parris intervened. "I'm afraid not, Miss Castro. After the investigation is far enough along, your property will be returned to you. In the meantime, I suggest you make a list of the items you loaned to the deceased. You could drop it by the station."

Her eyes sparked fire at this annoying man who was her father's age.

"If I could remember everything April borrowed from me, I wouldn't have to look."

Parris shook his head.

Melina looked to the Ute for support. And found a hint of sympathy there.

Parris's discomfort at playing the heavy showed on his honest face. "Sorry, young lady—I'll have to ask you to leave."

Melina flushed crimson with anger, but turned to go. And met a pair of men in neatly pressed gray suits. They were standing in the doorway. Blocking her path. No introductions were necessary. She was by now well acquainted with Special Agents Stanley Newman and George Whitmer. The latter escorted her into the hallway.

Newman closed the door behind him. "Well," the federal lawman said with an air of disapproval. He waited for a response. Something in the way of an apology for what was a trespass on a Bureau investigation. Ignoring Moon, Newman stared at the chief of police. "So what're you guys doing here?"

Scott Parris met the stare without blinking. "The murdered girl's apartment is in my jurisdiction. I'm conducting an official police investigation. You have a problem with that?"

"Hey, let's not get our tail tied in a hard knot." Newman tried to smile, but didn't quite bring it off.

Parris maintained the stare.

Eager to retreat from the confrontation, Newman turned to the Ute. "So, Charlie—what're you looking for?"

Charlie Moon looked over the man's head. "Nothing." *Already found it.*

Newman tried hard to appear amiable. "Look, I didn't mean to rattle your cages. But I wish you guys hadn't let that college girl into the apartment. She might've messed around with something that'll turn out to be important evidence."

The flimsy sketch in Moon's jacket pocket suddenly felt like a brick. It was a good time to change the topic of conversation. "What brings you and George here?"

The special agent hesitated. "We've come to see the girl."

Parris frowned at this news. "Miss Castro?"

"Yeah. She lives right down the hall."

Moon felt like having a little fun with the fed. "She a suspect?"

"In case you forgot, Miss Castro is our only witness in the Tavishuts homicide."

"You arrested anybody for her to ID?" Moon knew the answer.

"We'll make an arrest." Newman held a stubby finger near his thumb, making a crablike pincer. "We're this close."

"Glad to hear it," Parris said. And grinned.

Newman glanced toward the door. "Well, I'd like to hang around and beat my gums with you guys, but I got some police work to do for Uncle Sam."

They watched the door close behind the federal agent.

"I'm done here if you are," the Ute said.

Parris frowned at his partner. "So soon?"

Moon nodded. "Let's get outta this place."

They did.

Once they were in the parking lot, Scott Parris glanced back at the ugly apartment complex, then at his Ute friend. "Stan Newman is a by-the-book cop. I hope you didn't do anything up there that will come back to haunt me."

Innocence fairly oozed from Moon's pores. "Like what?"

"Like mess around with official evidence."

The Ute investigator removed the flimsy slip of paper from his pocket. "You mean like this?"

The chief of police stared in disbelief at the sketch of the Twin War Gods. "Please don't tell me you took that from the dead girl's apartment."

"Don't fret, pardner. After I get a copy made, I'll put it back. And if the feds don't find it, I could always drop 'em a little hint about where to look on her bookshelf—"

Parris slapped his palms over his ears. "I meant it—don't tell me."

"Okay." He paused. "But it's kind of interesting, these lines April drew by the Twin War Gods—"

"Damn it all, Charlie—why do you do these crazy things!"

The Ute thought about it. "That's exactly what my momma used to say."

• • •

Melina Castro seated the FBI agents at a spotless kitchen table. Her pretty face was calm enough. The student's clasped hands rested on the red oilcloth. Her fingers wriggled like an entwining of small white snakes.

George Whitmer, the more fatherly of the pair, smiled to expose a squarish-looking set of dentures. The effect was not particularly soothing to the young woman, who imagined a lunatic hippo breaking water to crush a canoe loaded with hapless Africans. Not that she had ever witnessed such a tragic event.

"Miss Castro," Whitmer said, "we very much appreciate your cooperation in this investigation."

Her fingers relaxed. "I've already told you everything I know about April's death. Why are you here?"

"A universal question," Whitmer mused. "Why are any of us here? What is the purpose of it all?"

Annoyed by his partner's lapse into whimsy, Newman assumed the role of interrogator. "Since we last talked, Miss Castro, I'm wondering whether you may have recalled anything about that night—when you encountered the man burying April Tavishuts's corpse."

"Like what?"

His sharp eyes surveyed the small kitchen. "Could be anything. Something you may've seen—or heard." This was generally a waste of time. But you never knew.

She felt a chill in the room. Hugged herself. "No."

"Okay. How about Miss Tavishuts? Anything you know about the victim might be helpful to our investigation. Like, were there any men in her life?"

She started to speak, then clamped her mouth shut.

"Miss Castro?"

"Well—there was this one thing." The white snakes began to wriggle again. "But it can't have anything to do with her death."

"Let me be the judge of that."

She rubbed her palms together briskly, as if to warm them. "April—she may have been . . . you know."

Newman shook his head. "No, ma'am. I do not know."

Staring at her doughy hands, she spat the word out. "Pregnant."

George Whitmer leaned forward. "You said 'may have been.' Do you have any direct knowledge that Miss Tavishuts was pregnant?"

Melina shook her head; the heavy yellow braid brushed her back. "But sometimes she was sick in the mornings."

"So'm I," Newman muttered, "but I am not with child."

Whitmer ignored his partner. "Did Miss Tavishuts tell you that she was expecting?"

"Not exactly." Now she met Whitmer's honest eyes. "But there was some campus gossip."

"She have a boyfriend?"

Melina half-shrugged the question away. "Maybe."

"You got a name for us?"

"No."

"That's not much help."

She rubbed her eyes. "I wish I hadn't mentioned it."

"On the contrary, you were quite right to bring it up," Whitmer said. "Anything else you'd like to tell us about?"

"No." She looked hopefully at the younger of the two federal agents. "Is that all?"

"Not quite, miss." Newman unzipped a leather briefcase. He removed a thick manila envelope that was secured with rubber bands. From this was disgorged an assortment of photographs. The federal agent pressed the Rec button on a microcassette recorder. He stated the location, date, and time to the minute. He named all those present. "Let the record show that Special Agent Whitmer will show Miss Melina Castro an exhibit of photographs, numbered one through thirty-four." The small reel spun slowly, converting compressions of air into complex magnetic patterns on the tape.

George Whitmer assumed his task. "Miss Castro, please inspect each of these photographs. If the person in the photo does not resemble the person you saw standing over April Tavishuts's grave, place the photo on your left. But if you see a face that looks like the suspect, place that photo on your right."

She stared blankly at each palm in turn. "I can never remember— oh yeah. The one with my wristwatch is the left." Melina smiled triumphantly at the other palm. "Then this must be my right."

Newman closed his eyes and imagined taking this taped evidence to court. A witness who doesn't know her left hand from her right. *Why me, Lord?*

Melina began with photo number one and proceeded without haste. The graduate student squinted at the images in turn, placed the photos on her left.

Newman was holding his breath.

At number nine, she paused. "That's Terry—Professor Perkins."

Whitmer nodded. "Does he bear any resemblance to the man you saw standing over the partially buried corpse of April Tavishuts?"

She shook her head quickly. "Oh no—of course not." Melina looked to Newman for support. "I mean, that's crazy . . ."

Whitmer reminded her of the protocol. "Then place Dr. Perkins's photograph on your left."

She did.

They watched her.

She frowned at the next photo. "Hmmm," she said. And placed number ten on her *right.*

Neither federal investigator showed any sign of interest. It was a matter of professional pride.

And so, as if nothing special had happened, Melina continued. And placed number thirteen on her right.

This brought an exchange of glances between the federal policemen.

The graduate student frowned at number seventeen and also placed it on the right-hand suspect pile. Then repeated this with number eighteen. And twenty-two. And so it went.

Newman exhaled his breath until he was completely deflated.

Melina continued the process until she had studied the last image and placed it on her left. "That's it."

Whitmer said nothing aside from a brief comment to the microphone. "Miss Castro has placed twenty-seven photos on the 'does not resemble' pile to her left, and"—his voice cracked—"seven on her right, which stipulates that they bear some resemblance to the suspect seen at the grave of Miss April Tavishuts."

Special Agent Newman was making a valiant attempt to contain his annoyance. He almost succeeded.

Whitmer spoke in a disinterested monotone, as if nothing untoward had occurred. "Miss Castro, just for the record, are we to understand that all seven of these images on your right resemble the murder suspect you saw that night?"

She nodded. "Sure. Well, sorta. You know."

"What is it about these individuals that reminds you of . . . ahh . . . the suspect?"

She riffled through the deck of seven faces. "Well, they're all *really old*."

Newman's voice croaked like a bullfrog's. "Old?"

"Well, yeah. I mean look at these geezers. They must all be at least in their forties. Some even older than that." She frowned with childish concentration. "Like I told you the first time we talked, the guy I saw that night was, like, really old."

Whitmer, who was fifty-seven, smiled benignly. "Could you estimate the suspect's age?"

Her head bobbed in an eager nod. "Fifty. Maybe even sixty."

Newman rolled his eyes at the ceiling. "And all seven of the individuals in the photos resemble the suspect?"

Another nod.

Newman aimed his finger at the bulbous device mounted on the tripod. "Please respond for the microphone."

"Yeah. Well, kinda. Like, I'm not saying one of these seven guys was actually the one I saw that night at the pit-house ruin—just that they sort of looked like him."

Newman ground his teeth. *What a dim bulb.*

Whitmer held the microphone close to his lips, stated the time of day and the fact that the interview was being terminated. He pressed the Stop button on the microcassette recorder and rewound it, played back a random section of tape to make certain they had a technically acceptable recording. Presently, they heard her voice again. "Sure. Well, sorta. You know . . ."

"Shut it off," Newman said through clenched teeth. There was a brittle edge of hysteria in his voice. With as much patience as his nature afforded, he explained the facts of life. The witness was sternly advised not to tell anyone that she had been asked to ID April Tavishuts's killer for the FBI. Not her mother. Not her priest or rabbi or psychiatrist. Not her closest friend. If the perp thought she had picked him out of the photo lineup, it might seriously jeopardize the Bureau's investigation. Maybe cause the killer to leave the country. Worse still—and he added this observation with a touch of malice—there was just the tiniest chance that the perp might decide to pay their supposed witness a visit.

She asked the obvious question: How big a chance?

Newman shrugged. "Who knows?"

Melina solemnly agreed to keep this interview a secret.

Whitmer assured the witness that she need not worry one hair on her head about the perpetrator of the crime harming her. Witnesses to crimes got rubbed out on TV dramas. But never in real life.

"Well, almost never," Newman added with a hint of a smile.

Almost? Her eyes grew large.

Whitmer urged her to relax. The FBI was hot on the perp's trail. Would probably have him in the jug within a couple of days. A week at the outside. He shot his partner a dark look.

Stanley Newman was repentant. "Even if it takes a bit longer to pick him up," he assured the witness, "the Bureau would see that you are protected."

Melina Castro reminded the federal policemen that her address was in the telephone book. Would the FBI hide her someplace until the killer was found?

Indeed they would, Newman assured her. The very moment the Bureau determined that her life was in the slightest danger.

The young woman closed the door behind them, listened to their footsteps recede down the hallway. "Well," she whispered, "I think I handled that pretty well."

A Bad Idea

George Whitmer made himself a bet. *It won't take Stan six steps.*

Special Agent Stanley Newman was precisely four paces from Melina's apartment door when the grumbling erupted. "Crap! What a waste of time."

Whitmer smiled. "Oh, I don't know. She picked out seven possible suspects."

"Right," Newman snorted. "Including the special agent in charge of the Denver field office."

The older agent snickered. "The boss does have a sort of criminal look about him. Sloping forehead. Beady little bloodshot eyes, set awfully close together."

Newman frowned at a set of graffiti-splashed elevator doors. "I don't like being shut up in a stinky little box—let's take the stairs."

"As long as we're going down." Whitmer closed the stairwell door behind them and paused to lean on an unpainted cinder-block wall. "Stan?"

"Yeah?"

"There's something on my mind."

There always is. "What's that?"

"Even though this young lady didn't recognize the perp, he's bound to have seen her and Dr. Silk. And by now, everybody in the state knows about the pair of women who stumbled on the murderous pothunter. Including their names. And where they live."

"The media," Newman said with a shake of his head. "I hate 'em."

"Dr. Silk didn't see anybody at the grave site. Her statement to that effect has been in the newspapers, on the radio and TV. So she's safe enough. But at our request, the grad student hasn't made a public statement about what or who she might have seen that night. Which could make the perp believe that she got a good enough look at his face to ID him."

Stanley Newman's stomach was churning bile. Whitmer had a nasty way of cutting right to the heart of bad news. "You really think he'd try to off this grad student?"

"You willing to bet her life he won't?"

Newman considered this a mean-spirited question. He did not reply.

"It'd be a long time—if ever—before we could get the paperwork approved to stash Miss Castro in a safe location. Especially since she's currently a useless witness. In the meantime, this murderous bastard could show up and slip a knife between her ribs."

"You got to stop worrying me so much."

Whitmer's silence boomed in his partner's ears.

"Go ahead, George. Say it."

George Whitmer said it. "You got to stop making promises we can't keep. Like telling Miss Castro the Bureau would protect her."

"Hey, what can I say—I work for the government."

Whitmer was about to rebuke his partner when he noticed Newman getting that cartoon look, as if a lightbulb had suddenly appeared above his head. With wiggly little lines radiating from it. He waited for the Eureka moment.

Newman banged fist against palm. "George—I got a really brilliant idea."

Whitmer sighed. *God help us.*

A Small Favor

Charlie Moon had just said good-bye to Scott Parris, who was heading away in his rusty red Volvo. The Ute was of the opinion that a man who was chief of police ought to drive a better-looking set of wheels. But the Volvo had sentimental value. The boxy sedan had been almost new when Parris and his bride spotted it on a Chicago auto lot. Helen was long dead. The man treasured her memory. And their automobile.

The Ute was sliding into his Ford pickup when he noticed the determined approach of the FBI agents. George Whitmer slowed his pace, then stopped a couple of yards behind his partner.

Stanley Newman took a long breath. "Charlie—"

"Yeah?"

"I need to have a word with you."

He's on to me. I should've put April's sketch back in the book. "Talk? About what?"

"Nothing much. A small favor."

The Ute's relief was masked by a fair-to-middling poker face. "From me?"

"No, wiseacre. I am hoping for some kindly assistance from Sitting Bull."

Moon seemed saddened by this news. "Well, that'll be a problem, Stan. He's not been seen in these parts for some time now."

"Don't give me heartburn, Charlie. I wouldn't ask you if there was any other way. Besides," he added seductively, "it'll be real easy. No sweat."

Moon regarded the special agent with a thoughtful look. "Stan, before I'd ever agree to do you a good turn, there'd be a condition."

"Which is?"

"You'd have to be seriously beholden to me."

Newman's innards made a pitiful mewing noise. "This is no joking matter."

The Ute tried hard to look serious. "I'm not joking."

"Okay." The federal agent raised his hands as one accosted by a robber. "You got it, Ace. I'll be in your debt."

Moon frowned suspiciously at the favor seeker. "For how long?"

Newman rolled his eyes at the blue Colorado sky. "Long as I live, Chucky." A buzzard circled above. *I'm dead meat.*

"You swear?"

"On my saintly mother's grave."

"Your mother's alive and well in Casper." He would pass on the saintly part. But it was rumored that the senior Mrs. Newman peddled dry-land real estate to gullible city folk on both coasts.

"Okay then, forget my mother's grave." Newman drew an invisible X across his chest. "Cross my heart."

"And hope to die?"

"In considerable pain. All alone in some rat-infested alley. With no one left to mourn my passing."

Moon brightened. "Okay. What's the favor?"

Special Agent Newman explained precisely what he required from his Ute friend.

Charlie Moon listened. And looked doubtful.

Newman hastened to point out that his proposal was one that the Bureau would be grateful for. More than that, if Charlie Moon agreed, his charitable action would be considered as one lawman's personal favor to another. Not only would Newman be beholden until his death, so would the nation's premier law-enforcement agency. *So help me, J. Edgar Hoover.* He spat on the gravel to solemnize this weighty vow.

The Ute, whose people had learned not to trust any solemn promise from the government in Washington, was wary. "For how long would this be?"

"Just a few days. Till we can make a more long-term arrangement."

The special agent, who knew his man, played his hole card. Stanley Newman just happened to mention that the Bureau would, of course, pay Moon for his trouble. Not that there would be any actual trouble. Merely a figure of speech. Ha-ha.

The owner of the Columbine asked the critical question: How much.

Newman shrugged. "Depends on what the bean counters will approve. But if you provide our witness with a decent room and three meals a day, I could probably get you something"—he squinted painfully, as if performing a difficult mental calculation—"say in the neighborhood of a hundred and twenty bucks per day."

The cash-poor rancher considered this a very nice neighborhood indeed. *Melina Castro could stay in the guest cabin I fixed up for Aunt Daisy. Meals wouldn't be a problem; Dolly Bushman could feed six kids her size on leftovers.* But a small voice whispered to him: *Don't do it.*

Charlie Moon—who needed the money—ignored the warning.

As Special Agent George Whitmer eased the sleek Ford Taurus out of the apartment building parking lot, he glanced at the rearview mirror. Charlie Moon was standing by his Ford pickup. Watching them leave. As if he knew they were not to be trusted. Whitmer suddenly felt as if he'd been party to a wrong deal. "Stan?"

"What is it?" *As if I didn't know.*

"I don't think you should've gotten Charlie involved in this."

Newman found a very old pack of chewing gum in his coat pocket. "Don't sweat it, George. It's a win-win situation—works for everybody."

"Bureau may not fund it."

"Hey, it's worth the risk."

"Charlie's taking all the risk," Whitmer pointed out. "And if he don't get paid, you've taken advantage of a brother lawman."

"Moon's not a real policeman anymore. He's more like a private cop." Newman popped a stale stick of Juicy Fruit into his mouth. "Anyway, it's not like I asked him to do something any upstanding citizen wouldn't be happy to do in the service of criminal justice."

Whitmer braked for a red light. "I still say it ain't right."

Special Agent Stanley Newman, his conscience tweaked by these righteous arguments, chewed the gum rapidly. "Okay, partner. Tell you what. If the bean counters disapprove the application to pay for our witness's room and board at Charlie's big ranch, we'll pay him out of our own pockets." *Say ten cents on the dollar* . . .

The older man laughed. "You made the promise, hotshot. Don't think for a minute you're going to pick my pocket."

CHAPTER 11

The Sun said: "My Sons . . . I know today that you will kill one of the members of your family." He handed the Elder Brother his weapon, which is also the lightning. . . .
—Sandoval, Hastin Tlo'tsi hee

Ghost Wolf Mesa

Her arms folded resolutely, Amanda Silk stood above the excavation, staring down at the slight man who wore transparent latex gloves. He was the latest in a string of government experts who had photographed, probed, and sampled the soil at the crime scene. The archaeologist intended to be intimidating.

She was.

Barney Felt looked up from his position beside the makeshift grave where April Tavishuts's calcined bones lay in deathly sleep. He squinted at the stark outline of this tall woman who stood with her back to the rising sun. Her form had the appearance of a cutout fashioned from black construction paper. He understood that Dr. Silk was the watchdog. She was present to make sure he did not go beyond the bounds required for the task at hand. "You needn't worry, ma'am. I'll be very careful." The forensics specialist grinned in amiable fashion. "I know how you archaeologists feel about folks disturbing these old ruins."

"How I *feel* has nothing to do with it," Amanda said evenly. "It is a matter of federal law."

His head bobbed as he nodded. "Yeah. I know about NAGPRA and all that." Barney glanced at the burned bones. "All I'm interested in is finding out how this young woman died. Maybe even getting lucky, finding some evidence that'll lead us to who killed her." *Then I'm outta here.*

The archaeologist felt almost sorry for the fed. "I understand that you have a job to do." She withdrew a respectful distance, sat on a slab of sandstone and watched him work.

The forensics expert moved slowly around the excavation, blinking at the disturbed earth.

Despite her professional concerns, Amanda Silk found this display immensely entertaining. He was crawling, his face inches from the ground. *All he needs is a big magnifying glass and a deerstalker hat.*

As if to oblige half her fantasy, Barney Felt produced a magnifying lens.

The archaeologist sighed. *He's almost too cute.*

"Hey," he said.

"What?"

He pointed with his nose. "What's this?"

She went to look. "It's a fragment of obsidian."

"It's real shiny," he said with boyish enthusiasm. "Almost like glass."

"Obsidian," the archaeologist said with a pedantic air, "is often referred to as volcanic glass. It doesn't occur naturally on the mesa. Someone carried it up here—probably at least a thousand years ago."

The FBI forensics specialist squinted as he moved the round lens for a perfect focus. "Absolutely astonishing."

"Not really so astonishing," Amanda said patiently. "The continent is littered with bits and pieces of artifacts much older than that."

"No. I mean what's on the *surface* of the obsidian."

She leaned to look more closely. "What do you see?"

The Bureau employee turned an impish face toward the archaeologist. "Why, the fingerprint, of course."

"You've got to be kidding."

"We who work for Uncle Sam's federal police force do not make idle jests about evidence. Particularly in a homicide."

"Then whoever buried the body must have touched the obsidian . . ."

"Sure. When the pothunter was digging, he must've found the volcanic glass. Picked it up, took a look at it, pitched it onto the pile of dirt."

She nodded slowly at this astounding piece of good fortune. "Of course. An unworked piece of obsidian has no value to an artifact thief."

Barney pocketed the magnifying lens, and rummaged around in his canvas tote bag until he found a camera in a leather case. He mounted the instrument on a small tripod, and took several close-up photographs of the obsidian artifact. "If our luck holds out, this bird's prints will be on file."

Amanda was beginning to find this man's work fascinating. "And if they're not?"

"Then we'll have to wait for a suspect." He looked up uncertainly at the watchdog. "It'd sure help if all of you folks who work at the archaeological site would volunteer to be fingerprinted."

Amanda nodded. "You may begin with me."

Barney used a plastic-tipped forceps to lift the obsidian specimen and drop it into a plastic bag. This was carefully sealed and marked with the date, time, and precise location of discovery. "What about the others—you think any of them will mind giving us their prints?"

"I'm sure they'll be happy to cooperate."

He removed a roll of film from the camera and slipped it into a black plastic cylinder. This evidence was stored in another marked plastic bag. "That's good to hear."

But in reality, Amanda Silk was not so certain. One or two of the academics were bound to protest. Privacy, civil rights, and all that sort of thing.

The Guest

Melina Castro sat at the table, watching the Ute prepare their supper. *This is a very interesting man.* "So you live all alone here."

"Pretty much." He switched on the gas oven.

"How big is your ranch?"

"Pretty big."

"How big is that?"

It was the sort of impolite question that a local citizen would never ask. Like: "How much money do you have in the bank?" Or: "How many cows do you have on this spread?" But he gave her a number.

Her face drooped in disappointment. "That's not so many acres."

"Square miles."

She was stunned into silence by this revelation. But only temporarily.

"So how many cows do you have?"

Enough was enough. "Not as many as I'd like to have."

"You must be incredibly rich."

He couldn't afford to laugh. "How d'you like your lodgings?"

She shrugged. "The guest cabin is—well, you know—okay, I guess."

"I fixed it up for a relative." *But it don't look like Aunt Daisy will be using it.*

"But there's no telephone. And no television."

"There's a radio," he pointed out. "And electricity. And indoor plumbing."

"I'm so terribly thankful for that." The sarcasm fairly dripped from her lips. "At least I won't have to light a whale-oil lamp to find my way to the outdoor privy." The young woman looked out the window, toward a dark grove of spruce. She shuddered. "I sure wouldn't want to live so far from town."

"Well," he admitted, "living on the Columbine has its drawbacks. Before going out at night, there are some precautions you should take." He turned up the flame under a well-seasoned iron skillet.

She imagined mountain lions lurking in the gathering shadows. "Please don't tell me I need to tote a rifle."

Moon shook his head. "You'll need shades."

"What?"

"Dark glasses."

"At night?"

"To prevent night blindness." He put the potatoes into the oven.

"I don't get it."

"Stars over the Columbine are extremely bright." He squinted at the beamed ceiling. "Been known to dazzle city folk."

Silly man. She checked her fingernails. They needed a touch-up. "You like being a rancher?"

"So far." He sprinkled salt and pepper on the prime beef.

"You ever been married?"

He shook his head.

"You got a girlfriend?"

Charlie Moon plopped the rib-eye steaks into the hot skillet.

She smiled. "Is she an Indian?"

Preferring another sound to her voice, he listened to the steaks sizzle.

The young woman looked Moon up and down. "How tall are you?"

"How do you want your steak?" He found a spatula in a cabinet drawer, flipped the rib eyes.

Melina Castro approached the stove to inspect the beef. "I like mine well-done."

"Me too."

"Just the thought of eating bloody animal flesh makes me want to urp up my kidneys." She opened her mouth, made a gagging motion with her finger.

"You're a very civilized young lady."

She appreciated the compliment. "It was sweet of you—letting me stay here till the FBI catches that awful man I saw at April's grave."

He wrapped a towel around the hot iron handle, slid the blackened skillet into the oven.

She gave him a squinty look. "You're some kinda cop, aren't you?"

"Used to work for the Southern Ute Police Department."

"That FBI agent said you were a private detective."

"Tribal investigator." Had a better ring to it. Like a cash register.

"What's the difference?"

"I work for the tribe." He spooned eight heaping measures of fresh-ground coffee into the percolator. Then two more for the pot.

"Will the FBI pay you for my room and board?"

"I sure hope so." But with the paperwork that would need approving, it was a long way from a sure thing. He glanced at her. "If you would care to contribute some cash for your lodgings, the management will gladly accept it."

"If you're not sure they'll pay you, then why're you doing it?" *Maybe because you got the hots for me.*

"Partly as a favor for Special Agent Newman."

Sure. A favor. Her mouth was engaged well in advance of her brain. "I thought—maybe you—uh—you know—well, you must get lonely out here—and . . ."

He put three extra spoons of coarse grind into the percolator.

She waited for him to say something. Anything.

He didn't.

Melina Castro assumed that this big, bashful fellow needed some prodding. So she put the spurs to him. "I thought maybe you found me—well—you know . . ." *Attractive.*

"Ahh—how do you like your steak, Miss Castro?"

Her lids narrowed to lizardlike slits. "You already asked me that—Mr. Moon."

"And what did you say?"

"Burn it to a crisp." *Bastard.*

"Oh yeah—well-done." Charlie Moon's mind balanced two thoughts. *It's going to be a long few days. But I expect the worst of it is over.* He was half right.

The wall-mounted telephone rang. Like a drowning man coming up for the third time, Moon grabbed for this bit of driftwood that Fate had floated his way. "Hello."

The gravelly voice on the other end was Pete Bushman's. "Hey, boss."

"Hey, Pete." Moon looked over his shoulder at the strange young woman. "What's up?"

"I thought you might want to know that you got a visitor comin' up the lane lickety-split."

Desperately in need of a chaperone, Moon welcomed this news. "Who is it?"

Bushman told him.

Fate had fixed an anchor around Moon's neck. The Ute slammed the receiver into its cradle, turned on his heel to glare at his guest. "Get out of here!"

She stood up, pale as a ghost. "Look, I'm sorry if I mouthed off and made you mad—"

He pointed at the back door. "Now!"

She was at the edge of tears. "You don't have to yell at me."

He took her by the arm. Gently, he thought. "Miss Castro, I promised Stan Newman that I'd keep his star witness stashed away where nobody would find her. But I have a visitor coming. So you head back to the cabin. Pronto!"

The circulation to her hand had been cut off by his grip. "Okay, I'll leave." She put on a pitiful look. "Without my supper."

He led her to the back door. "She'll get here any minute. Take the path through the spruce."

She? I knew it! "Is this visitor your girlfriend?"

"Scoot," he said, and pushed her out the door.

Melina flattened her nose against the glass. "Don't forget to bring me something to eat!"

"Heat up a can of beans," he muttered, and pulled a curtain across the pane. *Stan Newman is going to owe me big for this.*

Trouble

Camilla Willow held her platinum compact just so and frowned at the reflection of an astonishingly pretty face. "Charlie—you smeared my lipstick. And mussed my hair." She pressed a glistening golden tress back into place.

"Give me half a chance, I'll do it all over again."

Camilla smiled sweetly. "All in good time." She snapped the compact shut. "I bet you were surprised to see me."

"A little." *Like if a grenade went off in my pocket.*

She wrapped her arms around his neck. "Do you like surprises?"

"Hey, does the pope like Polish sausage?"

"I wouldn't know." She lifted her nose and sniffed. "It appears that I have interrupted your supper."

"Nothing that won't keep. Just burning me some beef."

She frowned. Sniffed again. "You know, I believe you are."

Before he could react, she was heading toward the kitchen. Helplessly, he watched her open the oven door. After a glance at the baking potatoes, Camilla found a pot holder. She pulled the iron skillet from the oven. "Charlie, these are quite overdone."

"You know I like 'em scorched."

She stood very still, staring at the steaks. Thinking about the pair of large potatoes. Camilla turned to stare at the place settings on the large table.

Moon prayed that she could not count to two.

"Charlie?"

"Yeah?"

"Is my unexpected arrival inconvenient for you?"

He managed a blank expression. "What d'you mean?"

"It would appear you were expecting someone for dinner."

"Fact is, I had a pretty young woman here for supper. But when I heard you were comin', I threw her out." *They never believe the unvarnished truth.*

She gave him a strange look. As if she believed him.

Moon forced a grin that hurt his face. *God help me.*

Camilla took another look at the table. "Why of course—Mr. Bushman called to tell you I was coming. And you hurried to make a place at the table for me."

He looked toward the ceiling. And heaven. *Thank you, God.*

"Every time I'm here, you're always preparing meals for me. Waiting on me hand and foot. Well, this visit is going to be very different from the others."

Charlie Moon had a nagging sense that this was a monumental understatement.

She pushed him toward a chair. "Now sit down. I'll take over."

"You're a determined woman." *Who once threatened to kill me if I ever lied to you. Or cheated on you.*

She hugged him, pinning his arms. "And you are such a kind, honest man. The sort of a fellow a woman can rely on."

To Moon's great relief, the meal proceeded without incident. They washed the dishes together.

Camilla Willow leaned on her beloved. "Charlie, there was a reason I didn't call first. I had to arrange this trip in a big hurry."

"Couldn't wait to see me?"

"Well, that too. But I have another trip coming up."

"Not too far away, I hope. Or for too long."

Her eyes moistened. "Some of both. I'm going on a journey with Uncle Eddie."

Moon groaned. Eddie Zoog managed the EZ Literary Agency. His specialty was gathering rumors about UFOs and monsters and ghosts and the like. Once Eddie had put together a few "facts," he contracted with one of Los Angeles's desperate, down-and-out writers to assemble a quickie book manuscript or screenplay. Most of these literary gems didn't sell, but on occasion one of the cable networks would fork over a hundred thousand bones for a hoax-of-the-week screenplay. Camilla's family held the mistaken notion that this bizarre line of work kept the Zoog from getting into serious trouble. The simple truth was that Eddie was a maniac who had a genius for conjuring up trouble from a vacuum. And because his niece owned the EZ Literary Agency, Camilla had no choice but to look after her eccentric uncle. Sometimes, she went along on her uncle's "research" trips. "What's he up to this time?"

She shrugged as if it were nothing at all. "Uncle Eddie has heard about some kind of pelt in Tibet. From the Yeti. He wants to bring it back to the States. Get the skin examined for DNA."

"It'll be a big yak," Moon muttered.

"It's no laughing matter," she quipped.

He slid two platters into the cupboard. "Why don't you let Mr. Zoog do this trip on his own?"

"Poor Uncle has awful luck." She smiled wanly. "Without me along to take care of him, he'd get into some kind of awful trouble. Maybe put in jail. Or even killed. I just know he'd never come back."

Moon smiled. "All the more reason."

"Don't pretend to be mean." She fluttered big eyelashes at him. "I know you adore my uncle."

Moon realized that this was very nearly true. Eddie Zoog was an odious man. A liar. A cheat. A fraud. A lunatic. Selfish to the marrow. But he did have a certain childlike innocence, a faith that the world was filled with hidden wonders just waiting to be discovered. This facet of the rough-cut man was strangely appealing.

"Charlie?"

"Yeah?"

"Let's go for a long walk in the moonlight." She gazed out of the large window. "The lake is lovely tonight. So romantic."

Moon also looked. Through his eyes, the mountain lake had taken on the character of a dark pit. On the far side was the guest cabin. Where the FBI's witness was stashed. A good-looking young woman. Whose presence he would rather not have to explain to his sweetheart. He felt a chill. "Looks cold out there."

"All the better," she said, snuggling up to him. "I have my man to keep me warm."

"That gives me a notion."

"What?"

"You and me, sittin' in front of the fireplace."

She gave him a strange look. "Charlie—why don't you want to go for a walk?"

He limped to the couch. "Big quarter horse stepped on my foot last week." This was the truth, though the limp was feigned. "And he did it on purpose. Mean West Texas animal."

She cocked her pretty head suspiciously. "I didn't notice you walking funny before."

"It's like the rheumatiz. Kicks up around sundown." He sat down with a great sigh of relief and stretched out his right leg. "There—that's lots better."

Camilla put her hand on his shoulder. "Sorry about your injury. Guess you'll have to take it easy."

"Hey, it's only my foot." He pulled her onto his lap.

She rested her face on his neck. "So what do you have in mind?"

"Something will come to me."

Camilla kissed his ear.

Charlie Moon decided that he was about the happiest man in the hemisphere.

The telephone rang.

The young woman, who was conditioned to respond to such electronic summonses, stiffened. It rang again. "It's the telephone."

"I figured it was."

Another rude jangle.

"It's ringing," she said.

"It'll stop."

It did not.

Camilla jumped up and ran to snatch the instrument. "Hello?" She listened to a startled cowboy. "No, you do not have a wrong number—this is the ranch headquarters." She nodded as if the caller could see her. "Yes, Mr. Moon is right here. Who's calling?" She pointed the telephone at her sweetheart. "It's one of your employees." She put her hand over the mouthpiece and giggled. "Say's he's the Wyoming Kid."

What's Jerome Kydmann want? Moon nodded. "That's who he is."

"You're not serious; you actually call this cowboy 'the Kid'?"

"Of course not," Moon said earnestly. "We call him 'the Kyd.' "

She frowned. "That's what I said."

"You said Kid. But I said *Kyd.*"

"Charlie, you're not making any sense."

"Sorry. I was just Kyding."

"Well, give it up, silly. Now who is he, really—doesn't he have an ordinary name?"

"Not as far as I know. Around here, Wyoming Kyd's his handle. He wears silver Mexican spurs, packs a Colt forty-four with a dozen notches in the grip." Moon was warming to the tall tale. "There are nasty rumors," he added in a half whisper, "that the Kyd has killed eleven men and a moose. That could be why he don't use his real name—he's a wanted man."

"Seems you and the Kid are both wanted men."

"You wanting me?" he asked hopefully.

"You're wanted at the barn," she smirked.

Moon glared at the offending instrument of communication. "What's going on at the barn that the Wyoming Kyd can't handle?"

"Something about a horse kicking planks out of the wall." She gave him the telephone.

The policeman-turned-rancher got to his feet. He listened to an excited report of equine mayhem. "Okay. I'll be right down." He slammed the phone onto its base. "Shoot." *Might as well be hauling in drunks.*

"What?"

"I'm going to shoot that damn horse." *And that drugstore cowboy.
What do I pay these people for?* And then he remembered. *This particular
cowboy-in-training is paying me. Tuition.*

She was enjoying this. "Don't be such a grouch."

"Hey, that animal's stepped on me once too often." He gave her a
quick good-bye kiss. "See you in a few minutes." Little did he know.

As he stomped away, Camilla noticed something peculiar about her
sweetheart. Charlie Moon wasn't showing the least sign of a limp.
After the door slammed, the young woman—who was quite good with
numbers—started counting things. Two steaks in the skillet. Two enormous potatoes in the oven. Two plates on the table. However she
manipulated these ciphers, they did not add up to a tidy sum. *After I left
the foreman's house, Charlie could have gotten a call from the Bushmans.
He could have put an extra plate on the table. But there wasn't nearly
enough time to bake another potato. Or burn a second steak to a crisp.* And
there was another thing. *Why doesn't he want to go for a walk by the lake?*

Camilla went to stand by the south window. Arms folded, she stared
across the surface of the shimmering water. And saw a faint, soft glow
of light. The reflecting gleam in her eye glittered with the hard sheen
of an assassin's dagger. The point of radiance was originating on the
opposite side of the lake. Where the guest cabin was located. *Who is
Charlie hiding from me? And why?*

Big Trouble

Melina Castro was hunched up on the small cabin bed. She was cold.
Lonely. And angry that she'd made such a fool of herself with a man
who was maybe twice her age. She was also furious with Charlie Moon
for throwing her out of his kitchen before she'd had a bite of supper.
Which reminded her stomach that it was in urgent need of victuals. It
gurgled in protest.

In short, the graduate student was not having a pleasant evening.
But compared to what this night had yet in store, her current situation
was, as she would have said herself, "Like, you know, not really so completely horrible."

Nevertheless, Melina sat on the bed, hugging her knees under the quilt. Feeling extremely sorry for herself. Staying for a couple of weeks in a real mountain cabin had seemed like such a romantic notion. But she was a city girl. And the place was so unnaturally quiet that she was able to hear the slightest noises. The scurrying of a mouse. The slight moan of wind in the chimney. Other, more sinister sounds were generated in her mind. She closed her eyes to imagine a more perfect place. Like the pizza and music store in the Hollywood Mall. She pressed fingertips to her temples and fell into a shallow contemplation. *I am an intelligent adult.*

We must all have our illusions.

I am the captain of my ship. Master of my soul. I will not let this crap get to me. I am woman. I am powerful. I am . . .

At the heavy knock on the door, she screamed like a banshee who'd had a boil lanced with the business end of a bayonet.

After hyperventilating, sufficient oxygen rushed to Melina's brain to help her realize who the caller must be. The young woman felt horribly foolish. She jumped from the bed, clad only in a skimpy nightgown, and padded to the door, already calling out to the landlord. "Charlie! Oh, I'm so glad you're here—I just couldn't stand being alone in this place another minute." As she turned the knob, the graduate student turned to light conversation. "So did your girlfriend hit the road already?" She opened the door, and was met by a frigid draft. She believed it was mountain air, and was half right.

Melina switched off the overhead light and stuck her head outside. "Charlie—where are you?"

There was no response. And no one to be seen. Except for an undulating glow of moonshine off the lake, there was only darkness.

Her voice quavered like a plucked string. "Hey—who's out there?"

The answer was a heavy, ominous silence.

The young woman slammed the door. Her entire body was quaking. *Ohmigod—who knocked on the door?* She was absolutely certain it was not Charlie Moon. The tall Indian had a quirky sense of humor, but he was not the sort to play a cruel prank like this. Maybe it was an animal. Some kind of nocturnal woodpecker. Or a deer had banged his antlers against the door. Sure.

Melina jumped into bed, pulled the covers up to her chin. Closed her eyes tightly. Counted to one hundred. But her imagination conjured up incredible terrors. She heard ghastly sounds. Creaking. Squeaking. Like rusty hinges whining. Slow footsteps across the pine floor. A draft. As if someone had opened a door.

And then all was quiet.

Gradually, she calmed herself. Invented comforting explanations. *An old shack like this makes all kinds of noises.* She allowed herself a deep sigh. Began to relax.

Felt a draft across her face.

It's the wind coming down the chimney. That's all. Just the wind.

There was a squeaking of boards in the pine floor. Footsteps?

No. It's just my imagination.

The imaginary footsteps squeaked on another board. Then another. Each time, a bit nearer her bed.

Trembling, Melina pulled the covers over her face. She whispered to herself: "I am not a child. I am a full-grown, educated, modern woman. I have a brown belt. Know how to kill a man twice my size with a single, swift blow from the palm of my hand. Not that I've ever actually done it, but I know how. I am not afraid. I have the covers over my face because it is cold in this shack. Well, maybe I'm just a teensy-weensy bit unnerved. Which is perfectly normal after some moron knocks on the door and runs away to hide. Probably one of Charlie Moon's idiot cowboys out to have a look at the college girl bedding down in the log cabin. No. I'm not really afraid. And I will prove it." She pulled the quilt down. Slowly. So that only a single eye would be exposed. Then, her body taut as the gut on a lyre, she opened the eye.

And saw it, hovering above her. The hideous face.

Melina shrieked, cast the covers aside, and hit the floor flailing her arms. In her mind, she was fully prepared to kill a man twice her size with a single deadly blow.

But her legs were not of a mind to hang around and pick a fight. Her highly intelligent feet had hit the floor running. And they did not stop. Once outside the haunted cabin, her toes barely touched the ground. She unknowingly chased a startled jackrabbit for half a furlong, until the panicked creature made a swift turn toward a thick stand of willow at the lake's edge.

· · ·

Camilla Willow slowed the rental Ford to seventy miles per hour. Stopped grinding her perfect teeth. And began to think.

Maybe I'm acting crazy. Charlie Moon is the sweetest man I've ever known. And the most honest. He wouldn't hide a woman from me. And that kid in the cabin is half his age. No. There's got to be a sensible explanation.

She slowed to sixty.

Dammit, I can't leave like this, close a door on this part of my life forever. I've got to go back. Talk to Charlie. A solitary tear made its path down her cheek.

Camilla jammed her foot on the clutch, shifted to second, then to low, hit the brake, did a screaming U-turn on the two-lane blacktop. *Oh, Charlie, I'm so sorry I didn't trust you. But I'm coming back!*

Charlie Moon mounted the back porch, kicked excess manure off his Tony Lamas, pushed his way through the kitchen door. He pitched his old black Stetson onto the massive pine table. The Ute was musing about how good it was to have someone to come home to. How sensible it would be to make that situation permanent. *Maybe I should ask her before she goes off to the jungles with Uncle Zoog. Maybe she'll skip the trip. Stay here with me.* The boots still smelled of manure. He sat down at the kitchen table long enough to pull them off. *Maybe Sweet Thing is snuggled up on the big couch by the fireplace. Waiting for me to come and snuggle up with her.* He smiled. *I could do that.* Moon padded into the parlor. And looked vainly for his woman. Sweet Thing was not on the couch. Nor anywhere else in the vast room. But her suitcase wasn't there either, so she must have taken it upstairs. He yelled at the ceiling. "Hey, sweetheart—I'm back from the barn." *That was romantic enough to turn any girl's head.*

There was no response.

Where is that woman? The big house had a strange, empty quiet about it. He told himself everything was okay. *She must be in her bedroom with the door closed, putting her stuff away.* Camilla had lots of silky, lacy stuff. Silent in his socks, the tall Ute went up the staircase three steps at a time. *Maybe I'll sneak up behind her and grab her and . . .*

But Camilla wasn't in her bedroom. Or his. Or the bathroom. Or anywhere else upstairs. *Now that's peculiar.*

A small coldness had materialized in his belly. Moon went downstairs, looked out a window. The little piece of ice in his groin grew to the size of a grapefruit.

Her car was gone.

But there had to be a reasonable explanation. Sure. She'd gotten a telephone call—probably a family emergency. So she'd left in a hurry. There'd be a note. He searched the parlor. The kitchen. The rest of the large log house. There was no note.

The policeman-turned-rancher-turned-tribal investigator sat down heavily at the kitchen table. *What happened? Why did Camilla leave without a word of explanation? What would make her mad enough to . . .* And then he guessed what must have happened. *Damn. This is going to take some serious fence-mending.*

He considered the situation. *I'll give Camilla time enough to get back to California and cool down. Then I'll call her cell-phone number. If she'll listen, I'll explain about the FBI asking me to hide a witness who's seen a murderer. If she won't listen, I'll write her a letter. And send some flowers. Sure. Flowers are good. But right now, I'd better go check on that young woman at the cabin. She is my responsibility.*

Feeling twice his age, the weary rancher got up and slowly pulled on the boots. *They stink. Like my life.* And his timing also stank. Charlie Moon opened the kitchen door just as the terrified woman vaulted up the porch steps and launched herself at him with a keening wail.

He listened patiently to the young woman's babbling. "Could you explain what happened again?"

Between choking sobs, Melina muttered about ghostly knocks at the door and no one was there and I hid under the covers and then this horrible face was looking down and I screamed and closed my eyes and ran and bumped into a tree and fell down and got up and ran and ran and ran until I thought my lungs would just burst and then there I was right at your door and oh God I'm so glad to be here . . . Following this preamble there was more of the same.

"I see," Moon said. And he thought he did. Camilla—for whatever reason—had hiked over to the cabin. She'd knocked on the door, discovered the pretty young woman inside, and somehow managed to scare the FBI's star witness half to death. Maybe three quarters. And now his sweetheart—who had leaped to the wrong conclusion—was gone. If he knew his woman, she wouldn't be coming back. A mere phone call wouldn't do it. Nor a letter. Not even flowers. *I'm sunk unless I can get Stan Newman to tell Camilla what Melina Castro was doing here at the ranch. But even if Camilla buys that story, she couldn't help being suspicious of what might be going on between me and this kid.* Which was foolish, of course. And then he noticed that this shapely young woman was dressed in nothing whatever except a flimsy nightgown.

And she noticed that he noticed.

"Hmmm," he said.

"Yes?"

"I think I'd better do something about you."

She gave him a wary look. "What do you have in mind?" *Not that I'd mind.*

"I don't suppose, after your—uh—little scare over at the guest cabin, you'd consider spending the night there?" He gave her—strictly above the neck—a hopeful look.

She wanted to ask whether he had totally lost his mind, but abbreviated the query: "Are you, like—crazy?"

Under the circumstances, he was not offended. It was a fair question. *I have, for the sake of a few dollars from the FBI—which I will probably never collect—lost the love of my life.*

Unnerved by the Indian's dark silence, she made a sensible counterproposal. "I'll sleep here."

"No," he said.

"I'm not going back to that—that haunted shack across the lake." She resolutely folded her arms and jutted out her small chin. "Never. Not if you got on your knees and begged me. Not in a million years. Not for a gazillion dollars. Twenty wild horses couldn't drag me—"

"I get the drift that you'd prefer to sleep somewheres else."

She brightened. "Then I can stay here?"

"I don't think that's a good idea."

She wiped a strand of hair from her forehead. "What's the matter—you find me irresistible? Afraid you won't be able to keep your hands off me?"

He nodded sadly. "You are just about more than a man can stand."

She patted her hair. "I thought so. So you'll sleep upstairs. I'll curl up here on the couch." She proceeded to curl up.

"I'll call Pete Bushman."

She made a face. "Your ranch foreman—the smelly old man with the fuzzy beard who's always breaking wind and spitting tobacco juice?"

"Him and Dolly have a spare bedroom," Moon said wearily. "They'll put you up for the night."

She pouted. "Then what?"

"Tomorrow, when you're—uh—calmed down, we'll talk about it." *After I talk to the FBI about finding another place for you.*

"I am perfectly calm," she said through clenched teeth. *You hateful man.*

Moon made the call to his foreman. Explained that the girl was somewhat uncomfortable in the cabin. Could she stay with the Bushmans for just one night?

Bushman's gravelly voice challenged him. "Why don't you put her up?"

Moon responded that the answer to this was all too obvious.

Pete made it clear he didn't want none of them nutty college girls in his home. She was probably on drugs, pregnant from a Hell's Angel, had a half dozen venereal diseases, and voted the straight Democrat ticket.

Knowing the power of avarice, Charlie Moon offered his foreman halvers on the FBI per diem.

There was a greenish glint in the foreman's eye. "How much is that?"

Moon told him.

"Hmmm," Pete said. And reminded the boss—who needed no reminding—that these college kids could be a big pain in the ass.

Moon was desperate. He offered Bushman the whole payment. *After it's collected.*

"Well," Pete said with a wary glance at Dolly, "it'll be up to my wife. If she goes for it, I s'pose it's okay with me."

Thus encouraged, Moon asked to speak to Mrs. Bushman. Dolly, who knew nothing of the payment, said he could bring the young woman right over. She would put fresh sheets and pillowcases on the cot in the loft bedroom. And fluff up the goose-down mattress. "Why, it'll be just like having our own daughter at home again." Moon thanked her. Dolly was a saint.

Last Chance

The closer she got to the heart of the Columbine, the more ashamed Camilla felt. Her man was already forgiven. *Charlie Moon is the best man in the world. And I've behaved like a complete fool. Didn't even give him a chance to tell me why that girl was in the guest cabin. There could be a hundred good reasons. A thousand.* She tried to think of one good reason. Couldn't. But it did not matter.

As she neared the Bushmans' home, Camilla realized how embarrassing this was going to be when the sun came up. She cut her headlights and coasted by, hoping they would not hear her pass. *Maybe I shouldn't say anything to him about it. Charlie is so sweet and understanding. If I don't bring it up, we can just pretend nothing happened. And things will be like before . . .*

"Let's go," Moon said.

The young woman got up from the couch. "Ouch!" She danced around absurdly on one leg.

"What is it?"

"I must've hurt my foot when I was running in the dark." Melina sat down, cocked her knee, aimed the long limb at him. "Can you see what's wrong?"

There was nothing at all wrong with what he saw. This was a well-proportioned feminine leg, all the graceful curves in just the right places. He tried hard to concentrate on the blackened sole of her foot. "Looks like a cut. But not a bad one," he added quickly. "Dolly will see to it. So let's get going."

Brute. She stretched out a hand. "Well, I can't walk to the pickup by myself."

"What does that mean?"

"That you'll have to help me," she cooed.

"Well, then, let's do it." He helped her up. And to the door.

Once again, Charlie Moon's timing stank.

Camilla cut the ignition, allowed the sedan to coast the final few yards to the ranch headquarters. *I'll walk in as if nothing's happened. If he asks me where I've been, I'll say I had an errand to run. None of his business*

what for. If he offers any explanation about that child in the cabin, I'll listen. And believe whatever he tells me. And that will be the end of it.

She was about to get out of the car when the front door opened onto the porch. Light flooded out, casting the two mismatched figures in stark profile. She stared in stunned disbelief. Charlie Moon had his arm around the girl's shoulder. And the shapely young woman who leaned on him was practically *naked!* Camilla didn't will the words she heard coming out of her mouth. "Well, that tears it, buster."

Melina Castro put her arm around the tall man's waist and peered into the moonless night. "Did you hear something?"

"Yeah." *She came back. But now she's gone. For good.*

"It sounded kinda like a car," the young woman said.

Sounded like my life's blood draining away.

Melina looked up at her protector. "But if it was a car, why weren't there any headlights?"

Charlie Moon knew why. For a brief moment, darkness had overcome the Light.

CHAPTER 12

Yietso, the Giant, lived at *Tqo'sedo* . . . the Twins went there and waited for him . . . there was a great blinding flash of lightning and it struck the giant.

The Twins went to the Giant and cut off his scalp. They saw that he was covered with flint armor . . . clothing made of stone knives.

—Sandoval, Hastin Tlo'tsi hee

Dry Bones

The chairman of the Rocky Mountain Polytechnic Department of Anthropology and Archaeology was by nature a garrulous man who enjoyed the company of his students. Particularly those who proved their worshipful respect by hanging on his every word. But these youthful members of the site survey crew were full of energy and tended to keep chattering long after there was anything worthwhile to say. On occasion, Professor Silas Axton tired of his disciples and would withdraw to conduct some private business. This was one of those times when he preferred to be alone with his thoughts. Having left the gaggle of graduate students up on the Crag, the scholar was shuffling along the west rim of Ghost Wolf Mesa. The place had many things to recommend it. For one thing, there was a measure of shade from the late-afternoon sun. For another, it was an isolated spot where one could be quite alone. And this edge of the mesa was a rather pleasant place, quite unlike the vertical cliffs to the east and south. While there was a drop of two or three yards in places, the remainder of the slope fell away from the sandstone tabletop in a gradual fashion and was well forested with ponderosa pine and towering picture-book spruce. Silas Axton paused by a massive sandstone outcropping that hung over the slope's edge, cocking his ear to hear the happy warbling of a mountain bluebird. And heard something else. An odd, grunting sound.

Axton's back went rigid. He moved forward cautiously, taking care not to step on a twig. And looked over the edge of the outcropping.

Not twenty feet below him was a man. Axton squinted. It was Dr. Terry Perkins, the impertinent paleoastronomer. Perkins was squatting like an aborigine, messing about with an oblong pile of rocks. From all appearances, he was making a large pile of stones into a smaller one.

Professor Axton posed two questions for himself: *What in blazes is he up to?* and *What should I do about it?* Being a methodical man, he considered his various options for almost a minute. Then smiled. Properly managed, this unexpected encounter would be great fun. *Too bad I don't have a camera with me.* The professor silently cleared his throat, then bellowed: "Aha—you slippery rascal. I have caught you red-handed!"

Perkins's alarmed response was more than Axton had hoped for. The younger scholar yelped, attempted to turn and face his adversary, tripped over his feet—and fell flat on his handsome face.

Axton leaned forward, hands resting on his knees, and guffawed at the comical sight. "So. Now we know what our brash young physicist does when he cannot discover a Stone Age astronomical site—he goes and builds himself one!" He shook his finger at the fallen man. "Shame on you, Perkins."

The paleoastronomer got to his feet and began to dust pine needles from his chic canvas jacket. "Good morning, Silas." *You silly old shit.*

"Well, don't keep me in suspense," the anthropologist boomed, "I imagine you'll have a remarkably opaque explanation for what you're up to."

Terry Perkins, having managed to regain some measure of dignity, glared up at his tormentor. "Not that it is any of your business—but I can explain what I am doing."

"Don't tell me—let me guess," the anthropologist said with biting sarcasm. "You have discovered a prehistoric rock cairn used by those ancient astrologers you're so fond of. But alas, it was not in quite the right place to align with Venus rising or Saturn occulting or something-or-other. And not a fellow to be defeated by mere facts, you are now in the process of moving this heavenly marker to a more suitable location. Now tell me, Terry, am I right?"

"This is no time for frivolity." The paleoastronomer had assumed a sour expression.

Professor Axton, who had suffered much at the younger man's barbs, thought Perkins a poor sport. But having had almost enough fun, he made a mocking bow. "I do apologize for anything I have said that may have offended in the slightest. Now tell me—what is so interesting about yon pile of pebbles?"

Terry Perkins took a deep breath. "It would appear that something is buried beneath them."

"Absolutely astounding—you have found the fabled Anasazi treasure. Tell you what. I'll keep your dirty little secret. For a half share."

"Don't be an ass."

"Very well. I'll settle for twenty-five percent."

"There's nothing here you'd want to cart away."

"I cannot bear the suspense—what have you found?"

Perkins turned to stare at the assembly of stones. "Bones."

"Of what species?"

"Human, I should think. Though tibias and clavicles are not my specialty."

"Which is to say—you have no sense of humerus." Axton chuckled at his joke; this made his belly shake.

The paleoastronomer glared up at the older man.

"Forgive me," Axton apologized. "I have been in a whimsical mood all day. But I now repent." He put on an ugly scowl. "Look up *solemn* in the dictionary, and you will find my likeness there." He leaned to squint at the makeshift grave. "These are *prehistoric* human bones, I hope."

Perkins sniffed. "Judging from the odor of decaying flesh, I'd say not."

"In that case," the anthropologist said with a dismissive wave, "they hold not the slightest interest for me."

Durango, Colorado
Three Days Later

Special Agent George Whitmer's desk was littered with reports from the Bureau's D.C. forensics laboratory. The federal lawman addressed his words to his partner. "There were slight traces of aromatic hydro-carbons found in the burned remains of the Tavishuts woman's body. Says here"—he ran his blunt finger across the paper—" 'Consistent with petroleum-derivative fuels.' "

Newman banged his fist on the older man's desk. "Aha—I knew somebody torched the body with gasoline."

"Not necessarily," Whitmer said. "The forensics scientists say the trace hydrocarbons could be explained by the old tent Charlie Moon put over the corpse. It was probably soaked with emissions from camp-stove fuels. Anti-wetting agents in the fabric. That sort of thing."

"Damn. Why did Moon have to interfere with the crime scene."

"To protect the evidence from the rainstorm," Whitmer reminded his partner.

Stanley Newman leaned on Whitmer's government-issue desk. "So what else have we got to work with?"

George Whitmer squinted through bifocals perched near the tip of a bulbous nose. "ME's report confirms that the latest corpse Dr. Perkins discovered at the Chimney Rock Archaeological Site was the Ute rancher who was reported missing last April—Mr. Julius Santos."

Newman straightened himself, hung his thumbs under tight red sus-penders. "Santos. The guy who went horseback riding."

Whitmer nodded. "Horse came back. Mr. Santos didn't."

"And his remains show up on Ghost Wolf Mesa."

"Just over the edge of the mesa," Whitmer said.

Newman ignored the technical correction. "At a location not all that far from where the Tavishuts woman was murdered. And he disap-peared weeks before her death. George, something bothers me about this."

"Right. Like why didn't we find his body when we had a couple dozen cops on the mesa looking for evidence in the Tavishuts murder."

"Maybe because we were searching for footprints, a murder weapon—a live suspect. We weren't looking for another body. And you generally don't find what you aren't looking for. What bothers me more is how this smart-aleck college professor happens to find Santos's remains."

Whitmer leaned back, entwining sausagelike fingers behind his neck. "Dr. Perkins claims he was walking along the edge of the mesa, looking for evidence of prehistoric astronomical markers. Maybe another petroglyph nobody had noticed before. Maybe a boulder with a notch in it. He just happened to look over the edge—and spotted the pile of rocks."

"So being an inquisitive sort of fellow," Newman mumbled, "Dr. Perkins climbs down to have a closer look. Under the rocks, he spots something that looks like a piece of cloth. So he starts taking some stones away. And finds some bones. Then Professor Axton comes along."

There was an uneasy silence while the federal lawmen mulled the testimony over in their minds.

Whitmer spoke first. "You think this Perkins geek knows something he isn't telling us?"

"Maybe."

A primly dressed middle-aged woman knocked lightly on the facing of the open door.

Whitmer didn't look up. "Come in, Marty."

She placed a blue folder on his desk. "This just arrived." The secretary left silently.

The older of the special agents thumbed through the report, then whistled.

Newman found this behavior mildly annoying. "Okay, George, what is it?"

Whitmer didn't offer his partner the document. "Another forensics report from D.C." He looked up over his spectacles. "Remember that fingerprint our tech found on that flake of obsidian at the murder scene?"

"Of course not. I've completely forgotten about the single piece of hard evidence in the hottest reservation murder we've had in twenty years."

"And the dead girl's stepfather—Alvah Yazzi—remember the burned powder and stuff we found in that old Navajo guy's empty clothes?"

"Come on, George, give."

Whitmer managed to look quite smug, as if he'd done the laboratory analysis himself. "Forensics has come up with a match for the print. And they've got some really interesting things to tell us about the ashes and bone chips in Yazzi's duds."

"So tell me."

"If I told you, Stan, you wouldn't believe a word I said." Whitmer offered his partner the forensics report. "So you'd better read it yourself."

Newman scanned the document. Then read it more carefully. "George, this is really weird. We'll have to rethink this case. Right from page one."

The older agent nodded. "Charlie Moon has our witness stashed up there on his ranch. We'd better check on the both of 'em."

Newman, who had the Columbine number memorized, punched it into his cell phone. There were four rings before he heard the Ute's recorded voice. "Damn. I'm getting his answering machine."

"I imagine Charlie's out on the range somewhere." Whitmer said this with a wistful look. "I bet he's doin' some neat cowboy stuff."

"Sure," the Easterner muttered. "He's probably down at the old corral, punchin' a cow." He heard the end of Moon's recorded message, and a beep. "Charlie—this is Stan Newman. There's some important new developments in the Tavishuts homicide. Soon as you hear this, call me at the Durango office—or buzz me on my cell phone." He pressed the Off button. "We'd better head up to Charlie's ranch."

Whitmer was already pulling on his jacket. "I bet him and that student are sitting out yonder by a campfire somewhere. Singing somma them sad old cowboy songs."

Newman snickered.

Whitmer raised an eyebrow at his contemptuous partner. "I bet you couldn't name one cowboy song if your life depended on it."

"I could name a couple of 'em—just in case your life was in danger too." Newman checked the clip in his 9mm automatic. " 'Bumbling Tumbleweeds.' 'Low Riders in the Sky.' "

The older man sighed. "I think we'd best be careful out there."

The Badger Hole

It was a dark purpose that drew Daisy Perika on her trek into the Canyon of the Spirits. The Ute shaman—despite stern warnings from her Catholic priest—was seeking an audience with the *pitukupf*. Despite the scoffings and snickerings of younger members of the Southern Ute tribe, Daisy knew that the dwarf was quite real. For as long as she could remember—and probably for hundreds of years before she was born—the little man had lived in a badger hole in the Canyon of the Spirits. No one knew for sure when he had first attached himself to the People. But the *pitukupf* was a source of considerable power to the shaman. And almost as important, the dwarf was a source of information. Nothing went on among the People that he did not know about. Daisy—who was full of years—had enjoyed a long and profitable acquaintance with the peculiar little fellow. There were protocols to be followed, of course. You did not visit his home without a gift. Today, she had brought a bag of pipe tobacco, two candy bars, and a roll of green cotton cloth that he might use for making himself a new shirt. She had even added a half spool of brown thread, a fine steel needle, and a plastic thimble. If you wanted to get serious help from the dwarf, you could not skimp.

On the way into *Cañon del Espíritu*, the elderly woman had stopped several times to rest. Now at her destination, Daisy leaned on her stout oak staff, breathed hard. She wiped sweat from a dark, furrowed brow, then looked up at the sandstone walls towering three hundred feet. It would be pleasantly warm up there on the top of Three Sisters Mesa. But here in the cradle of the canyon, under soft covers knit from shadows, the remnant of winter slept. Dreaming frigid dreams of next October. Icy winds. Heaping drifts of snow.

Grunting at the painful stiffness in the small of her back, Daisy half-leaned and half-squatted to drop the gifts into the entrance to the *pitukupf*'s cavern. The well-meant offering was swallowed up, sinking down the earthen throat into the dark innards of the dwarf's underground domicile.

Hoping the cranky little man would be pleased, Daisy shuffled away to the company of a fragrant juniper. She seated herself on a flat outcropping of gray limestone left behind by an ancient sea. The weary woman leaned against the trunk of the twisted tree and closed her eyes, unaware of a bluefly that buzzed busily around her forehead. Within moments, her breathing was even. Quite soon after this she fell into a deep, restful sleep. And the shaman did dream.

Floating in front of her, Daisy saw the kindly face of Father Raes Delfino. The little Jesuit's features were sorrowful to know that this troublesome member of his flock was straying once more. "Daisy, Daisy . . . what am I to do with you? I have warned you, so many times—it is dangerous to commune with the pitukupf. He is not of our Lord's kingdom."

"I wasn't actually communing," the dreamer protested. "I just brought him some things to eat. Pipe tobacco. And cloth for a new shirt."

"Ahh," the priest said with a wry smile, "and you did this with not the least thought of receiving anything in return from the dwarf-spirit?"

"That's just the way it was," the shaman said earnestly. "It was Christian charity that made me want to help that poor little fellow."

There was a loud noise, like the sound of a branch snapping. The image of the priest vaporized. Daisy Perika opened her eyes. The shaman was not—as she had expected—in the eternal twilight of the dwarf's underground cavern. She was sitting on the limestone shelf, under the juniper. It seemed that she had slept for some time. The shadow of the tree reached almost to the canyon wall; the evening sky had the mottled gray texture of sour milk. She was disappointed by her failure to communicate with the little man. But it was getting late in the day— no time to linger in this place where the spirits of the dead walked. With the intention of getting to her feet, Daisy reached for her walking stick.

And then she saw him.

The *pitukupf* was seated on a piñon stump not two yards away. As was his way, he pretended not to notice the presence of his visitor. Having impaled the discarded wrapper on a cluster of yucca spears, he was munching on a candy bar.

"Nasty little litterbug," she muttered.

And so they sat opposite each other. Time, gauged only by the rhythm of Daisy's heartbeat, passed slowly.

Finally, she spoke. "I hope you like the stuff I brought you."

The *pitukupf*, having consumed the candy bar, scratched his belly. And belched loudly.

Being a civilized woman, she found this behavior offensive. But being sensible, she understood that though the *pitukupf* was extraordinarily powerful, immeasurably old, and extremely peculiar, he was also a helpless product of his gender—a little man much like other men. And so Daisy wisely decided to accept this small vulgarity as an expression of appreciation. Or at least an acknowledgment of her gift. She resumed her monologue. "Nice weather, we're having. For this time of year."

He grunted.

So she got right to the point. "You may not know that April Tavishuts was killed over at those Chimney Rock ruins." She had no doubt that he knew. But he was a taciturn little fellow. And one way to get him talking was to suggest that there might be something of importance to the People that he did *not* know. This ploy never failed to tweak his vanity.

He took a deep breath, puffing up his chest.

"Nobody knows who killed poor April," Daisy said.

Using an archaic version of the Ute tongue that even the Ute elder could barely follow, he told her that *who* had done the killing was unimportant. *Why* it had been done was what mattered.

Daisy did not agree, but she kept her lips pressed together.

The dwarf told his visitor why two terrible crimes had been committed. Why a horseman had died at Chimney Rock. Why April Tavishuts had met her terrible end. The cause he described was a tale about a single creature. An old man. A gray wolf.

The shaman listened intently.

His story completed, the *pitukupf* pointed a crooked finger at the earth.

The shaman looked at her feet, and saw viscous steams of blood flowing by. At a great distance, she heard anguished cries from those whose throats had been slit. She began to tremble.

The little man pointed at the sky.

Almost against her will, Daisy Perika looked up.

Great drops of rain—the size of a man's fist—were falling.

She asked what this could mean.

The dwarf told her.

Daisy was greatly relieved to hear that these were White Shell Woman's tears—shed for the sacrificial victims of the Anasazi priests. But even as the Ute elder watched, each of the precious drops of fluid was transformed into a fiery coal of blue-white fire.

As the flaming cinders fell to earth, the shaman saw more. Much more.

Columbine Ranch, the Foreman's House

Dolly Bushman was a kindhearted woman, slow to anger. And not given to complaining. But her man was getting on her nerves. She let her knitting drop into her lap. "Peter."

Pete Bushman did not hear her. He was engrossed in his noisy work with the number two bastard file.

"PETER!"

The Columbine foreman glanced up from the crosscut saw, which he had been sharpening tooth by tooth. "Eh?"

"Go do that somewhere else."

He feigned an innocent expression, which was hidden under the bushy beard. "What's the matter?"

"That awful noise is driving me to *distraction*."

"Where'n hell's that," he drawled. "Somewheres down south of Grouchyville?"

"If you don't stop," she said with a menacing gesture of the knitting needle, "I'll push this thing in one of your ears and pull it out of the other. Without hitting anything in between."

He was trying to think of a snappy response when the telephone rang. Pete Bushman bunched his bushy eyebrows at Mr. Bell's invention.

"You get it," Dolly said, clicking her needles.

"Why?"

"I got it last time it rang."

"But that was on Tuesday."

"PETER!"

"Okay." He got up, grumbling under his breath about how Dolly had turned out to be just like her cranky old mother who had driven her husband to drink. Which made him think about a small taste of black-berry wine. He pressed the black plastic device to a hairy ear. "Yeah?" A pause. "Oh. It's you."

Dolly wondered who might be calling. She realized from his tone that it was someone her husband didn't like. Which did nothing what-ever to narrow things down.

He scowled. "No, I don't know where he is."

There was a lengthy silence as Pete Bushman listened, occasionally interrupting as he tried to slip a word in.

"Well, when he gets back I'll—"

"Lissen, there's no need to—"

"He don't generally tell me where he's headed and I don't—"

He gave the instrument a pop-eyed look, slammed it onto the cradle. Dolly looked up from her knitting. "Who was it?"

The Columbine foreman took his seat before the fireplace. He stared at the crosscut saw as if wondering what on earth it was.

"Pete, who was on the phone?"

He snorted. "That nasty old woman."

Dolly sighed. "Does she have a name?"

"There's a few I could give her."

"All right—*don't* tell me."

"It was the boss's Injun auntie. You know the one—Dizzy Pear-Creek."

"Daisy Perika," Dolly said. "What did she want?"

The old cowman waved his thin arm dismissively. "Some foolishness about the boss. Said she'd called the big house, got his machine. Wanted to know where he was and right now. I told her I didn't have no idea. Then she commenced to yellin' at me—like I was some kinda sorry-assed nincompoop."

"I know where Charlie is." Dolly made this announcement with a superior air. "He stopped by on his way out. It was right before lunch. I fixed him a cheese sandwich."

Bushman shot a yellow-eyed look at his wife. "It's a wonder he didn't stay and eat us out of house and vittles. That's the hungriest redskin I ever saw."

"Charlie's a nice man." The needles clicked rhythmically as she worked. "I wonder why Mrs. Perika was so upset."

Bushman chuckled. "Because she's an old fool. You know what she told me to tell him when he showed up?"

"Now how in the world would I know?"

"I'm to tell the boss not to go nowheres near that place where that Injun girl was murdered."

The needles stopped clicking. "Those old ruins at Chimney Rock?"

He nodded. "Charlie Moon's auntie says if he does, he'll die sure as possums eat grapes."

Dolly set her knitting aside. "Pete."

"What is it now?"

"That's where Charlie told me he was headed. Chimney Rock."

The ranch foreman did not like to hear bad news. He pulled a tobacco-stained mustache. "You sure that's what he said?"

She was already pulling her coat on. "Get the pickup started right now, so it can warm up."

"Now, Dolly, you lissen to me—that's over a hunnerd miles and Charlie's got a good four-hour head start. Hell, he's prob'ly already on his way back here by now." He took a deep breath. "And besides that, all we got to go on is a crazy old woman's—"

She gave her husband a withering look. "Peter Bushman, are you so bone lazy that I have to go by myself?"

CHAPTER 13

The Elder Brother threw the being down over the cliff where his own children were waiting. There was a great shouting below. Someone said, "Mine is the head." Another said: "Mine is the heart." And so on, for they wanted different parts of the body. But when the body reached the ground they all stepped back. "This is the body of our father!" they cried. But the mother told them to go ahead and eat.
—Sandoval, Hastin Tlo'tsi hee

Followed

As if protesting this brutal exposure to abrasive asphalt, the thinning tire-skin whined in painful complaint. Charlie Moon was unaware of the rubbery objection originating beneath his aging Ford pickup. His attention was focused upon something more important. Something his aunt Daisy would have understood. Something that embarrassed him. A bad feeling.

It started in his socks. A dull tingling at the tips of his toes. Crawled up shin and thigh to drop a sour nugget in his gut. And moving still upward, the writhing thing ignited a warm prickling in his spine, a warning tickling in his brain. There was this whisper: *Somebody's back there. Behind you.*

He glanced at the cracked rearview mirror, and saw no automobile headlights. No airborne hag straddling a broomstick. Nothing. And so he responded to the voice: *There's nobody back there.*

He was mistaken.

Now it seemed as if the *follower* spoke to him. *You can't see me—but I'm here. And when I'm ready* . . .

Being a rational man, Charlie Moon understood that no one had spoken to him. With a tooth-grinding set of his jaw, the Ute forced himself to ignore the dark messages.

He slowed to turn at the entrance to Chimney Rock Archaeological Site. Rather than let the engine idle as he got out to unlock the gate, Moon killed the ignition. He told himself this decision had nothing whatever to do with the sense that he was being followed . . . and wanted perfect quiet, so he could listen for any sound of his imaginary pursuer. He buttoned his jacket against the chill and stood still as a post. He heard nothing except the passing growl of a big Durango-bound semi a few miles to the north on Route 160. Within moments even this was gone. Now there was nothing whatever to hear. Aside from the sudden *whuff-whuff* of an owl's wings as the goggle-eyed night hunter passed close overhead. Looking for the unwary rabbit—or something else?

The Ute looked up at the shadowy form. *Don't call my name tonight* . . .

The owl went about its nocturnal business. Whatever that was.

The tribal investigator opened the gate, eased the creaking pickup through the site entrance, then got out to slam the heavy bar against the post. He dropped the steel locking pin, snapped the padlock shut. And felt some small satisfaction. *If someone is tailing me—he'll have to get through that.*

Wrong again.

The drive up the winding gravel road to the mesa top took less than ten minutes. Only one camper was in the parking area. There was a feeble yellowish glow in the window of Amanda Silk's small trailer. *Probably shouldn't bother her.* But he was unaccountably lonely. *Maybe she'd like some company.* After a moment's hesitation, he knocked on the door.

The yellow light dimmed. "Who is it?" she barked.

"Charlie Moon."

Curtains parted in the small window; the fuzzy outline of a face appeared as if an Impressionist portrait had miraculously manifested itself on the glass. The painting stared at him for a long moment. Then vanished. The light in the camper increased. A latch snapped, the aluminum door opened with a sly creak. And there she was, bathed in the light of a Coleman lantern. Long locks of stringy hair draped onto her thin shoulders. A tattered red terry-cloth robe was wrapped snugly around her frame. Amanda's feet, shod in green gum boots, protruded comically from under the warm garment.

Moon tried not to smile. He was almost successful.

She smiled back at him. "Well, I may not look like a movie star, but I stay warm."

He shifted his weight from one leg to the other. "I was just passing. Thought I'd stop and say hello."

"Come in." She pulled on a belt to cinch the heavy robe tightly around her long waist. "And close the door behind you."

As on his first visit, the small trailer lurched and creaked as he stepped inside. He shut the flimsy door gently.

Amanda hung the light on a hook that was screwed into the varnished plywood ceiling. The lantern swung in pendulum fashion. "How've you been?" she asked.

"Good enough," he said.

"Sit down," she pleaded, "before you poke your head through my roof."

The tall Ute eased himself into a chair across from his host. The cluttered table provided a surface for simple meals and reading old books and recording the results of work well done. He wondered how the scientist could manage to read or write in the dim glow of lantern light.

As if she had read his mind she said: "I've got twelve-volt electric lights. I use the Coleman to conserve my storage battery."

It was not hard to tell what she had been doing when he arrived. There was a half cup of black coffee, the remains of a cheese sandwich on a plastic picnic plate.

"You want something to eat?"

"No thanks." He sniffed, eyed a cup on the table. "Coffee smells good, though."

She poured her guest a cup, and pushed the fat plastic hippopotamus across the table.

He twisted the hippo's head, helped himself to several spoons of sugar. After the sweetener was stirred into the coffee, he had a taste. *Strong enough to get up and walk.*

Amanda Silk seated herself and began to squint at an open ledger. It was bright blue, and appeared to be quite new. "I suppose you've heard about the Ute man's body that Professor Perkins found on the site. A Mr. Santos."

Moon nodded. "I've heard."

She rubbed her pale hands together. "This is getting to be a creepy place. I can't wait to see the last of it."

"I'm kinda surprised you're still here."

"My work at Chimney Rock is important. But I'll be done in a few days." Taking up her fountain pen, the archaeologist proceeded to scratch meticulous entries onto the lined page. She would occasionally pause to sip at the tepid black coffee, or take a small bite from the stale sandwich. Crumbs fell onto the lapel of her robe.

The Ute was comfortable with the silence.

In the darkness, there was a sudden stirring. Without disturbing the brooding silence, a shadowy figure moved through the night. And like a great black moth, was drawn to that solitary pinprick of light on Ghost Wolf Mesa.

When her sandwich was finally consumed, Amanda Silk swallowed the last gulp of black liquid from the stained china cup. She looked across the table at her guest. "So. What brings you to the mesa?"

Moon leaned back in the chair. "Still haven't worked out what happened to April Tavishuts. Thought maybe if I came up here again— walked around some . . ."

She nodded. "I know what you mean. You want to get in touch with the atmosphere."

Atmosphere? "Yeah. Something like that."

The shadowy appearance moved across the parking lot on four legs. At the source of the light, it stood on two.

• • •

Resting her elbows on the table, the archaeologist leaned forward. The muscles under her cheeks went taut, pulling a thin smile across pearly-white teeth. "You've got some trouble boiling in your brain. I can see it bubbling there behind your eyes."

Moon—who valued his privacy—half-closed his eyelids. "There's always trouble someplace." Amanda Silk was not an easy woman to trade stares with. The Ute looked over her head at a row of books on a small shelf. A tattered dictionary. *Hiker's Guide to Copper Canyon*. Several novels. He was interrupted by a gasp. There was a startled look in the woman's eyes. She was staring over his shoulder—at the window, where she'd pulled the curtains back. Moon turned to look, and saw nothing but a velvety-black portrait of night. "What is it?"

Amanda Silk hurried past him, yanking the tiny cotton curtains across the pane. Her hands trembled. "Somebody was out there—looking in at us!" She shuddered. "It was a scary face. All wild-eyed—and ugly as original sin."

With a suddenness that raised him from his chair, the Ute recalled his sense of being followed to the mesa. If a man was interested in staying alive, he learned to pay attention to his hunches. And to ugly faces women saw in darkened windows. The trailer creaked and swayed as he took a single step to the door. As he stepped outside, the heavy revolver was ready in his hand. The small parking lot was washed in bright moonlight. Charlie Moon waited for his pupils to dilate.

Aside from a fat raccoon scampering along a path among the ruins, there was no sign of life. Apart from the whisper of a breeze in the piñons, not the slightest sound. Moon holstered the sidearm.

Amanda moved outside cautiously, looking around with large eyes. Satisfied that there was no immediate danger, the woman tugged urgently at Moon's coat sleeve. "Did you see anything?"

He shook his head.

The archaeologist sucked in a deep breath, then exhaled. "I absolutely did see a face in the window—it was not my imagination."

"I believe you."

She cocked her head like an inquisitive spaniel. "You *know* something about what's been going on up here, don't you?"

The Ute didn't respond.

"Tell me about it."

Moon felt the breeze touch his face. "I think April drove up here that evening, stopped her car, went to have a look at the pit-house ruin. Somebody was already here—digging. But I don't think it was a pothunter."

It was hard, staring at this shadowy man. She looked away. "Do you know who it was?"

"I have some notions."

Amanda Silk pushed her hands deep into the pockets of her robe. "So what do you intend to do?"

Moon stared into the deepening purple twilight. On the Crag, smoky blue mists swirled over the temple ruins. Only a few steps away, a congregation of piñons stood like giant black mushrooms. They leaned slightly toward the Ute investigator, as if eagerly awaiting his reply to the archaeologist's question. "Think I'll go have a look at that pit house. The one where April's body was found."

Amanda shuddered. "Why on earth would you want to go to that awful place?"

He shrugged. "Maybe it'll help me think of something."

She held her breath for a few heartbeats. "Then I'll go with you."

"I don't think that'd be a good idea—"

"Well, I'm certainly not going to sit here in my trailer while some ugly-faced Peeping Tom is roaming around. Wait here while I get some proper clothes on."

Before Moon had an opportunity to press his objections, Amanda Silk was already inside her camper, slamming the aluminum door. While he waited, the Ute felt eyes staring holes in his back. He assured himself that this was a product of his imagination. Must be something about this place at night—made a man feel like a malevolent *something* was out there. Waiting for a chance to pounce. But that was foolishness.

Despite the beams of creamy moonlight, their path was patched here and there by the blackest of shadows. The archaeologist—her thin frame now swallowed in a bulky canvas coat that hung to her ankles—stayed close by the Ute's side.

Moon found a small flashlight in his jacket pocket; he pressed the switch and swept the beam along the path.

"No," she rasped, "turn it off. If there's somebody out there, it'll make us just that much easier to follow."

To allay her fears, he pocketed the flashlight.

And on they went, wending their way among piñon, juniper, bristly clumps of yucca spears.

Amanda glanced uncertainly over her shoulder. *I do! I feel somebody back there in the darkness, watching us.* But she said nothing more to her companion about this uneasiness. *Charlie Moon would just think I'm a silly woman. But ever since I saw that ugly face in the window, I've been in a terrible nervous state. What I need is a good night's rest.* And so she trudged on. But this morbid conviction would not depart from her: *I will not live to see the sun come up.*

A few yards behind them, a pair of eyes watched. There was a low, menacing growl.

In the patchwork of ivory moonlight and ebony shadows, the remains of the thousand-year-old pit house took on the character of a macabre mirage. Least real of all was the rectangular trench in the center of the crumbling ruin. Moon asked the archaeologist to stay put. The Ute investigator approached the rectangular trench where April's corpse had been found. In the moonlight, the pit looked wider. And much longer. He squatted, looked in. There was nothing to see but blackness. *Might be a yard deep. Or a bottomless pit.*

Amanda Silk stood close behind the Ute policeman, her cold hands jammed deep into the ample pockets of the long overcoat. By sheer force of will, she had managed to put away the nagging sense that— from somewhere in the inky darkness—a pair of brutish eyes stared at her. "It's all nonsense," she whispered. "There's nothing out there. I'm just being silly . . . like Chicken Little."

Charlie Moon heard these mumblings. He was turning his head. "What did you say—"

The sky fell on him.

• • •

The Ute investigator regained a small portion of his consciousness. He found himself in a strange, cramped bed. Underneath was a mattress of cold, hard soil. Heavy stones for a cover. A pungent scent of pine needles.

His head seemed clamped in an iron vise. Someone was turning the screw.

The least effort required an enormous expenditure of will and energy. He managed to open his eyes. There—just above him—sailing across velvet waves of a diamond-speckled sea was White Shell Woman, coolly aloof from the troubles of this world.

What's that? Something was hovering over him. He blinked, hoping to wash the specter away.

It remained—a dark, amorphous shadow between his grave and the starry sky. In the center of this singular darkness, a Cyclops eye appeared . . . flickering with fire.

The Ute tried to move. Could not. *It's over.*

The shadowy thing leaned toward him. The fluttering flame grew larger. Then, almost simultaneously, a guttural growl, a snapping of teeth—a gut-ripping shriek.

God Almighty. Charlie Moon closed his eyes. *Let it come.*

It came.

The Journey

The world was rapidly passing away—to become the fading memory of a receding dream.

Now, he was enveloped by a cool, painless . . . nothingness.

The thing was finished.

Charlie Moon felt his soul slip from his body. As the spark lifts in the warm currents above waning campfire embers, so did his spirit rise from the dark, dank pit-house grave. He was as a fluff of eagle feather, carried aloft on the soft evening breeze.

But he did not soar far above the sandstone forms of the Twin War Gods—or near those fiery remnants of exploded stars whence his very atoms had been assembled. Neither did he pass through myriad dancing, swirling galaxies, nor was he whisked through ephemeral worlds of curved space, twisted time, and manyfold dimensions. He was not destined to enter a parallel universe, if such strange places there be. He was infinitely beyond such inconsequential things.

The Ute found himself in a misty twilight country, tucked between a cleft of hills. There were no horizons here. The sky—if there was a sky—was a swirl of colorless mists. He heard no hum of insect, no call from bird in flight. Stunted tree, mottled sky, flinty earth—parched grass—all was gray. He found a little-used path and made his way along it. Searching. If there were days or hours in this place, he could not find them. And so he walked. And walked.

Precisely where it was supposed to end, the path terminated—at a railroad track. He kneeled to touch the rail. The steel was rusty from disuse.

What do I do now?

A shelf of speckled granite jutted from the hillside. He sat on it.

A damp breeze swept over this netherworld. The sky was cleared of mists. And then the first touch of color—an enormous tangerine moon rose slowly, majestically, over the hills. He watched. And waited.

Faraway up the tracks, a shrill steam whistle rose above the rhythmic clickety-clack of iron wheels on steel rails.

Moon got up to watch it come—rounding a hillside, bathed in amber moonlight. A hulking great engine trailing a plume of black smoke and sixteen cobalt-blue coaches. Ninety miles an hour and not slowing. *It's going to pass me by.*

But great wheels—spitting red sparks—braked screechingly on the rusted rails.

Cinders and ash sprinkled from the smokestack. A uniformed conductor opened a creaky coach door. The railroad official's blue uniform was freshly laundered and ironed, his polished shoes glistened with moonlight. A billed cap decorated with gold braid perched on his head. The bewhiskered man gestured anxiously at the prospective passenger. "Don't just stand there—get onboard!"

The Ute gratefully accepted this gruff invitation.

"Seat yourself," the conductor instructed, "I'll be back in a couple of shakes." The uniformed man hurried away, glancing at an enormous pocket watch, muttering about timetables and schedules, how railroading was not one whit of what it used to be when he worked the L&N.

The coach, like the conductor, was from an earlier time. Large rectangular windows were curtained in red velvet. The seats were upholstered in rich brown leather, polished from use, cracked with age. There was only one other passenger. The elderly man seated just across the aisle was outfitted in worn cowboy boots, a brown raincoat, and a slouch felt hat with a small blue feather stuck behind the band. Braids of snow-white hair sprouted from under the brim of the hat, spilling over the man's shoulders like twin waterfalls. Moon's fellow passenger looked oddly foreign. And yet familiar.

Charlie Moon hesitated, then leaned toward the aisle. "Nahum Yaciiti—is that you?"

A brief smile played at the corners of the Ute elder's mouth; he glanced at the new arrival. "It's me all right."

The old shepherd had disappeared years ago when a tornado touched down at his place on the banks of the Animas. Most of his small flock had perished. And though his body was never found, Moon had always supposed that Nahum's corpse had been washed down the river, buried in a sandbar. A pious (but highly imaginative) Hispanic neighbor swore that she had seen his body spirited away by a band of angels. Some of the People believed this might be so—the man was known to be a Saint of God. The more sensible members of the tribe speculated that Nahum's body had been taken away by his relatives for a traditional burial in the badlands east of Bondad. Any way you sliced the pie, this old man was supposed to be dead. *And so am I. Or maybe this is a dream. But everything seems . . . solid. Real.*

The elder drummed his fingers on the varnished maple armrest. "Something on your mind, Charlie?"

"Nahum, I don't know where I am. Or what's happening."

"You're on the train. Headed for a destination."

"Where . . ." He wasn't sure he wanted to know.

In any case, his inquiry was interrupted by the conductor's sudden appearance from the rear coach. He offered Charlie Moon a broad, friendly smile. And an open palm. "Ticket please."

Moon searched his pockets. "I don't seem to have one."

The conductor's smile was replaced by a melancholy expression. "Sorry, sir. You got to have a ticket to ride the Blue Train."

"Well, I'd be glad to buy one, but I don't seem to have any money on me . . ."

"It's all right," Nahum said. He showed the conductor a sizable red rectangle. "Charlie's ticket is prepaid."

The conductor's smile was born anew. "Well, now—that *is* good news." He reached for the ticket.

Nahum withdrew the crimson rectangle. "I'll be holding it for him."

"Oh—I see." The conductor made a deferential nod to the shepherd, then turned to Moon. "Have a good journey, sir." He pulled the watch from his pocket, flicked open the golden cover. "We'll be pulling into the City at first light."

After the conductor had passed into a forward coach, Moon offered his companion a curious look. "Nahum, what're you doing here?"

The Ute elder turned away, peering out the window as if he could see all manner of fascinating things in the gathering darkness. "It's unusual for one of our people to take the train. Most of 'em come by horse. Or they walk, or follow the white buffalo—or they just—" He chuckled at some private joke. "But you always were different." He turned to smile across the aisle at the younger man. And answer his question. "I'm here to meet you."

"I'm glad to see you." Moon was hesitant to ask the cardinal question. "But what am *I* doing here?"

Nahum's eyes widened in mock astonishment. "You don't know?"

Moon studied his hands, flexed his fingers. Nothing ghostly about them—they looked like genuine flesh and bone. "Guess maybe I do know." *Just don't want to say it out loud.*

"Well?"

"Last thing I remember, I couldn't move. And somebody was standing over me. There was this little flame . . ." The next words were hard to get past his lips. "So I figure I'm . . . dead." *There—that wasn't so hard to say.* Moon frowned. "But I don't *feel* dead."

Nahum considered this. "Neither do I." There was a lengthy silence before the Ute elder spoke. "We need to talk about some things." And so the old man talked.

The young man listened.

Nahum Yaciiti told Charlie Moon about new things. For the former things were passed away.

CHAPTER 14

The Twins said: "We have killed the Giant, Yietso."
First Man said: "No one can kill the Giant."
—Sandoval, Hastin Tlo'tsi hee

The Jasmine Room

The founder of the clan had been the principle citizen of Granite Creek. Great-Grandpa Snyder had made his stake in those boisterous days when silver was king and ten thousand rowdy miners squandered their wages in two dozen saloons and twice as many brothels. After the precious metal was drained from the mountain's veins—and the miners had departed to chase after other avaricious dreams—the Snyders remained. The family mansion, situated on the creek among a grove of cottonwoods, was home to a family comprised of assorted scoundrels, wastrels, lunatics, soldiers, politicians, scholars—even the occasional saint. There had been memorable parties in the palatial home, with orchestras and operas imported from St. Louis, New York, and Vienna. It had been a wild, sordid, violent, romantic era. But that was quite another time. Alas, all the eccentric characters of the Snyder clan are long since departed to their respective rewards. Nothing remains of them but photographs of solemn Victorian faces hung in heavy frames along the dim hallways. The gay character of their mansion is also a ghostly memory. The business conducted on the premises nowadays is of a decidedly serious nature.

FBI Special Agent Stanley Newman entered the vast lobby that had once been a magnificent parlor. The gathering place held the largest crowd it had seen in more than a century. Several dozen members of the Southern Ute nation were under the domed ceiling. A congregation of elders was seated on rare and costly antique couches and chairs; a few were leaning slightly forward, as if ready to bolt should the owner of this uncomfortable furniture confront them. Younger Utes milled about, muttering among themselves in low voices. All now claimed some sort of kinship or friendship with Charlie Moon, though some of those present had been arrested by the former tribal policeman. Whether dealing with foul-mouthed drunk or tribal chairman, wife-beater or wide-eyed child, Moon had always been a fair man.

The middle-aged woman behind the cherry desk wore a pinstriped suit and an expression of quiet superiority. The federal policeman flashed his ID. Unimpressed by this display of credentials, she peered through tiny rimless spectacles at the man in the suit. "Yes?"

Newman pocketed his ID. "I'm here to see Charlie Moon."

Her thin lips curled in a perfunctory smile. "I should imagine so." By way of explanation, she added: "Mr. Moon is, at the moment, our only . . . client." The management—which considered itself quite progressive—enforced a strict policy. All employees wore conservative suits. Those who were serviced on the premises were referred to as "clients." The facilities had been carefully remodeled to disguise the actual business conducted. The receptionist pointed a manicured finger to indicate the south wing. "You will find Mr. Moon in the Jasmine Room." Under the former management, the rooms had been identified with mere numbers. Now they were Jasmine, Whippoorwill, Lupine, Shady Brook . . .

Stanley Newman thought about knocking. But that was hardly necessary. He reached for the white porcelain knob. Before he could grasp the implement, it turned in his hand. He backed off. The door opened.

Daisy Perika's small, hunched-over form emerged slowly, as if every step required a concentrated locomotive effort.

Poor woman. She looks a hundred years old. "Hello, Mrs. Perika."

Charlie Moon's aunt blinked at the pale *matukach*, her deeply furrowed face registering an inner confusion.

He managed a weak smile. "I'm Stanley Newman. FBI."

She stared.

Newman cleared his throat. "I'm Charlie's friend."

Daisy Perika dismissed this with a snort. Everybody claimed to be Charlie's friend. She shook her finger at him. "I told my nephew for years—he should get out of the police business. He never listened to me, not once. Said he had to earn a living and police work was what he liked. Then, just like a gift from God in heaven, a fine ranch property falls into Charlie's lap. So what does he do, the big jughead? Go and grow some hamburger like a normal human being? Does he listen to his aunt, who has always give him good advice?"

Newman was uncertain whether she expected him to respond to these questions.

She did not. "No, sir, he don't." Daisy banged her walking stick onto the carpet with a soft thump. "First chance he gets, he's up to his armpits in murders and witchcraft and God only knows what else." She turned to glare at the closed door. "And look where it's got him." Without a good-bye to the FBI agent, she marched away down the hall toward the crowded lobby, muttering dark syllables Newman could not hear.

Stanley Newman entered the Jasmine Room. Though modified for its current function, such necessities as were required were cunningly disguised. Against the south wall, there was a maple wardrobe flanked by an enormous chest of drawers. A crystal chandelier hung from the precise center of the plastered ceiling. It was just large enough to be impressive, but not so massive as to offend good taste. Centered under this sparkling array of lights was a circular oak table. It was about the right size for six hands of poker, Newman thought. The north end of the large room was dominated by an overstuffed couch perched on gracefully curved maple legs. There were three matching chairs. This might have been a sumptuous bedroom in a wealthy person's home. As once it was. Now it was something else entirely.

The federal policeman saw Charlie Moon's long frame resting near a mullioned window that overlooked the river. *Maybe Charlie enjoys the view.* He was pleased that Moon was not alone in the room.

A rumpled-looking Scott Parris wore a three-day stubble over a glum expression. Charlie Moon's best friend was staring intently at a watercolor of purple asters in an alabaster vase.

Newman faked a small cough.

Parris turned. "Morning, Stan."

"Hi." Newman glanced toward the still form. "Too bad about Charlie."

"Yeah." Too bad.

The federal agent stepped softly across the thick carpet toward the place where Moon lay. Though the room was distinctly chilly, the Ute's form was draped lightly in a pink satin sheet. Newman stood there, staring at the still face. All things considered, Charlie looked fairly presentable. Newman turned to Moon's best friend. "Old buddy, you look like death warmed over. And that's a compliment."

Scott Parris rubbed at bloodshot eyes. "Police work is getting me down."

"Why don't you go find some breakfast." Newman slapped him on the shoulder. "I'll keep watch here."

"Thanks anyway. I'm not hungry."

The fed glanced at the form on the bed. "He said anything yet?"

"Nothing that makes any sense. But the doc says he's getting stronger."

Moon grunted.

Parris was at the bed in one second flat. "Charlie?"

The patient blinked bleary eyes. "Scott . . . that you?"

His friend grinned from ear to ear. "Well. You're back."

"What day is it?"

Parris told him.

Moon took a deep breath, exhaled slowly. "I been out that long?"

"You've suffered a serious head injury. For a while, it was a close thing. Once or twice, we thought you'd left us."

From some far place, Moon thought he heard a lonely whistle blow. *The Blue Train* . . .

"So how do you feel?"

"Like my head exploded." Moon's fingertips explored the satin sheet. He tried to raise his head from the pillows, but was unable to perform this simple task. "Anybody been here to see me?"

Parris knew who *anybody* was. "I haven't been able to get in touch with your sweetheart. Camilla's away on an extended overseas trip."

The Ute didn't respond to this news.

"But you got a visitor here now. Besides me, I mean."

"Who?"

"Serious-looking fellow in a gray three-piece suit."

Moon almost grinned. "Newman or Whitmer?"

"The mean one."

"Hah—Newman."

The fed looked over Parris's shoulder. "Maybe it's just as well your sweetheart's not here. I doubt she'd be able to look at you."

"I'm bunged up pretty bad, huh?"

"Nah," Parris said. "Nothing broke but your noggin."

The FBI agent grinned. "Damn lucky thing it wasn't a vital organ."

"Did they cut into my head?"

"I hate to be the one to tell you," Newman said with a happy smile, "surgeon took about a cupful of scrambled brains out. Which is more than some of us thought you had."

"Thank you."

Parris seated himself by the bed. "Lucky thing you didn't lay out there all night."

"Out where?"

So you don't remember. "Up by Chimney Rock."

The Ute relaxed his mind, allowed the drifting pieces to come together. "Oh yeah." *Ghost Wolf Mesa. Coffee with Amanda Silk. Something ugly looking in her trailer window . . . following us to April's grave?* "Who found me?"

"Far as we know," Newman said, "a dog."

"Run that by me again."

The FBI agent consulted his notebook. "Here's how it went down.

Mr. Bushman got a call from your aunt Daisy, who was certain you were in mortal danger."

Moon sighed. "How'd she know?"

No one had an answer to that.

Newman cleared his throat. "Mr. Bushman and his wife drove all the way down to Chimney Rock, just to see if you were all right."

"Good people," Moon said.

The federal lawman flipped a page. "Bushmans stopped when they spotted your pickup on the mesa, then they heard a dog howling over in the ruins. Mr. Bushman went to see what all the fuss was about. Didn't actually see the dog, but he did find you. More dead than alive. From the knees up, you were stuffed in a hole in the ground. Same hole where the Tavishuts woman's body was found. And there was something kinda peculiar. You were covered with sticks and pine needles—looked like some kind of ritual burial." He closed the notebook. "That's about it." But it wasn't.

"What about Amanda Silk?"

Newman responded in a monotone. "What about her?"

"She was with me."

The special agent looked out the window. A puffy shawl of cumulus was draped over the shoulders of a sprawling, spruce-studded mountain. "Mr. Bushman also found Dr. Silk."

"Found her where?"

"Where she'd fallen. Halfway in the trench—practically on top of you." *Face all pale and twisted.*

"Dead?"

"I sure hope so," Newman grunted. "She was buried yesterday."

Again, Moon tried to move his head; a dull pain thudded behind his left ear. "How'd she die?"

Not easy. Newman watched the ivory blades of an antique ceiling fan rotate slowly. "Her heart stopped beating."

The injured man was not in a mood for word games. "*Why* did her heart stop?"

"I asked the medical examiner about that," Newman muttered, "and he said . . ." Like a faint trail in a thick forest, the syllables slipped away into the shadows.

"What'd the ME say?"

Newman clamped his mouth shut.

Scott Parris's face wore a hollow, haunted expression. "Charlie, it's kinda technical. When you're feeling better, you can talk to the medical examiner yourself."

Moon was silent for a while before asking the obvious question. "You have any idea who murdered Amanda?"

As if his hands were suddenly cold, Newman began rubbing his palms together. "We don't know for sure she was . . . ahh . . . murdered, Charlie. At least not in a legal sense."

"You have any idea who conked me on the head?"

The special agent's blush matched the pink satin sheet on Moon's bed. "Not exactly."

"You got any evidence at all?"

The fed studied his highly polished shoes as if he'd never seen them before. Tiny lights from the chandelier sparkled back at him. "Well, there was that dog Bushman heard howling. We found a couple of paw prints at the edge of the—uh—excavation where you were dumped."

"So you're looking for somebody who owns a dog."

Newman was still looking out the window. "Big dog."

Charlie Moon rubbed gingerly at the thick patch of bandages on his skull. "That don't narrow it down much."

The fed glanced at Moon. "Mr. Alvah Yazzi owns a big dog."

Owns? Moon tried to see through the bandages. "Then you're sure he's not dead?"

"Not unless a great big truck's run over him." Newman relished this image.

"You got a warrant out on Alvah?"

"I'm working on it." Newman felt a choking sensation, pulled at his tie. "There's no law against scattering some wood ashes and chips of animal bones in your clothes. Not unless hoaxing your death is part of a conspiracy to commit a crime. Or," he added with a steely edge to his voice, "the hoax is for the purpose of evading prosecution for a felony. You hear about those fingerprints on the obsidian chip at the excavation site?"

"Word gets around."

"They turned out to be Mr. Yazzi's."

Moon thought about this. "I can't see that old Navajo messing around in the ruins."

"It's plain enough if you're willing to look at the facts, Charlie—Mr. Yazzi was the man those two women saw at his stepdaughter's grave that night." The special agent's face relaxed into an expression somewhere between satisfied and downright smug. "So that explains why the old sonofagun went to so much trouble to convince us he'd burned to death in his clothes. Must've thought by the time the Bureau caught on to his ruse, he'd be in deep hiding. He's probably somewhere on the Navajo Reservation. But wherever he is, we'll find him."

Moon thought the federal agent was being unduly optimistic. If Alvah Yazzi was holed up on the Big Rez, the FBI and the National Guard and All the King's Men would have a hard time flushing him out. "So what's Yazzi's motive for murdering his stepdaughter?"

Newman started to say something, then swallowed the words. "We're working on that."

Moon felt like changing the subject. "Anybody else come to see me?"

"Your aunt's been checking on you," Parris said. "Tribal chairman stopped by a couple of times. Chief of Police Whitehorse was here yesterday with Father Raes Delfino. The Bushmans come in almost every day. Dolly keeps bringing you things to eat. Just on the off chance you wake up hungry."

Moon brightened at this news. "Like what?"

"Nothing special. Apple pies. Deep-dish peach cobblers."

"Sounds good."

"They were," Parris said.

"I been to the Columbine," Newman said. "Some of your seedy-looking cowboys been asking about you. Couple of 'em look like their ugly kissers oughta be on wanted posters. One of 'em is a wetback if I ever seen one." He grinned. "Maybe I should drop a hint to the immigration boys that you're hiring illegals."

"Don't go messing with my help," the Ute muttered. "Good cowhands are hard to find."

Newman assumed his stern, official look. "And there's this kid who looks like he ain't old enough to get a tricycle driver's license. Claims he's paying tuition at the Columbine to learn how to be a sure-enough cowpoke." The federal lawman gave the patient a one-eyed squint. "You got a state license to operate a cowboy school, Charlie?"

Moon ignored the rude question. "Where's Melina Castro?"

"We've offered to move her to another location," Newman said. "But she's gone to stay with a friend. I wonder—are you concerned about the welfare of our witness, or the outrageous fee you're expecting to collect for her room and board?"

"Speaking of money, when do I get paid?"

"Don't worry about it—we're the government—you can trust us." The federal agent was in remarkably good humor. "Check's practically in the mail." Newman's gut-wrenching laughter tailed off into a coughing fit.

Scott Parris couldn't help smiling. "Speaking of visitors, Charlie—there's a dozen or so hard cases you locked up at one time or another hanging out in the lobby. They keep asking me, 'Is ol' Charlie Moon dead yet?' "

Newman had partially regained his composure. "You might as well know, Charlie—there's a ten-dollar pool going on when you'll give up the ghost."

"I was holding six A.M. this morning," Parris said.

"Tough luck," Newman said. "I got two A.M. tomorrow. Hey, who knows what'll happen? Charlie might still cash in his chips shortly after midnight."

Moon ran his fingers over the bandages on his head. "Is there any good news?"

The visitors considered this question.

Newman could not come up with anything positive.

"Your aunt Daisy's in the lobby," Parris offered.

"I said *good* news."

"I'll tell her you said that."

"How's she taking this?"

"Old woman's madder'n I've ever seen her. Figures the whole thing's all your fault. Soon as you're well enough, I expect she'll kill you."

"Thank you for cheering me up, pardner." Moon had a look at the elegant room. "This don't look like Mercy Hospital."

Parris shook his head. "You only spent a couple of days in Durango.

You're in my jurisdiction now—bunked out in Snyder Memorial. The annex, no less. The Ritz of Colorado's intermediate-care facilities."

Moon raised an eyebrow; even this simple gesture was painful. "Who's gonna pay the bill?"

Parris shrugged. "Barter with 'em. Maybe you can ship the joint a couple head of prime beef." The attorney who managed Moon's taxes was seeing to the finances.

The FBI agent glanced at his wristwatch without noting the time. "Look, Charlie—I got some other stuff to do. I'll talk to you later, after your head clears up. When you've got all your thoughts together, we'll want a statement—okay?"

"Don't slam the door on your way out. I've got an eye-popping headache."

Special Agent Newman closed the door ever so softly.

Moon tried to think of just how to broach the sensitive subject. "I got to ask you something."

Parris rested one scuffed boot on the bed frame. "Shoot."

"When you and Stan Newman was talking at the same time, I couldn't make out what you was saying. Do you think this conk on the bean has made me kinda . . . dumb?"

"Nah. Injury had nothing to do with it. You've just finally realized your limited potential."

"Thank you kindly," the Ute said.

"Don't mention it. But you owe me a favor in return."

"I'll do my best. As long as it don't involve any hard thinking."

"I figure you had a good reason to go up to Chimney Rock. So don't hold out on your buddy."

Moon's vision was hazy. "We all alone now?"

"Like two skunks at church."

"Then I'll tell you about the pictograph."

"I'm listening."

"Whoever made the sketch in stone was a sort of magician. A conjurer."

"Maybe you could enlarge on that just a bit."

"It was a matter of misdirection."

Parris slapped his forehead. "Oh, now I get it."

"You're faster that I thought."

"I was being sarcastic."

"Oh."

"Go ahead. Explain."

"Remember what was sketched on the sandstone?"

Parris scratched at the stubble on his chin, and tried to recall the memory of what he'd seen in a newspaper photo. "It was—lemme see. Oh yeah—these two little guys."

"The Twin War Gods," Moon said.

"Hey, I knew that. And they're holding spears."

"One of the spears was pointed at Companion Rock, the other at Chimney."

"So?"

"The petroglyph was a sign, pardner. Telling whoever could read it where the Anasazi priest had stashed something or other."

Parris shook his head at the injured man. "You don't really believe those old tales about hidden treasure."

"Somebody did."

"So where was this treasure supposed to be?"

"Somewhere near that pit house—the one where April was buried."

"And where you were assaulted."

"Very same spot."

"And where we found Dr. Silk's body."

"So I'm told."

"So how'd you figure this out?"

"April Tavishuts told me," the Ute said.

Parris chuckled. "Your aunt Daisy will be overjoyed to hear you've had a conversation with a dead person."

The Ute recalled his encounter with Nahum Yacitti. "It was April's sketch. The one we found in her apartment."

"What's this 'we' stuff—I had nothing to do with that particular misdemeanor."

"Felony," Moon said.

"Don't get technical. Anyway, it wasn't me who filched that evidence from her apartment."

"I was just trying to give my pardner some of the credit for a good piece of police work."

"Very generous of you."

"Thanks. D'you remember what was on the paper?"

"Sure. Her sketch of the petroglyph. And a couple of penciled lines."

"Those lines were aligned with the spears," Moon said.

The Granite Creek chief of police crinkled his brow into deep furrows. "What am I missing here?"

Moon licked parched lips. "Can I have a glass of cool water?"

"Sure. Right after you tell me what you know."

"Pardner, I'm really thirsty."

"I got a bag of salted peanuts in my pocket."

"Okay. The spears are pointing at the pit house."

Parris poured iced water from a crystal pitcher into a cranberry-glass mug. "I sure hate to correct a man whose brain is all scrambled. But you already said those spears were pointing toward the stone pillars— which is to the northeast. And the pit house in question is to the southwest of the pictograph." He put the glass in the Ute's outstretched hand. "Why're you grinning at the ceiling?"

"Like I already said, the sketch was a misdirection." Moon took a short drink. Then a long one.

"What kind of misdirection?"

"Whoever drew that nifty little picture must've been laughing up his sleeve." Moon emptied the mug. "He went to a lot of trouble to find a nice, flat sandstone outcropping for his sketch that was *between* the stone formations and the burial site. The pointy end of one spear is aimed at Chimney Rock, the other one at Companion."

"So?"

"Try to remember what you learned in grammar school."

"Always clean up your mess. Don't throw erasers or spitballs. Oh yeah—'Don't dip the little redheaded girl's pigtail in the inkwell.' "

"That's good. But what'd you learn about parallel lines?"

"Everybody knows that—they never cross."

"And nonparallel lines?"

Parris was beginning to get it. "The lines those two spears make— they cross at the pit house where Miss Tavishuts encountered the pothunter—and you almost met your Maker?"

The Ute's nod was barely perceptible.

"And April Tavishuts was the first one to figure this out?"

Moon closed his eyes. Tried to remember April's face. He couldn't. "April must've been the second one to catch on."

"So who was first?"

"Now that's the question."

"If somebody knew where the lines crossed," Parris countered, "then why dig all over the mesa—why not concentrate on the sweet spot?"

"I'm not sure, pardner. Maybe our treasure hunter didn't want to make it too obvious where he thought the Anasazi treasure was buried. And digging in a whole buncha places would make it look like ordinary pothunters at work. Which is what the NAGPRA committee believed. That's why Amanda Silk was contracted to check out the vandalism."

"I am impressed with this complicated line of reasoning. Especially from a fella who's recently suffered a serious brain injury."

"All praise—however slight—is gratefully received."

"So?"

"So what?"

"So what did our treasure hunter find in the excavation that was worth killing for?"

"I don't know if he found anything at all."

"Then it might still be there."

"If it ever was."

"If there wasn't anything to find, then your clever converging-line theory is . . . well, just wrong."

"If it's wrong, I disclaim it," Moon said.

"Maybe whoever bopped you was just a run-of-the-mill pothunter, digging all over the mesa. Maybe they picked that particular pit house because it looked like a promising spot to unearth a snazzy Anasazi pot. Maybe the Twin War God spears are in the sketch just to point at those big rock towers. Maybe the fact that the lines cross at the pit-house grave is a coincidence."

"Pardner, you could *maybe* a fella plumb to death."

"Three or four hard cases in Boot Hill have said the same thing. But you have to admit—there's a strong possibility you were on a snipe hunt."

"Maybe." *Maybe the pictograph is a hoax. Just like Amanda said.*

"But even if it's wrong, I like your converging-line theory. It proves you have a knack for plane geometry. And a fertile imagination."

"You're altogether too kind."

"It's one of my serious failings. And speaking of kindness, I guess it's about time I told your grieving aunt that you've regained consciousness."

"I'm feeling awful weak," Moon said in a wan whisper. "Slipping away . . ."

"I'll tell her you're sleeping."

The Ute's voice was stronger. "She'd just bang me on the shins with her walking stick till I wake up."

"Then what should I do?"

"Tell her I'm dead."

Prognosis

The physician, a slight man rattling around inside a starched white smock, leaned against the foot of Charlie Moon's bed. He cuddled a clipboard under folded arms. "I'm Dr. Kenny—your neurologist. Last time I came by, you were not entirely with us."

The Ute—who was sitting in a chair—wondered whether Kenny was the doctor's first or last name. "Nurse tells me I'm about to be set free."

The doctor smiled. "Over the wall." He glanced out the broad window at a sunlit lawn edging the riverbank. "After almost two weeks, I suppose this place does begin to feel like a prison."

Moon was pulling on his socks. "I'm ready to be in the world again."

Like a discriminating shopper considering the quality of a melon, Dr. Kenny regarded his patient's head with a doubtful expression. "You have suffered a serious concussion."

"I'm feeling pretty good." The Ute looked up. "And I sure don't want to hear any bad news."

The slender man shrugged under the loose-fitting smock. "You're progressing as well as could be expected. CAT scan showed nothing remarkable. How's your appetite?"

The seven-foot Ute was extremely tired of macaroni and cheese. Lime Jell-O with seedless, tasteless grapes. Green peas that tasted like the grapes. Cardboard meat loaf. "I could eat a five-pound beefsteak. Burned to a cinder or still bloody, wouldn't make much difference."

Dr. Kenny—a vegetarian—found this imagery stomach-turning. The neurologist shifted subjects. "Has your memory of events at the time of the trauma improved?"

Moon, pulling on the second sock, shook his head. "Still pretty fuzzy."

"How about the—ahh—visual phenomena you described to the intern?"

The Ute smiled. "You mean the hallucinations?" Wearied from the exertion of dressing himself, Moon leaned back in the comfortable chair. "I still see some lights." He didn't mention the oddly shaped shadows that occasionally cavorted at the edge of his visual field.

"Given the nature of your injury, that is not unusual. It should get better."

"How?"

"How what?"

"How better? Will it all go away—or will I start to see pretty women dancing on my bed?"

The physician laughed.

"When'll I be completely well?"

"Hard to say. The visual phantasms should become less frequent over the next few weeks. Though you may experience recurrent symptoms even months from now." The physician made a scribbled note on the clipboard. "Have you noticed any other phenomena?"

"Like what?"

"Oh—anything at all that you consider unusual."

Moon gave the doctor an odd look. "Sometimes this feeling comes over me."

Dr. Kenny leaned closer. "What sort of feeling?"

Apparently embarrassed, the patient looked at his socked feet. "It's kinda hard to describe."

The doctor waited patiently.

"It's like . . . like I'm not *me* anymore." Moon looked up. "You know what I mean?"

The physician nodded. "I think so. You have the sense that you're . . . someone else. We call it post-concussive disassociation." Once a thing was named, it took on an air of familiarity. One might become almost comfortable with it.

"Not exactly someone else," Moon said. "More like some*thing* else."

Now this is interesting. The neurologist had once had a head-trauma patient who imagined she was a coat hanger. "What sort of something else?"

Moon set his jaw. "Something like . . . an animal."

The physician's Adam's apple bobbled as he swallowed. "An animal." *How delightful.* He could imagine publishing a socko *JAMA* paper on this. "What sort of animal?"

"Big hairy one."

The neurologist paled.

There was a long silence while Charlie Moon managed to pull on his bull-hide boots.

Eventually, Dr. Kenny cleared his throat. "It is my understanding that you live on a ranch. In a rather large house—by yourself."

"That's right."

"I think it advisable that until these—ahh—symptoms clear up, you should not be alone."

"I'm not all that much alone. I see my ranch foreman and his wife almost every day. And the ranch hands. And my buddy Scott Parris drops by from time to time."

"Do you have any relatives."

Moon grimaced. "My aunt Daisy."

"May I have your permission to speak to some of these individuals about your illness?"

"Sure, Doc." Moon buttoned his shirt. "Only don't bring up that thing about the big hairy animal. Wouldn't want them to worry."

Symptoms

Dr. Kenny was seated behind an immaculate rosewood desk, his spare figure centered in a picture window that looked out onto a hedged garden. His gray eyes darted between Charlie Moon's medical charts and the four persons in his office. He thought it fortunate that they had been present to visit the patient on his final day at the hospital. "I appreciate you ladies and gentlemen coming to my office on such short notice." He frowned at the bearded cowboy. "Mr. Bushman, I understand that you'll be driving Mr. Moon back to his ranch."

The Columbine foreman, pulling absently at his tobacco-stained beard, grunted something unintelligible that was intended as an affirmative, and taken as such.

The neurologist looked down his nose at the elderly Indian woman, who seemed half asleep. "And you are Mr. Moon's aunt?"

Daisy Perika nodded.

This poor woman looks barely able to take care of herself. He turned his attention to the handsome couple. Dr. Kenny needed no introduction to Scott Parris or Anne Foster. He was well acquainted with the Granite Creek chief of police and the town's eminent journalist. "Mr. Moon," the neurologist said in measured tones, "is recovering from a serious injury. As he lives alone, it is my hope that his friends and family will keep an eye on him during his recovery."

"I'll be checking on Charlie from time to time," Parris said.

Bushman jammed his hat onto his head. "Me and Dolly—that's my wife—we see the boss fairly reg'lar when he's at the ranch. 'Course if he's off somewheres doin' some work for the tribe, why we may not lay eyes on him for days at a time."

"What sort of work does Mr. Moon do for the tribe?"

"Charlie's an investigator for the Southern Utes," Parris said.

The physician did not like the sound of this. "I will advise him to avoid any work for at least several weeks."

"I could come and take care of my nephew," Daisy said. She shot a dark look at Bushman. "If I'm allowed to."

The ranch foreman met her hard gaze with one of his own.

The neurologist smiled at the Ute woman. "That would be very helpful, Mrs. Perika. But I must tell you that patients who are recovering from an injury such as Mr. Moon has suffered may . . ." He hesitated, reflecting on the delicate issue of doctor-patient confidentiality. "They sometimes exhibit peculiar symptoms." He paused to let this sink in.

It did. Four pairs of eyes stared holes in the doctor.

Anne Foster broke the tense silence. "Peculiar symptoms—what exactly does that mean?"

Dr. Kenny—who toyed with a gold-plated fountain pen—did his utmost to sound casual. "In Mr. Moon's case, it is possible that there could be unusual discomforts. Even though the injury is to the cranium, referred pains may be felt in an arm or a leg. The effect is temporary. There is, of course, memory loss associated with the time interval shortly before and after the traumatic event."

There was a collective sigh of relief.

"That is not all," the neurologist added.

They waited for the big boot to fall.

He dropped it. "There may be other, more bizarre symptoms."

"Like what?" Scott Parris said hoarsely.

Dr. Kenny cleared his throat. "Personality disorders. Delusions. Disassociatons. He may experience auditory or visual hallucinations."

"Hah," Daisy said with a derisive snort, "you're telling us Charlie's likely to start acting crazy."

"I would certainly not use that term." The physician shot the old woman a flint-tipped look. It bounced off like an arrow that had struck a wall of granite.

"I knew it," she muttered. "He'll never be right again."

"I do not mean that it is *likely* that this patient would exhibit these particular symptoms. It is merely possible. Furthermore, such phenomena as I've described are actually not all that uncommon for a severe concussion of this type and—"

"Rattle-brained as an overworked woodpecker." Daisy threw up her arms. "I always knew it'd turn out like this. Charlie ought to have listened to me and give up police work for good. Now," she said darkly, "he'll be like one of them punch-drunk fighters. Wandering around the streets of Durango, begging for loose change, drinking cheap wine, talking crazy talk."

The neurologist found himself taking a professional interest in this peculiar old woman.

Free at Last

Charlie Moon was packed and ready to go, waiting for the sheaf of paperwork that would discharge him from Snyder Memorial's intensive care annex. He was not alone.

Pete Bushman leaned against the doorjamb.

Scott Parris stood by the window, staring out at a beautiful day. The mountains never changed. But men were different. He was wondering whether Charlie Moon would ever be the same.

Anne Foster, her large eyes anxious, sat on a small couch.

Daisy Perika was hunched forward in an antique rocking chair, clicking her knitting needles. "Myra drove me up here to the hospital," she said to her nephew.

Moon frowned. "Myra?"

"Myra Cornstone." Daisy looked up from her work. "She came to see you a coupla days ago. Don't you remember?"

"I must've been taking a nap." Moon seemed to be in deep thought. "She a short girl—kinda plump?"

Daisy blinked owlishly at him. "Myra's a head taller'n me. And thin as a grass snake."

"Oh."

There was a long silence.

"I've been thinking," Daisy said.

Moon's stomach churned at this unsettling news. *What I need is to get home. Have a few days of peace and quiet.*

"Don't you want to know what I've been thinking?" There was an unmistakable tone of accusation in her question.

"Sure." *Go ahead. Ruin my day.*

"I've been thinking about how you're always after me to come up and stay with you. Keep you company on that big ranch."

Charlie Moon pretended not to hear.

"I thought I should go up and get that big house cleaned up for you."

"You don't need to bother." Moon glanced at his foreman, who had backed into the hallway. "Dolly Bushman takes care of the place when I'm away."

Daisy leaned close and whispered, "That foreman's silly wife—you let her mess around in your house?"

"Dolly is a very nice lady."

"Well, there's another reason I'd like to go up there." *Not that I'd ever tell you.*

"What's that?"

"Your doctor thinks you need some looking after."

"I'll be fine."

Daisy was not about to give up. "And I thought I'd go and put some of my things in my little log house across the lake."

Moon looked blankly at his aunt. "The guest cabin?"

"Sure. The one you fixed up for me. Sometime, I might want to come and stay for a few weeks. So I need to put some pots and pans in the kitchen."

"There's plenty of cookware there already."

"I need my own stuff," she snapped. "I'll get someone to drive me up."

Moon knew when he was whipped. "That won't be necessary. I'll come get you." *When I'm good and ready.*

CHAPTER 15

There was a plan from the stars down. . . . They planned that
the rainbow should be used for a path whenever there was a
deep canyon to cross; and it was to be thrown over a river and
used for a bridge.

—Sandoval, Hastin Tlo'tsi hee

Expert Opinion

While his visitor watched, Charlie Moon squatted in front of the
massive fireplace. The rancher nestled a fat pine log into a bed of
amber embers. The damp wood hissed. Popped. Sizzled.

Fizzled.

"Some Indian," his guest smirked. "Can't even get a fire started."

The Ute took iron rod in hand, spurred on the mulish fuel with an
urgent prodding. "Go," he muttered.

The wood would not.

Moon aimed his pointed weapon, made a vicious thrust into barkish
skin. The pine whined, weeped resinous blood. Flames came to lick the
wound.

Having had his way with the log, the Ute seated himself on a couch. Poker in hand, he waited for his guest to say what was on his mind.

Dr. Walter Simpson, snuggled in a cushioned rocking chair, had removed his ankle-high suede boots. The medical examiner stretched his short legs, the better to toast a pair of size-five feet in the hospitable warmth of Charlie Moon's hearth. He wriggled chilly toes under monogrammed silk socks. "So, my land-rich friend, how's the ranching business?"

"It'd better get better," Moon said, "or I'll have to take up another trade."

Simpson shifted his rump in the chair, and treated himself to an old man's rheumatic groan. "It's a helluva long way here from Granite Creek. And it'll be twice as far back."

"I would've been glad to come to your place."

Simpson's mouth curled into an elfin grin that was almost hidden by the underbrush of a silvery-white mustache. "I realize how much you enjoy encountering the bloody, mangled cadavers in my quaint basement morgue. But I thought I should have a look at your famous ranch." He reached for a ceramic mug, inhaled a sip of hot apple cider. "I'll need some serious coffee before I hit the road. It's hard driving after dark since my cataract surgery."

Moon took the hint. "You could stay at the ranch tonight."

"I would not want to impose on your hospitality."

"Sure you would."

"What's for breakfast?"

"Eggs fried in pig grease. Slab of honey-cured ham. Red-eye gravy. And my special homemade green-chili biscuits."

Simpson's mouth watered. "Real biscuits—made from scratch?"

"I grind the wheat on a vermiculite metate. Just like Grandpa used to do."

"You talked me into it."

They heard the melancholy call of a lonely coyote. The soft whisper of night wind in the eaves. Then, the heavy sound of silence.

Moon seemed mesmerized by the flames flickering in the fireplace.

The physician gave the Ute a sideways glance. "You doing okay, Charlie?"

"Sure."

"Suffering any symptoms from your head injury?"

"Nothing I can't live with."

The medical examiner cleared his throat to make way for the professional voice. "Tell me what you remember."

Moon tapped the poker on the pointed toe of his boot. "About what?"

"Start with how you got your injury."

"There's not much I recall." *And nothing at all I want to talk about.*

"Then you don't know anything about Amanda Silk's death?"

"I was hoping you'd tell me how she died."

Simpson stirred a cinnamon stick in the cider. "I'll give you three guesses."

"How about a hint?"

A sly mask slipped over Simpson's face. "Okay. It's one word."

"Heartfailure."

"That's two words."

"Not if you say it fast."

"Try saying . . . catecholamines."

"That would've been my second guess."

The medical examiner's voice took on a pedantic tone. "Catecholamines are primarily comprised of adrenaline and noradrenaline."

"Any half-wit knows that."

"Not just any half-wit. But evidently, that blow on the skull has improved your mind." Simpson licked the cinnamon stick. "But in my attempt to flatter you, I have digressed. Where was I?"

"Showing off."

"Well, of course." The medical examiner smiled amiably. "But please be more specific."

"Something about adrenaline. And catching coal mines."

"Ah, yes. Catecholamines." Dr. Simpson's bespectacled eyes took on a dreamy look. "Dr. Silk must have suffered an incredibly stressful experience. This results in a multitude of physiological responses. The whole point is to make the fight-or-flight mechanism kick in. The one of particular interest in Dr. Silk's case involves the hypothalamus. That organ signals the adrenal glands to start squirting catecholamines into the bloodstream—which increases the ability of the blood to coagulate. This same chemical also makes blood vessels constrict. All of which helps prevent excessive bleeding." The medical examiner enjoyed the sweet sound of his own voice far more than the ethereal song of violin or harp. "This response is very handy if you are running from a hungry grizzly who is right behind you biting big chunks outta your ass." Simpson paused to chuckle.

The Ute was engrossed by the second act on that small stage where dancing flames were impersonating something. Or other. It was a dark, lurid performance. Charlie Moon forced himself to look away from the fireplace.

The medical examiner frowned at his host. "Charlie—you listening to what I'm telling you?"

"Sure."

"Good." The ME tapped a cinnamon stick on his ear. "As mandated by God's grand evolutionary plan, mammalian heart cells are provided with marvelous channels that enable calcium to flow in. These channels are controlled—among other means—by the release of catecholamines. Which is a highly useful response. Unless you get *too much* calcium in the heart muscles."

Moon heard the hall clock chime the half hour. "You telling me Dr. Silk died of a calcium overdose?"

Simpson nodded at the fireplace. "It is a fairly rare physiological phenomena, but in instances of extreme stress, massive amounts of catecholamines are released. This can cause excessive levels of calcium to flood the heart-muscle fibers." He swirled the lukewarm cider residue, then downed it in one gulp. "Dr. Silk's heart fibers seized up completely. The heart muscles became rigid—almost like stone." To demonstrate, he gripped the empty mug until his knuckles turned pearly white.

There was a lengthy silence while firelight flickered on their faces.

"She have a weak heart?"

Simpson stared unblinkingly into the flames. "The woman had coronary arteries an Olympic athlete would be proud of."

"So what's the bottom line?"

"Charlie, I cannot even imagine the extreme nature of the external stimulus that led to the archaeologist's demise." The ME closed his tired eyes, rocked himself gently in the cradle of the leather-backed chair. "But the internal evidence is beyond dispute. The unfortunate woman was frightened to death."

CHAPTER 16

He traveled southward . . . he found a ragged old man. The Elder Brother was about to kill him when he said: "No, my Grandson, you must not kill me, even though I am *Tie en*, Poverty . . ." The Elder Brother . . . let him live.

—Sandoval, Hastin Tlo'tsi hee

Pie Thief

Charlie Moon's aunt had telephoned several times, insisting that she come and "look after him" until he was better. Assuring Daisy Perika that he was doing quite well did nothing to dissuade the elderly woman. And though he needed some solitary time, maybe a visit to the Columbine would be good for her. Might even help her realize that she could spend some time away from her little home at the mouth of *Cañon del Espíritu.* Which was all to the good. So he decided to drive south to the reservation and get her.

A light wind was moving in from the northwest, pleasantly rippling its way through the willows along the river. Moon pulled on a wool-lined denim jacket, pressed the familiar black hat down to his ears. The novice rancher stood on the west porch. He had a long, satisfying look at this sweet land that was his. Pete Bushman had trucked in sixty head of purebred Herefords. They were dotted along a thousand-acre pasture on the far side of the river, where the fresh breeze made rolling waves in the blue-green sea of grass. A day's walk away, blue granite mountains raised craggy heads heavenward, to be crowned with an iridescent wreath of swirling ice crystals. The Ute felt very close to Paradise.

But the sun was high; there was work to be done.

Shaking off the mesmerizing spell of the land, Moon headed toward where his pickup was parked. The F150 waited under a pair of ancient cottonwoods that leaned against each other like friendly drunks. As he opened the cab door, the Ute thought he sensed something behind him. He turned to see Sidewinder. The lanky dog looked half starved and was moving slowly, as if all his muscles ached. Though not particularly fond of the eccentric animal, Moon was in a generous mood. He opened the cab door. "Want a ride?"

The hound turned up his nose at the offer. Sneered.

Moon shook his head at the peculiar creature, then got into the pickup. The machine had not been driven since it was returned from Ghost Wolf Mesa. He twisted the ignition key. The engine turned over slowly at first, then picked up speed as a film of oil lubricated the cylinder rings. But it didn't start. He turned the ignition off, tapped the accelerator pedal several times, then tried again. Six cranks and the gasoline fumes ignited. "Right," he said. It would be good to be on the road again. He did not realize that this small delay in starting the truck had allowed something to happen. Something trivial. Something that would change his life forever.

Moon headed down the graveled lane, over a fast-running creek that fed the river. From force of habit, he pulled over at the foreman's house. By the time he was halfway across the dusty yard, Pete Bushman had emerged, on the porch. Moon waved. "Good morning."

"It'd be good," the grizzled foreman said, "if we could get some rain. The south pastures ain't growing nothin' but black rocks and spiny-cactus and blood-suckin' ticks."

"You sure know how to cheer a man up."

"I forgot to mention a fine crop of locoweed."

Moon looked toward the clouds hanging over the mountains. "The rain'll come."

"If you're goin' into town," Bushman said, "maybe you could pick up some supplies we're needin'."

"You got a list?"

"I'll make you one." The foreman turned to open the screen door.

Moon removed his hat and followed his employee inside.

Dolly Bushman was already pouring coffee. She invited the boss to have a chair.

The Ute expressed his appreciation and seated himself at the kitchen table, where all business was conducted.

Pete Bushman licked the tip of a stubby lead pencil before laboriously scribbling a column of necessaries that included salt blocks and veterinary supplies for the stock. For the human population of the Columbine, one hundred pounds of flour, fifteen pounds of coffee beans, a bucket of lard, ten pounds of bacon, twenty pounds of sugar, a fifty-pound sack of pinto beans, and miscellaneous canned fruit. He added cookies to the list, specifying gingersnaps, which were the foreman's favorite. For the ranch itself, two hundred feet of Manila rope, fifteen pounds of two-inch roofing nails, a bundle of welding rods. And a bucket of tar.

"Well," Dolly said to their employer, "it sure is good to have you back on the Columbine."

"Thank you." Moon stirred a generous portion of sugar into his coffee. "Glad to be back. If it wasn't for you and Pete, I might not—"

"Shush," Dolly said sternly. "We won't hear another word about it."

"There is one thing," the Ute said. "After you found my pickup on Ghost Wolf Mesa, I understand you heard a dog."

Dolly nodded. "Awfulest howling I ever heard. That's what led Pete to where you was. It was like that animal was drawing us . . ." A tear trickled down her cheek.

"You didn't actually see the dog?"

Pete Bushman shook his head. "I don't think it was no dog. I think maybe it was—" He checked himself at a look from his wife. "Maybe it was just the wind—whistlin' in a holler tree."

Dolly wiped the tear away, then patted Moon's shoulder. "So where are you headed?"

"To pick up my aunt. She's been calling every day. Wants to come take care of me."

"Well, I expect that'll be nice for you." She said this with no hint of enthusiasm.

"No," the Ute responded, "it'll be like hugging an armload of prickly pears. But I doubt she'll want to stay all that long."

The expression on Dolly's face betrayed her relief.

Moon looked to his foreman. "How're things going with the new stock?"

Pete Bushman didn't look up from his list. "Them beeves is doin' just fine, thank you."

Moon got the point. Foremen were indispensable. Ranch owners were a damned nuisance.

Dolly held a jar of apricots up to a dust-streaked shaft of light from the south window. "Well, there is one thing."

Her husband shot her a warning look. And for good measure, he growled.

Dolly ignored him. "Somebody's been prowling around at night. Has to be one of them cutthroats Pete hired. A couple of 'em ain't worth the powder it'd take to blow 'em to Kingdom Come." She smiled. "But that young man from Rhode Island is very nice. So I'm sure it wasn't him that stole the pie."

Moon looked up from his coffee. "Somebody stole a pie?"

"Bernanner cream." Pete Bushman said this with a hollow-eyed expression of deep loss.

Dolly pointed to the scene of the crime. "Scoundrel took it right off my windowsill."

The Columbine foreman scowled. "I expect that jumble-headed chowhound snatched it."

"Window's too high," his wife said. "And besides, Sidewinder never takes any food from my kitchen."

Moon grinned. "Why's that, Dolly?"

Her eyes sparked fire. " 'Cause that old mongrel knows better than to mess with me." She suggested that the boss help himself to a freshly baked brownie.

He helped himself to three.

The good woman happened to look over Charlie Moon's shoulder. And out the window to where his Ford F150 was parked. "Oh, my goodness—speak of the Devil."

Moon was turning to see which devil.

"No," she whispered urgently, "don't look."

He didn't. "What is it?"

She laughed. "It's old Sidewinder, bless his ornery heart."

"He must've followed me."

She refilled his cup with coffee. "I expect he got in the back when you wasn't looking."

"He's in the truck?"

She nodded. "But don't let on you know he's there. It'd hurt his feelings."

"Well, I offered him a ride and he turned me down cold." *Damned annoying dog.*

"It's just his way," the kindly woman said.

"That old dog," Pete Bushman said, "is fond of pickups. 'Specially Fords. He'll hitch a ride ev'ry chance he gets."

"Well, he won't be stealing no more rides in my truck," Moon grumped.

Pete Bushman looked up from his ciphering. "Dogs is like chillern."

"Like what?"

The man's hearing must have been buggered up by that whack on the head. "Chillern," Bushman said. Loudly. "You let chillern or dogs do something one time, they figger they can do it again whenever they wants to."

Moon turned to look out the window. The hound's massive head, which had been hanging over the edge of the truck bed, immediately popped out of sight. "Excuse me," he said. And headed for the door.

Moon leaned on the tailgate. The pickup bed contained the ordinary items one would expect to find in a cow-ranch pickup. A bale of alfalfa hay. Tool box. Coil of rope. Tattered horse blanket. Under the blanket was a large, hound-shaped lump. Sidewinder had made a dogged effort to conceal himself. And was fairly successful. Except for the ropelike tail protruding from under the blanket.

"Sneaky mutt. You get outta there."

The form did not move.

The Ute tried again. "Hey—Sidewinder."

Hearing the sweet sound of his name was too much. The tail, which had a sentimental mind of its own, did a half wag before it was stilled by an urgent command from the hound's canny brain.

The Ute grinned. And gave the tail a yank.

The animal squirmed around under the blanket, then poked his long muzzle out to give his supposed master an embarrassed look.

Moon eyed the dog. "Think you're pretty smart, don't you?"

Sidewinder grinned.

Charlie Moon pulled the blanket away, and discovered that the F150 was more than transportation for the animal. The pickup bed was apparently a favorite spot for the hound to relax. Gather his canine thoughts. Chew on things. There were, in fact, several chewable items the hound had collected. Fractured ham bone. Battered tomato soup can. Mangled cowboy boot. And something else.

Under the hound's watchful eye, Moon reached to get it.

A low growl began to rattle in the animal's innards.

"Show me just one tooth," the Ute said evenly, "and I'll tie your tail in a knot."

The growl persisted.

"Then," Moon growled back, "I'll drop you off the ledge into Burro Canyon. That's a good two hundred feet," he added. "A long, long way to fall."

Sidewinder seemed to appreciate the gravity of the situation. The growl was transformed into a pleading whine; the so-far, knotless tail thumped against the truck bed.

Charlie Moon turned the remains of the shapeless blob over in his hand. It was mostly plastic, but a small metal tube dangled from the wreckage. "What was this before you tried to eat it?"

Sidewinder opened his mouth, canted his head sideways. And howled.

He gave the homely beast a long, thoughtful look. The dog stared back with large, pitifully sad eyes. With the suddenness of the first lightning strike in a gathering storm, Moon experienced a wonderful clarity of mind. One piece of the dark puzzle fell into place. Then another.

The Bushmans kept up their vigil at the window, peeking through a yellowed lace curtain at the boss.

Pete's tone was openly suspicious. "Why's he talking to that dog?"

Dolly looked over her husband's stooped shoulder.

The foreman shook his head. "The man's daft from having his brain all scrambled."

"Everybody talks to dogs," she said. "Look, Pete—the dog said something to Charlie!"

The husband sighed. *Charlie Moon's not the only one around here that's loco.*

Dolly Bushman jerked at her husband's sleeve. "Get away from the window, Pete. He's coming back."

The Pie

They had been sitting at the table for a full three seconds when Moon rapped his knuckles against the door frame.

"Come on in," Pete bellowed. "I thought you was on your way to pick up your aunt Dizzy."

"Daisy," Dolly muttered to her husband.

The Ute leaned on the back of a chair. "Decided to put it off for a day or two."

Pete Bushman shot the boss a sly look. "Don't got the stomach for it, huh?"

Dolly slapped his arm. "Pete—hush that kind of talk."

"I've got something else on my mind," Moon said.

They waited to hear what.

He told them.

Dolly stared at this unpredictable man. "You got *pie* on your mind?"

Moon nodded.

"Well, you're in luck," she bubbled. "I still got a peach cobbler in the cupboard." She pointed at the table. "Now you sit yourself down. I'll get you a helping."

"Don't bother to cut it," Moon said. "I'll take it with me."

Pete Bushman went goggle-eyed. "You want the whole damn thing?"

"You bet." Moon pressed a twenty-dollar bill into his hand. "And thank you."

The ranch foreman eyed the likeness of Andrew Jackson. *Fine-looking man. Nice head of hair.*

Dolly snatched the greenback from her husband, pushed it into Moon's coat pocket. "You'll not pay for anything from this kitchen."

Bushman fell into a sulk. "And what am I supposed to eat when I want me a piece a pie?"

Moon grinned at Mrs. Bushman. "Let him eat cake."

They stood behind the window curtain, watching the boss crank up his pickup.

"Well, that's just the damnedest thing," Pete Bushman said. "Took the whole pie. And you gave him the money back."

"It's all right," Dolly said softly.

"Why'n hell is it all right?" the old man barked.

"For one thing, he always says thank you. And for another, Charlie Moon is a big man. I expect he eats a whole pie at one sitting."

The ranch foreman thought about this. And decided that maybe his wife was right. She generally was. But on these cool nights, a hot dish of peach cobbler was just the thing. And Andrew Jackson *was* a fine-looking man.

Just as the sun was dropping behind the cloud-shrouded granite peaks, Moon removed the warmed-over pie from the oven. Cut himself in for a quarter share. And enjoyed it. When his dessert was finished, he left the remaining portion in the kitchen. Sitting on the windowsill. Cooling.

CHAPTER 17

He walked on and he found an old, old woman. He was about to kill her for she was *San*, Old Age, but she stopped him and said: "No, no, my Grandson, do not kill me. . . . Know that it will be the old people who will tell the young people what happened in years past. . . ." The Elder Brother knew that wisdom walked with old age, and he let her live.

—Sandoval, Hastin Tlo'tsi hee

Durango, Colorado
FBI Field Office

Charlie Moon sat across the desk from Special Agent Stanley Newman. The Ute investigator was concentrating on a list itemizing what had been found in Amanda Silk's camp trailer immediately after the archaeologist's unusual death. Similar items were listed by category. "Clothing." "Kitchen Utensils." "Native American Artifacts." Food was broken down by storage location—pantry cabinet, refrigerator, and so on. Printed reading matter was listed by category—professional journals, magazines, textbooks, reference works, her ledger, and last, a few novels.

From the corner of his eye, Newman watched the Ute investigator study the computer printout. The federal lawman nervously twirled a ballpoint pen in his hand while he waited for Moon to say something.

The silent seconds stretched into a minute. Two minutes. It seemed like hours to the impatient man from New Jersey.

Moon turned a page. "You sure everything's here?"

Newman bristled at this. "Of course."

The Ute looked doubtful. "Maybe if I could have a look at her stuff . . ."

Newman swallowed a mouthful of bitter resentment. And managed a civil reply. "The Bureau no longer has access to the personal effects of the deceased. Two days ago, we released everything to Dr. Silk's nephew."

Damn! Always a day late and a dollar short. "Where could I find this nephew?"

"Probably where Dr. Silk's personal property is—at her home. Unless her nephew has carted it all off by now."

"Where'd she live?"

Newman resisted the temptation to suggest that Uncle Sam's FBI was not the Ute's personal investigative organization. He forced himself to relax. Looked out the south window. "She lived down in New Mexico. Chama."

Moon got up to go. "Thanks."

The FBI agent could not resist a parting shot. "Sure you don't need anything else, Mr. Moon? There must surely be some other service the Bureau can provide."

The tribal investigator took a long, thoughtful look at the fed. Hesitated. Then removed a slim piece of yellow cardboard from his shirt pocket. "Could you validate my parking permit?"

Angel's Cafe

Charlie Moon's entire attention was focused on a thick sandwich.

Tribal chairman Oscar Sweetwater's small form occupied the opposite side of the booth. The elderly Ute sipped at a glass of tepid buttermilk. And watched wistfully as the young man made short work of a double bacon cheeseburger. With the works. Oscar took a nibble from the corner of a saltine cracker. "Glad to see you forked-end down."

"Thanks."

The waitress punched a Willie Nelson number on the jukebox. The Utes listened until the Texan's melancholy wail had ended.

The chairman tapped a horny fingernail on the scarred Formica. Stared unblinkingly at the tribal investigator. "So."

Moon looked over his sandwich.

"How d'you like your job, Charlie?"

"Okay."

"Just okay?"

"I'll like it better when I get paid."

"I'll see they cut you a check." Sweetwater's smile gave way to a thoughtful frown. "I been wondering . . ."

Moon waited for the chairman to complete his thought.

"About those murders at Chimney Rock . . ." The old man's voice trailed off into a hoarse whisper; he coughed into a paper napkin.

Moon drained his coffee cup.

The chairman cleared his throat. "I been wondering where your investigation is going."

The tribal investigator banged his palm on the side of a stubborn ketchup bottle. "South."

Oscar took a sip of buttermilk, making himself a thin white mustache. "Too bad."

Moon clarified his remark. "New Mexico."

"What's down there?"

"Chama."

A neon Coors sign sizzled and snapped in the fly-specked window.

The chairman licked off the mustache. He remained respectfully silent until the tribal investigator had finished his meal. "Know what I think?"

Charlie Moon shook his head.

"The *matukach* are right."

"About what?"

"Us."

The young man raised an inquisitive eyebrow.

"We are a taciturn people."

Moon grunted. *Only when I'm eating.*

Chama, New Mexico

The Ute pulled the Ford pickup under the tired, drooping branches of an aged maple. The house on the shady street was a century-old adobe covered with cracking stucco and thick mats of a vine heavy with hard red berries. The structure would have been nice to look at except for the pale-yellow two-car garage that had been attached to one end— seemingly as a malicious afterthought. Amanda Silk's camp trailer was in the driveway, beside a Chevrolet Suburban with Delaware plates. There was a large hand-lettered sign nailed to the whitewashed trunk of an oak.

YARD SALE — CASH ONLY
ABSOLUTELY NO RETURNS

A dozen people milled around aimlessly. An elderly, toothless man was departing with a satisfied smile under his nose, a brass spittoon under his arm. He looked up at Moon. "Afraid you're too late—it's been picked over. All the good stuff's gone."

The Ute investigator hoped this wasn't so.

In the garage, a bald, chubby man sat at a card table—counting greenbacks into a shoe box. The tribal investigator—assuming the innocent manner of a hayseed looking for a bargain—wandered around the garage. He peered into cardboard boxes of meticulously labeled potsherds, examined rusty garden tools, inspected a greasy pop-up toaster. The melancholy residue of a life snuffed out.

The bald man watched the potential customer poke around in a box of books. "Wanna buy something?"

"Maybe. You a member of Dr. Silk's family?"

"Yeah. I'm her nephew."

"The one who sells the plastic gizmos?"

The nephew's mouth drooped into a petulant scowl. "The term in the trade is FNP. Functional Novelty Products."

"I saw some of your functional novelty products in your aunt's camp trailer. You got any of 'em here?"

"Could be." *There really is one born every minute.* He rummaged around, found a paper bag, offered it to Moon. Inside was a wind-up alarm clock. A tin of sheet-metal screws. A collection of ballpoint pens secured with a rubber band. A *Saturday Evening Post* dated January 1947. Also a plastic mule that served as a pepper grinder. And a pot-bellied hippo.

"This all you got?"

"If you was lookin' for something in particular, maybe I could find it for you."

Moon told him.

The nephew shook his head. "I don't remember seein' nothin' like that."

Moon continued his search. Fifteen minutes later, he found a cardboard soup box containing a half dozen books. A bottle of aftershave shaped like a 1937 Plymouth. A plastic whale. "What're you asking for this box of stuff?"

"Depends." The nephew said this with a cagey look. "Somma this material could be valuable to the right collector. You a dealer?"

"Nope." Moon put the box back where he had found it.

The salesman didn't want to have to haul this junk to the Dumpster. "Okay. How about, say—thirty bucks for the whole kaboodle?"

The Ute investigator checked out a leaky garden hose. "Fifteen."

"Let's say twenty."

Moon turned away. "Let's say fourteen."

The man's eyes popped. "Waitaminute. You already offered fifteen."

"Thirteen."

The nephew raised his hands in a gesture of defeat. "Okay, okay—don't get sore. It's a deal."

Charlie Moon had started his pickup when he noticed the expensive sedan pulling to the curb across the street. The automobile had Colorado plates, which was not unusual in northern New Mexico. But yellow Mercedes were uncommon in Chama. And the driver of the luxury car looked familiar. As did his passenger. *Well now.*

Moon watched them cross the street. The paleoastronomer seemed tense and preoccupied. Possibly with the pretty young woman who was holding his hand. Or maybe with more important business. Neither of them saw Moon until he stepped from behind a maple trunk. Melina

Castro almost bumped into the Ute; she quickly released the professor's hand.

Charlie Moon tipped his black Stetson. "Small world."

"Hi," she said in a brittle tone. "How're things on the ranch?"

"Quiet. Peaceful." *Since you left.*

"I'm glad you're—uh—okay and all." Melina's words spilled out. "I mean—you know—after being almost killed and everything."

"Me too."

Professor Perkins seemed to be playing catch-up. "Oh yes—you're the fellow I met at Chimney Rock. The Indian police official."

Moon nodded. "You were going to give me some of your technical papers to read."

"Oh, right. I'll—ahh—have to get your address." The paleoastronomer looked past Moon at the small crowd milling around the garage sale. "We—uh—thought we'd drop by and . . . and . . ." It was as if Perkins had finally used up his vast supply of words.

Moon decided to help. "I bet you came here to buy something."

The academic cleared his throat for another attempt at speech. "Well, yes, actually. Amanda had quite a fine collection of Anasazi artifacts. Thought I might make a small purchase—something to remember her by."

"You may be too late," Moon said. "I'm told all the good stuff is gone."

Melina Castro's mouth twisted into a counterfeit smile. "Did you buy anything?"

Moon nodded.

The paleoastronomer was regaining his customary composure. "Get yourself some of the good stuff?"

The Ute's dark face was unreadable. "I hope so."

CHAPTER 18

> The . . . Elder Brother met . . . a creature of bluish color. "Do
> not kill me," he said. "I am Death, Grandson. Spare me, for if
> every creature lived there would be no place on earth for youth
> and laughter." The Elder Brother left him with the others.
> —Sandoval, Hastin Tlo'tsi hee

Under the Earth

Except for the dog, Charlie Moon thought he was entirely alone on
Ghost Wolf Mesa. The sky was crystal clear from here to the end of the
rainbow, the air crisp enough to break between your fingers. Moreover,
a pair of magnificent red-tailed hawks soared lazily overhead. A man
would not want to go overboard and claim this was a perfect day. *But
it's close enough.*

The Ute left his pickup at the edge of the graveled road. Alternately
followed and led by Sidewinder—who managed to sniff at everything—he headed through clumps of piñon and juniper to the spot
where the wandering child had found the petroglyph. The important
artifact was now covered with thick Plexiglas, set in a sturdy frame of
redwood two-by-fours. A sign under the transparent cover sternly

warned of dire consequences for the sorry soul who might even think of molesting this ancient sketch in stone. Mess with the Twin War Gods and the U.S. government will stop your clock.

Sidewinder slobbered on the plastic-shrouded shrine.

Charlie Moon studied the squat figures, each grasping a spear in his stick-hand. The Ute smiled. About a thousand years ago, a crafty old Anasazi fellow had probably enjoyed his little joke. And wished he could have come back someday and watched the fun when folks tried to decipher his simple picture. Maybe this same artisan had been the architect of the Great Pueblo out on the Crag. That structure had non-parallel sides. And as April Tavishuts had told the Indian tourists, lines drawn along the slightly cockeyed outer walls converged over here on the mesa—precisely at the mysterious stone basin. But why? And what was the purpose of the hemisphere chiseled into the sandstone? More puzzles yet unsolved. And that was good, Moon thought. It would be a far poorer world if there were no riddles left to ponder. Like what made gravity work. And why the world was filled with so-called ordinary people who never gave up—no matter how tough life got. These were very deep mysteries indeed.

Moon left the petroglyph, traversed a rocky ravine, then made his way up a gentle slope dotted with dwarfish oak and scented pine. With the lanky dog trotting at his side, he walked another hundred yards. There at his feet was the pit house. The excavation—once so precisely geometric—was already crumbling into shapelessness. A ruin within a ruin. What had the murderer found? Maybe nothing. Scott Parris might be right. Maybe the fact that lines drawn through the pictograph spears converged at this spot was a meaningless coincidence. If that was true, Julius Santos, April Tavishuts, and Amanda Silk had all died for nothing. *And I took a ride on a train with a dead man.*

His brain still ached from time to time. And there were other reminders of the concussion. Sharp twinges of pain from places in his body that had no reason at all to hurt. Flashes of light at the periphery of his visual field. Recently, on a quiet walk in Black Mule Canyon at the east end of the Columbine property, he had even experienced a hallucination. Thought he saw one of the *pitukupf* clan pop his little head out of a hole in a hollow pine. Moon smiled at the embarrassing memory.

He sat down by the excavation and stared into what had almost become his grave. As if staring could help. *This is dumb. I should go get Aunt Daisy, head back to the ranch. Later on, I could phone Camilla. See if she's back from her travels. And if she's still mad at me.*

But the unsolved problem nagged at his aching brain. What if there *was* something here. If the pothunter hadn't found it, it'd probably stay in the ground for ages to come. Maybe forever. Until a few billion years hence when the sun grew hugely fat and hungry and swallowed the earth whole.

Sidewinder flushed a cottontail, chased it for fifty yards. Then came back, his tongue lolling happily from a panting mouth. Moon wondered idly whether dogs were capable of worrying.

In an instant, the hound lost his happy expression. Lowered his head. Stared at something Moon could not see.

"What's bothering you, old boy?" The Ute reached out to rub the animal's neck. The rippled muscles were taut as spring steel.

"You spot another rabbit?"

The hound whined, pawed at the earth.

This is a sure-enough strange dog. "What's the matter—"

Before all the words were out of his mouth, the hound leaped into the excavation and started to dig furiously.

"No," Moon yelled, "get outta there."

The dog, dirt spraying out between his hind legs, ignored this command.

Moon grabbed Sidewinder by the scruff of his neck and pulled him from the excavation. As the animal was withdrawn, his front paws continued to flail vainly at empty air. The Ute held the dog's face close to his own. "When I say NO, you better know I mean it."

Sidewinder whined and looked sideways at the hole.

"You are a stubborn creature." Moon carried the hound back to the pickup and locked him in the cab. The malefactor securely imprisoned, he returned to the excavation. "Well, that animal sure made a mess." *I wonder what possessed him.* Now, there was a silly word. Nothing *possessed* him. Sidewinder was just a regular dog. Nothing but drives and instincts. With about enough working brains to fill an acorn hull.

Moon knelt by the hole in the ground. He was wondering how he would explain this canine vandalism when he noticed something. On the bottom of the excavation, Sidewinder's furious digging had uncovered a slab of smooth, black stone. Looked like basalt. *But this is a solid sandstone mesa. There can't be any basalt up here. Not unless someone brings it . . .*

There was no two ways about it. What he had in mind was illegal. Seriously illegal. He did it anyway.

Moon scraped away rocks and sand from the basalt slab. He got a grip on one edge, lifted the black stone. Under it was more sand. He removed a thick-bladed knife from a sheath on his belt and scraped away at the soil. About two inches down, the blade encountered something. Moon laid the knife aside and proceeded to remove the soil with his hands. He touched something hard and smooth. It was a bluish-tinted circular disk. Baked clay. Very carefully, he removed more sand. The lid sat on a ceramic pot.

Moon paused to consider his discovery. It was bad enough to dig here at all. It was a serious offense to remove an Anasazi artifact from its original burial site. If he was going by the book, he should notify the U.S. Forest Service authorities in Pagosa. They would notify the NAGPRA committee. On the other hand, this might be important evidence in an ongoing murder investigation. And despite all the jurisdictional squabbles—and the fact that this property was administered by the U.S. Department of Agriculture—Chimney Rock Archaeological Site was within the boundaries of the Southern Ute Reservation. And he was a duly appointed official of the tribe—gathering evidence in the murder of tribal member April Tavishuts.

A man who feels a strong urge to break the law will think of a multitude of good reasons to do it.

Charlie Moon felt a strong urge to examine the artifact that someone was willing to kill to possess. So he resumed his work, gently removing sand from around the almost spherical vessel. When he lifted the object from its resting place, the Ute was in for a surprise. This was not Anasazi ware. The pot—like the lid—was made of a light blue clay. The delicately applied lines and swirls were bright red. These were clearly not Anasazi geometric designs. Circling the outside of the vessel were nine blood-red anatomically correct male figures, their hands raised as if in rapt supplication. The tenth man, taller than his comrades, was notable for more than his size. The only object on the pottery painted white, this human form had the head of a wolf.

Moon weighed the pot in his hands. Twenty-five, maybe thirty pounds. So the ceramic wasn't the Anasazi treasure, just a container. The good stuff was *in* it. All the more reason to notify the authorities. *But what'll I tell them? That I moved a basalt slab and dug up a pot?* No. That wouldn't do.

Best thing would be to put it back.

But it wouldn't hurt to have a quick peek. And so the Ute removed the lid. Looked inside. Stared at it. *Where on earth did you come from?*

As the truth slowly dawned, he realized that this was an improper question.

CHAPTER 19

Then he chanted. And the first chant he used was this:
Ponder well what you think of me.
I am he who killed the monsters.
—Sandoval, Hastin Tlo'tsi hee

The Invitation

Daisy Perika had heard the painful creaking of Charlie Moon's pickup shortly before it topped the crest of the nearest ridge. The Ute elder realized that her hearing was not so keen as it used to be. Only three or four years ago, she would have heard him coming a mile away. She busied herself at the stove. He would want some coffee.

By the time he knocked on her door, a pot of brackish brew was bubbling over a blue ring of propane flame.

Moon removed his hat before ducking through the six-foot door. "Good morning."

She was very pleased to see her nephew, but old habits die a hard death—so she snapped at him: "You're too late for any breakfast."

He made another attempt. "It's a really fine day out there."

Daisy responded with a doubtful grunt.

Accustomed to this sort of welcome, Charlie Moon took his customary seat, managing to fold his long legs under the small kitchen table.

Daisy poured the scalding coffee. Most of it went in his cup. She brought a crockery sugar bowl to the table, slammed it down. "So what brings you out here?"

He winked at her. "Woke up this morning feeling fine. Thought I'd do something nice for myself. But what? And then it come to me—I'll go visit my favorite aunt."

The old woman fought off a smile. "I'm your *only* aunt."

"That's what makes you so special." He dumped five teaspoons of sugar into the oily black liquid and stirred. "You still want to visit the Columbine?"

Daisy's heart fluttered with excitement. "Ahh—what would I do up there?" She hoped he had no idea.

"I thought you wanted to put some of your stuff in the guest cabin—so it'd always be ready whenever you want to come see me. But if you'd rather go someplace else, we could—"

"No, never mind. I know how proud you are of that big ranch—always wantin' to show it off." She directed a pained expression at her youthful relative. "You sure it's not too much trouble for you to have an old woman in the way for a day or two?"

He paused, as if thinking it over. "You will be an awful nuisance." Moon flashed her an ivory smile. "But I'm feeling big-hearted today."

Daisy Perika waved a sooty-black skillet at him. "Don't get smart with me, you big jughead—or I'll make you a round hat out of this flat frying pan."

The Journey North

Daisy Perika stretched her neck to peer over the F150 dashboard. Far ahead, a row of sawtoothed peaks ripped through the clouds. "We almost there?"

Moon swerved to miss a bounding jackrabbit. "Another half hour to the turnoff."

"I'm hungry."

"There's some Fig Newtons in the glove compartment."

She helped herself to the stale cookies. Then: "I need to pee."

"I stopped for gas in Granite Creek. Why didn't you—"

"Because I wasn't ready."

He slowed the pickup. "I'll pull off the road by some bushes."

"Don't bother." She exhaled a practiced martyr's sigh. "I'll just have to hold it."

Moon thought it best to change the subject. But what would the old woman want to talk about? Something gloomy, of course. He recalled his aunt's dismal prediction that she was not long for this world. "So. How're your toenails growing?"

What a peculiar thing to say. Daisy turned to stare at him. "What?"

She's already forgot about it. "Never mind."

A ten-mile silence ensued. Moon wondered whether he should tell his aunt about the object he and the dog had unearthed at Chimney Rock. The tribal elder knew all of the old Anasazi legends. He knew what it was—but Daisy might even have some idea what it was *supposed* to be. After some consideration, he decided he couldn't trust his aunt to keep his secret. *No, I'll have to handle this thing by myself.*

A boisterous west wind pushed its muscular shoulder against the pickup.

The old woman's head gradually fell back against the seat. Her mouth gaped open. She began to snore.

A roaring gust flung a bushel of sand and grit at the windshield. Daisy's head jerked up; she raised a hand as if to shield her face. "What was that?"

"Texas sleet."

As Daisy watched the sand grind away the surface of the glass, she wondered whether she should tell her nephew what she had learned from the *pitukupf*. Not that Charlie Moon would have the least interest in what the little man had to say. Her nephew did not even believe in the existence of the dwarf. But the shaman had a nagging feeling that she should tell him anyway. She took a deep breath. "Before you was almost killed at Chimney Rock, I had a talk with someone."

"Anybody I know?"

"No." *Sad to say.* "But he lives in *Cañon del Espíritu.*"

Oh boy—here it comes.

"In a badger hole," she added with a stubborn jut of her chin.

"Is that a fact." This would be embarrassing.

"He told me what all that mischief at Chimney Rock was about."

It would be best to humor the old woman. If she got to telling one of her fanciful tales, it'd keep her mind off a full bladder. "Well, I'd like to hear what he had to say."

She shot him a suspicious glance. Charlie Moon never liked to hear about the dwarf. *Just wants me to talk about anything but needing to pee. But I'm going to have my say.* "The trouble started a long, long time ago. With them old Anasazi wizards who did all that strange stuff in that big temple up on the Crag."

"Wizards," he muttered.

She nodded. "What they wanted was always the same thing—power. Problem was, they got *too* powerful. They was able to control those spirits that live in stones and trees and the wind. For a while, they could even make the weather do what they wanted it to."

"Well," Moon said. Not knowing what else to say.

"Then came the awful drought. Lasted for years and years. Those Chaco magicians, they did all kinds of things to make it rain. Mostly, they stuck cactus spines through their tongues for blood sacrifices. Stuff like that."

Ouch.

"They were peculiar people," she said, and added: "From Mexico."

Moon eyed the oil pressure gauge. *Down some. Rings must be going bad.*

"Most of their sacrifices were made to White Shell Woman. That's what they call the moon."

He wondered where the money for repairs would come from. *It'll need valves too. Might be cheaper in the long run to put in a whole new engine, with all the trimmings. Or at least a short block.*

Daisy hated to mention the really awful things—talk about such terrible evil could bring bad luck. Like painful boils and stomach ulcers and vomiting. But Charlie Moon needed to hear this. "They tried all kinds of sacrifices to get some rain. But no matter what they did, the rain didn't come. Then, those priests got desperate. And went too far. They started killing human beings."

Moon glanced uncertainly at his aunt. What was she muttering about?

"They burned people—while they was still alive."

Poor old thing must be having nightmares.

"The reason they did these bad things," the shaman explained, "was to make White Shell Woman cry—so her tears would fall from the sky and make rain for the corn and beans and stuff."

Corn and beans sounded good. With a big chicken-fried steak. *Better keep her talking.* "Did it work?"

"Wait till I get to the end of the story," she said with a testy look, "and you'll find out."

"Take your time."

"Finally, White Shell Woman did begin to cry. But not for those Anasazi priests—she was cryin' for those poor people who was being murdered."

"That's good."

"No." She shook her head. "That's bad."

I bet you're going to tell me why.

She was. "It happened like this. When White Shell Woman cried, her tears wasn't water like those old priests had hoped." Her old eyes flashed. "When they hit the ground, they was pieces of fire. Like red-hot embers."

Moon felt the hairs on the back of his neck stand up.

"One of them burning tears landed down by Stollsteimer Creek," she said. "Only they didn't call it that back then." Unaware that she now had her nephew's full attention, the old woman continued as if talking to herself. "Them priests, they waited till it had cooled down. Then, they wrapped it in some cured deerskin and took it up to the temple on the Crag. The priest who was head honcho, he knew what the burning tear meant. It was a sign that White Shell Woman was very angry with them. They had to leave the temple. So they started packing up to go south. Back to Chaco. Then all the way down to Mexico. But after everyone else was gone, the oldest wizard, he stayed behind."

Moon found a scratchy voice. "Why'd he do that?"

She was surprised at this expression of interest, which seemed genuine. "Because he had to hide White Shell Woman's tear close to the

Twin War Gods. Someday, way off in the future—when the time was right—he intended to come back for it. But old men are forgetful."

Charlie Moon was staring at the sand-strewn road that stretched out toward home. But he was thinking about White Shell Woman's white-hot tear that had scorched the earth.

Daisy continued. "That old priest knew that things change a lot as time passes—even the land. So he was worried that when he came back a long time later, he might not be able to find the spot where he buried it. That's why he made that drawing of the Twin War Gods on the sandstone—to help him find it again. And covered it up with lots of dirt. But something went wrong."

Moon heard himself say: "Somebody found the petroglyph."

Daisy gave her nephew a searching look. *Maybe you do understand.* "This person understood the drawing—and knew where the old priest had hidden White Shell Woman's tear." She pursed her lips and frowned. "The thought of finding a treasure can make almost anyone act silly. It can make a bad person crazy enough to kill a person who interferes with their plans."

The wind hurled a parched tumbleweed against the windshield, causing the old woman to gasp. "What was—"

"Utah rosebush."

She attempted to recover from this distraction. "Where was I?"

"Something about treasure hunters."

Well. He is listening. "For all these years, that old Anasazi wizard has been guarding the place where he hid White Shell Woman's tear. But after the bad person found out where it was buried, Julius Santos was called up to Ghost Wolf Mesa."

"Called by who?"

"You shouldn't ask."

"Sorry."

Daisy continued. "Julius was supposed to stop the bad person from digging up what the old wizard had buried. But he didn't get the job done." She glanced at her nephew. "So that old Anasazi wizard showed his Twin War Gods drawing to that little Zuni girl—who showed it to you."

"Why would he do that?" *Why am I having this dumb conversation?*

"So another person—a good person—would understand what the

War Gods' picture meant—and find White Shell Woman's tear before the bad person laid hands on it."

Moon stared through the windshield into the windswept sands. *A good person. Like April Tavishuts?* It almost made sense. But April hadn't found anything but trouble. And like Santos, she had ended up on the far side of that deep river. He heard his aunt's voice droning on.

"But even with two dead, another person was called to find White Shell Woman's tear. That person is supposed to hide it in another place." She aimed a sharp look at her nephew.

Moon pretended not to feel her eyes. But he did. Like a pair of darts stuck in the side of his head.

The tribal elder drew in a deep breath. "You got anything you want to tell me?"

"Yeah. We're almost to the Columbine gate."

Sand-laden wind screamed around the cab.

Daisy frowned at her reflection in the windshield. It frowned back. "If a person should see that old Chaco wizard, he'll usually look like a reg'lar man. Dark—skin like beef jerky. But when he wants to, he can grow hair white as snow—and walk on four legs." The mere thought of the albino wolf made the tribal elder shudder.

It's my own fault. I shouldn't have got her started.

The sun slipped behind a mile-thick bank of dark clouds. A long, dismal shadow ripped over the wide valley.

Just ahead, Moon caught a glimpse of something in the road. Something trotting along on four legs. He braked the pickup to a crawl. As the beast paused to look toward the headlights, its eyes reflected bright red—twin embers. The pale form stood quite still for a moment, then loped across the road, down the bank into a shallow arroyo. And was gone.

It was a coyote. Moon gritted the sand between his teeth. *Just an old, gray coyote.*

Daisy Perika had not seen the creature. "A long, long time before you was born—I think it was about nineteen and thirty-something— there was some *matukach* scientists who came to Colorado with Franklin D. Roosevelt's WPA. They was working up on Ghost Wolf Mesa, digging in those old kivas and pit houses. You want me to tell you what happened?"

Any way I could stop you?

"One day—just about sundown—one of 'em let out this awful scream. Then just flopped over on his face. Dead as a doorbell."

"Knob," he mumbled.

"What?"

"Door*knob*." He frowned. Or was it "dead as a door*nail*"?

Daisy stared blankly at her nephew. *First, it's some nonsense about toenails. Now he's babbling about doorknobs. Must be his head injury.* Thinking it prudent to act as if his behavior was perfectly normal, she groped for a moment, then picked up the thread of her tale about the scientist who had perished at Chimney Rock so long ago. "From what I heard, that white man must've gave up the ghost fairly close to where April Tavishuts's body was found." *And where you got the sense knocked outta your head.* "And you know *how* he died?"

Not intending to reply, Charlie Moon was surprised to hear the thought slip past his lips. "Scared to death."

"Oh," Daisy said. "You already heard that story."

To block any other stray words that were inclined to escape, he clenched his mouth tightly shut.

Her wrinkled face settled into a satisfied smirk. "You know what I think?" She didn't wait for a response. He might just say *doorknob* again. "I think somebody has already found White Shell Woman's tear. And intends to keep it for himself."

Moon attempted an innocent expression. His reflection in the windshield sneered back at him. A brutish mug on an FBI most-wanted poster.

CHARLES "GRAVE-ROBBER" MOON
DESPICABLE ARTIFACT THIEF — DESECRATOR OF SACRED SITES
USE EXTREME CAUTION WHEN APPROACHING
SUBJECT UNHINGED BY BRAIN INJURY — MAY BE ARMED
P.S.: FORMER SWEETHEART SAYS SHOOT THE BASTARD
ON SIGHT.

His aunt's voice interrupted this melancholy fantasy. "It could be very bad for the person who took White Shell Woman's tear if they don't do what that old Anasazi wizard wants them to do—*very* bad."

Moon didn't ask.

Needing no encouragement, the tribal elder explained precisely what the old wizard expected of the person who had removed the precious artifact from its hiding place. And if he refused, what the terrible consequences of such folly would be.

Moon almost wished he'd left her at home. Almost. But he had woke up this morning with a pocket full of silver dollars. And the day was not yet spent.

Unhinged

By the time Charlie Moon delivered his aunt to the Columbine, the groaning moan of the hardworking wind had abated to a weary sigh. But the Ute still had sand in his mouth. He brushed his teeth. An hour later he had a fine lunch under his belt, and felt much better. Furthermore, he had managed to dismiss his aunt's fanciful tale. He inquired whether she would like to go for a short ride, take her things over to the cabin.

Daisy Perika agreed; asserted that she was looking forward to spending the night there. Charlie Moon's ranch headquarters was too big. Too many dark corners. Reminded her of a museum. Or a barn.

Leaving the sandblasted F150 to heal in the therapeutic shade of the leaning cottonwoods, Moon drove the Expedition along the lane that led across one of the Columbine's smaller fenced pastures. It was barely a half mile wide. He had the windows down, the better to inhale the sweet mountain air.

Daisy Perika was straining for her first glimpse of the log cabin that lay across the lake and just beyond a spruce-lined ridge. "Well, that was a fairly decent meal you fixed. Pork chops. Pinto beans. Fried squash." She glanced sideways at her nephew. "I didn't know you could cook anything but beef steaks."

"Had lots of practice."

"Sure. You've been a bachelor a long time."

Moon absorbed this body blow with a grunt. *Wonder what Camilla's doing right now.*

Penetrating the stand of blue spruce, the arrow-straight ranch road was transformed into a meandering serpent, gliding stealthily beneath thick evergreen branches.

The sudden change from bright high-altitude sunlight to deep shade startled the old woman—it was as if a prankish magician had snuffed out the sun. Black-looking moss was spread like a lumpy carpet under the scented trees. A furry Something scurried along in the emerald twilight, startling a patch of delicate ferns into a shiver of excitement.

The air was corpse-cool, and unhealthily damp. Daisy pulled the woolen shawl tighter across her shoulders. She wondered whether death was like this. Would the dangerous journey from Middle World to Upper World pass through a dark, cold place where loathsome creatures lay in wait for the unprotected soul? *The next time I see Nahum Yacitti, I'll ask him what it was like to make the crossing.* More than once the old shepherd had returned from Upper World to talk with the Ute shaman. *Maybe when it's my time to go, Nahum will come to take me across.* "Charlie?"

He lifted his boot off the accelerator pedal, shifted the Expedition to low. "Yeah?"

"How are you feeling?"

"Fine. Why do you ask?"

"Oh, that head doctor—he said your injury might cause you to—well . . . have some problems."

"I'm doing as good as can be expected." He tapped the brake pedal as a mule deer bounded across the lane. "There are some peculiar symptoms I have to get used to."

This didn't sound good. "Like what?"

"Odd things."

"How odd?"

"Sometimes . . ." He sighed. "Sometimes I *see* things."

Getting something out of this man was hard as pulling a mule's back teeth. "What kinda things?"

His eyes seemed to glaze over. "Things that aren't there."

"Oh." She didn't dare ask. Not while they were in this dark forest.

"And sometimes," he added, "I have a hard time controlling my temper."

Charlie Moon didn't have a temper. "Sounds like you're not quite yourself."

"Last week," he said matter-of-factly, "I shot a John Deere tractor."

"You did?"

"Five times."

"Why?"

"That was all the live rounds left in the chamber. I'd plugged a contrary fence post with the first one."

"No, I mean why did you shoot a *tractor?*"

"You don't want to know." The big Ute ground his teeth and muttered under his breath. "Damn machine had it coming."

She scooted an inch closer to the car door. Away from him. "Well, I hope you start getting better real soon."

"Doc Kenny says I'll eventually be fine. But getting over a brain injury takes time."

The lane left the small forest, and so did they. The reentry into sunlight pleased the Ute elder. It was like passing from death into life.

Moon braked to a stop by the sturdy cabin. He helped the elderly woman from the Expedition and began to unload her cardboard boxes from the rear seat. He nodded to indicate the cabin's front door. "You can open up for me. Use that key I gave you."

She fumbled in her purse. "Well—it's not here. Must've left it at home."

A ring of keys was in the ignition switch, but Moon had an armload of boxes. "Why don't you try it?" he said.

His words had been masked by a gust of wind. Daisy squinted, as if this would help her to hear. "What?"

He used his chin to point at the cabin door. "Doorknob."

She stared oddly at him. *He's doing it again.*

Moon stared back. *Poor old woman must be going deaf.* He set the boxes down, turned the knob. And stared thoughtfully at the unlocked door. "Guess I should keep this locked. We've been having a problem with a prowler."

"A prowler—way out here?"

"Hasn't done any real harm yet. Just swiped a few things."

Probably just a bear. "What kind of things?"

"Nothing much. Horse blanket from the barn. Sack of apples. Couple of pies."

Daisy felt her skin tingle. "All sorts of riffraff is running around these days."

He frowned at the elderly woman. "Maybe you should stay up at the ranch house tonight."

She dismissed this suggestion with a wave of her hand. "I'm not afraid of no pie thief. Besides I've got things to do here." *Things you don't need to know about.*

"Well, I suppose it'll be all right. We strung a phone line out here last week. Anything disturbs you, you can ring me at the big house."

Daisy pulled a wicked-looking butcher knife from a box of cooking implements. "If any sneak thief comes messing around here, I'll have his liver for breakfast."

They passed through the living room to the small kitchen. Daisy found a blue cotton cloth in one of the boxes and spread it over the stout redwood table. Moon started to open a box marked "Food." She slapped his hand. "Don't be messing around with my stuff."

"Just thought I'd help you—"

"I don't need no man's help. I can do this job by myself."

He eyed the "Food" box. "Well, if you're sure."

"I'm sure. Now hop in your fancy car and get along back to that big ranch house."

"Okay. But you keep the doors locked. I'll come and pick you up for breakfast."

"I can make my own breakfast. Now get going."

Charlie Moon turned, took three steps toward the door, then stopped cold.

"What is it?"

He raised a hand to silence her. Then stood perfectly still.

Daisy could feel her pulse throbbing in her neck.

Slowly, the Ute rancher turned.

"What's wrong?"

He answered in a whisper. "I heard something."

"What was it?"

"Don't know. But the noise was down there." He pointed at the floor. "In the cellar."

"Probably just a squirrel," Daisy said. But she was trembling like an aspen leaf in a brisk wind.

Moon approached the cellar door. "Okay," he boomed, "come on out."

There was no response.

He gave his aunt a look that brooked no argument. "Go outside. Get in the car and lock the doors."

But Daisy Perika could not make her feet move.

Charlie Moon removed a heavy, long-barreled pistol from underneath his jacket.

Daisy, who did not know he was armed, gasped. "What are you gonna—"

Moon glared at the cellar door. "Come out now. Or I'm coming in after you."

He's acting crazy! Her whole body seemed to shudder. "No, don't—"

But her nephew had already opened the door. She heard the boards creak as he took several steps down the darkened stairs.

"I'm counting to three," he said to the darkness. "One." A pause. "You better show yourself." Another pause. "Two."

"Charlie," she said, "don't shoot, it's just—"

"Three." There was a rafter-shaking *boom*. The smell of spent gunpowder wafted up the cellar stairs. It was mixed with dust and the smell of old potatoes.

She waited, too deep in despair to pray that nothing really bad had happened down there. It was too late for that.

A minute passed.

Two minutes.

A grim-faced Moon finally appeared at the head of the stairs. He stuck the revolver under his belt. "You'd better wait in the car." He looked around. "I need to find a shovel."

"Who did you shoot?"

He hesitated. "It's best if you don't know."

"You better tell me." *Then we can get our stories straight. I'll claim it was self-defense.*

Moon glanced down the stairs. "I gave him a chance. He should've come out."

"Oh my God in heaven." Daisy collapsed on a kitchen chair. "It's all my fault."

"Thieving bastard had it coming to him. I bet he was after my stash of Vidalia onions."

"Oh, poor old Alvah," she wailed.

"Who?"

Daisy was wringing her hands. "Alvah Yazzi."

Moon seemed bewildered by all this. "How would that Navajo get into my cellar?"

"It was me and Louse-Marie LaForte," she moaned. "We brought him up here in her old car. I gave him my key to the cabin."

Moon stared holes in her. "Why would you go and do a thing like that?"

"Because he asked me." Daisy rested her face in her hands. "After April was killed, Alvah set it up to look like he was dead—then he hid in *Cañon del Espíritu*. But he ran out of food he could manage without his false teeth. He came to my trailer late one afternoon, but I wasn't at home. So that numbskull Navajo climbed onto the top of my house. For a while, he sat up there—watching for me. Then he got tired of waiting, and laid down on the roof and fell asleep. Later that night, he woke up—and started banging on the side of the trailer to get my attention. I come within a inch of shootin' him. When I found out who he was, I said, 'What in the world is the matter with you, Alvah— waking me up in the middle of the night.' That's when he told me what'd happened. And begged me for help. So I started taking food up the canyon to where he was hiding. Then one day, he saw you followin' me—and watched you eat the breakfast I'd left for him." Daisy glared accusingly at her nephew.

Moon avoided her eyes. "I thought you was leaving the food for . . . ahh . . . the little man."

"Hmmpf," she said. "Anyway, after you almost found him, Alvah Yazzi figured that *Cañon del Espíritu* wasn't a good enough place to hide. That's when he begged me to help him get him away from there—to someplace safe."

"And so you and Louise-Marie carted him up here. To my ranch."

She nodded. "We put him in the trunk of her old car. He was mad as a yella hornet when we finally let him out. Said he'd almost died of suf-focation and the heat and from being bumped around like an old sack of apples." The Ute elder grunted. "Just like one of them Navajos. Do

him a big favor and all he can do is find something to complain about."
She offered her nephew a sorrowful look. "And now he's dead. And
you killed him."

"Well," Moon said slowly, "not exactly."

"You just wounded him?"

"Not exactly."

"What are you trying to tell me?"

"Alvah's not down there."

Thank God. "Where is he?"

"Down in New Mexico, I expect. Or Arizona. Somewhere on the
Big Rez."

A suspicious expression spread over her dark features. "Charlie
Moon—who was it you shot down there under the house?"

"You mean in the root cellar?"

"No, I mean on toppa the chimbley. Now tell me."

"Okay. It was Mr. Rutabaga."

This made no sense at all. "Who's he?"

"A Swede." *Scandinavian member of the turnip family.*

"Is he hurt bad?"

"Just a flesh wound."

Daisy Perika opened her mouth as if to protest, then clamped it shut.

"Well, it was dark. I couldn't get off a good shot."

"Charlie Moon—I am going to tell you something. And I want you
to listen to me with both ears." She pointed a trembling finger at her
nephew. "You have completely lost your mind."

"Could be." He grinned at his aged relative. "Maybe it runs in the
family."

She glared at him. "What do you mean by that?"

"Well, I have this aunt who brought a Navajo outlaw up here and
hid him on my ranch. Without asking my permission."

"Alvah hadn't done nothing bad. That poor old man was just
afraid."

"Afraid of what?"

"Of the witches who'd murdered his stepdaughter. Alvah figured
they'd kill him next."

With Aunt Daisy and her ilk, there was always a witch to blame. "It
wasn't witches who killed April Tavishuts."

"That's what I told Alvah. Witches aren't responsible for *all* the bad things that happen."

He stared at the enigmatic old woman. *Maybe she's smarter than I give her credit for.*

The Ute elder shook her head. "But a sensible Ute girl should've known better than to mess around those old ruins. The spirit of that old Anasazi wizard has been prowling around Chimney Rock for ages. It was him that lured April into the ruins."

Moon sighed. *Sure. If it's not a witch, it's a ghost.*

"Don't look at me like that."

"Like what?"

"Like I'm a silly old woman." She frowned at the cabin floor. And painted herself a lurid, bloody picture of what was in the cellar. "Can we please get outta here?"

"Sure. We'll head back to the big house. I'll fix you a bedroom upstairs."

"Don't bother. You can take me home."

"But you just got here." *And it's a long drive south . . . and a longer drive back.*

"My business here is done. I come to see if Alvah was still hanging around, but he's gone. Besides, I could never catch a wink of sleep this far from home."

"Sure you could. I'll fix a special pillow for you—stuff it with peach fuzz."

The old woman told him where he could stuff his peach fuzz.

Charlie Moon had endured sufficient abuse for the day. "Okay. Home you go."

"And there's another thing," she snapped.

With Aunt Daisy, there was always another thing.

She jabbed an arthritic finger at his silver belt buckle. "Since your mother and father died years ago, I've been the closest thing to a parent you got. And I want you to know, Charlie Moon—I'm disappointed with you."

"I do something wrong?"

"You shouldn't of shot that poor foreigner in the cellar. Maybe he *was* a pie thief—but all he wanted was something to eat."

CHAPTER 20

> . . . many of them practiced black magic; when they left their homes they traveled in the form of the coyote, the bird, the wildcat. . . . Evil grew among them.
>
> —Sandoval, Hastin Tlo'tsi hee

A Fine Madness

Anne Foster leaned on her man. "I hope Charlie's okay. His aunt is really worried about—well—you know."

Scott Parris gave his favorite redhead a reassuring one-armed hug. "He'll be fine." He rapped gloved knuckles on the heavy door. No answer. He opened it, poked his head inside. "Hey, Charlie—you in there?"

Moon's bass voice boomed through the house. "In the kitchen."

Parris and his fiancée headed across the cavernous parlor, then down a dimly lighted hall to the kitchen. The Ute was unwrapping a package of brown butcher paper. He paused to shake Parris's hand.

Anne gave Moon a hug. "How are you?"

He shrugged under the embrace. "I'm getting by." Moon frowned down at the top of her head. "You look different."

She backed away and posed. "It's my new hairdo. How do you like it?"

"Always liked your hair," he said to the shapely woman. "It's your best feature." *Almost.*

"She's been to Colorado Springs," Parris grumped. "In the ten-dollar-a-minute part of town."

"Got my fingernails done too." Anne displayed a delicate hand.

"Nice," the Ute said.

"And my toenails."

Moon looked down his nose at her hand-tooled cowgirl boots. "I'll take your word for it."

Parris laughed.

Anne made a face at both of them, then glanced at the steak. "Did we arrive at supper time?"

The Ute had not looked a timepiece in the face for three days. "You're lookin' at a free man. I eat when I get hungry, go to bed when I'm sleepy." He stuck a meat fork into the steak, plopped it onto a platter. Then added a dash of salt. "Don't this look good?"

She twitched her pretty nose. "It looks *raw.*"

"Since my injury, my taste in meat is kinda . . ." Moon searched for the right word. Found it. "Different."

The puzzled woman watched their host leave the kitchen with the platter. He was halfway down the hallway when she called out, "Charlie, where are you going?"

"Outside."

"What for?"

He seemed not to hear the question. "There's more steaks in the refrigerator. Why don't you get some of 'em broiling."

She turned to her sweetheart with a worried expression. "Charlie is acting awfully strange."

Scott Parris—long accustomed to his friend's occasional eccentricities—snorted. "Compared to what?"

"Don't be flippant," the pretty woman said. "Poor man has been through a lot. His girlfriend dumped him. Then the head injury." She nodded to agree with herself. "I think his aunt is right. It's been too much. Unsettled his mind."

"Hmmpf," Parris said, intending to close the discussion with this observation.

Anne frowned in the direction of the front porch. "I think you should go check on him."

"I think I should tend to my own business."

"Then I'll do it myself." With a toss of her strawberry mane, his sweetheart charged down the hallway.

Scott Parris watched her go. Once she had her head, there was no turning her. He opened the refrigerator and sniffed at the pathetic remains of a peach cobbler.

Anne Foster surreptitiously parted the curtains at a tall window, just enough to accommodate one eye. It was almost dark outside, but she could see Charlie Moon plainly enough. The Ute was stalking back and forth like a caged cougar, the platter of raw meat in his hand. Moreover, he was muttering to himself. Alarmed, she hurried back to the kitchen.

Scott Parris, who had arranged several steaks on the broiler, looked around to see his intended. Her face wore a peculiar pinched expression. "What's wrong?"

"It's Charlie—he's behaving strangely."

"Oh." *Now where does he keep the potatoes.*

Anne's lip trembled. "Scotty, this is serious."

"I'd rather you didn't call me Scotty." He opened a cabinet under the sink. "Aha." Big bag of Idaho spuds.

She stamped her foot. "Listen to me."

This got his attention. And got her a hug. "What's botherin' you, darlin'?"

Anne pointed toward the front porch. "Your best friend is out there with a chunk of raw meat—pacing back and forth like some kind of wild animal."

"So?"

She stared in disbelief. "That doesn't bother you?"

This woman sure is pretty when she's mad. "Should it?"

"Don't just stand there—*do* something."

He gave her a long, earnest look. "You want a great big man-sized spud with eight eyes—or a puny little plum-sized tater?"

Anne wanted to kill him. "I want you to go outside—talk to Charlie Moon."

He selected a handsome potato. "Why don't you talk to him?"

"Well, I think I'll do just that."

The Error

Anne Foster paused at the door that opened onto the porch. Called to the man outside. "Charlie?"

"Yeah?"

"May I join you?"

There was no response from Charlie Moon.

She opened the door. And stepped onto the porch.

The Snake

Anne Foster stood very still. She watched the Ute pace back and forth on the long porch. Thick planks squeaked under his boots. From time to time, he would pause to sniff at the beefsteak on the plate. And lick his lips.

She pulled the jacket tightly around her shoulders. "It's absolutely frigid out here."

"You should go back inside with Scott," Moon said gently. "I bet he's in the kitchen. Brewing up some fresh coffee."

"Charlie—there's something I want to tell you."

"What's that?"

"I want you to know that Scott and I are here for you. If there's anything you'd like to talk about."

"I appreciate that."

Anne hesitated to mention Moon's former sweetheart. "I know life has been, well—hard on you lately."

"Life is tough," he admitted. *And tougher if you're stupid.*

A shooting star flashed briefly over the mountains. "Oh," she said, "make a wish!"

I wish you'd go back inside.

Anne tried to see his face. *The poor man is suffering so terribly.*

Moon seated himself on a pine bench, placed the platter in his lap. *Now, that's better.* She sat down beside him. "It's a pretty night."

The Ute grunted.

She sighed. "A night like this makes me feel—so very young."

Moon sensed a shadowy presence. "Makes me feel hungry." He grabbed the raw steak with both hands.

Anne stared in horror. "Charlie—what on earth are you doing?"

The Ute snarled. And began to gnaw at the bloody slab of beef.

A coldness that had nothing to do with the thermometer crept up her spine. "Charlie—please don't—"

He glared in her direction with one wild eye. "It's mine—all mine. You can't have any."

Very deliberately, she scooted away. *His aunt was right. Charlie Moon has completely lost his mind.*

He grinned over the steak.

"Charlie—please stop. You're scaring me."

Being a kind man, he thought about sparing her the inevitable.

Too late.

The Big Scare was already coming, hell-bent for red meat. It thumped in on all fours, out of the darkness, ripping along the porch, leaping over her lap, over Moon's knees—neatly snatching the steak from his grasp.

Anne threw her arms over her face and shrieked. And shrieked.

Scott Parris was on the porch in four seconds flat.

It took the men some time to calm her.

Anne was finally able to get a few words past trembling lips. "Ohmigod—ohmigod—what *was* that?"

"Sidewinder," Moon said.

She gasped for breath. "A sn . . . snake?"

"Sidewinder's a dog," Parris explained soothingly, "just a harmless old hound."

Anne glared into the darkness, toward the chewing sounds that were punctuated with satisfied grunts. "A dog? But why did he pounce on us like that?"

Moon flashed a smile in the darkness. "He wanted the beef I had on my plate."

She sat very still for some time. When Anne did speak, her words were crisp and quite to the point. "Charlie—you purposely lured me out here for the scare of my life."

"He asked you to stay inside," Parris reminded his sweetheart.

"Well, of course he did. Because he knew that would make me want to come out and see what he was up to." She shot a dark look at her fiancée. "And you were in on it. Up to your knobby knees. You two are such *children*."

Knobby? "Honest, honey—"

"Don't lie," she snapped. "That just makes it worse."

Parris raised his hands in a defensive gesture. "But I didn't know nothing about—"

"And don't use double negatives." She closed her eyes and cringed. "You know how that grates on my nerves."

Moon grinned. "Maybe he means just what he says."

"Yes," she said. "Like he *did* know something."

Parris scowled at his Ute friend. "Please don't help me, Charlie."

"She's on to us," Moon said with a solemn shake of his head. "You might as well confess."

Scott Parris promised himself he'd get even with the Ute. This pledge made, he gave up the dispute with Anne. He was, he said, very sorry. And would make it up to her. *Anything. Imported Dutch chocolates. Two dozen roses. Well . . . maybe a dozen.*

Anne was slightly mollified by this strategic withdrawal from the field of battle. But one issue still bothered her. "Charlie—why didn't you just throw the steak to that—that horrible animal?"

"It isn't his way." Moon cast an affectionate glance toward the dark place where the hound was noisily crunching a bone. "Old Sidewinder don't care for handouts. He prefers to grab his food and run."

The Code of the West

Anne had retired to an upstairs bedroom. The men, bundled up in warm jackets, remained on the porch, seated in sturdy redwood chairs. The corrugated steel roof temporarily blocked their view of the moon as it ascended behind them, but ripples of silver light reflected off the rolling black river. If this were not sweet enough, the mountain lake was transformed into a glassy sea of shimmering quicksilver.

Time passed slowly, as time should. Charlie Moon and Scott Parris were as content as men can be in this troubled world.

Parris's voice cut through the mile-thick silence. "Charlie?"

"Yeah?"

"You're my best friend."

"That's right."

Parris smiled in the reflected moonlight. "Bein' as we're such good buddies, I think we should talk."

"About what?"

"You know what."

"I guess you mean your love life," the Ute said. "Okay. Pour your heart out. Tell me why you and that redhead haven't done the big I Do."

"None of your business. Besides, that's not what—"

"You been engaged for about six hundred years. And me—I'm supposed to be your best man. And your best friend to boot. So if there's something gone sour, you should tell me."

"Well, there's lots of reasons. If you really want to know—"

"Never mind. I'm not the sort of man who wants to poke around in his pardner's private business."

Parris choked back a sigh. "Sometimes Anne kinda gets on my nerves."

"Gimme a f'r-instance."

"Well, she's always correcting the way I talk. Like I don't never say nothing right."

Moon sighed. "Ain't that always the way."

Parris took a deep breath. "Keep this under your hat—but I found out she's an English major."

"You should not make an accusation like that without evidence."

"She keeps the sheepskin hid in a closet. But I've seen it with my own eyes."

"When you first met the woman, she should've told you about that right up front."

They enjoyed a long silence.

"Charlie, sometimes I wonder if I really want to be married."

"Pardner, I'd just as soon you kept all this personal stuff to yourself. It is the Code of the West," Moon added in a flinty tone. "A real cowboy don't talk about his woman problems."

Scott Parris curtly reminded the Indian that neither of them were cowboys.

"I got cowboys working for me. So it's the same difference."

The Ute's Tale

Like the black river flooding the earth, Night flowed on toward the west.

Parris cast a glance at the Ute. "Tell me what happened at Chimney Rock."

"Well, it all started about a thousand years ago."

"Hold on. Give me the short version."

"Okay. I figured out who murdered Julius Santos and April Tavishuts—and came awful close to sending me across the river."

"Then I assume you know who's responsible for Dr. Silk's death."

Moon nodded. "But he'll never see the inside of a jail."

Parris waited. "That's it?"

"You wanted the short version."

"I would not complain if you fleshed it out some."

"Okay. It got started last winter. The archaeologist—Amanda Silk—she was doing some contract work at the Chimney Rock site. One morning, whilst out for a refreshing stroll, she practically stumbles over the edge of that Twin War Gods petroglyph. It takes her most of a week—"

"Wait a minute—how did you come to know about this?"

"The more you interrupt, the longer this'll take."

"I retract the question."

"Where was I? Oh yeah. One morning last winter, Dr. Silk finds the petroglyph. Takes her most of a week to clean off the topsoil. These archaeologists do things awfully slow."

"So do you."

"When Amanda Silk is finally able to see the whole picture, she realizes right off she's found a very unusual petroglyph. She has this funny feeling—like it was trying to tell her something."

"About what?"

"The old legend."

"Which old legend is that?"

"There are several versions," the Ute said. "But in all of 'em, an Anasazi priest hides something close to Chimney Rock. Something important."

"So what does the archaeologist do?"

"Well, she thinks and thinks and thinks about the petroglyph. But exercising her brain don't get her nowhere fast. Then, one fine morning after a good night's sleep, she sits straight up in her bunk and bingo! She knows what the little men in the drawing are trying to tell her."

"She comes up with the converging-lines-from-the-spears theory?"

"You bet. Before breakfast, she goes and makes some sightings. Within an hour, she's worked out pretty much where the artifact must be buried. Now Dr. Silk has never had a shot at the big time—and this smells like an opportunity to make a big name for herself."

"I still don't see how you know what she smelled."

"If you keep making me forget where I was, I'll have to go back and start over."

"I won't do it again."

"Anyway, Dr. Silk makes up her mind to keep this important discovery to herself—at least for a while. So she covers up the petroglyph with the same dirt she'd removed."

"To make sure nobody finds it."

Moon nodded his black hat. "But the poor woman has a run of hard luck. Wind keeps blowing the dirt off her big secret. She keeps putting it back."

Parris sighed. "Life can be tedious."

"And it just gets tediouser. Dr. Silk knows she'll never be able to get a permit to excavate at the pit house. Especially not to look for the legendary Anasazi treasure."

"Sounds like she's in a tough spot."

"It does look pretty bad. She needs some kind of legal excuse to dig up this mysterious Anasazi artifact so she can publish a paper about it.

Then she has this brilliant notion. Amanda tells the NAGPRA committee that pothunters have been digging in the Chimney Rock ruins. Because she has a contract for dealing with such issues, the committee authorizes her to check out the damage the vandals have done. Now as long as she's careful, Dr. Silk can dig pretty much where she wants. But she has to be able to make the case that it's where a pothunter has already dug. If somebody spots her making a fresh hole in the ground, she is in deep trouble. But she's got one thing working in her favor. It'll be several weeks before the site opens for the summertime tourists. So, expecting some privacy, she starts to dig some random 'pothunter' holes to make her story hold up in case somebody from the NAGPRA committee eventually shows up to check things out. All the time, she's getting closer and closer to where she really wants to stick her shovel into the ground."

"Sounds like she's got a pretty good scheme going."

"And it could've worked. But life is unpredictable, pardner. No matter how careful you lay your plans, something always goes wrong. While Dr. Silk was hard at work one day, I believe she had an unexpected visitor."

"That missing horseman?"

Moon nodded. "Julius Santos went missing before Amanda Silk lied to the NAGPRA committee about the vandals digging at Chimney Rock. I'm betting he showed up and caught her red-handed while she was faking one of those 'pothunter' holes. Santos could've messed up her whole plan and then some. I figure she spooks his horse—which throws him and runs off. Before Santos can get up, she bangs him on the head with her shovel."

Parris could imagine the grisly scene. "Then she drags him to the edge of the west slope, dumps him over. Piles rocks on his body."

"She probably planned to bury him more permanently when she got some spare time. But at the moment, Dr. Silk is lots more interested in digging things up than putting them under the sod. Who knows when another unexpected tourist will interrupt her work? So she starts excavating right on the spot where she thinks the Anasazi priest buried his precious whatever. But right away, she has more bad luck, which puts an end to her digging. The Chimney Rock Archaeological Site is opened early for Native American Day. That's when the little Zuni girl wanders away and finds Amanda's secret petroglyph."

"And the kid shows it to you."

"That she did. And now that it's public knowledge, somebody else is bound to figure out what Dr. Silk already knows. She is pretty upset. She expects either Professor Axton or that paleoastronomer—" Moon searched his injured gray matter for the name.

"Professor Perkins."

"Yeah, Perkins—she expects one of those guys will understand what the spears mean right away. But they don't. It is a clever graduate student who works things out."

"Sure," Parris said. "April Tavishuts."

"And on the night April was killed, Dr. Silk—whose cell phone was on the blink—doesn't expect anybody from the university survey team to show up for a week or so. She decides to do some excavating late in the day. But whatta you know, here comes more trouble. What with the discovery of the Twin War Gods petroglyph, Professor Axton has decided to begin his project early. And April Tavishuts—who is anxious to check out the spot where she thinks the Anasazi whatzit might be buried—is the first member of the survey team to show up. Alvah Yazzi and his dog are in the car with her."

"Why'd the Navajo come along?"

"Alvah's old Chevy pickup is broke down and he needs some wheels while his stepdaughter is working at the mesa. He hitches a ride to Chimney Rock so he can drive April's car back to his place."

Parris nodded at the darkness.

The darkness nodded back.

Moon did not notice this exchange. "So up the road comes a car carrying triple trouble for Amanda Silk. April Tavishuts, her stepfather—and the old man's dog. Once April tops the mesa, she pulls her car off the lane. She is going to check out the coordinates she's worked out from the Twin War Gods petroglyph. Find out what those tilted spears are trying to tell her." Moon paused to consider the convergence of nonparallel lines. And the ill-fated crossing of human pathways. "A big thunderstorm is brewing, but that don't stop April. She follows her compass heading, and ends up at the very spot where Dr. Silk is currently hard at work."

Parris was beginning to see the picture Moon was painting. "April doesn't hear Dr. Silk digging from the road—for the same reason the archaeologist doesn't hear the car coming up the mesa. The thunderstorm is making too much noise."

"That's the way I figure it, pardner."

"And while his stepdaughter goes to check out her triangulation, Mr. Yazzi stays with the car."

"You bet. April couldn't have dragged that old Navajo into the ruins if she'd had six teams of Tennessee mules for the job. When April gets back, she intends to drive up to the parking area and unload her camping gear. After which Mr. Yazzi will take her car back to his place."

"Only she doesn't come back."

Charlie Moon tried to remember what the young woman looked like. The single image he could summon was a profile of a very still face. In the grave. "When April discovers her hero digging in the pithouse ruin like some common artifact thief, there must've been a nasty confrontation. Accusations. Threats. A struggle. April is struck on the head by Dr. Silk's shovel. Now the archaeologist has a corpse to deal with."

"And a ready-made hole in the ground."

"I don't think Amanda Silk intended to leave April's body in the fresh excavation—the very spot where she is hoping to unearth whatever the Anasazi priest has buried. But it's a handy solution for the moment's problem. And she needs some time to think about where to move the body so it'll never be found."

"So she covers up her victim in the temporary grave, heads back to her camp trailer."

"And all the while, Alvah Yazzi is wondering why his Ute stepdaughter is taking so long. Eventually, the old man calls for April. Naturally, he don't get any answer. Feeling the way he does about the ruins, the Navajo elder suspects something really awful has happened. Ghosts or witches must've grabbed her. It takes all the nerve Yazzi has to make himself go look for April. But he'd never have found where she was in the dark—not by himself."

"You're guessing that Mr. Yazzi's dog sniffed out the new grave."

"No guessing about it. That's exactly what happened. The Navajo's dog starts digging—uncovers just enough of April's leg for Alvah to recognize his stepdaughter's boot. The old man stands there for a long time, scared to death. A right-thinking Navajo knows that it is extremely bad medicine to mess around in Anasazi ruins. Especially at night. And it's a worse taboo to touch a freshly dead body. But what if she's not quite dead yet—what if she was buried alive?"

Scott Parris filled his lungs with a deep breath.

Charlie Moon's disembodied voice continued to tell the tale. "So, stone by stone—a handful of dirt at a time—Alvah begins to uncover his stepdaughter's body. About the time he gets started, Melina Castro shows up and sees April's car parked by the gravel road. By now, the worst part of the storm has passed over. Things have quieted down some. When Miss Castro gets out to have a look at April's parked car, she hears the sounds of Alvah digging up his stepdaughter with his bare hands. Thinking she's got a pothunter cornered, she hurries away to enlist Dr. Silk's help. At first, Dr. Silk isn't sure what she should do. She probably decides she'd better go along just in case the graduate student finds something incriminating."

"If necessary, she's ready to whack another young lady over the head."

"I wouldn't bet a thin dime against it, pardner. So they go off looking for whatever is out there. About the time the Navajo gets the dirt off April's face, the pair of women show up. There's a big flash of lightning. And right in front of 'em is Alvah Yazzi."

"Not burying his stepdaughter like the grad student thought—but digging her up." Parris shook his head. "But if he's innocent, why does the old man run?"

"Pardner, put yourself in Alvah's moccasins. Imagine you're a traditional Navajo. It's dark as the bottom of a tar bucket. Thunder is booming like Death's drum. You're trespassing in the Anasazi ruins. Standing in a fresh grave. Right over a corpse that's still warm. You're asking yourself this urgent question: Where is the witch who killed my stepdaughter? The answer comes in a flash of lightning, a crash of thunder. You look up and see these two ghostly-pale women, practically standing over the grave. Looking down at you. You telling me you'd have taken off your hat and said, 'Good evening, ladies—out for an evening stroll?' "

Parris silently conceded the point.

"Alvah Yazzi believes he's seen a couple of white-faced witches who killed his stepdaughter. Figures he's next on their list. So he's gone like a shot. His dog already has a fifty-yard lead. It never enters Yazzi's head that he could end up being a murder suspect."

Parris could visualize the old man's fright. "But Mr. Yazzi has a lucky break—neither one of the women can ID him. Melina Castro don't recognize his face. Dr. Silk don't even see him."

"That's not what the old Navajo thought. And we'll never know for sure whether Dr. Silk saw April's stepfather, but I'd bet ten to one she did. And after the old man runs like a jackrabbit with his tail on fire, Amanda Silk decides to keep quiet. Pretend she didn't see him."

"Sure," Parris said, "if the poor bastard who flees from the scene of the homicide isn't identified immediately, maybe he'll have enough time to get away to where he can't be found. And the longer Alvah evades the authorities, the more solid a murder suspect he becomes. If the archaeologist keeps quiet, nobody'll even think of suspecting her."

"And once the body's removed from the grave," Moon said, "it'll be Dr. Silk's job to see whether any harm was done to the ruin. Which adds support to her legal excuse to go back and excavate for the Anasazi treasure."

"Looks like her luck is finally changing for the better."

"Sure does. But things are looking bad for Mr. Yazzi. After the Navajo catches his breath and starts the long walk home, he's got some time to think about his awful predicament."

Parris was shaking his head. "Wait a minute—"

"You're interrupting the flow of the story, pardner."

"Excuse me. But why does the old man walk? If he's in such a big hurry, why don't he drive the car home?"

"The ignition key is on April's body."

"Oh. I didn't know that." Parris began to reconstruct the events of that dark night. "So it must've been Dr. Silk who set April's corpse on fire while Danny Bignight was having a pee." That delectable story had been repeated in every cop shop within a hundred miles.

"The woman was not short on nerve."

"Why'd she want to burn things up?"

"Don't know for sure. But one of April's fingernails was broken.

Maybe when Amanda undressed for bed late that night, she found a scratch somewhere. Figured bits of her skin might be under April's fingernail. She had to destroy any DNA evidence before the medical examiner showed up."

"She use gasoline to get the blaze started?"

The Ute investigator shrugged. "Or Coleman lantern fuel. Rubbing alcohol. We'll never know for sure."

"A very thorough planner. Not a lady I'd want to have out for my blood."

"Alvah Yazzi felt the same way. By the time that old man and his dog got home," Moon said, "he'd already worked out a plan to protect himself."

Parris rocked in his chair. "Sure. He rigs up some ashes and bone chips in his clothes—so if the witches come calling, they'll believe he's already dead."

"But *brujas* are hard to fool, pardner, so that Navajo left plenty of his personal items behind with the phony corpse. Wallet, money, keys, dentures—just about everything. And to make double-sure the witches don't wise up to his scheme, he don't even take his dog with him when he goes into hiding."

"Seems like he thought of everything."

"Almost everything, pardner. He even remembered to bring some food along. But without his false teeth that old Navajo had a lotta trouble gumming peanut brittle and buffalo jerky."

That sounds good. Parris searched, found a rock-hard fragment of beef jerky in his coat pocket. From the feel of it, the petrified tidbit was covered with lint and grit and a variety of other disagreeable debris. *Disgusting.* He stuffed the morsel into his mouth.

Moon continued. "This is why Alvah Yazzi goes to see my aunt Daisy—to get her to provide him with some chewable grub."

Parris ground his molars on the gob of desiccated cow flesh. "Can I ask now?"

"Sure."

"How d'you know so much about what Yazzi was doing?"

"He told me."

"When?"

"Same evening he stole a pie off of my kitchen window. I followed

Yazzi to his hideout. He was holed up in the guest cabin—the one across the lake."

"His truck was broke down. How did a man afoot get all the way to the Columbine—hitchhike?"

"In a manner of speaking. When *Cañon del Espíritu* got too hot for him, my aunt Daisy—with some help from a friend—brings Alvah Yazzi to the ranch. She stashes him in the guest cabin, tells him if any-body comes poking around he's to hide in the root cellar. Which is where he was hunkered down the night Miss Castro was in the cabin. By and by, Yazzi needs to relieve himself. He intends to slip outside once she's asleep. But right about this time—for no apparent reason—the young woman screams like a banshee. This makes Alvah suspect that she is demented."

"Why does the grad student scream, Charlie?"

"From what she tells me later, somebody knocked on the door and this startled her. It had to be Camilla, who wants to find out who I'm hiding in the cabin."

"Uh-oh."

"My very words. But when Miss Castro opens the door, she don't see nobody. So after a while, she settles down again. By now Yazzi really needs to empty his bladder. So one step at a time, he sneaks up the stairs from the cellar. Opens the door into the kitchen. The young woman seems to be asleep at last. He slips out the back door and has a five-minute pee."

Parris was regretting the third cup of coffee. "He must've been quite relieved."

"You can say that again."

"Once was enough." He got up. "Please excuse me."

The Ute waited.

Parris returned, plopped into the chair. "Where were we? Oh yeah—the college girl is inside the log cabin, nestled in her snug little bed. The Navajo elder is outside in the cold."

Moon shifted to a more comfortable position. "By now, Mr. Yazzi has had some time to think about one thing and another. And, pardner, you know what thinking does for a man."

"Gets him worried. About one thing and another."

"Every time. That old Navajo starts to wonder about this peculiar woman in the cabin. There is something familiar about her scream. Sounds an awful lot like what he heard when the two witches appeared in a flash of lightning at April's grave—and shrieked at him like bloody murder. What if she's one of those witches who killed his stepdaughter? Maybe she followed him all the way to the Columbine with blood in her eye. If there is a *yee naaldlooshii* in the cabin, he's got to find another place to hide. One way or another, he's got to find out who Screaming Woman is. So Yazzi cranks up his courage and sneaks back inside. She seems to be asleep, so this looks like his chance to have a good look at her face. Alvah leans real close. Right about the time his nose is close enough to touch hers, Miss Castro opens her eyes. Poor thing sees his ugly kisser and hollers like she's woke up in a tub fulla scorpions. The old Navajo high-steps it for the back door, Melina shoots out the front. She don't slow down till she is bangin' on my door. Next day, I check out the cabin. Nobody's there. But after sleeping under the stars for several nights, Alvah Yazzi moves back in. He has gotten attached to the comforts of living indoors—and to the canned food in the pantry. Without his chompers he can't eat the potatoes and raw onions and rutabagas in the cellar."

"Rutabagas?"

"Dolly Bushman bought two bushels down in Salida."

Parris grimaced. "Why?"

"I think they were on sale." The Ute had a bitter taste in his mouth. "I never did like rutabagas. Matter of fact, I shot one of 'em."

Parris would let that dog lie. "So tell me what happened that night when you got clubbed on the head."

"When I showed up at her camp trailer, Amanda Silk must've decided that I was getting a little bit too close to the truth."

"Or maybe she just don't like you. You tell her any of your long-winded tales?"

The Ute ignored this petty barb.

"So while you two are standing by the excavation, Dr. Silk whacks you on the head?"

"There was nobody else around to do any whacking." Moon rubbed at his skull; the ridge of scar tissue was still tender. "I must've fell into the excavation. Then she covered me with those big rocks and pine needles." He paused to contemplate the close call. "The woman was going to burn me alive."

"Why?"

"I'm not sure. Maybe to make it look like the same pothunter who set fire to April Tavishuts was also responsible for my death."

Parris thought this made sense. "Sure. Nobody suspected Dr. Silk of killing Miss Tavishuts. FBI cops would have fingered Mr. Yazzi for the crime." Parris wondered what he'd do if Charlie Moon wasn't here anymore. "So what stopped the archaeologist from lighting the pine needles?"

Moon allowed himself a moment before speaking. "My dog."

Parris raised a doubtful eyebrow. "Sidewinder?"

"I didn't even know he was there. But that peculiar old chowhound must've hitched a ride in my pickup." *Had to have been him who reared up on Amanda's trailer and looked into her window.* "I figure he follows us out to the pit-house excavation. Sees her conk me on the head. Then he comes a-runnin' through the brush, makes a leap, and nails his teeth into that candy-cane lighter—"

"Wait a minute. Which candy-cane lighter is this?"

"A novelty item. Dr. Silk's nephew sells 'em. She used it to light the stove in her camp trailer." *Or whatever else needed lighting.* "Anyway, when Sidewinder snatches it from her hand, Amanda Silk must think he is the well-known Anasazi Ghost Wolf come to swallow her whole—toenails, eyeballs, and all."

"This must've frightened the woman."

"Scared her to death." Moon was staring at a spot under the cottonwoods. A place where the shadows danced.

"Did anybody see your dog at the mesa that night?"

"Not as far as I know. But it must've been Sidewinder howling at the pit house when the Bushmans found my truck. Which is how they found me. Later on, that old hound could've hid in the back of my pickup till Pete Bushman brought it back to the ranch. Or maybe Sidewinder got scared off when the police cars and ambulance showed up, then walked all the way home." He paused. "Dogs do that kind of thing."

"Charlie, I don't mean to nitpick—but did you actually see Dr. Silk with this candy-cane lighter in her hand, ready to set fire to the pine needles?"

"Well . . . not exactly."

"Did you see the dog snatch something from her hand?"

"I wasn't conscious when it happened." *Maybe I was already on the Blue Train.*

"Then how can you be sure that's how it happened?"

"Weight of evidence. I know she had the candy-cane thingamajig, because I've seen her light her stove with it. The FBI didn't turn up any kind of butane lighter on or near her corpse." He raised a hand to ward off the expected objection. "And you're right, that don't prove Sidewinder had taken it away from her. But the FBI also didn't find the candy-cane lighter in her trailer—I checked Stan Newman's inventory list. And it wasn't at her nephew's garage sale. When I asked him about it, he was sure he hadn't seen it."

"Okay. The candy-cane lighter is missing. But that doesn't prove that your amazing dog snatched it from Dr. Silk's hand." Parris waved his arms. "I mean, this is a lot of arm waving."

Moon held his tongue.

Which made his friend suspicious. "If there's something you haven't told me, I'd like to hear it."

"You'll have to keep this under your hat. I found what was left of that candy-cane lighter in the back of my pickup, pardner. That's where Sidewinder keeps some of his toys."

"So what'd the FBI forensics experts say about this piece of physical evidence?"

Moon hesitated. "I never showed it to the feds."

"Why not?"

"You know how those guys are."

"I don't follow your drift."

"Pardner, whenever the U.S. government gets involved in a citizen's business, just about anything can happen. And it's usually something bad." Moon looked toward the mountain ridge.

"Like what?"

"They might confiscate my dog. For evidence or something."

"Arrest your mutt?" Parris laughed. "Surely you're not serious."

"They got Sidewinder's paw print at the pit house. Right where Dr. Silk dropped dead."

"You don't know for a fact that it's your dog's print."

"I sure don't intend to take Sidewinder into Stan Newman's office for a comparison."

There was a grin in Parris's voice. "Sounds like you're getting sweet on that old hound."

Moon exhaled a long sigh. "He'll do."

"You still haven't told me how you come to know so much about Dr. Silk's personal business." Parris grinned. "Or is this about ninety-nine percent guesswork?"

"That *matukach* woman was a meticulous scientist. Wrote down what she did in a ledger. Kept it in her camp trailer."

Parris raised a hand in protest. "Just a minute. Hold on. Whoa, there."

"You fall off your horse, pardner?"

"Please don't tell me that this highly educated, presumably intelligent person recorded detailed evidence of her capital crimes."

"Oh, no. Dr. Silk was way too smart for that. But there was a lot of incriminating information in her book."

"Like what?"

"Well, an entry from last March about her discovery of the Twin War Gods petroglyph. And just a few days later, her idea about what the tilted spears must mean. Following that, pages and pages of sketches. Trigonometry. Compass headings."

"If this record book was in her trailer, why didn't the FBI find it?"

"They found the new one."

"Please explain."

"Well, pardner, first time I visited her camp trailer, Dr. Silk had this big green ledger. And it wasn't half filled. Should've lasted her for a long, long time. But the next time I had coffee at her table, she was scribbling in a *blue* ledger. Way I see it, right after she kills April Tavishuts, the archaeologist buys herself a new ledger to keep in the trailer, stashes the incriminating one at home. Once April's body is found, she doesn't want anyone reading her research notes. Her motive for murder was right there in her own handwriting. And to top it off,

Amanda's last entry in the original ledger was on the day April was murdered."

"So where did Special Investigator Moon find this remarkable piece of evidence?"

"Garage sale."

"You're making this up, aren't you?"

"Nope. I bought the ledger in a box full of junk down in Chama, where Dr. Silk's nephew was selling off her stuff."

"Okay. You're sure Amanda Silk is the felon. But the FBI's looking for Mr. Yazzi."

"They're not looking so hard since I gave 'em Dr. Silk's original ledger." Moon waited for a compliment. And waited. "So?"

"So what?"

"So what do you think of my investigation?"

"Give me a moment."

"You are a deliberate man."

"I am trying to think of an appropriate superlative."

"Then take your time, pardner."

Parris considered and rejected several explosive adjectives. Then hit on one that was just right. "I'd say . . . adequate. Yeah. Your investigation was adequate."

"That's the best you can do?"

"Okay. Your investigation was *stupendously* adequate."

"Now that's more like it."

Parris looked up at the stars. An artificial satellite passed north to south. Russian, he thought. Spying on America. *Hello, Ivan—here's spit in your eye.* He spat. The missile fell far short.

The Hallucination

Scott Parris had spent some time turning Moon's theory over in his mind. "I find the whole thing hard to believe. Three people dead—all because of some scratches on a rock."

The Ute stretched his long legs into a bath of creamy moonlight. "It makes perfect sense to my aunt Daisy. She claims that petroglyph was made a thousand years ago by an Anasazi priest—to help him find what he'd hidden."

"So what do you think, Charlie? Is there a fabulous Anasazi artifact buried on Ghost Wolf Mesa?"

"Not now, there ain't."

Parris stared through the midnight at his friend. "You found it?"

"With some help from my dog." Charlie Moon told his friend a tale about a prehistoric ceramic. Inside the clay pot was a twenty-six-pound iron meteorite. A flaming tear shed by White Shell Woman? Perhaps.

"Digging up stuff like that is against the law," the Granite Creek chief of police observed. "A man could get into big trouble."

"Only if he gets caught."

"So you figure you're in the clear."

"Maybe," Moon said. *Maybe not.* Something was moving in the moon-shadow cast by a leaning cottonwood.

They heard iron hinges creak behind them. Anne, a long winter coat covering her silk pajamas, materialized in the doorway. "Well?"

There was no response from the men, who did not understand the question.

She pulled the coat more tightly around her slim waist. "Are you two going to sit out here till daylight?"

"It is a fine night for sitting," Parris said.

Anne closed the door. They heard her feet padding up the stairs.

Parris tried to wiggle his toes. Couldn't feel them. *Maybe they're frostbit. About ready to turn black and fall off. I could get gangrene and die. Anne would never let me forget it.* In an effort to scare some feeling back into his feet, Parris banged his boot heels against the sturdy porch planks. "Charlie, there's something I got to discuss with you."

"Discuss away, pardner."

"Your aunt is concerned about your injury. She wanted me to find out whether . . . well . . ."

"Whether I'm doing better?"

"Well, that wasn't exactly the way she put it." Parris folded his hands in prayerful fashion. "This is kinda hard for me."

"Just tell me what she said."

"I would rather not."

"But being the silver-tongued devil you are, I bet you can think of a polite, civilized way to represent Aunt Daisy's concerns about the state of my mental health."

"Lemme see. Okay, here goes: Has your brain turned to turnip mush. Do you see a bullfrog in a top hat dancing on you knee. Should I hide your sidearm before you do something incredibly stupid."

"Is this true-false or multiple choice?"

"Look, I got to tell her how you're doing. So level with me—is that whack on the skull causing you any serious problems?"

"You mean did I shoot up my John Deere tractor?"

"Mrs. Perika did mention the incident in passing."

"Alleged incident. In my whole life, I have never aimed a loaded firearm at any farm equipment. Besides, a rancher's tractor is his friend."

"Shame on you for teasing your elderly relative."

"Had to convince her I was crazy enough to shoot an old Navajo in my root cellar. Only way to get Aunt Daisy to admit what she'd done." *And it was the most fun I'd had in months.*

"I'm willing to bet Alvah Yazzi had already told you that Mrs. Perika brought him to the Columbine."

"He had," Moon admitted. "But the confession was good for her soul."

"You have evaded my question."

"Which question was that?"

"Is your head injury causing you any problems?"

"None worth mentioning."

"Go ahead. Mention."

"It won't help none."

"I am your best friend," Parris said evenly. "I will damn well find a way to help."

Might as well humor him. So Charlie Moon told Scott Parris about the apparition. Ever since Aunt Daisy had planted the poisonous seed of suggestion—which was well fertilized by the fantastic tale the Zuni child had told him—the noxious weed had grown and flowered in his imagination. It was not real, of course—this wispy apparition of a leathery-faced old man, his gaunt frame draped in a feathered blanket, the skin of an albino wolf draped over his back. The hallucination generally began with the first touch of twilight. The wizard would materialize a dozen yards or so beyond the porch, his lips moving in a silent chant, bare feet dancing a slow, shuffling step. Four to the right. Four to the left. Over and over again. This somber demonstration would continue as the sun fell behind the granite peak and the mountain's black shadow exploded across the valley to envelop the Columbine. Sometimes, after many hours, the dancer would arch his thin back like a rainbow of sinew and bone—reach down to flatten splayed fingers onto the earth—and shake off the form of man. What was left would assume the shape of a pale four-legged creature. Head hung low, black tongue lolling over teeth made for tearing flesh, cracking bone. This shadow-animal would pace back and forth where the wizard-priest had danced. On occasion, it would stop to glare at the Ute. Moon would watch the nonexistent creature into the small hours. And think his troubled thoughts. *Ugly-looking devil . . . scary enough to frighten someone to death?* As the rising sun touched the mountains, the apparition would depart. For a time.

According to Aunt Daisy, the phantom's visits would not cease until the precious object Moon had removed from the pit house was buried again. But not on Ghost Wolf Mesa. This time, White Shell Woman's tear must be concealed on the long saddle of sandstone rubble stretching between the Twin War Gods. Though the apparition was no more than a malignant fantasy infecting his wounded mind, Moon knew of no other way to evict the imaginary guest. This being the case, he had followed his aunt's instructions to the letter. But the shaman's therapy had not succeeded. The phantom still came to torment him. "And that's about it," Moon said in conclusion. "Guess my brain needs more time to heal." The Ute was unsettled by a flickering shadow under the cottonwoods. He closed his eyes to keep out the darkness. Too late. The darkness was already inside.

Parris shook his head. "Never thought I'd live to see the day—Charlie Moon visited by a haunt."

"Yeah. You were always the spooky one."

Parris chewed on this. And the jerky. "I don't much like that word, Charlie."

"Spooky?"

"It makes me seem, well . . . peculiar."

Charlie Moon pondered the issue. "How about—you were always the *perceptive* one."

"Well . . . I guess perceptive is sorta okay. If that's the best you can do."

"How about stupendously perceptive?"

Parris nodded. "Now that's more like it."

The Exorcist

Time passed smoothly, unsevered by the ratchet-hatchet of ticks and tocs. And it came to pass that the whole disk of ivory moon was visible to the men. About to roll off the porch roof.

Scott Parris was oblivious to the pale, pockmarked face. He chewed contentedly on the cud of beef jerky. And thought about all he had heard. And seen. "Charlie?"

"Yeah?"

"This old geezer-priest draped in the wolf skin—you say he shows up every single night?"

Moon was staring at the porch floor. "And stays till the sun comes over the mountain."

"So you can see him right now."

The Ute allowed himself a quick glance. "Afraid so."

"What you need is plenty of rest." Parris drummed his fingers on the chair arm. "Why don't you go upstairs and hit the hay."

"Won't do any good."

"You don't mean—"

"Yeah. He comes with me."

"Right into your bedroom?"

The haunted man nodded. This hallucination had no sense of propriety.

"Must make it hard to get a night's sleep."

"It don't help a whole lot."

"So what're you gonna do about it?"

"Wait him out," Moon said. *When I get well, he'll go away.*

The broad-shouldered man pushed himself to his feet. Clenched big hands into knobby fists. "Well that does it—I have had enough."

Moon was staring helplessly at the dancing phantom. "Going up to bed, then?"

"Not just yet." Parris's voice was soft as kitten fur. "I have had a crawful of this Anasazi intruder. Anyone who makes trouble for my buddy has got me to deal with." The policeman slipped a hand under his coat. Callused fingertips crawled across the tread of a corduroy shirt—toward the shoulder holster.

This odd behavior piqued Moon's interest. He inquired about his friend's intentions.

Parris produced a short-nosed Smith & Wesson revolver. "I am going to shoot Mr. Wolf-Man a new rectal orifice."

"I—uh—don't think you oughta do that."

The gunman rolled the cylinder under his thumb. It was fully stuffed with five .38-caliber copper-clad slugs. "Why not?"

"A gunshot'll scare your fiancée."

Parris turned to his left. He raised the weapon, took careful aim at a spot where a long moon-shadow snaked its way to the base of a cotton-wood tree. "Give me a better reason."

"Well, sensible folk hereabouts might think you've lost your mind."

He cocked the pistol. "Trust me, Charlie. I know how to deal with this trespassing badass."

The Ute felt the skin prickling on the back of his neck. *He's kidding.*

Scott Parris closed one eye and looked down the barrel. "Hold still, you scraggly old bugger. Right . . . that's it." He whispered thirteen words.

He's not kidding! "Shooting at it won't do no good. It's not real—"

The lawman pulled the trigger. The hammer fell. In the perfect still-ness, the explosive report boomed as the very crack of doom.

There was a startled yelp from Anne's upstairs bedroom.

The Ute—who had been holding his breath—exhaled a raspy sigh.

The Granite Creek chief of police blew an imaginary wisp of smoke off the tip of the stubby barrel, holstered the sidearm. "Don't bother to thank me."

"For what?"

Parris pointed.

Moon leaned forward. Squinted. "He's gone."

"Damn right. And he'll stay gone."

• • •

A sleepy-eyed Anne Foster cracked the door. Peeked out onto the porch. "What on earth was that awful noise?"

"Gunshot," Parris said. He patted his jacket over the shoulder holster.

The lovely woman brushed a scarlet lock off her cheek. "What did you shoot?"

Her fiancé spat a parabolic arc of jerky juice. "Hostile Indian."

"Okay—*don't* tell me." She slammed the door. *Lunatics!*

The Question

Having completed trillions of tireless circumnavigations, White Shell Woman glided serenely toward that vast emptiness beyond the granite peaks.

Scott Parris was likewise serene in the shadows. And smugly satisfied with himself. Moreover, his toes were now toasty-warm. He attributed this touch of grace to his victory over Darkness.

Charlie Moon stood stock-still, staring off into the shadows. A small, sensible segment of his mind knew better than to ask the question. But the inquiring majority of that convoluted organ wanted to know. He turned to his friend. "Pardner, there is one thing that puzzles me."

"Only one?" Parris cocked a bushy eyebrow. "Me, I am mystified by all sorts of stuff." He tilted his happy face skyward to smile at the rotating swirl of fiery spheres. "I wonder whether space just goes on and on forever and ever, or is it curved and twisted so that if a fella could eyeball it out there far enough, he'd see the back of his head. And that's just for starters. There's urgent questions about multidimensional string theory—quantum gravity—parallel universes. Not to mention the conundrum of entangled photons."

"What I wonder about is—"

"And does toad frogs cause warts? Well, if you ask me, the jury is still out on that one." Parris stretched out his arms as if to embrace the Infinite Unknown. "My friend, this old universe is stuffed chockful of deep mysteries wanting solutions. Big questions waiting for big answers."

"Well let 'em want and wait." Moon squinted at the Big Dipper. "I got something in my mouth that needs saying."

Parris tapped his boot heel on a redwood plank. "The floor is yours."

"What you did for me, pardner—I appreciate it."

"Please. I am modest to a fault. Praise—however well deserved—makes me blush."

The Ute hesitated to raise the troublesome issue, but the thing must be said now or never. "I just don't understand how it worked."

"There's no real mystery, Charlie." The gunslinger tapped a finger on his temple. "The sudden, loud noise reset your brain back to normal. Kinda like shock therapy."

Moon counted a dozen heartbeats. "There's something more I need to say."

"Say it."

"We been pardners for a long time."

Parris nodded. "That we have."

"So what's mine is yours. My pickup truck. My last greenback dollar. Even my brand-new John B. Stetson hat."

"I appreciate that, Charlie."

The Ute took a deep breath. "But there's some things a man don't share—not even with his best friend."

The policeman frowned. "Like what?"

"Well . . . like his woman. Or toothbrush."

There was an audible smirk in Parris's reply. "Well, I don't see what the problem is. Now that Camilla's given you the kiss-off, you don't have no woman for me to covet. And I already own a three-dollar toothbrush."

"This is not about women. Or toothbrushes."

"Quit dancing around the cow pie, Charlie—say what's on your mind."

Moon's words came slowly. "A sick man's hallucination is kinda personal—not something he cares to share. Not even with his best friend."

The white man pushed himself to his feet, walked stiffly to the edge of the porch. "Well, if that don't take the cake—now Charlie Moon thinks us sane and healthy folks can see his illusions." He turned toward the Ute. "That's just about the damnedest notion I ever heard."

Moon could not see his friend's face in the blackness. "Then how'd you know where to shoot?"

Parris hesitated. Then floated a sly Cheshire grin. "Spooky, ain't it?"